THE MAN ON
THE STREET

THE MAN ON THE STREET

TREVOR WOOD

Quercus

First published in ebook in Great Britain in 2019 by

Quercus Editions Ltd
Carmelite House
50 Victoria Embankment
London EC4Y 0DZ

An Hachette UK company

A CIP catalogue record for this book is available
from the British Library

HB ISBN 978 1 78747 836 7
TPB ISBN 978 1 78747 916 6

10 9 8 7 6 5 4 3 2 1

Typeset by CC Book Production
Printed and bound in Great Britain by Clays Ltd, Elcograf S.p.A.

MIX
Paper from
responsible sources
FSC® C104740

Papers used by Quercus are from well-managed forests and other responsible sources.

For Pam and Becca, with love, always x

1

Leazes Park, Newcastle, June 1, 2012

Jimmy didn't have a watch. He liked watches well enough, but these days they were more use as currency. The last time he'd found one, in a bin behind one of the big houses in Jesmond, he'd swapped it for some dog biscuits. It didn't matter because he could always tell what time it was – or near enough as made no difference. Like now. It was somewhere between 3 and 3.30 a.m. He used to be more precise, always within ten minutes one way or the other he reckoned, but since they brought in the late licensing laws, the mixture of noise and light from the bars and clubs had messed with his head a bit and he was sometimes out by an hour or more. It was easier here though, quieter. Leazes Park wasn't his normal patch, but he liked to keep on the move. It was harder to hit a moving target.

His favourite spot when he first came back to Newcastle, five months ago now, was just behind Greggs in the main street. The warmth generated by the ovens seemed to stick around all night. When you were hungry, though, the lingering smell of cheese pasties could drive you insane. On the plus side, you sometimes found a few in the bins, past their sell-by date but good enough for the likes of him and Dog. Then some bastard put spikes in the ground to stop people crashing there.

This wasn't a bad spot though. The late-night revellers tended to stay clear. No one wanted to walk home through a dark park, not even the nut jobs, so the chances of someone pissing on you in your sleep were pretty low, unlike on the street where you were invisible by day and a wanker-magnet at night.

He'd found a spot under an old beech tree behind the tennis courts where he and Dog could rest up where no one could see him. He could see them, though. There were others here, some he knew, some not. It used to be same old, same old, but new faces on the street were common now, more so during the day when the pretend beggars appeared, but even at night the numbers were growing.

He could make out a shape on the bench near the path that ran along the top of the bank, on the far side of the court, underneath the only lamp post still working. At least they hadn't fucked with the benches. A lad from York had told him that the council there had bolted armrests onto the middle of them to stop people sleeping there.

Gadge reckoned one of the Polish lads used to crash in a tree on the edge of the park, for safety. Daft bastard broke his arm when he fell out. Good job the hospital was just across the road. Jimmy didn't really believe that one; Gadge told a good story, but mostly that's what they were, stories.

A crack from somewhere behind him made him jump. Jimmy sat up, hugging his sleeping bag around him and putting a restraining hand on Dog who was on his feet, growling softly. He looked around. Though the moon was hidden by thick clouds, his night vision was working well, one of the bonuses of sleeping like a . . . whatever the opposite of a baby was. An old man? A dead man? That couldn't be right; dead men sleep great.

There was nothing to be seen. A false alarm. He patted Dog on the head and the mongrel terrier curled back down near his feet.

Jimmy watched as the figure on the bench stirred in his sleep and rolled over. It was Deano. The Cossack hat was a dead giveaway. Gadge called him 'the Twat in the Hat', but Deano didn't seem to mind. He reckoned it was well toasty. Jimmy watched as Deano pulled his hat over his ears and rolled back, his face turned towards the bench, the hulking shadow of the football stadium behind him, towering over the four-storey town houses that flanked the park. That's when Jimmy heard the voices. Men, at least a couple of them, laughing in the distance.

Sound travels miles in the park at night, so at first he wasn't sure where they were, but then he caught a glimpse of two men through the trees by the lake, heading down past the derelict pavilion, their bright green, high-vis jackets standing out in the darkness. Coppers, Jimmy thought. The bane of his life – even though he used to be one, sort of. It was like they could smell him. He pulled himself further back beneath the tree, well out of sight of the path.

'I wouldn't touch her with a bargepole,' one of them said.

'You haven't got a bargepole, mate,' the other said, laughing, 'more like a Twiglet.'

'Piss off, Duke,' the first man said. As they came closer Jimmy could see them more clearly through the mesh fence surrounding the tennis courts. Laughing boy seemed huge, like a wardrobe on legs.

'What have we got here?' the small copper said, spotting Deano on the bench. They were now standing underneath the lamp; Jimmy recognised the big one. He'd got previous. Dog started to stir again, but Jimmy calmed him with another pat.

'You can't sleep here, pal,' the big copper said, nudging Deano with his baton. Deano didn't move.

'Oi!' he shouted, nudging him harder. 'Get up!'

Deano rolled over slowly and looked up at the pair standing above him.

'Come on, cloth ears, get moving or you'll get my boot up your arse.'

Dog growled again and the smaller copper turned and peered across, towards the noise. Jimmy edged even further back into the shadows, dragging a reluctant Dog by his collar, hoping he wouldn't start barking.

'Can I stay here just for now?' he heard Deano say in his child-like voice. 'It's nice.'

'No you bloody can't,' the big copper said, hauling Deano off the bench and, in one movement, hurling him down the steep bank into some thorny bushes next to the court fence.

'Steady on, Duke, he's just a kid,' the other one said.

'Just a kid, my arse; he's as old as you.'

Deano clearly knew better than to complain. He scrambled out of the bushes, crawled up the bank and headed back to the bench.

'Where you going?' the big copper said.

'Get my stuff,' Deano said, pointing at a small rucksack tucked under the bench.

'No you're fucking not,' the big copper said.

'But I need—'

The kick caught Deano straight in the balls. As he fell, a second kick caught him on the side of the head.

'For Christ's sake, Duke,' the smaller copper said, grabbing his friend's arm. The other man shrugged him off, pulled out Deano's rucksack and heaved it over the iron railing that edged the park. He laughed and glanced down at Deano who was quietly wiping blood away from his face.

'Now piss off, you scrounging git.' He aimed another casual kick at Deano, but the lad didn't need telling twice. He leapt to his feet and legged it off towards the gate at the top of the path.

'Have a nice day!' the mean bastard shouted.

Jimmy watched as the two policemen headed off, to make sure they left the park. He'd learned the hard way that when you stick your head above the parapet it gets shot off. But the guilt of inaction still burned in his throat; even Dog had moved away from him.

'Bollocks to you, Dog,' Jimmy said. 'Not my fight.'

2

The Pit Stop, Newcastle, June 4, 2012

The scratches were visible on the back of Deano's hands. He hadn't mentioned the kicking he'd got and Jimmy wondered if Deano knew he had been there, watching, doing nothing.

Gadge was telling one of his stories, something about a Salvation Army woman wanting to save him. Jimmy was only half listening, finishing his soup, which didn't taste of anything in particular but was at least hot. The Pit Stop's kitchen was open three nights a week and they sent a mobile van out on two other nights, so he never needed to go hungry.

'So she gave us a Bible and said, "This will save you,"' Gadge said. 'I looked at her and smiled. "That's exactly what I need," I said. You should have seen her face. It was whats-a-name . . . beatific.'

Deano nodded as if he knew what Gadge was on about. Over Deano's shoulder Jimmy could see the small TV in the corner. On it there was a huge crowd of people waving tiny

Union Jack flags, all standing in the Mall; Jimmy recognised it from back in the day, when he'd had to attend a Remembrance Day service in Whitehall. Doing his duty. Now there was a huge stage smack bang in front of Buck House. On the stage there was a fat man in a beefeater costume stamping his foot.

Gadge was on a roll now; there was no stopping him once he got going.

'I took it off her – the Bible, that is – and opened it up, pretending to read it, like. She's still smiling, as if the Lord himself had stuck his tongue up her fanny. "Thank you, missus," I said, and gave her a big smile right back, all grateful and that.'

'What did you do then?' Deano asked. He'd probably forgotten that Gadge had told this story before. It was a Catholic priest last time.

'What do you think I did, Deano? I ripped out a bunch of pages and threw them on the fire. "That'll keep it going for the whole night," I said, holding up what was left of the good book. The Sally Army lass was squealing like a pig, trying to grab the rest off us. You should've heard the language. Made us blush.'

Deano thought it was the funniest story he'd ever heard. Like he did last time. And the time before that.

On the TV Jimmy could see the Queen on stage, holding what looked like a giant diamond. She placed it in a stand and a huge flame shot up into the air. Within seconds fireworks had filled the night sky behind Buck House.

'Am I boring ya?' Gadge asked. Jimmy shook his head.

'You're boring me, ya gobshite.' A new voice. From his right. Jimmy turned and looked at the speaker. Long, straggly light brown hair and black teeth. A smell of cheap lager and sausages. He was wearing a grey army greatcoat that looked like it had actually been through a war or two.

'Is that right, Goldilocks?' Gadge said to the newcomer. Gadge was practically square: short and wide, but muscular, not fat. The long beard made him look friendly, but he could look after himself. All around them people were starting to move away. A stainless-steel salt cellar was knocked off the table and rolled along the floor. One of the younger volunteers hovered, unsure whether to get involved.

Someone had turned the sound up on the TV; there was a loud bang as a huge firework exploded. Jimmy flinched.

'Pussy,' the stranger said.

'Him or me?' said Gadge.

'Both.'

'He doesn't mean nothing, Gadge. You d-didn't mean nothing, mister, d-did you?' Deano said, his voice trembling with worry, his big urchin-like eyes opening wide – a look that earned him more money than most on the streets.

'What if I did?' Goldilocks said, and placed his hands flat on the table, as if preparing to leap across at Gadge. Another firework exploded.

'You didn't,' Jimmy said, taking a tight grip on the man's left arm. The stranger turned to look at him. Jimmy was holding a fork about eight inches above the man's outstretched fingers. The man tried to pull his arm away but Jimmy was too strong. He stared at Jimmy for a moment, then looked down.

Jimmy let go of Goldilocks' arm. He thought about saying something, something conciliatory maybe, to give the man a chance to save face, but he'd already done more than he should have, trying to make up for not helping Deano the other night, so he kept schtum. Defeated, Goldilocks pushed his chair back, got up and moved away. The young volunteer breathed a sigh of relief and went back to wiping a table.

Gadge laughed. 'Fuck off with you, Goldilocks, before my man Jimmy kicks off for real. You wouldn't like him when he's angry.' Somehow Gadge always knew stuff. Jimmy didn't have a clue how he knew stuff. But he knew stuff alright.

Jimmy reached over and grabbed Goldilocks' left-behind plate. He made sure no one was looking and put it under the table where Dog leapt on it greedily.

Back on the TV the Queen was giving it her best Mona Lisa smile while behind her a thin, glamorous woman with dark brown hair grinned inanely.

'Eeeh, look, it's wor Cheryl with the Queen,' Maggie, one of the older volunteers, squealed. 'Isn't she canny?'

One or two people glanced up from their food but no one cared enough to answer.

'He's filth, I reckon,' Gadge said, nodding at Goldilocks, who was now sitting on his own in a corner of the room.

'A copper?' Deano said.

'Aye, undercover.'

Jimmy thought about the man's teeth. Gadge saw conspiracies everywhere, you name it: the moon landings, Princess Di, 9/11 – none of them what they seemed.

On the TV the fireworks had reached a crescendo, lights exploding all over the London sky. Someone, Maggie probably, had turned the volume up to the max and the room was filled with the sound of 'Land of Hope and Glory'.

Jimmy hadn't seen a sign of either for a long time.

3

Falkland Sound, 1982

The ship's tannoy breaks the threatening silence.

'Brace for impact.'

Jimmy has been expecting it. The Argy Skyhawks have been buzzing over them like deadly mosquitos all morning, but hearing the words out loud still comes as a shock. That morning, one of the lads in the mess had been banging on that 'not knowing' was the worst thing, but that was a pile of shite. Knowing is worse. Knowing is much fucking worse. The tannoy crackles back into life.

'Brace, brace, brace.'

This time Jimmy reacts. He dives behind the ladder which leads up to the upper deck and wedges himself in, his back set firm against the bulkhead, knees pulled up tight to his chest, feet jammed under its base. For the first time in his brief life he's glad he is a short-arse. Christ knows where Red is, but it's every man for himself now. 'Man, eh?' he imagines Red saying. 'You've barely started shaving.'

The impact of the first bomb hurls the stern up in the air. Jimmy shoots forward. He flings his right arm out to stop his head crashing into the underside of the ladder. Jesus, that hurts. The second explosion is bigger. The ship lurches violently to the right. This time his head smashes into the bottom of the steps. Inside his anti-flash hood he can feel blood streaming down his forehead into his eyes. Most of the lights have died, but through the blood he can still see thick black smoke pouring down the passageway towards him. It is getting so hot his ears are starting to sweat.

He jams his eyes closed and takes a deep breath to suck in some clean air before the smoke overwhelms him. A sickly-sweet smell – like burning pork – hits him. The gut-wrenching screams echoing down the passageway, from where the rest of the first-aid team are stationed, tell him exactly what that means. He puts his hands over his ears to drown out the noise of both the screams and the clanging alarm which has just started to ring.

The ship is vibrating noisily, like a giant tuning fork. A brief image of Bev in widow's black flashes into his head. He mutters a prayer to a God he usually mocks, but before he has got to 'Hallowed be thy name' he feels a tug on his shirt. He opens his blood-sticky eyes. Red's face is inches from his, his mouth opening and closing silently. Jimmy takes his hands off his ears. The siren has stopped. His friend's high-pitched Scouse accent penetrates the hissing and crashing of the ventilation pipes collapsing around them.

'Move it, lad, get up top.'

Jimmy shakes his head, but Red drags him out by his No. 8 shirt and pushes him around to the front of the steps.

'Go! Fucking smoke'll kill you.'

Jimmy clambers up, flinching as the heat of the handrail bursts through his thin gloves. He looks up. There is a sliver of daylight above him filtering through the smoke – the hatch cover has been ripped from one of its hinges and has fallen to one side. He squeezes through the narrow gap.

What the hell? There should be an airlock at the top with two doors but the inner door is lying on the deck and the outer has been obliterated, nothing but smouldering jagged metal, the grey paint bubbling and blistered. He lurches through the gaping hole and emerges on the port side of the ship. It stinks of sulphur and fear. Red pushes past Jimmy and races through the smoke towards the flight deck. Jimmy stands and stares over the side of the ship. A headless body is caught in the netting.

A muffled shout jerks him back into action. He turns and chases after Red who has grabbed a fire hose and is aiming it at the flames shooting out of what remains of the hangar. Water dribbles from the nozzle.

'The fire main's shot,' Red shouts. 'I'd be better off pissing on it.'

Amid the smoke Jimmy can see metal debris scattered everywhere. A brief gust of wind momentarily clears his view and he sees something else, something bigger, lying on the flight deck. He runs towards it but trips and falls, crashing onto the deck. He turns and sees a pair of overall-clad legs sticking out from a fallen section of the hangar roof: one of the flight crew. He jumps to his feet and tries to pull the poor sod out, only half succeeding. Both legs have been severed just above the knee, and whatever – whoever – they had been attached to is still under there somewhere. The vomit comes before he can remove his hood and half of it goes back down his throat. He rips the hood off and spits the rest out.

A feral scream comes from the back of the ruined hangar.

Red drops the now dried-up hose and runs towards the scream. There is a small pop and then an ear-shattering explosion. Chopper fuel.

A fireball hits Red square in the chest, shooting him backwards through the air like a blazing rag doll, crashing into the guard rail. For a moment he hangs there, a vaguely human shape in a haze of flame, a pair of orange and black arm-like shadows windmilling for balance. And then he's gone.

4

The Quayside, Newcastle, June 5, 2012

Jimmy woke up with tears running down his cheeks. He didn't know why. Dog was sitting up, staring at him, confused. Jimmy had probably been crying out in his sleep. Bev used to banish him to the spare room when it got too much.

He could see the names of various cities embossed on the side of the open roof: Hull, Antwerp, London, Malmö, Copenhagen. Places the ships used to go, when there were ships, when there were shipyards, right there, on the river, where his dad worked before he got laid off. Now there were only bars and expensive works of art, like this place, the Swirle Pavilion – a future folly, with its sandstone walls, a golden globe hovering above its open top like a satellite or something. It was one of Gadge's favourite sleep spots, but he had a bed for the night, in a hostel, with real sheets and everything, so tonight it was Jimmy's. The open roof could be a pain but it was June, so it was worth the risk.

Someone was talking, arguing even. He sat up and looked

through a gap between two stone pillars. Two men stood about thirty yards away, by a two-bar rail that ran along the river, just down from the dormant cruise boats, their long shadows framed in the towering arc of the Millennium Bridge.

The man facing away from Jimmy was tall, over six foot, wearing a black donkey jacket, big boots, a black-and-white-striped bobble hat on his head, maybe a glimpse of a beard when he turned his face. He reminded Jimmy of a bricklayer friend he used to have, his shoulders somehow too big for the rest of him.

The other man, facing towards him, was shorter, about Jimmy's height. He was slighter too, wearing a denim jacket and light-coloured chinos, longish dark hair, maybe a moustache, a black bag – like a school satchel – slung over his right shoulder. A social-worker type, Jimmy thought, and he'd met enough of them to know.

There was no one else around. The nearby bars and restaurants had long since kicked out their punters. About 4 a.m., Jimmy guessed.

The men were closer together now, talking, the smaller one shrugging occasionally, slightly unsteady on his feet. Jimmy wondered if it was a gay hook-up, but if it was, they were in the wrong place. Everyone knew Dog Leap Stairs was the place for that. Anyway, none of his business.

He lay down again, drifted off.

Flames everywhere. He's in bed. An empty space beside him. Where's Bev? Burning curtains fall to the floor, setting fire to the bed covers. He

leaps up, naked, sweating. Where is she? The doorway is ablaze . . .
and the window. A woman's scream from somewhere. The stairs? He
runs through the doorway, feeling no heat, no pain, straight into the
back of Bev who is standing on the landing. But it's not the landing.
It's the flight deck, the South Atlantic all around them. He spins her
around. Her hair is on fire, lips and nose melting.

'Get help,' she whispers, locking him in a fiery embrace.

Jimmy woke again, bathed in sweat this time, heart
pounding, ready to burst out of his chest like the Alien, his
hands beating at the non-existent flames, his eyes searching
for Bev but seeing only the stone pillars and the open sky.
Dog stirred at his feet, disturbed by both his movement and
the raised voices outside, angrier now than before. Frag-
ments drifted over.

'I saw you . . .'

'. . . fucking incensed . . .'

'. . . none of your business . . .'

'. . . your system . . . it's wrong.'

Jimmy took a deep breath and let it go, then another and
another, until he felt his heartbeat start to slow. A cellmate
had once told him that thinking of a happy place would
help. 'Like where?' he'd asked.

Suddenly there was another shout, indistinct this time.
Then a cry of pain and a muffled thud, something heavy hitting the ground. Jimmy froze, not wanting to get involved,
still regretting his confrontation with Goldilocks. Whatever
was happening, it was someone else's problem. Under his
breath, he started to repeat his self-taught mantra.

'Not my fight. Not my fight. Not. My. Fight.'

The silence bothered him more than the shouting and he wished the voices would start up again. Then he heard another noise, a dragging sound, that same heavy thing being pulled along the ground. But not towards him, away from him, towards the river. Now he wished it was silent again.

'Not my fight,' he whispered.

To his relief the dragging sound stopped. The loud splash that followed was worse though. Jimmy took one more deep breath, sat up slowly and looked across to where he'd last seen the men. The bricklayer was on his own now, his back to Jimmy, standing at the rail and peering at the river. The other man – the social worker – had vanished, his satchel now lying on the ground. After a few minutes, the tall man turned, picked up the bag and left.

As soon as he was out of sight, Jimmy went to the rail, Dog at his heels, and looked over. There was nothing to see. Just the black waters of the River Tyne, still as a grave.

Bloody buskers. Jimmy opened his eyes and stared at the blue sky through the open roof. A seagull screeched. The busker continued to whine on about somebody he used to know. Jimmy seemed to hear that song every day. The sound of the summer, he'd bet people called it. Dog yelped somewhere nearby.

Then he remembered. The bricklayer and the social worker. A fight of some kind, maybe. A splash. He sat up quickly and looked out of the pavilion. The optimistic early-

morning busker had set up in front of the cruise boats.
A street sweeper was driving his truck slowly along the
path and one or two over-keen commuters were making
their way into work. A normal day. Not a crime scene. No
dead body floating in the river. No police tape. Nothing had
changed.

Dog was chasing the seagull. Or maybe it was the other
way around. It was hard to tell: one swooped and the other
leapt, meeting somewhere in the middle. Dog came off
worse this time, tumbling to the ground before turning
and running back to the pavilion. A tactical retreat. Jimmy
grabbed a handful of dog biscuits from the front of his
backpack and held his palm out to the grateful terrier. The
seagull looked on, perhaps considering whether it could
take the pair of them. To Dog's obvious disgust, Jimmy
tossed one of the biscuits to the bird, who caught it in
mid-air and immediately gulped it down.

Jimmy stared at the water, the light bouncing off it to
the Sage, a giant mirrored music hall on the other side of
the river, and back again. He could smell coffee. Glancing
behind, he saw that a mobile food van had set up shop on
the road behind the pavilion.

He turned back and watched as a tall, balding man in a
black jacket stopped next to the busker. The man dropped a
coin in a biscuit tin on the ground, and then turned to walk
towards the pavilion. Jimmy pretended to be busy with his
bag, waiting for the man to say something, but he walked
straight up the steps, past him, and out the other side,
heading for the offices across the square. Jimmy watched

him and wondered if it was the same man he'd seen in the middle of the night; wondered if he'd even seen a man in the middle of the night. He'd had stranger dreams, lots of them, but something told him this one was real.

The man stopped at the coffee van and ordered something, turning to look at the river as he waited, his elbows resting on the counter. Jimmy adjusted his position so he could keep an eye on him without making it obvious. The man was certainly big enough and the jacket looked similar, but it had been dark and he'd been half asleep.

Once his coffee was ready the man remained at the van, sipping carefully, occasionally glancing over at the pavilion. Gadge reckoned Jimmy was paranoid but he knew that people were always looking at him. He could feel it even when he couldn't see it. And this time it wasn't just a feeling. The man nodded as if to acknowledge him.

Jimmy began to gather up his stuff, ready to run, but there wasn't time. The man had thrown his empty cup into a small bin outside the van and was walking back over to him. Jimmy stuffed his sleeping bag into his rucksack but the man was already at the steps, pulling something shiny out of his pocket, shiny like a blade. He walked up the steps and stopped, his black Doc Martens brushing against the edge of Jimmy's rucksack, and dropped a couple of coins onto the ground next to Jimmy.

'Get yourself a cup of tea, mate,' he said.

5

Grey Street, Newcastle, June 8, 2012

Friday night. Jimmy and Gadge sat in a doorway staring at a middle-aged woman in a skin-tight pink dress taking a piss in an alley.

A moment earlier she had tailed off the back of a hen party, stumbled into the narrow gap between a karaoke bar and a low-rent fast-food joint, hiked her dress around her waist and squatted down. Four feet from the main drag.

'Divvn't fancy yours much,' Gadge laughed.

The woman looked up.

'Porvorts!' she shouted, raising her middle finger at them, while still, somehow, maintaining her balance on her haunches. Gadge saluted her back with his can of Tennants.

'Guilty, pet,' he said.

The trail of urine crept out of the alley and ran down the pavement in a manky echo of the Lort Burn, an open sewer that followed the same route back in the day. Or so Gadge said. Jimmy didn't do history.

'You can't escape history,' Gadge said, 'specially not in this city, bonny lad. It's everywhere.'

Jimmy looked around, and shook his head. Not any more. Aside from the hen party, most of whom seemed to be dressed as slutty air stewardesses, there were drunks everywhere, lying at the foot of Grey's Monument, staggering into walls and, in one case, sitting on top of a parked car shouting scripture at passers-by.

'Do not judge or you too will be judged,' the car-percher shouted, as a fake fire engine cruised past, a second hen party hanging out of its windows and doors, their squeals almost drowned out by someone murdering 'Should I Stay Or Should I Go' in the karaoke bar. You should go, Jimmy thought.

'It's like a modern-day Hogarth painting,' Gadge said. Jimmy shrugged. He didn't do art either.

'I wish you'd stop talking for a minute, Jimmy, it's hard to get a word in,' Gadge said, pulling more of their shared blanket onto his side of the doorway. It was a nice enough summer evening, but Gadge always seemed to feel the cold more than Jimmy.

'Still thinking about that thing by the river, are you?' Gadge said.

'Aye,' Jimmy said. He hadn't thought of much else. It was why he was sitting with Gadge and not in the company he normally preferred: his own. Safety in numbers. What had he seen, really? Not a murder exactly. A man was there and then he wasn't. That was all, wasn't it? Maybe he just ran off. Nothing he could do about it anyway. He wished he'd never said anything to Gadge, but his story had been so sketchy that even Mr Conspiracy himself had quickly lost interest.

'You could always run it by those two, see what they think,' Gadge said, nodding towards a pair of policemen walking up the other side of the street. 'Mind, they'll probably fit you up for it.'

The woman in the pink dress finished her business and tidied herself up, pulling her dress back over her arse. She stumbled out of the alley straight into the arms of the two policemen.

'Steady on, pet,' one of them said, grimacing at the acrid smell as he helped the woman stay upright.

'Jesus Christ,' his colleague said, glancing down at the stream of piss running past his black boots.

'Needs must,' the woman said. 'What goes in must come out, eh, lads?'

'She reminds me of my third wife,' Gadge muttered.

Jimmy had heard many a tale about Gadge's wives, none of them pretty – the tales, that was, not the wives. Jimmy would bet they'd all been lookers. Gadge blamed them for most of his ills. His business, a software-development company – another thing that Jimmy didn't have a clue about – had been divvied up between the three of them a piece at a time. Gadge didn't entirely blame the 'bitches' coven' for how he'd ended up though; mostly, he blamed Steve Jobs, who – according to Gadge – had stolen his idea for the iPod. Hence his nickname – a shorthand version of Inspector Gadget.

'I should give you a caution,' one of the policemen said to the woman.

'Hey, if you're gonna arrest someone, you should do them,' the woman said, pointing at Jimmy and Gadge. 'Fuckin' porvorts. One of 'em was 'aving a crafty wank just now.'

Jimmy started to get up, ready to be moved on, but then he saw *her*, in the distance, walking up the street towards him, arm in arm with a tall, tanned man in a grey suit. Bev. His Bev, laughing as the man whispered in her ear. Her hair was longer than he remembered from the last time he'd seen her, a month or so ago, when he'd watched from behind a wall as she moved into her latest new home, looking happier than he'd ever made her. She was so clearly better off without him that he'd vowed to stay out of her life rather than mess it up again.

Seeing her again was pushing that vow to its limits. He watched as she leaned into the man, her head resting lightly on his shoulder. Jimmy knew what that felt like and he still missed it.

As the couple got nearer, he realised he was wrong. A mistake he made at least once a week. It wasn't her.

'Who was that?' Gadge asked, as Jimmy turned to watch the happy couple disappear up the street.

'No one,' Jimmy said.

6

Byker Medical Centre, Newcastle, 1985

The room is so cold that Jimmy's nipples are erect. He's embarrassed and tries to cross his arms to hide them, but he's standing up so that feels weird.

'You can put your T-shirt back on,' the police doc says, taking his stethoscope from around his neck and dropping it on the desk.

Jimmy grabs his top from the back of the chair and pulls it on as quickly as he can as the doc flicks through some notes.

'Amateur boxing, eh? Still doing it?'

Jimmy nods.

'You're in good shape,' the man says.

'Thanks.'

'Physically, that is. It's your mental condition the recruiters are concerned about.'

'I'm fine,' Jimmy says, but instantly regrets it as the doc looks a bit pissed off.

'That's for me to decide,' he says curtly, putting down one piece of paper and picking up another.

'You were in the naval police?'

'I was a Leading Regulator.'

The doc frowns again, as if he's not used to being corrected. 'That *is* the naval police, isn't it?'

Jimmy thinks about explaining the differences but they're small and he's done enough damage so he just nods.

'Thought so,' the doc says, smiling to himself. 'How did you find the interview last week?'

The correct answer would have been 'a piece of piss' but Jimmy doesn't want to appear cocky.

'It went OK, I think,' he says. The Deputy Chief Constable, who'd asked most of the questions, had definitely been impressed with his knowledge of the law, arrest procedures and stuff like that. And he'd smashed the observational-skills test out of the park.

The doc skims through his notes.

'You did well. They liked you.'

Knew it, Jimmy thinks, but he just smiles. Keep things on the level. It had been Bev's idea to apply for the police, to use the strengths he'd developed in the Navy. She knew that he was bored out of his skull stacking shelves in the local Presto. And an old mate had told him that ex-military personnel were almost guaranteed entry – so much so that they wouldn't mind that he barely scraped the height requirement. He'd stood on his tiptoes just in case.

'It says on your discharge papers that you have good leadership skills,' the doc continues.

Jimmy supposes that's true. He likes telling people what to do right enough.

'You're exactly the kind of man we're looking for . . . but . . .'

Jimmy knew there'd be a *but*. There is always a *but* these days.

'. . . the medical discharge is worrying. *Psychologically unfit for duty*, it says. Tell me more about that.'

'My ship was bombed . . . my friend was killed. It threw me for a while. But I'm OK now,' Jimmy says.

And then the bell starts ringing. It sounds ridiculously loud in the small room and Jimmy immediately tries to put his hands over his ears – but not before he hears the doc say, 'It's the fire alarm.'

Jimmy sees the package on the floor as soon as he enters the flat. He puts down his six-pack of Carling Black Label and picks it up. There are several different addresses scrawled on it and crossed out. He rips it open and something shiny falls onto the threadbare carpet. A medal. The MOD had invited him to a presentation ceremony down in London months ago but he hadn't bothered to reply. Didn't want the fuss. Or the memories.

He examines the medal. It's fake silver with the Queen's head on one side, surrounded by something in Latin. He turns it over. The Falkland Islands' coat of arms is on the other side. He thinks about biting it – he's seen athletes do it at the Olympics – but he's no idea why, so doesn't. He's about to put it on the side table when he sees the blue, green and white striped ribbon hanging out of the torn packet. Jimmy attaches the ribbon to the medal, pins it on the white T-shirt he wore to the medical, sits down in his chair, turns on the TV and opens his first can of the day. The other five pints were on tap at his local around the corner.

On the TV, a man from the Open University with lank, greasy brown hair is explaining that a hole has appeared in the ozone layer. Jimmy understands about one word in three, so his gaze occasionally slips to the dusty photo of his wedding which sits on top of the TV cabinet: Jimmy in his No. 1 uniform, Bev glowing in a vintage red velvet number, wearing a smile that he hasn't seen for a while. Last time was when they bought the flat – using most of the lump sum he got with his medical discharge.

'Psychologically unfit, my arse,' he mutters to himself.

A Christmas edition of *Grange Hill* is on now and Jimmy is laughing at the French teacher's obvious wig. Five empty cans are scattered at his feet. When Bev walks into the front room he jumps to his feet and salutes, spilling warm lager on the carpet.

'Front room ready for inspection,' he says, though it clearly isn't.

'How did it go with the doc?' she asks.

He can see the hope in her eyes, how much she needs him to say, 'Great. I start next month.' Can't bear how disappointed she's going to be when she finds out he bollocksed it up; that he threw himself under the doc's desk and started crying like a baby when the fire alarm went off. He tries to think of something to say, an explanation that won't make him look like a twat, but in the end just shakes his head.

Her shoulders drop immediately.

Jimmy takes a swig from his can and offers it to her. She frowns.

'What do you think you're doing, Jimmy?' she says.

'Celebrating,' he says. 'I'm a hero.' He points to the medal, still hanging from his shirt. 'For services to Queen and country,' he says.

'Congratulations,' she says, slumping on to the sofa. 'I've had some news as well.'

He stares at her, curious, still holding the can out.

'I'm pregnant,' she says.

7

City Library, Newcastle, June 23, 2012

The City Library was a home for the homeless; warm with comfortable seats. The staff weren't exactly welcoming – apart from the old woman with the weird name that Jimmy could never remember – but they didn't kick you out unless you stank or swore at them. He and Deano usually went there a couple of times a week – which was ironic as the kid couldn't read a word. Jimmy had been sneaking in more often though, since the night at the river, checking the paper, looking for news of a body or something. There'd been nothing.

The last time they'd been in, Gadge had got himself banned for throwing a copy of *Down and Out in Paris and London* at the librarian who'd recommended it. And for telling her that he'd rather wipe his arse with it than read any more. At least it meant there was someone to look after Dog. Jimmy didn't like leaving him tied up outside.

Deano was off his face again, hadn't moved for ages, just

sat, staring at the wall. Special K, Jimmy reckoned. He was probably buried deep down inside a K-hole, like a dishevelled Alice in Wonderland, enjoying a world way different from the shitty one he lived in. Maybe that was where Jimmy had been that night, over two weeks ago now, off in a K-world of his own; a world where people got thrown into rivers. But he hadn't taken anything for a long time. Although one of the bastards might have put something in his food, he supposed. Some people just liked to mess with your head. Even a tiny bit of horse tranquilliser could do that. That Goldilocks would be the sort. He knew that was shite though; he hadn't been wasted that night, just half asleep.

Deano blinked a couple of times and smiled – a welcome-to-La-La-Land smile. Jimmy didn't begrudge him his moment of happiness. He'd heard lots of sob stories, but Deano's was one of the saddest. The poor kid was a twelve-year-old trapped in a man's body, didn't know what the hell was going on half the time. When he was fourteen he was locked up for breaking and entering – because he was tiny the bigger kids would get him to climb through windows and let them in to rob the place. Deano was the one who kept getting caught and eventually he got put in a secure kids' home. By the time he came out his mum had done a runner with his baby brother. He never saw them again. Been on the streets ever since. How he'd survived was anyone's guess but if he kept doing ketamine, it was only a matter of time till he'd jump off the Tyne Bridge, thinking it was an Olympic diving board. Wouldn't be the first.

'You alright, love?' someone said.

Jimmy turned around. The old librarian with the funny name had crept up on him. He should be more vigilant. Just because someone looked like your gran it didn't mean they were harmless. He stared at her badge, tried to work out what it said. A-O-I-F-E. She saw him looking.

'It's Ee-fa,' she said, laughing. 'No one ever gets it right.'

'Ee-fa,' Jimmy repeated.

'Perfect,' Aoife said. She glanced at Deano, concerned. 'Is he OK?'

'He's fine. Just tired.'

'OK.' She raised an eyebrow but seemed willing to let it go for now. 'You look like the responsible type. Keep an eye on him.'

Jimmy nodded and she walked off. She was obviously as mad as a box of frogs if she thought he looked responsible. A convict was what he looked like: scarred, pale, jumpy. Definitely not responsible.

'S'proper lush,' Deano sighed, pointing at the blank wall.

Jimmy picked up the paper and flicked through the news pages: the Queen's impending visit to the North East, an obesity scare and a big story about fracking at the coast – whatever 'fracking' was – but no dead bodies found floating in the Tyne.

Deano was snoring gently now, a sliver of drool hanging from the corner of his mouth. Jimmy looked around but there was no sign of the librarian, so he left him to it and went back to the paper. A headline on page seventeen, next to a picture of a young girl caught his eye.

GIRL IN MISSING DAD PLEA

A young Newcastle woman today issued a heart-wrenching plea for her missing father to get in touch.

Carrie Carpenter, 22, who works as a nurse at the Freeman Hospital, said that her dad Roger, from Heaton, has been missing for more than two weeks.

'We were supposed to meet for a drink,' Carrie said, 'but he never turned up and I haven't seen him since. No one has.'

Roger Carpenter, 45, an environmental campaigner and part-time lecturer at Northumberland University, is divorced from Carrie's mother, Alice. He moved out of the family home four years ago, but he and his daughter have remained close.

'We meet up regularly, once a fortnight at least, to catch up, hear each other's news,' Carrie said. 'He wouldn't just disappear without getting in touch, so I know something's happened to him but the police aren't interested. They just say he's an adult and it's up to him what he does.

'If anyone knows where he is, or has seen anything of him, could they please contact me on Facebook.'

A Northumbria Police spokesman said that the investigation was 'ongoing'.

It was probably nothing. The timing of the man's disappearance was about right, but that was all. Jimmy was going to turn the page when he saw what he'd missed first time around.

The girl in the photo was Carrie Carpenter, her fair hair tied back in a ponytail, a concerned expression on her face. She looked much younger than her twenty-two years. More importantly, he now realised she was holding a small, dark-framed photo of her missing father in front of her. Jimmy studied the photo-in-a-photo closely. It was a head-and-shoulders shot, clearly posed, as if for an ID card or something. In it, Roger Carpenter was smiling, laughter lines spreading out from his eyes and mouth. He had long brown hair and a moustache; aside from the smile, he looked like a typical social worker.

8

Ouseburn Valley, Newcastle, June 26, 2012

Sinking into the pitch-black water. Lungs bursting. Ears screaming. Jimmy tries to swim but can't. Getting deeper and deeper. Something . . . someone . . . holding his legs. Looks down. Can't see a thing. Pulls his feet up. A headless body, arms entangled around Jimmy's feet. He kicks out, once, twice. Free. Tries to swim up, water thick as tar. Six strokes, seven, eight, still no light above. Can't hold on, stars filling his vision. Breathes. Filthy water fills his mouth, pouring in, choking him. One more stroke, a glimmer of light, closer, another stroke. He bursts through the surface, spitting the foul liquid out. Air. Light. Smoke. Oil. Nothing else. Just ocean. Miles and miles of ocean. Then, a noise in the distance. A rumbling sound. Getting louder. Getting nearer.

Daylight. Jimmy woke up, sweating, as the Metro train rumbled over the railway bridge, sixty feet above his head.

'*Namaskar.*' The tall, bearded Sikh bowed his head, put the palms of his hands together as if in prayer and pressed his thumbs to his forehead. Gadge followed suit. Jimmy was a step behind, watching his friend and following his every move, glad that one of them knew the ropes.

'Welcome to the gurdwara,' the Sikh said, before moving aside to let them pass.

Gadge headed straight to a small room just off the entrance hall. A bench stood on one side of the room and on the other, the wall was lined with shelves, most of which were covered in shoes. It reminded Jimmy of a bowling alley he'd been to when he was a kid.

'Take your shoes off,' Gadge said.

'Why?' Jimmy said.

'It's respect, man, cleanliness and that.'

Gadge had already removed his trainers. Jimmy did the same and then, seeing the state of his socks, took them off too; he made a mental note to take his laundry to the drop-in centre that afternoon. His feet were aching from the long walk across the Town Moor, past the cows, with Dog straining at the leash. But at least they were clean. Good job he'd nipped into the Pit Stop for a shower to get rid of the night sweat.

They placed their shoes on one of the shelves and headed back out of the room where a young Sikh woman handed them each an orange scarf.

'*Shukriya*,' Gadge said.

'*Koi nahi*,' the young woman replied.

Gadge tied the scarf around his head. Jimmy copied him. As he did, he noticed the large noticeboard on the wall. Pinned between adverts for Punjabi lessons and a festival commemorating the martyrdom of some guru was a poster headed 'Have You Seen This Man?' Underneath the heading was a larger version of the photo he had seen the girl holding in the paper. Despite the enlargement he still had no idea if it was the man he'd seen on the Quayside.

'Oi, slow coach!' Gadge shouted.

Jimmy looked up. Gadge was halfway down the corridor, urging him to catch up. He hurried along and followed his friend into a large room where several Sikhs were sitting on the floor, cross-legged, each with a metal tray of food in front of them.

'Just do what I do,' Gadge said.

Jimmy followed him to a counter at the end, where they both picked up trays of food and went to sit down near the other men.

'This is definitely free?' Jimmy said. 'I'm not going to have to wash up or owt?'

'Why aye, man,' Gadge said. 'They call it *langar*. It's a Sikh tradition; they like to share stuff, all men are equal and shite.'

'What is that?' Jimmy asked, pointing at a dollop of orange gunk that filled a quarter of the tray.

'Dhal, man. Lentils, and spices and stuff, tomatoes probably, bit of turmeric. Just grab the paratha, the flatbread, and dip it in. Eat, man, before it gets cold.'

Jimmy had no truck with religion, but maybe some were better than others. He dug in.

'Good, eh?' Gadge said, picking a crumb of something from his beard. Jimmy nodded. He had barely eaten for two days, fretting too much about what he should do, and so whatever this was he was going to enjoy it. He was so hungry that he'd reluctantly agreed to leave Dog tied up outside. Free food was free food.

'If you try and take him in there, they'll probably chuck him in a pot,' Gadge had said. Jimmy was pretty sure that was bollocks.

He wished his old man could see him now. The miserable bastard had been a card-carrying racist and if it wasn't for the fact he was already dead, the idea of his son eating in a Sikh temple would have given him a heart attack. Even the idea of a Sikh temple existing in Newcastle would have been enough to start the palpitations.

He tried to imagine what it would have been like to have had any kind of relationship with his dad, like that Carrie lass seemed to have, meeting up for a chat and a drink and that. But he couldn't. His dad had liked a drink right enough, but he tended to talk with his fists.

'Have you listened to a word I've said?' Gadge said.

'What?'

'I'm talking about the Queen's visit, man, how she's descended from lizards. Shouldn't say owt really. People who speak out get disappeared, ya knaa.' Gadge looked around to make sure no one else could hear him. 'I'm putting me life at risk here, trying to warn you about stuff, the least you could do is listen,' he added.

'Sorry,' Jimmy said, yawning, 'just tired. Didn't sleep much.'

'Bollocks, man, I knaa what's gannin' on. I saw the thing

on the noticeboard. It's that lass from the paper, isn't it? Been bothering you for days.'

Jimmy wished he'd kept his gob shut. Gadge never let anything go; he liked to worry away at stuff until it was sorted.

'Why don't you get in touch with her?' Gadge said. 'Can't hurt.'

'I don't know how.'

'Aye, but I do.'

'You shouldn't be in here!'

Jimmy couldn't believe he'd let the old librarian sneak up on him again. She was like a ghost.

'He's barred,' Aoife said, pointing at Gadge.

'But I've got to do me searches,' Gadge said.

'Your what?'

'Job searches. Thirty-five hours a week searching or I lose me benefits.'

To Jimmy's surprise Aoife was nodding in sympathy.

'They make you jump through hoops, don't they?'

'Aye,' Gadge said, his voice cracking. 'It's demeaning for a man of my age. And I can't afford to go to an Internet café because the bastards withhold your money until you've done it. It's a vicious circle.'

The triple whammy of obscure regulations, volumes of paperwork and hostile staff was enough to put most street people off trying to claim benefits – they preferred to take their chances with a begging bowl. But not Gadge. Beer money was a powerful motivator for Jimmy's friend.

'My man Jimmy here has no idea how hard these things are – he's got a private income,' Gadge said.

Jimmy's 'private income' was the small pension he'd been awarded when he was medically discharged from the Navy back in the day. Gadge liked to take the piss out of him for it.

Aoife looked Jimmy up and down and laughed.

'Aye, right.' She sighed. 'The boss'll kill me for this, but he's not here at the moment so you're lucky.' She pointed at Gadge. 'Five minutes and then you've got to go. No more, mind, and you'd better be on your best behaviour, no cursing and definitely no book-throwing.'

Gadge looked suitably sheepish. 'Thank you,' he said.

Aoife wandered off and they returned to business. Gadge had already set Jimmy up with an e-mail account and got him on to Facebook before Aoife had interrupted them. He'd amused himself by making Jimmy's picture an image of Charlie Chaplin in his tramp guise.

'I cannot believe you didn't knaa what a mouse was, Jimmy lad. There are bairns living in the Kalahari desert who knaa more shite than you. Watch and learn, son,' he said. 'What was the lass's name?'

'Carrie,' Jimmy said, 'Carrie Carpenter.'

Gadge entered the name in a box at the top of the Facebook page and a list of four people appeared, each with a small photo.

'Recognise any of them?' Gadge said. Jimmy looked closely, trying to remember the picture from the paper.

'That one, I think,' he said, pointing at the third one

down. Gadge clicked on the name and a page came up with the girl's name at the top. Underneath that was the picture from the paper, Carrie holding the photo of her dad.

Gadge whistled in appreciation.

'Not too shabby, Jimmy lad. I can see why you'd want to get hold of her, like.'

'Piss off, Gadge, it's not like that.'

'Whatever you say, son.' Gadge moved the little arrow thing and clicked on a box that said 'Message'.

'What do you want to say to her?'

'I don't know. Is it private?'

'Aye. Just between you and her.'

Jimmy thought for a moment.

'Tell her that I think I might have seen her dad. On the night of the Queen's celebration thing. But I'm not sure. It might not have been him.'

Gadge typed in the message and hit send.

'There you go son, all done.'

Jimmy could see Aoife heading back up the stairs.

'You'd better go,' he said to Gadge.

'What about you?' Gadge said.

'I'll just wait a minute, see if she replies.'

'It'll probably be a while, ya knaa. Could be days.'

'Aye, but even so.'

'OK, catch you later.'

Once Gadge had left, Jimmy sat down at the screen and tried to remember how it all worked. He grabbed the mouse and moved the little arrow up to the box at the top, took a deep breath and typed in another name. He wasn't sure of the surname she'd be using now but he had to start somewhere.

One click and there she was. Top of the list. Older now, obviously, but it was unmistakably her. He'd know her anywhere. He smiled at the knowledge that she'd kept his surname.

He clicked on the photo and her page came up. Another photo, more recent, by the look of it, taken in a bar, hugging and smiling with a group of friends, drinks in their hands. She looked happy.

Jimmy moved down the page, soaking it all up, more photos, a band playing on stage, a cat lying on a bed, a boy with a stud piercing in his eyebrow. And finally, from a couple of weeks ago, a group of students standing outside a building he knew well, Newcastle College. He'd slept in a Portakabin in the car park once.

There, in the middle of them, her arms around the shoulders of the people beside her, was his daughter, Kate.

9

The Royal Victoria Infirmary, Newcastle, 1986

Bev's screams are deafening. Jimmy instinctively moves to put his hand over her mouth to quieten her down but stops himself at the last moment. The midwife would definitely not approve. Not to mention how Bev would react. But still, it's tempting. He knows she should have taken more drugs but she's been reading one of those natural childbirth books and is sticking to gas and air.

He's sitting on the edge of the bed, holding her hand tightly as the gap between the contractions narrows. Bev is sweating buckets now, her face shiny and red, contorted in pain.

She screams again and suddenly he's back there. The smoke and heat, the cries of men dying in agony, the smell of burning flesh, pipes bursting all around him.

'Are you OK?'

Jimmy opens his eyes. The midwife is staring at him, concern etched on her face, her hand on his shoulder. He blinks, re-orientating, his eyes darting from side to side. It's safe here, he's fine. He nods.

'Yes.'

'Good, I don't want you fainting on me; I've got enough on my hands.'

Bev moans again, a deep, guttural sound, animalistic. He squeezes her hand.

'Nearly there, love,' he says.

'He's right, pet, very close now,' the midwife confirms. 'One last big push and you'll be done.'

Bev grabs the mouthpiece and breathes in a final gulp.

'You ready?' the midwife asks. Bev nods.

'Let's go, then. Start pushing again.'

Jimmy can feel Bev's body tense as she strains to push the baby out, howling as she does. He squeezes her hand.

'Again,' the midwife urges.

'Fuuuuck!' Bev screams as she pushes.

'And again.'

Another howl and another push.

Jimmy leans in close to Bev, desperately trying to say the right thing.

'You're doing great, love, keep going.'

'Fuck off, you bastard,' she screams in his face, pushing once again, her upper body lifting off the bed as she does.

'That's it, love, keep going, I can see the baby's head. D'you want to have a look?' The midwife taps Jimmy on the shoulder. 'I'm talking to you, love.'

Jimmy shakes his head. 'No thanks, I'm good.' He's not

though, not good at all. He's so nervous that he thinks he might throw up.

'Push then, darling, come on, a few more and you'll be done,' the midwife says.

Bev cries out again, the sound muffled by her clenched teeth.

'And again, nearly there!' the midwife says.

Bev rolls onto her side, her face away from Jimmy, and he can see her whole body clenching as she pushes one more time, groaning with the strain.

He tries to pat her on the back but she shrugs him off. Suddenly, her low moan is interrupted by another sound, a much higher pitch.

'She's out!' the midwife says.

She, Jimmy thinks, she said *she*.

Bev rolls onto her back again and the midwife thrusts the baby onto her chest for her to hold, wiping away the blood and slime as she does. The baby is sliding around, mewling, until Bev wraps an arm gently around her, as the midwife continues to clean up. Bev's weeping now, sobbing loudly, a mixture of joy and relief, Jimmy thinks.

He's staring at this little creature, with her tiny tuft of jet-black hair plastered to her scalp. He counts the fingers and toes – ten of each. That's good.

And then she opens her dark blue eyes and Jimmy falls instantly and irrevocably in love.

'Hello, Kate,' he says, knowing for sure that he is going to get his shit together properly now. Everything is going to be great from now on.

10

Jesmond Dene, Newcastle, June 28, 2012

The goats smelled like shit. Jimmy sat as far away from them as he could, wishing they were meeting somewhere else, wishing he hadn't agreed to meet her at all. A well-dressed, middle-aged woman walked past him, nose turned up, looking anywhere but at him. He thought about following her, just for the crack. Thought better of it – not the time to piss about.

He used to come to Pets Corner when he was a kid. His mam would bring him, just to get out of the house, away from Dad and his moods. She always had a thing for pigs.

A dog-walker was dragged past him, four leads straining, all different breeds, big and small, yapping like crazy, pulling the poor sod faster than he wanted. Dog ignored them, happily settled under the bench. Jimmy looked towards the park entrance, but there was nowt – a couple of pushchairs, a jogger way off in the distance. Maybe she'd changed her mind.

Behind him, the hens kicked off, clucking over some seeds chucked into the pen by an old woman carrying a shopping bag. Jimmy glanced at the 'No Feeding the Animals' sign. Good for her.

Dog stirred underneath his legs, interested in the birds behind him, itching to chase them. Jimmy stood up, looked around; still nothing. Probably for the best, anyway. Nothing good ever came from getting involved in other people's shit; he'd learned that lesson alright. He grabbed Dog's lead and walked towards the river that ran along the side of Pets Corner.

As they reached a small bridge a little girl came tearing around the bend from the other side, closely followed by a man, her dad, he guessed. The girl was looking behind her, trying not to be caught, so didn't see them until it was almost too late. Dog yelped but just before she was about to run into them, the chasing man scooped her up in his arms. The girl clearly thought it was hilarious, giggling and wriggling, trying to shake herself free.

'Sorry about that, mate,' the man said, 'can't take your eyes off them for a minute, can you?'

'Sholda,' the girl demanded, 'sholda, sholda.'

The man laughed and hoisted her onto his shoulders, keeping a tight grip on her legs.

'Birdies, birdies,' she chanted, pointing towards the animal pens.

'No rest for the wicked, eh?' the man said and headed off.

Jimmy watched them go, trying to remember if he'd ever brought Kate there, pretty sure he hadn't. Bev did all that stuff. He shook his head as if to clear it; if he dwelled too much on the things he regretted, there'd be no space for anything else. The little girl was clapping with glee as she and her dad neared the goats.

Bollocks, Jimmy thought, I'll give it five more minutes. He headed back to the bench.

The jogger was by the gates now – a girl, young woman, whatever. The sun was in Jimmy's eyes so he couldn't really see her. She stopped by a man with an ice cream and took out her earphones. They seemed to be talking but it was hard to tell from so far away.

Jimmy watched. Could that be her? She left the ice-cream guy, moved past the large, gateless pillars guarding the entrance and walked towards him, then sat on the next bench, a yard or two away, looking around. It was definitely Carrie; she was prettier in the flesh, even though her cheeks were flushed from the jogging. He saw her check him out and wince, edging away. She glanced at her watch and looked around, restless, uneasy, a bit pissed off even.

In for a penny.

'Hi,' he said. She jumped a little.

'Hi,' she said. Tentative. Understandable, he thought, glad that he'd brushed his hair and had a shave that morning.

'I'm Jimmy,' he said. She looked across at him, eyes wide.

'You? You're Jimmy?'

'Aye,' he said. She tried to keep the disappointment from her face. Failed.

'I was expecting . . .'

He made her work for it.

'. . . someone, um, different, you know. Sorry,' she added.

''Salright,' he said, 'used to it.'

That was a lie. You never got used to it.

Carrie got up and moved over to his bench. He appreciated the gesture.

'You said in your message you knew something about my dad?'

'I don't know. Maybe.'

'How do you know him?'

'I don't,' Jimmy said. Carrie frowned and looked down at her muddy trainers. She hadn't yet learned to hide her feelings. Not like him.

'I don't have any money,' she said.

'What?' he said, puzzled. She lifted her head, glared at him, clearly seething.

'I can't pay you, if that's what you think.'

'I don't want money.'

'What then? You better not be pissing me about.'

He could feel his anger building. Knew he should have kept out of it, stayed in the shadows.

She was standing up now, holding her earphones, ready to leave.

'You know what,' she said, 'forget about it. I'm done. It's all . . . shit.'

'Wait—' Jimmy said.

'Everyone thinks he's just gone off with another one of his slappers – Mum, his boss, the police. Maybe he has, maybe I'm the stupid one for caring.'

'Look,' Jimmy said, trying to slow her down. It didn't

work; she was pacing furiously now, ready to go, her voice getting higher, close to tears.

'I thought . . . I thought that I might be getting somewhere. Your message didn't seem like the others, the trolls who were, I don't know, just messing with my head, I thought—'

'I think I saw something,' Jimmy said. She stopped pacing around.

'What? What did you see?'

'I don't know. Something, someone. Could have been your dad. There was a fight . . . not a fight, an argument.'

'Argument? Where? When?'

'On the Quayside, night of the fourth of June, late though, morning of the fifth really, I suppose.'

He'd looked the date up in the library, remembered the Queen's Diamond Jubilee thing on the telly in the dining hall earlier that same night.

Her face lit up, she sat back down.

'That's bang on, that's right in between when I saw him last and when he stood me up. What was he doing?'

'Steady,' Jimmy said, trying to gather his thoughts. 'I'm not even sure it was him. Describe him. How tall was he?'

'*Is* he. Don't say *was*, he's not dead.'

I really hope not, Jimmy thought. 'Sorry,' he said.

'He's short. An inch shorter than me.' Carrie stood up again to show him. 'I tease him about it all the time.' She sat down again, excited now.

'He has long brown hair, like in the photo, nearly always wears a denim jacket, has a bunch of them. I'm always checking out the vintage shops for him.'

She was on a roll now; Jimmy could almost see the hope bursting out of her as she searched her memory for something else, something to clinch the deal.

'His satchel! He takes it with him everywhere, I bought it for his last birthday. His black satchel. Did you see that?'

Fuck, Jimmy thought, closing his eyes. Fuck. Fuck. Fuck. He opened his eyes again. She was even closer now, staring right at him.

'You saw him!' she said.

Jimmy hesitated but couldn't stop himself; her desperation was a steamroller, crushing his resistance in its path. He nodded.

'Maybe . . . I think so. I think I saw him.'

She reached for his hand. He pulled away. Not ready for that.

'You said there was an argument. What was he doing? What did you see?' she asked.

'Not much. I was half asleep. If it was him, he was by the river, arguing with another man, a big guy in a black jacket and a bobble hat.' She shook her head as if to say, *Could be anyone.*

'What happened? Where did he go after that?' she asked.

'I don't know . . . he didn't.'

'What do you mean? He must have gone somewhere?'

Jimmy looked at his feet. He could end it all here. Not his fight. Little white lie. Move on. She grabbed his hand, held it tight this time.

'I need to know, Jimmy,' she said. He looked up at her.

'I think he went into the river,' he said. He saw the

confusion on her face. It wasn't the answer she was expecting or hoping for.

'What?' she whispered. Then louder. 'What do you mean? You *think* he went into the river. Did he or didn't he?'

'I don't know, didn't really see it. There was a struggle, I think. A splash.'

'Was he pushed or what? Did you actually see him fall in the river?'

'No, it's just—'

'Just what?' she shouted, tears rolling down her face.

'Well, he was there, and then he wasn't. The other man left. I told you, I was half asleep.'

'What did you do?' He pulled his hand from hers, turned away.

'I looked in the water,' he said quietly. 'Couldn't see anything, it was dark.'

'Is that it? Did you tell anyone? What else did you do?'

'Nothing,' he muttered.

'Why not?' she shouted.

'I was . . . hiding.'

'From what?' She jumped to her feet. Jimmy looked up at her, his fear replaced by shame as he saw how much she was hurting.

'From everything,' Jimmy said.

'You have to go to the police,' Carrie said, wiping her face with her sleeve. 'Tell them what you just told me. You have to!'

Jimmy realised he'd been shaking his head, only slightly, but she'd noticed.

'I'll come with you,' she added, 'help explain. They need to hear this.'

'I can't,' Jimmy said.

'Why not?' she asked.

How could he explain it? She'd run a mile if she knew the real reason.

'There's been . . . in the past . . . I've done some bad stuff.'

'But—'

'I just can't, OK.'

Carrie screamed in frustration.

'You OK, Carrie?'

Jimmy looked up. The guy with the ice cream was standing there, just a bit of the cone left in his hand.

'I'm fine, Mike,' she said. Mike didn't seem convinced but let it go.

'It's just that I need to get off?' Mike said.

'Can you give me ten minutes more?' she said.

'Sure.' Mike gave Jimmy a quick once-over before walking back to the gate.

'Boyfriend?' Jimmy asked. She gave him a strange look. Hesitated.

'No. Just a mate,' she said, 'keeping an eye out for me, just to be on the safe side.' She sat back down.

'Please,' she said, 'you have to help me.'

'Me and the police don't get on,' Jimmy said.

'I said I'll come with you.'

'They won't believe me. They never do.'

'They didn't believe me either, doesn't stop me trying.' More contact. Her knee brushed against his.

'Have you got kids?' she asked. He thought about lying, knew where she was heading.

'Kid,' he said, 'a daughter. A few years older than you.'

'Imagine I was her, looking for you,' she urged.

He'd tried to do that already. Couldn't. He wasn't even sure that Kate knew he was still alive; or even remembered that he'd ever been alive.

A scream came from the pens behind. Dog leapt out from beneath the bench as Jimmy spun around. He breathed again. One of the goats was right up against the fence, standing on its hind legs, its front hooves scraping against the wire. It screamed again, as near to a human scream as made no difference. Dog jumped at the fence and the goat pulled away.

'I should get going,' Jimmy said. 'Dog'll be hungry.'

He tried to get up, but Carrie was holding on to his sleeve.

'He's my dad, Jimmy.'

She didn't know he was more trouble than he was worth. That he would let her down like he had everyone else. How could she?

'Help me, please. You're my only hope.'

If that was true, she really was in trouble.

Sod it. Jimmy nodded.

Pilgrim Street Police Station, Newcastle, June 28, 2012

'Get that filthy mutt out of here.'

Jimmy hesitated, still automatically inclined to follow orders from people in uniform, but Carrie wasn't having any of it, charging up to the angry desk sergeant.

'You again?' the sergeant said, grimacing.

'Is DS Burns in?' Carrie asked.

'No, he isn't, and I'm serious, the dog can't be in here. Health and safety,' the sergeant growled.

Dog cringed at the outburst and Jimmy started to back out but Carrie held on to his arm. Two bored-looking teenagers sprawling on a bench by the wall sat up, no doubt hoping it was going to kick off.

'Who else is dealing with my dad's disappearance?' she said.

'How many times, pet? You can't keep coming in here. No one is dealing with your dad's "disappearance" as you call it. No crime, no police involvement.'

'There's new evidence. We want to make a statement,' she said.

'Oh, *we* do, do we? Who's we when they're at home?'

Carrie pulled Jimmy forward. 'Me and Jimmy. My dad was attacked. He's a witness.'

The sergeant looked at Jimmy properly for the first time and laughed. Jimmy looked away.

'This is your witness?' the sergeant asked. 'Nice to see he's made the effort to dress up.'

He sniggered and glanced at a civilian typist sitting behind him for approval. She ignored him. He turned back to Carrie who wasn't giving him an inch.

'You're serious?' he said, pointing at Jimmy. '*He's* your witness?'

'It's rank in here,' one of the teenagers on the bench said. His mate laughed.

'Can I speak to your superior?' Carrie said to the sergeant.

'No, you can't,' he said. 'Look, love, here's the deal. If Jimmy here wants to make a statement, that's fine, up to him. I'll get one of the lads to take him through. But let's be clear. There's no "we" involved. You can step outside and take that manky mongrel with you. If Jimmy really wants to make a statement, that is?' He gave Jimmy an intimidating glare, clearly expecting him to back down.

Every bit of Jimmy wanted to turn and walk out but he held his ground, conscious of Carrie's pleading look coming at him from the side, aware of how much she needed him to do this.

'I'd, um, like to make a statement,' he said.

The sergeant sighed.

'Right. You,' he said, pointing to Jimmy, 'take a seat on the bench, someone will fetch you in a minute; and you,' pointing at Carrie this time, 'take that bloody dog outside.'

'Thank you,' Carrie said, mainly to Jimmy. 'Will you be OK?'

Probably not, Jimmy thought, but it was way too late to back out.

'I'll be fine,' he said, handing Dog's lead to her.

'Don't worry, I'll look after him. We'll go for a walk,' she said. 'I'll be back in a bit, see how you're getting on.'

Once she'd gone Jimmy sat down on the end of the bench. The nearest teenager made a show of edging away.

'Fuckin' neighbourhood's going to shit,' the kid said, staring at Jimmy, making his mate laugh so hard that snot hung from his nose and he had to wipe it off with his sleeve.

'Cheesy bastard,' his mate muttered.

It was the smell thing that always pissed Jimmy off the most. When you had to live in a floating tin can with 250 other men your personal hygiene had to be spot on – unless you wanted a hatch cover dropped on your fingers accidentally on purpose. Even though he'd long since left the Navy, he still made sure he showered at least every other day and did his laundry twice a week – more than most, he reckoned. He knew the clothes he got from the Pit Stop store weren't exactly box-fresh but they were as clean and tidy as he could get them.

'Should have made him go outside and let the dog stay,' the first kid said, laughing again.

Enough, Jimmy thought. He opened his eyes wide, turned and feinted as if to butt the nearest kid, but pulled back at the last second, barking loudly instead.

'Ruff, ruff,' he barked, into the kid's ear.

'Nut job,' the kid shouted, leaping up from the bench.

'Oi,' the sergeant yelled, 'behave yourselves or I'll throw you all out.'

Jimmy smiled at the kid, who stayed standing, his back to the opposite wall, making sure he could see what Jimmy was doing. Jimmy growled under his breath. He knew how to do crazy; he'd had plenty of practice.

Jimmy knew it was going to be a waste of time when he saw who they sent to take his statement. One of the coppers from the park. Not the nasty bastard who had beaten Deano up; the smaller one, who had done nothing to stop it. Not that Jimmy could point the finger. He knew the type though – don't rock the boat and that; Jimmy'd been one himself for a long time. This one said he was called PC Stevens.

Stevens led the way down a corridor, which reeked of disinfectant, to a small, bare room, furnished with just a desk and two chairs. He told Jimmy to sit down and sat opposite him, putting a pad of paper and a pen on the desk in front of him. Jimmy shuddered at the memory of the last time he'd been in a room like this. The beating he'd taken. Black boots stamping on him. He'd pissed himself that time.

'Sergeant Williams said you wanted to make a statement,' Stevens said. Jimmy could almost smell the apathy and imagined the man dragging himself into work each morning, as if he was carrying a sack of coal on his back.

'That's right,' Jimmy said.

'I'll just take a few notes first, if that's OK?'

PC Stevens picked up the pen and scribbled on the side of the pad to make sure it was working.

'Name?' he said.

'Jimmy.'

'Jimmy what?'

'Just Jimmy.'

'Any relation to Just Jack? Or Just William?' Stevens said, laughing.

Jimmy stared him out, said nothing.

'I'm going to need a surname.'

'Stevens,' Jimmy said.

'Are you taking the piss?'

'No. It's a common name.' Stevens gave Jimmy a look, trying to work out if he was being insulted, but decided life was too short. He sighed and started writing.

'Address?'

'Don't have one.'

'I'll put No Fixed Abode, shall I?'

'If you like,' Jimmy said.

Stevens wrote something down. Jimmy tried to see it, but the policeman covered it with his hand.

'Right. Now, what did you want to make a statement about?'

'I saw a man pushed into the River Tyne, down by the Quayside.'

'Did you now? When was this?'

'Early June, night of the fourth, or maybe the morning of the fifth.'

Stevens snorted.

'That's more than three weeks ago.'

'I know.'

'Why has it taken you so long to report it? There's no reward or anything, if that's what you've been told.'

Jimmy bit his tongue. He was getting pissed off with people thinking he wanted money. First Carrie and now this twat.

'Well?' Stevens said.

'I've been busy,' Jimmy said.

'Doing what?'

'This and that.'

PC Stevens put his pen down and glared at Jimmy.

'If I wanted to talk to a sarky twat I could have stayed at home and had a cuppa with the missus. So let's start again. Did you know the man you saw pushed into the Tyne?'

'No,' Jimmy said. 'Not then, but I think I know who it was now.'

'And who is that?' PC Stevens picked up the pen again.

'His name's Roger Carpenter. His daughter reported him missing a few days after I saw the fight.'

'What fight?'

'I saw two men arguing.'

'And can you describe these two men?'

'Aye. The man I saw pushed in was about five foot six. He had long brown hair and was wearing a denim jacket. The other man was taller, over six foot, and bigger; he looked like a bricklayer.'

'A bricklayer?'

'That's what I said. His upper body was big, like he did a lot of heavy lifting.'

'Could just have been a gym bunny?'

'S'pose so,' Jimmy agreed.

'What about the men's faces? Can you describe them?'

'It was dark. I think the big man had a beard.'

'You *think*?' Stevens sighed.

'I was a long way away.'

'And you saw the bigger man push the other man ...' Stevens glanced at his notes, 'Mr Carpenter, into the river.'

'Sort of.'

'What do you mean "sort of"?'

'I didn't see it, I heard it. They were arguing – there was a tussle of some kind and then a sound like someone being dragged along the ground. And a splash.'

'A splash?'

'It's the noise that's made when something falls into water.'

Stevens jabbed his pen at Jimmy's face. 'One more crack like that and I'll take your eye out, capiche?'

Jimmy nodded.

'So, what you're telling me is that you didn't actually see the man being pushed? Or going into the water? Is that right?'

'Yes,' Jimmy said, 'but there wasn't anywhere else he could have gone. If he'd run off, I would have seen it.'

'Did you see anything else?'

'The big man took the other man's bag. A black satchel. It was lying on the ground. He picked it up and took it with him.'

'Is that it?'

'They were arguing – before the splash – something about the system, something wrong with the system.'

Stevens rolled his eyes but made a note anyway.

'That it now?' he said.

Jimmy nodded.

Stevens stood up.

'OK, we're done.'

'Aren't I supposed to sign something?' Jimmy said. He'd been taught to always get the witness to sign a statement before they left – it saved you having to get them in again at a later date.

'Not at this stage. I've made a note. If CID want a full statement, they'll call you in.'

Jimmy frowned; that should be interesting. Stevens was sharper than he thought.

'Don't worry, son, if they want you, they'll find you.'

There was no sign of Carrie or Dog in or out of the station. The two teenagers had gone as well, which was probably a good thing. He wouldn't have been surprised if they'd hung around outside, thinking him an easy target; would have enjoyed proving them wrong.

'Jimmy!' A woman's voice. Carrie. He looked around and saw her sitting at a table outside a café bar, about thirty yards up on the other side of the road, one of the city's token efforts to go all Mediterranean, which only worked if you ignored the heavy traffic and the shit weather.

As he got nearer, he realised how much she reminded him of the photos of Kate he'd seen on Facebook, from a certain angle anyway, the same hair and build, the same open, trusting look. Was that why he was doing this?

Carrie was nursing a drink, some kind of lager, he guessed. She didn't look old enough to drink – probably still had to carry ID with her to get served. Dog was underneath the table, lapping from a bowl of water, didn't even acknowledge him.

'What did they say?' Carrie asked.

'They made a note.'

'Is that it? A note?'

He nodded.

'No photofit or anything like that.'

Jimmy shook his head. 'I did say.'

Carrie was quiet, her head bowed. Jimmy could see a small tremor in her shoulders, like she wanted to cry but was trying to control it. She was too young for this shit. Eventually she looked up again.

'You think he's dead, don't you?'

'I don't know what I think,' Jimmy said. She waited for more. He could see she wanted, no, *needed* an explanation.

'I have these, um, dreams ... nightmares, whatever,' he said. 'Vivid, like the real thing. Sometimes, the next day even, I find it hard to know what was real and what wasn't.'

He could tell she didn't really understand. Not many people did.

'You'd think you'd know, wouldn't you?' she said. 'If someone you loved wasn't there any more, you think that you'd feel it somehow, and sometimes I think I do. But that feeling's not real, is it? It's just hope, that's all . . . just hope.'

Jimmy said nothing, what could he say? He hadn't had a conversation like this for years. Maybe never.

'Everyone thinks my dad's a fuck-up,' she said, 'that's why no one else cares.'

Jimmy still said nothing. Could see she had to work through it.

'But they're wrong. He was a rubbish husband, I know that, but if you met my mum, you'd kind of understand. She's not an easy woman to live with. They bring out the worst in each other. But he's a great dad, fantastic even. Never missed anything I did as a kid, school sports days, Christmas shows, you name it. He spent hours helping me revise for my exams.' She smiled at the memory.

'He's the kind of man . . . if you've got a problem, he'll try and sort it, you know what I mean? He's a fixer. He's never ever let me down. That's how I know something bad has happened this time.

'Trouble is, it's not the first time he's gone off. He thinks he's some kind of player, that's why Mum chucked him out. Everyone thinks he's with some woman somewhere. Even my friends reckon I'm wasting my time, that he'll just turn up one day with his tail between his legs. But he's always been there for me and now I have to be there for *him*.'

'Any port in a storm,' Jimmy said.

'What?' Carrie said.

'I used to be in the mob . . . the Navy,' he corrected. 'It's what the lads said when they'd pulled.'

He could see he'd surprised her. No one ever really considered that people on the street might have had a proper job some time.

'You were in the forces?' she said.

'Aye. I used to have to keep the lads in order, maintain discipline and all that.'

'Like military police?' she asked, smiling at the obvious irony.

He nodded. He'd long grown out of explaining the differences. People liked simplicity.

'Any port in a storm,' she repeated, like she was trying it out to see if it fitted, nodding as she realised it did.

'Sums him up.' She sighed. 'Maybe they're right.'

'Don't give up on him,' Jimmy said before he could stop himself.

She stared at him, clearly surprised by his directness, though not as surprised as he was. There were questions in her eyes and something else, something shared, something Jimmy couldn't quite recognise – it had been too long. He looked away.

'Why shouldn't I?' she said and started gathering her things to leave. Dog raised his head. Jimmy wondered if he was considering switching teams; wouldn't have blamed him. 'Thanks for trying,' she said. 'I appreciate it.'

'No bother.'

'I owe you one. Do you want a beer or anything?'

'No thanks. I don't drink.' He saw the puzzled look on her face. 'Used to,' he said, 'didn't agree with me.' Or with other people, he thought.

Grainger Park Boxing Club, 1988

The bell sounds. Round two. Jimmy bounds off his stool. Williams is slow to react and Jimmy's in. He throws a quick combination, left, right, and forces the other man back. Jimmy steps forward and hits him again, a straight left jab followed by a right cross which catches Williams on the top of his head, driving him against the ropes. Jimmy knows he's got him, moves in for the kill, but the guy's holding on, trapping his arms. Jimmy's chin is on Williams's shoulder and he can see Bev on the front row, shouting at the referee to sort it. She must have got a babysitter at the last minute.

Jimmy gets in closer, trying for a gut punch to break the hold, but before he can throw it the bastard's butted him, cutting his left eye. Blood seeps down his cheek. The ref pulls them apart and sends Jimmy to his corner. Micky patches him up quickly with some magic glue and sends him back out. Most refs would have stopped the fight, but this is Grainger Park, Jimmy's home patch; the ref wants to get home in one piece and the crowd are baying for more blood. Williams's blood.

Jimmy's into him again straight away, jabbing and moving. They both know the end is nigh but Williams grabs him again, holds him in close. So close that Jimmy can see the blood on his mouth guard. When he looks up, Williams winks, but it's not Williams's face, it's Red's, his hair on fire, his mouth opening and closing with no sound coming out. Jimmy blinks and Williams's mocking gaze returns. The bell rings for the end of the round. Jimmy shrugs off the man's grip and smashes him in the side of the face with his elbow. Stunned, Williams lets his hands drop and Jimmy's all over him, hitting him with everything, over and over and over. He can hear shouting and there's a woman screaming and the bell's ringing and someone tries to pull him off but he keeps going, pounding and pounding, blood spraying his arms and chest, pounding and pounding until he can barely lift his gloves and someone finally drags him away.

Williams is slumped against the ropes, his face a vivid scarlet mess of pulped flesh, his nose broken and pointing towards his right cheek, his white vest unrecognisable. There are men piling into the ring but through the growing crowd of bodies he can see Bev's seat. It's empty. She's gone.

Several beers later, Jimmy gets home. As soon as he's through the door he can tell from the silence there's no one in. He grabs a can from the fridge, pours the ice-cold lager into a pint glass and goes to slump in his favourite chair.

He's spent so much time sitting there recently he can see an outline of his body in it, his shoulders clearly marked in the back, his arse cheeks in the seat. He settles down into his own body-mould, puts his glass on the side table and closes his eyes.

Freezing. Pitch dark. In his pyjamas. Baby Kate in his arms, crying. A ridge under his toes. Looks down at his feet. Roof tiles. Barefoot. Wind catches his hair, smoke rises up from beneath the gutter. Sirens clanging in the distance, getting nearer. Moves to the edge. Flames shooting out of the windows below. A crowd gathering on the ground. Two men hold a sheet, shouting something up at him. Kate's cries getting louder. A muted 'Drop her' reaches him through the surrounding noise; 'Drop her' seems to echo around his head. He looks over once more, holds Kate out over the edge of the house, takes a deep breath and lets go.

'You OK?'

Jimmy opens his eyes. Bev is standing in front of him, concern on her face. He blinks a couple of times, gets his bearings.

'Fine.'

'You were screaming. I could hear you from outside the house.'

'Was I? Just a dream.'

'People don't scream in *dreams*, Jimmy.'

'I do. Where you been?'

'Kate was restless. The sitter had got her up. I took her out in the pushchair to settle her down.'

Jimmy nods. It's a regular occurrence – it's a toss-up which one of them wakes up the most in the night, him or Kate.

'Is that man going to be OK?' Bev says.

'Which man?'

'The one you beat to a pulp.'

'Wasn't that bad. A few cuts. Usual stuff.'

'That wasn't usual, Jimmy. I was there, I saw what you did.'

He wills her to stop talking about it, still rattled to the core by both the fight and his latest nightmare.

'You could have killed him.'

Jimmy can feel her slipping away from him. He searches desperately for something to say, something to explain what happened, something to close the growing gap between them, but he's running on empty. There's nothing there. 'I'm sorry,' he says. It's the best he can do.

'You should speak to the doctor. See if he can help.'

'Doctor's shite, man, can't do anything.'

'You don't know till you try.'

'I have tried.'

'Once.'

'That was enough. Waste of time.' Jimmy takes a sip of stale beer. Puts the glass down again. He can feel his head starting to pound. Bev waits him out.

'There's nothing wrong with me. Just need a bit of time to sort myself out.'

'You've had years, Jimmy.'

'There's nothing wrong with me.'

'You need help.'

'There's nothing fucking wrong with me!' he screams, flinging his arm out and sending his beer glass smashing into the wall, inches from the side of the kitchen door. The open kitchen door where two-year-old Kate stands, mouth open in shock, beer splashes flecked on her white sleepsuit, a small trickle of dark red blood running down her cheek from the tiny cut an inch away from her bright blue eye.

13

The Pit Stop, July 1, 2012

Deano had tried on every coat in the room and thrown most of them on the floor: a puffa jacket, a ragged parka, minus the hood, something that looked a bit like a small purple tent and countless others. Some had been too big, some too small and some just right. It's like the three bears, Jimmy thought as he glanced out of the window again.

Ever since going to the police station he'd had a strong sense of being watched, and on the way to the Pit Stop that morning it had been even stronger. He'd been there for half an hour now but was still on guard. A few minutes earlier he thought he'd caught a glimpse of someone standing in a nearby doorway, a blond guy, watching the building – but when he'd looked again there was no one there.

I'll be waiting for you.

Where did that come from? Hearing voices now, was he? He shook his head and turned back to watch his friend. The clothes, aside from those discarded by Deano, covered the dining room's four long trestle tables. Jimmy was always surprised by the quality of things people donated. Some of them were as good as new, designer labels and everything, bought and then quickly rejected. Jimmy wasn't that bothered but it was good to see Deano excited by something other than his next hit. The kid had been trying to clean himself up – it was only about a week in, but it looked like he might be getting somewhere.

'What about this?' Deano said, holding up a gold number.

'Too big,' Jimmy said.

'Not for me, you twat,' Deano said. 'For you. You could do with some bling.'

'I'm alright, thanks,' Jimmy said, pulling his trench coat tighter.

'That's minging, man; it's older than you.'

Jimmy looked down. The kid was right – the coat was clean, but way past its best. He had one last glance out of the window before moving away to sift through a pile on one of the tables.

'Try it on, man,' Deano said, still holding out the gold jacket.

'No chance. I'd look like a fucking Stylistic.' Jimmy's mum had loved them.

The reference was lost on Deano, who shook his head and tried it on himself, checking out his reflection in the aluminium shutters above the counter.

'Fresh,' he said.

Jimmy delved deeper into the pile and pulled out a plum. A green waxed Barbour jacket which seemed like it had come straight from the factory, just across the water in Shields. Must be a second, he thought, unable to imagine how minted you'd have to be to give a practically new one like that away. He shrugged his coat off and tried it on. Great fit. Deano looked up and laughed.

'Going 'unting are you, Jimmy?' he snorted. 'Giddy-up.' He slapped his thigh and started galloping around the room, neighing and laughing like a drain as he dodged between the tables, Dog running behind him, like he was a fucking beagle or something.

The door opened and Maggie, the volunteer, poked her head in. Jimmy assumed that she'd come to tell them to keep the noise down, but she didn't say anything to them, just looked behind her and said, 'He's in here.'

She held the door open and ushered a visitor in. Carrie. Jimmy frowned. He hated surprises. Wondered if she'd been the one following him.

'Hi,' she said.

Deano was staring at her as if she was a creature from another planet, which, in a way, she was.

'Close your mouth, Deano,' Jimmy said. 'You'll catch a fly.'

Deano blushed and went over to one of the tables, pretending he was still looking for a coat, watching her out of the corner of his eye. Carrie walked over towards Jimmy and put her hand on his arm.

'I need your help again,' she said.

14

The Quayside, Newcastle, July 1, 2012

Jimmy stopped talking as a young family walked past, all licking ice creams. No need for kids to hear this death stuff, life would turn to shit soon enough.

He watched them head along the river towards the bridges until he lost them in the sun before turning back to face the journalist who had finally finished scribbling in his notebook.

'Let me get this straight. You didn't actually see him go into the river?' the young reporter said.

Jimmy shook his head. In the open air the lad looked about fifteen. Jimmy could see a drop of dried blood on his shirt collar and little cuts on his chin where he hadn't yet learned to shave properly.

'Where else could he have gone?' Carrie said. 'He didn't just vanish into thin air.'

As they argued, Jimmy slumped onto a bench and watched

Dog playing his favourite chase-the-seagull game, wishing he had the energy to join in.

They'd met the journalist in a nearby pub about an hour before. Walked past him once, thinking he was too young to be the person they were looking for, before he'd shouted over to them, recognising Carrie from the earlier piece in the paper. Once they'd done the introductions he'd gone straight for the jugular.

'Why would anyone want to kill your dad?'

Young but merciless, Jimmy thought. Carrie seemed stunned and for a moment Jimmy thought she was going to punch the lad, but she quickly recovered.

'Who said *killed*? We don't know he's dead.'

'You told me on the phone that your man here saw him pushed in the river.'

'That's right, sort of, but I didn't say he was dead.'

The journalist looked out of the window, where you could just get a glimpse of the Tyne if you stretched a little. He didn't look convinced.

'OK, I'll rephrase my question: why would anyone want to push your dad into the river?'

'He's made a lot of enemies,' Carrie said. 'He's an environmentalist, always sticking his nose into things, trying to expose stuff. Maybe he upset the wrong people. Got in the way of something.'

'Names?' the journalist said, pen poised.

'I don't know. Building companies, businessmen – anyone

who's tried to mess up the environment with their shitty developments. It's all in the public records, look it up.'

'I did. He doesn't like progress much, does he?'

'Depends on what you think progress is, doesn't it?'

'Seems to spend a lot of time campaigning against stuff. How does he make a living?' the journalist asked.

'What's that got to do with it?' Carrie said, clearly exasperated.

'I don't know yet. Just trying to build up a picture.'

'He lectures part-time at the uni, if you must know.'

'In what?'

'Environmental studies.'

The journalist snorted. 'Should have guessed.'

'Some people care about the future of the planet!'

Jimmy tried to imagine what it was like to care about such things. He found it hard enough to care about his own future; caring about the fate of an entire planet seemed a bit of a luxury to him. He'd obviously let it show as Carrie slapped him hard on the arm.

'Thought you were on my side.'

'Sorry,' he said, wondering how she could read his thoughts so well, thinking he'd have to learn to hide them better.

'Where did he live?' the journalist asked.

'*Does*,' Carrie emphasised, 'where *does* he live?'

'Alright, sorry, where *does* he live? He can't have much money lecturing part-time.'

'He lodges with his boss from the university, Andrew

Lang, most of the time, but he sometimes stays with other friends to give Andrew and his wife a bit of a break.'

I'll bet he does, Jimmy thought, remembering what that was like, being an unwanted house guest, though he doubted Roger had been sofa-surfing.

'Got a lot of friends, has he?'

Girlfriends, Jimmy thought, remembering what Carrie had told him outside the cop shop.

'Yes, he has, actually,' Carrie said, giving Jimmy a warning glance – *don't mention the women* – somehow reading his thoughts again.

A seagull squawk brought Jimmy back to the present. Dog had given up the chase and was settled by his feet. Carrie and the journalist were still arguing the toss.

'I'm not sure there's a story here – maybe your dad just walked off. *Maybe* your man Jimmy here just dozed off for a moment – he was half asleep, after all.'

'The fight woke him up though – didn't it, Jimmy?'

That was right. Probably. He was tired. Couldn't remember exactly how things had panned out but didn't want to let the girl down. She needed him to remember.

'Yes,' he said, 'that's right, um . . . ?' The lad had introduced himself in the pub, but Jimmy hadn't been paying attention, still unnerved about talking to a reporter.

'It's Brian,' the kid said, a hint of annoyance in his voice.

'Right, sorry,' Jimmy said.

'And you've reported this to the police?'

'Yes!' Carrie said.

She was getting frustrated now; Jimmy could hear it in her voice. Had heard it a lot since he met her.

'But they're not looking for him. Or this . . .' – he glanced at his notes – 'bricklayer guy?'

'For God's sake, how many times? They just talk about a "lack of resources" and how he's a "grown man", whatever the hell that means,' she said. 'If we can get another piece in the paper, maybe someone will come forward to support Jimmy's story, then they'll have to do something, won't they?'

Jimmy could hear the lack of conviction in her voice and he could see that Brian noticed it too. Carrie even seemed to recognise it herself. She sighed.

'Will you write something or not?' she said.

Brian looked down at Jimmy.

'I'll need a photo.'

'That won't be a problem,' she said. Carrie glanced at Jimmy for confirmation.

'No,' he said.

'Jimmy?' Carrie said.

He shook his head. He didn't like having his picture taken, never had. Didn't think it was stealing your soul, shit like that; just didn't fucking like it. But this wasn't that. This was different. His picture in the paper would be like holding up a sign saying, 'I'm back, come and get me.' And people *would* come.

'We could do it in silhouette,' Brian said, 'keep it anonymous if that's what you're worried about. Editor won't use the story if there's no photo.'

'Please, Jimmy,' Carrie said. 'I really need you to do this.'

He looked up at her. It would be like kicking Dog. He nodded.

'OK. Just silhouette though, nothing else.' Carrie smiled at him, touching his arm in thanks.

'Great,' the journalist said, reaching into his bag and pulling out a camera. Looked pretty flash to Jimmy, not that he knew much about it. Not that he knew much about anything. He remembered a song that Bev used to sing, something about not knowing much about stuff: history, biology, French and that.

'Jimmy?'

He looked up; Brian was scratching his head, looking irritated.

'I said, can you stand up and put your hands on the rail, look out to the river maybe?'

He did as he was asked but it made no sense really; the sun was in his eyes so he couldn't see a thing. They should come back at night if the guy wanted to keep it real.

Brian stepped to one side and started taking pictures, moving around to change the angle.

'Can you point at something,' he said.

'Like what?' Jimmy said.

'Anything. Doesn't matter what. As if you've seen a body.'

'I didn't see a body though.'

'Doesn't matter.'

Does to me, Jimmy thought, but pointed anyway, spotting a plastic bag drifting along the Tyne and following it with his finger.

A loud scream. Jimmy flinched, then looked up. A young girl was travelling down a zip-wire that ran from the top of the BALTIC art gallery, all the way across the river, to a temporary platform about a hundred yards downriver from where they stood. The girl screamed again as she gathered speed, helpless in the face of an unstoppable momentum.

He knew exactly how she felt.

15

A front room, Newcastle, 1989

Jimmy wakes to the sound of raised voices from the kitchen. Looks at his watch. 7.30 a.m. He rolls over, buries his head in the cushions and tries to go back to sleep but it's useless.

'I want him gone,' a woman says.

'Why?' a man says.

It takes Jimmy a moment to identify the voices. He's been sofa-surfing for nine months since Bev chucked him out and all the sofas seem the same, too narrow and too short to sleep properly. He gets there in the end. Gary and Liz.

'He frightens the kids,' Liz says. 'They're scared to go in the front room in the mornings.'

'He's got nowhere else to go.' Gary this time; he's right. Jimmy's heard this same conversation or a variation on it in at least three other houses. He's tried hard not to outstay his welcome each time but he's run out of friends. Not that he had many. Gary's the last one, and he was a stretch. Used to work with him at the supermarket.

'I don't care,' Liz says. 'We've done our bit.'

'But—'

'No buts, Gary. I want him out of here by the time I get home.'

'That's not fair, love.'

'Him or me, Gary.'

As the row continues, Jimmy gets up and quietly pulls on his clothes. It takes him a couple of minutes to find one of his trainers, but he eventually sees it on the floor, hidden underneath a copy of the *Sporting Life* he nicked from the bookie's the day before. He scribbles '*Thank You*' on a scrap of paper and puts it on the table, picks up a small rucksack, glances around the room to check that he isn't leaving anything behind and goes, shutting the front door gently behind him.

He bangs on the door for the umpteenth time, but there's still no answer. She's changed the locks; none of his keys works.

'You should go home before someone calls the police.'

He turns around. The next-door neighbour. Jill . . . or Julie, or something like that. He's never really spoken to her before.

'This *is* my home.'

'Not any more. Bev doesn't want you here, Jimmy.'

'You don't know that.'

'I do. We talk. You frighten her.'

It's a low blow. Only words, but it has the same effect as an actual punch: knocking the wind out of him.

'Did she actually s-say that?'

The woman nods. He feels sick. Sits down on the door-step.

'You should go.'

'Where?' he asks, somehow hoping she might have an answer because he really doesn't. She doesn't say anything, stands her ground. He doesn't look at her, just stares at her feet, willing her to leave him alone before he loses his shit again. That's the last thing he needs right now. He's been trying so hard to keep it together.

A child's cry makes him look up and there she is, Bev, walking towards the house, a pushchair in front of her. He stands up, goes to move towards her but the grim look on her face halts him in his tracks.

'What are you doing here?' she says.

'I wanted to see you. And Kate,' he says, edging towards the pushchair.

'Shall I call the police?' the neighbour says.

Bev hesitates. It's only for a second but Jimmy sees it and it's devastating. He slumps back down on the step, his head in his hands. It's not going the way he imagined.

'No,' Bev says, eventually. 'I'll be fine.'

'I'll just be next door if you need me.'

'Thanks, June,' Bev says.

The neighbour goes back into her house. Kate is crying loudly now.

'She needs to get some sleep.'

'Can I put her to bed?' he asks.

'No, Jimmy, I'm sorry. We've spoken about this. Get

yourself sorted out and we can talk about you spending more time with her.'

'And about moving back in?'

'One step at a time.'

'I'm trying my best, love,' he says. And it's true. He cleaned himself up at the swimming pool after leaving Gary's; he's even had a shave. And that's not all.

'I've been to the doctor,' he says.

'And?'

'He told me to stop drinking.'

'And have you?' she says.

He looks at the ground, thinks about lying but knows that would be worse. He looks up at her, shakes his head.

'Not completely, but if you let me move back in, I will, I promise. I haven't had a drink in nearly a week.' It's only a couple of days, actually, but it feels longer. 'I'm on the mend, Bev, I really am. I had an interview at B and Q last week.'

He hadn't got the job. Lost his rag when they asked him why he'd left the Navy, but she didn't need to know that. Not just now.

Jimmy gets to his feet, moves towards her, hoping for some small sign of affection, but she backs off. He feels it like a slap.

'Can I at least give Kate a hug?' he says.

He thinks she'll say no, but after a moment she nods. He leans into the pushchair and lifts his daughter out; holding her tightly until her cries get louder and her wriggling is so vigorous he nearly drops her.

'She's too tired,' Bev says, 'give her to me.'

He gives up the struggle and hands her over to Bev. Kate buries her head in her mother's shoulder and the sobs die down a little. Bev opens the front door and guides the push-chair into the hallway one-handed before turning back to him.

'Get yourself sorted properly, Jimmy,' Bev says. 'Then maybe we can talk again.'

'I will,' Jimmy says, but he's talking to a closed door.

The pub is full now. Jimmy's been there since first thing, was sitting on the doorstep when they opened. That was twelve hours ago. He's been measuring the time in half-pints, eking them out to save what little money he has left.

Aside from the barman he hasn't spoken to another soul since Bev closed the door on him. Hasn't got a clue where he's going when they kick him out. He's the last man standing, seeing off the rest of the early drinkers – the doleys and the pensioners. Now he's surrounded by a younger, livelier crowd, the karaoke lot. Thankfully, the young lass slaughtering 'Another Day in Paradise' will be the last of them; the DJ's ready to pull the plug. Jimmy's drunk enough to joke to himself that she's singing his song, but not so far gone that he tries to join in. A bell rings.

'Last orders,' someone shouts.

Jimmy thinks about getting in one more half for the road, which also makes him laugh, as that's probably where he's going. On the road. Get away from this place for a while. Try and clean himself up for good. Maybe even get another job somewhere where his reputation doesn't get in the way.

The singer screeches over the noise of people grabbing a final drink, urging him to think twice. Jimmy ignores her advice, his mind made up. He drains his glass, grabs his rucksack and walks out.

He stops immediately outside as the cold hits him; it had been sunny when he walked in. Which way? He pulls out one of his few remaining coins, tosses it in the air, catches it in his right hand and places it on the back of his left. Tails. He turns right; no real idea where he's heading, just walking, hoping for a sign. He looks up at the sky, wondering if there's a star he could follow like the shepherds in the Bible. Or was that the wise men?

Ten yards ahead of him he sees a young couple walking side by side, early twenties, the girl tall, the bloke stocky, with a rolling walk which reminds Jimmy of being at sea.

It's like he's gone back in time; on shore patrol, making sure the lads kept out of bother and got back to their ship safely. He can tell at a glance that the bloke's a bit pissed, so he follows the couple at a distance, a memory of breaking up a street fight in Portsmouth between the matelots and the civvies seeping back into his head.

There's a shriek from up ahead. The bloke has grabbed a fistful of the girl's hair and pulled her head towards him. They've stopped walking, so Jimmy is getting closer.

'Let go,' the girl screams.

'Fucking slag,' the bloke shouts, pulling her head further down.

'I didn't do anything, Kev, promise.'

'You were licking your lips like he was a fucking doughnut.'

In the struggle they've flipped round so they're now facing Jimmy. Kev has a cigarette in his free hand and is jabbing it towards the girl's face.

'Made you hot, did he?' Kev shouts.

'Get off,' she screams. 'You're hurting me.'

'Let her go,' Jimmy says.

Kev looks up, seeing Jimmy for the first time.

'Mind your own business,' he says.

'I can't,' Jimmy says.

'Just fuck off, mate.'

Jimmy is close now, close enough to flick his arm out and knock the cigarette out of Kev's hand into the road.

'What the fuck!' Kev loosens his grip on the girl's hair. She pulls away. He puts his face right into Jimmy's.

'D'you want some, pal?' he yells.

'Leave it, Kev,' the girl says, trying to pull him away. He backhands her across the face, knocking her into the road where a passing car swerves to avoid her, its horn blasting as she screams in fright.

Kev barely glances at her.

'Well?' he shouts, so close to Jimmy that his spit hits him in the face. Jimmy doesn't blink, just stares at him, willing him to back down. He doesn't, putting both hands on Jimmy's chest and shoving him to the floor.

'Now piss off, you twat,' Kev says and turns to the girl, who is sitting in the road, sobbing now. He grabs her by her hair again and pulls her towards the kerb, like a caveman, ignoring her wailing as her knees scrape along the tarmac.

Jimmy jumps up and grabs Kev in a bear hug, locking his arms in, breaking his hold on the girl's hair. She crawls towards the pavement as the pair of them spin back into the road.

Kev thrusts his head back towards Jimmy's face, trying to break free, but Jimmy's too strong. He lifts him off his feet and hurls him onto the bonnet of a parked car, right in front of a gathering crowd, who cheer as Kev slides off the now-dented bonnet and onto the pavement on the other side.

Jimmy is about to walk off when someone jumps on his back. The girl. For fuck's sake.

'Leave him alone, you bastard,' she screams. She's scratching at his face, her nails digging deep; he can feel blood trickling down his cheek. He wrenches her off, holding her at arm's length as she kicks out at him.

'Calm down, love,' he says. 'It's over. We're done.'

He's wrong. He's grabbed from behind again. Kev is back. Bouncing off the car should have taken him out of the fight but the alcohol's obviously masking the pain. Jimmy turns and reacts instinctively as a wild swing heads towards his face. He throws up his left arm to block the punch and smashes Kev square on the jaw with a fierce right uppercut, knocking him off his feet. He flies backwards and crashes to the ground, a loud CRACK as the back of his head smashes into the kerb. He lies completely still, a pool of blood slowly appearing from under his head.

The girl runs past Jimmy, kneeling next to her boyfriend, shaking him.

'Wake up, Kev,' she screams. 'Wake up.' Nothing. He doesn't move. Neither does Jimmy, the pool of blood getting bigger and bigger and bigger until he can feel it soaking into his trainers.

A man comes out of the crowd and kneels down next to the girl. He grabs Kev's wrist, feeling for a pulse. He doesn't seem to find one.

'Someone should call the police,' the man says.

'He is the fucking police,' the girl screams, pointing at Kev.

16

Newcastle College, July 3, 2012

Jimmy stood in the shadows of a monkey-puzzle tree, just behind the bike sheds, staring at the glass doors which formed one of the college's many entrances. Two days in a row he'd been there, hanging about with no luck; maybe he'd got the wrong place? One of the security staff had been giving him funny looks earlier but had let it go, for the time being. There were so many buildings there, scattered around haphazardly, that it was almost impossible to know where to start.

A gust of wind blew his hair into his eyes. He pushed it back behind his ears, fed up with how long it was getting, thinking he should do something about it. He'd always worn it short before, ever since they'd shaved his head on the day he joined up.

Then he saw her. His breath quickened and he had to put his hands in his pockets to stop his legs shaking.

Kate was with two other students, a skinny boy and

another girl – though 'girl' was the wrong word to describe
Kate and her friends now. He supposed he should try and
think of them as adults. It was hard to remember that when
you hadn't seen them grow up.

She was carrying one of those brightly coloured satchels
that he'd seen a lot of recently. What was it with all the
satchels? Maybe everything makes a comeback eventually.
There was hope for him yet.

Kate moved down the steps, talking with her friends.
Even from the other side of the road he could see she had
changed from the photos on Facebook. Her hair seemed
shorter and fairer, though with the orange beret perched on
her head it was hard to tell for sure. She looked a lot like
Carrie from that distance. And she'd lost weight but not in
a worrying way. She looked . . . healthy . . . happy.

Kate laughed and hugged the boy, before heading off on
her own, the boy watching her go. Jimmy waited until he
stopped watching then came out of the shadows, crossed
the road and followed her, Dog beside him. He pulled his
new Barbour jacket tight to protect him from the wind
and kept his head down, avoiding eye contact with anyone
passing by.

He had to keep Dog close as the poor thing hated traffic.
Jimmy didn't know why, but he knew as well as anyone that
the past could be a right bastard. He had no real idea what
Dog's past held but he could guess. They'd come together
under Byker Bridge one night, not long after Jimmy had
come back to the city. Both were wary at first, Dog of
humans in general and Jimmy of a forlorn-looking critter

with large gaps where his fur should have been. Eventually they'd each taken a chance on the other and had been together ever since.

Kate was clearly in no hurry, meandering through the college and the surrounding streets until she hit Westgate Road, with its parade of cheap cafés and motorbike shops. She stopped to look in the window of a bakery and he wondered if she still had a sweet tooth – probably not, from the size of her. She was about four when he last knew such stuff about her; another reason he still thought of her as a girl. He waited, pretending to do up his laces, even though his boots didn't have any. She moved off again and he continued to trail her, still keeping his distance.

She stopped again, at a crossing this time, and he slowed up, waiting outside a newsagent's, already too close for comfort. He would have edged back but a group of bikers studying the new machines outside the showrooms were blocking his way and they'd been reluctant to let him past in the first place. Suddenly the wind picked up again and her beret flew off. She tried to grab it, but it sailed behind her, towards Jimmy. He stopped, glancing anxiously around to see if he could get out of the way, but the path was still blocked behind him and the road too busy to cross.

Kate ran after her hat and almost caught it, but the breeze picked it up again and blew it straight at Jimmy and Dog. It would have flown past them if Dog hadn't leapt up and caught it in his mouth. Jimmy had no choice. He bent down and picked the beret out of Dog's mouth. The temptation to hold it to his nose and get a scent of her was enormous – he used to love the smell of her freshly washed hair – but he resisted. He looked up and she was standing right in front of him. He held the hat out. She smiled. She still had a great smile; got that from her mother. Not a hint of recognition though.

'Thanks,' she said, taking the hat.

Jimmy's mouth went dry; so many things he wanted to say but no words available to say them.

'Cute dog,' she said. 'What's his name?'

'Um, Dog,' he croaked.

She laughed.

'Must have taken you ages to come up with that,' she said, crouching down to pat Dog.

As she did, Jimmy heard a screech of tyres and a scream. Over her shoulder he could see the bikers scattering as a black car narrowly missed them, mounted the kerb and headed straight towards him and Kate. She looked back, alarmed by the noise, went to stand again but slipped, falling towards him. Jimmy grabbed her coat and pulled her back into the newsagent's doorway, both of them stumbling against the door, leaving Dog alone on the path, seemingly frozen to the spot, his lead trailing on the floor. Jimmy leapt forward and yanked him out of the car's path. As the car roared past, clipping an advertising stand on its way, Jimmy saw a flash of blond hair from the driver's seat. He tried to read the number plate but the car was moving too quickly and the plate seemed to be covered in mud.

He turned around to check on Kate, but she was already being comforted by a couple of the bikers who had run over to make sure she was OK. He could see she was fine, a little shaken, sure, but no real damage. No one came to check on him. The newsagent came out of his shop and picked up the advertising stand. The headline on it read: 'Homeless Man Sees Murder.'

Jimmy got up, walked into the shop and picked up the paper. The bastards had used his photo. Not a silhouette, as Brian had promised, but a side-on shot of him pointing at the river. They had used his photo and someone had tried to kill him, nearly taking out his daughter instead. He didn't believe in coincidences. He'd come forward as a witness and now he had a target on his back. One thing was for sure – from now on he had to keep as far away from Kate as possible.

17

Pudding Chare, Newcastle, July 4, 2012

A mechanised street sweeper clanked noisily down the lane. Jimmy was already awake, huddled in the doorway of a shabby Indian restaurant. Hadn't slept a wink. Unlike some, he thought, glancing down at Dog who was crashed out by his feet, twitching like a Taser victim.

He reckoned it was about 6 a.m.; the sun had been up for quite a while, the pavement was warming up nicely and the first commuters had started to appear, heading down the narrow lane towards Central Station, coffee and newspaper in hand.

The staff entrance to the *Chronicle*'s offices was just opposite where he lay and he'd been watching carefully as the day shift started to amble in, half asleep. He could tell the journalists from the commuters before they turned into the entrance – they were the ones dressed like shit. He didn't think he'd have to wait much longer, betting that junior reporters didn't get a lie-in.

The sweeper neared the doorway, stirring Dog from his dreams of rabbits or seagulls, maybe. Jimmy reached into his rucksack and grabbed a handful of dry dog food, placing it on the ground in front of him. Dog watched warily until the sweeper went past before leaping on the food. Half a dozen people, the discharge from the latest early-morning bus, had been trailing behind the vehicle down the narrow lane from the Bigg Market, hidden from Jimmy's sight. The first three were definitely commuters: smart, well-pressed suits; the others journalists: stained, baggy trousers and cheap jackets, some of them with patches on the elbows. At the back of them, walking on his own, head down, oblivious, was Brian, the lying, shit-for-brains, so-called reporter. He had a briefcase in one hand and a cup of coffee in the other.

Jimmy clambered over Dog, who was now focused on filling his belly, and stepped out into the middle of the lane. Brian glanced up, suddenly aware that someone was blocking the light, and then jumped back, his cup of coffee slipping from his hand, sending dark brown liquid over the pavement.

'W-what do you want?'

Jimmy held up the previous day's paper like a baton.

'Seen this?'

Brian's eyes widened and he backed away.

'I can explain—'

Jimmy whacked him round the head with the rolled-up paper.

'Jesus!'

'Sil-hou-ette,' Jimmy shouted, emphasising each syllable with a prod of his makeshift weapon. 'You used my photo. You showed my face.'

'I know, I'm sorry, but my editor insisted.'

'You fucking promised me.'

'It wasn't my call.'

'Funny you didn't mention that before.'

Brian held his hands up, pleading guilty.

'You're right.' He paused, clearly considering how much to say. 'I'm sorry. I should have told you that I didn't have the authority. I needed the story. My probation period's nearly up and it's not been going that well.'

'Probation period?'

'I'm just a trainee.'

'A trainee! Does Carrie know?'

'I don't think so. I certainly didn't tell her.' Brian looked sheepish. 'It doesn't mean I can't help her.'

Jimmy waved the paper in his face.

'She doesn't need your kind of help. You put people in danger.'

Brian looked sceptical.

'I'm not sure that's fair.'

'They've already come after me.'

'Who's they?'

Where to start? The blond driver who'd tried to run him over seemed the obvious place. But he wouldn't be the only one – others would follow, people he'd hurt in the past, people like Kev, his family and friends. Now they knew he was back, they'd be looking for him. Some of them already had been, he knew that; he'd seen them out there in the doorways and the alleys, lurking in the shadows. And that was before this idiot put his picture in the paper.

He looked back at Brian. The cub reporter had pulled a pen and paper out of his briefcase, ready to take notes.

'You've got to be kidding me,' Jimmy said, jabbing him roughly in the shoulder with the paper.

Brian jerked away, but as he did, he tripped over his own feet, falling heavily to the ground into the spilled coffee.

He flies backwards and crashes to the ground, a loud CRACK as the back of his head smashes into the kerb. He lies completely still, a pool of blood slowly appearing from under his head.

Jimmy slapped the side of his own head, as if trying to dislodge an insect from his ear.

'Are you alright?' Brian asked.

Jimmy blinked a couple of times, regaining his focus. Brian was back on his feet and brushing himself down, rubbing hard at the coffee stain on his trousers.

'What?' Jimmy said.

'You've gone white.'

'I'm fine,' Jimmy said, his head clearer. 'Sorry about that,' he added, nodding at the stain.

'Don't worry about it, you're right to be pissed off. I'm sorry about the picture. Really sorry. But I might be able to make it up to you.' He started to smile, clearly pleased with himself.

'I doubt that.' The kid had no idea.

'I've been doing a bit of research – into Carrie's dad – I think I might have found something.'

'Like what?' Jimmy said.

'It's not much but I've hardly started. That's why I haven't said anything to Carrie yet.'

'Show me,' Jimmy said.

Brian started to dig around in his briefcase, chattering away as he searched.

'Carrie said her dad was a bit of a troublemaker, and you reckoned you saw him on the Quayside on June the fourth – so I started from that date and worked backwards, looking to see if anything had been going on. I found out there was a big demo at the City Council offices that afternoon – something to do with a planning application. I haven't nailed it all down yet but I do have some photos. Here they are.'

He pulled a small handful of photos out of the briefcase and handed them to Jimmy, who looked at the first one – a group of protestors standing outside the council building waving placards. Right in the middle of the group, standing next to a woman with bright red hair, was Carrie's dad, looking exactly as Jimmy remembered: a denim jacket and light-coloured chinos, longish dark hair, and a black satchel slung over his shoulder. Maybe he could rely on his memory of that night, maybe it all happened exactly as he remembered. Maybe he wasn't crazy after all. He looked at the other photos, four in total, all similar, all with Roger front and centre, standing next to the red-headed woman. A germ of an idea started to niggle away at him.

Not my fight.

This time he batted his inner voice away. The girl needed

help. A conversation couldn't hurt. Then he could step back into the safety of the shadows.

'Like I said, I've got a lot more digging to do but it's a start, isn't it?' Brian said eagerly.

'Can I keep these?' Jimmy said.

'I don't know, um, there's, um, copyright stuff and I don't think the editor would like—'

'Thanks,' Jimmy said, putting the photos in his pocket and walking off.

18

Newcastle city centre, July 4, 2012

The flaming torch flew up towards the overhead street lights, spinning around three times until it reached its peak and started to descend again. As it plummeted towards the ground it was snatched out of the air by a man riding a unicycle. The large crowd circling him clapped and hooted.

'Don't try this at home, kids,' the man said, his golden top hat glinting in the sunlight.

Wanker, Jimmy thought, as he passed the crowd, searching for Carrie's face among the other onlookers who were sitting outside Starbucks.

'Over here.'

He turned and saw her, sitting alone at a small table, cup of coffee in hand. Her other hand was bandaged from her wrist to her knuckles.

'Looks nasty,' he said, taking the empty chair beside her.

'Just bruising really. You should see the other guy,' she said.

'What happened?'

`Someone tried to mug me.'

'What? When?'

'Last night, when I was leaving the hospital. It's an occupational hazard on lates. I normally get a porter to walk me to my car, but there was no one on the desk when I left. Someone grabbed me by the arm. Nearly crapped myself.'

She gave Jimmy a weak smile. He wasn't fooled, she still seemed shaken.

'He won't try it again. I really smacked him one, right in the face.' She held her bandaged hand up. 'Hence the bruising. Knocked the little blond twat on his arse and sprinted back into the hospital.'

Little blond twat. The same guy who'd tried to run him over? Had to be. Missed him then went for Carrie. Someone really didn't want anyone talking about her dad.

'Anyway,' Carrie said, 'I was surprised when I got your message. I didn't expect to see you again. Thought you didn't want to get involved.'

Jimmy told her about the car, leaving out any mention of Kate. That was personal.

'Shit,' she said. 'You don't think the attack on me was random then?'

'Not if it was the same guy.'

'Jesus. Not just a mugger.'

Jimmy shook his head. She shuddered; no doubt imagining what would have happened if she hadn't escaped.

'Did you get a good look at him?' he said.

'Not really, like I said, blond, short – a bit older than me maybe? A couple of people ran back out to the car park but he'd gone.'

'Definitely short though?'

Carrie nodded. Not the bricklayer then. Someone working with him? Some kind of conspiracy? Jimmy shook his head – he was spending too much time with Gadge.

'Is there CCTV?' he asked.

'No. It's out of action. We've been complaining about it for months – maybe they'll fix it now.'

Jimmy glanced up at the camera high above them on the other side of the street; they were all over the city now. He wondered if any of them worked or whether they were all just for show. Another cheer went up from the crowd gathered around the fire juggler.

'We should tell DS Burns,' Carrie said. 'We've stirred things up with that story in the paper. It proves that there's something going on. The police'll have to take notice now.'

Jimmy doubted it. Been there, done that.

'Anybody else see what happened?'

'No, but with us both having similar stories . . .' She tailed off. 'He still won't believe us, will he? Not without proof. He'll just *make a note*. We need something else.'

'Yes, we do.'

Jimmy pulled out the photos of the demo.

'Have a look at these – a present from Brian. He owed me for putting my picture in the paper.'

She studied the photos carefully, reaching out tentatively to touch the image of her dad, as if he was sitting there in person. Jimmy pointed to the red-headed woman standing next to Roger. She was waving a *Save Our Greenbelt* placard.

'D'you know her?'

'Nope. Never seen her before.'

Jimmy was reluctant to push it; he didn't want to upset her, but Carrie seemed to sense he had more to say.

'What is it, man? I can take it, I'm a big girl.'

'Well, you said your dad was a bit of a womaniser, didn't you?'

'More than a bit.'

'I think they might be a couple. She's standing next to him in every photo, and in one of them' – he shuffled through them until he found the right one – 'it looks like they're holding hands.'

She held the photo up to the light.

'Maybe,' Carrie said. 'He never tells me when he's seeing someone. I don't want to know.'

'If they were though . . . she might know what he was planning to do that night.'

'Why wouldn't she have come forward?'

'Maybe she didn't see your appeal.'

'Or she's married,' Carrie said. 'Wouldn't be the first time.'

'She's got a university scarf on.'

'And? Perhaps it was cold.'

'Or she works with him?'

'Bit of a leap – you can buy them anywhere.'

'Most relationships start at work.' He'd read that somewhere once and it rang true for him – he and Bev had met when they were both working weekends at a supermarket.

'Easy enough to find out,' Carrie said.

She took a laptop out of her bag and quickly pulled up Northumberland University's website. Jimmy watched, bemused, as her fingers clicked away, opening another page: About Us – a list of staff, by department and with photos. Geography seemed the obvious place to start and on the third page, she found her: Norma Weston, Faculty Registrar.

'Boom!' Carrie said.

The woman was younger in the photo and her hair was a dull brown, but it was definitely the same woman.

'So, d'you think I'm right? They were a couple?' Jimmy said.

'Maybe. But that's easy to find out too.'

'Really?' Jimmy said, glancing at the laptop.

'Not on there, you dick.'

'How then?'

'We go and ask her,' Carrie said.

Jimmy could feel himself getting sucked in; so much for just having a conversation.

'We?'

'Of course.'

'I don't know about that.'

'You used to be in the military police, didn't you? You know how to question people. You can help me find out what's going on.'

'It's not that simple.'

'Some bastard attacked me! I'm not going to sit here and do nothing. You were attacked too – by a lunatic in a car. Why wouldn't you want to do something about it?'

Where to start? How about: *because getting involved in someone else's fight always ends with me in a fucking prison cell.* Way too direct and way, way too much information. He took the roundabout route instead.

'Because I always make things worse.'

'My dad's disappeared, Jimmy. How much worse can it get?'

19

HMP Acklington, 1990

Jimmy lies on the bed in his cell staring at the graffiti on the ceiling, trying to ignore the grim stench leaking out from the bucket in the corner.

He's got dibs on one of the two top bunks; he's been there longer than the others, his trial date continually being moved back, and nobody makes someone with his rep sleep on the bottom – beating a copper to within an inch of his life has given him respect. Not self-respect, mind; he still fucking hates himself.

On the plus side, if it hadn't been for the quick work of the paramedics, he'd probably be facing a manslaughter charge instead of ABH. He'll still get five years, his brief reckons, due to 'aggravating factors' – beating up a policeman, even one who's off duty, abusive, and pissed out of his mind, most definitely counts as one of those. They even reckon he had a motive – resentment at the police for turning down his application; as if he had the energy to be so vindictive.

His three cellmates are way down the food chain in comparison: an arsonist, a wife-beater and a petty thief who got caught one time too many with his hand in the till. There's an unwritten rule that there should only be two men to a cell but, as the tired joke goes, the rule isn't worth the paper it's written on. One of the screws cracks it a lot, still thinks it's funny, but he's wrong.

Jimmy's cellmates are out in the yard, exercising. They only get an hour a day out of the cell so they've taken advantage of it, but Jimmy prefers the peace and quiet of their absence.

There's a click at the door, it's being unlocked. A screw – the not-nice one, not the not-funny one – shouts out 'Visitor' and a head pokes around the door; a head with a dog collar underneath it.

'Have you got a minute?' the dog collar says.

Jimmy laughs. Can't help it.

'To be honest, I'm a bit busy, padre. Maybe you could come back another time?' The man looks puzzled, not sure whether to take this seriously or not.

'Only kidding, man,' Jimmy says. 'Got all the time in the world, padre, all the time in the world. Come in, pull up a chair.'

Dog collar's face brightens, looks like he gets the joke this time; there are no chairs.

'Great.'

He enters the cell, leaves the door open though – you can't be too careful where a stone-cold thug's concerned, even with the Almighty on your side. He grimaces at the smell and perches on the edge of the bottom bunk opposite Jimmy, as far away from the bucket as he can get. He's very young, fresh-faced, not long out of whatever they call padre school, Jimmy reckons.

Jimmy levers himself off the top bunk in one move – practice makes perfect – lands feet together on the floor like an Olympic gymnast and sits down opposite his visitor.

'How are you holding up?' the dog collar says.

'I'm peachy,' Jimmy says, giving him a beaming, reassuring smile.

'I've been looking at your file.'

Jimmy says nothing. Leans his head to one side, curious to hear what's coming next.

'Have you considered talking to a psychiatrist? We have a visiting consultant who comes here three days a week.'

'A shrink?' Jimmy says.

'Um, yes.'

'There's nothing wrong with me,' Jimmy says, wiping snot from his nose with his sleeve; one of the four men in the cell always has a cold, it gets passed around – it's Jimmy's turn this week.

'Don't get me wrong, Jimmy – you don't mind if I call you Jimmy, do you?' Jimmy shakes his head. 'It's just that looking through the notes, I think it's possible you might have PTSD.'

'What's that when it's at home?'

'Post-traumatic stress disorder.'

'None the wiser, padre.'

'Used to be called shell-shock. In layman's terms, it's a,

um, condition, that some people suffer from after they've been involved in, or maybe just even witnessed, a horrific incident. Like, um, you.'

'Is that right?'

'Yes, it's a sad fact that around ten per cent of current prisoners are veterans, many wrongly committed in my view, because of their PTSD. The condition means that after such an . . . incident, they may behave, um, erratically and, as such, in essence, it can – and should – be used as a defence . . . in some cases.'

'Defence?' Jimmy says.

'Yes.'

'Have you met my brief?'

'Um, no, I haven't had the pleasure.'

'It's not a pleasure, padre, believe me. The best legal aid can buy, apparently. He wouldn't know a defence if it tapped him on the shoulder and shouted "Boo".'

'Would you like me to talk to him?'

'No.'

'Why not?'

'Because there's nothing wrong with me.'

Jimmy stands up and paces around the cell. The dog collar is clearly getting a little concerned but is trying his best to hide it. Failing, but trying his best. Jimmy doesn't mind his shortcomings; it's a shit job he's got in here, trying to talk religion to the Godless.

'I nearly killed a policeman,' Jimmy says eventually.

'Yes, but it was unintentional – and you didn't know he was a policeman.'

'Doesn't make him any less damaged. They reckon he'll always have to walk with a stick. And that's down to me. I know he was a twat, but you can't go around beating up all the twats, there'd be no one left. I punched him. It was my responsibility – you understand.'

'Yes. However—'

Jimmy stops pacing. Turns to face the dog collar.

'Let me finish, padre. All my life I've been told you have to take your lumps. D'you know what I mean?'

'I think so.'

'My dad used to beat the crap out of me. But I was a cheeky little twat, so I took the beatings. I took my lumps. It was the only thing he liked about me, I reckon, that I took them. With no complaints.'

The dog collar is giving it his sad face now and looks as if he might interrupt again, so Jimmy presses on.

'Then I joined the Navy – and guess what – they preached the same thing. Take your lumps. Hold your hands up. Re-spon-sibility. You understand preaching, don't you, padre?'

The dog collar nods.

'Well then. Consider me a convert. A true believer. So excuse my French, but you can take your PTSD and stick it up your arse. The door's over there.'

The padre knows better than to argue. He leaves without another word and the door shuts behind him. Jimmy hears the lock turn. He knows fine well that once his visitor has left the wing there's every chance the not-nice screw will come back in and beat the shit out of him. Not just for dissing the padre – the screws are much less impressed with what he did to Kev than the inmates and they like to give him the occasional kicking just to reinforce the point. But that's OK. He was the same back in the day, always hated the lippy ones on the other side of the cell door when he was on guard duty.

And, anyway, if there's one thing he knows how to do, it's *to take his lumps*. He's at least got that to cling to.

20

Northumberland University, July 4, 2012

They walked straight past the receptionist like they belonged there, going through two doors before hitting a problem. Jimmy pushed at the double doors in front of them, but they stayed closed.

'Bollocks,' he said. Carrie smiled and pulled out a card from her purse. She placed it against a scanner on the wall and the doors clicked open.

'How did you do that?'

'I'm a student,' she said.

'I thought you were a nurse?'

'Student nurse, spend half my time here, the rest doing shifts at the hospital. You'd know if you'd asked.'

Jimmy shrugged. It wasn't the kind of conversation he had any more. Nobody he knew did anything.

As they walked through the corridors, they passed a security guard going the other way, the ageing-bouncer sort. He glanced at Jimmy, but didn't stop. Eventually they found a noticeboard with pictures of the Geography staff on it. Norma Weston was in Room 132. Two doors away.

They were about to knock when a student came out of the office. He held the door open for them, so Carrie walked straight in, Jimmy slowly following behind.

Norma Weston was sat at her desk, her back to the window. She was sipping from a plastic cup, a folder open in front of her.

'Can I help you?' she said, smiling at Carrie. Then she saw Jimmy and the smile disappeared.

'I'm Carrie Carpenter; I think you know my dad, Roger.'

Weston nodded, her eyes still firmly on Jimmy. She cleared her throat before answering.

'Yes, a little, we're, um, colleagues.'

'Colleagues? You know he's disappeared?'

'Yes, well, sort of.'

Jimmy could see a newspaper on the windowsill behind her. It was the one he'd been pictured in.

'You read about what I saw?' he said.

'Yes.' She grimaced slightly, like she'd just smelled sour milk. 'D'you really believe someone attacked him?'

Jimmy nodded. He may have doubted it before, but the doubts had gone. Having someone try and run you over had that effect.

'You were with him on the day he disappeared, weren't you?' Carrie said.

There was a long pause. Jimmy ticked it off a mental list of things he was looking out for.

'I wouldn't say *with* him,' Weston said. 'There was a

demonstration, at the council offices; there were lots of us there.'

'Have you spoken to the police?'

Weston took a sip from her cup and glanced at her computer before answering.

'No.'

'Why not?' Carrie continued. 'You might have been able to tell them something useful.'

'Look, what do you want exactly? I'm a little bit busy at the moment.'

'D'you know why he might have been attacked? Or who by?'

Weston sighed. 'No, of course not. I don't even know he *was* attacked,' she added, glancing accusingly at Jimmy.

Carrie took a breath. Jimmy could sense her anger building; she was going in hard. She dropped a photo on the desk. The woman barely glanced at it.

'You seem close,' Carrie said, pointing to the photograph. 'Were you shagging him?'

'How dare you talk to me like that?' Weston said, a redness creeping up her neck. She rubbed the side of her face as if trying to halt the blood flow. 'I'm married.'

'That never stopped my dad.'

'You should leave. Now.'

'Has he been in touch with you?' Carrie pressed.

'No. Now get out before I call security.'

'Was he worried about anything?'

The woman hesitated. For a second Jimmy thought she was going to say something, but then she picked up the phone.

'Security, please.'

'I'm a student, I'm allowed to be here,' Carrie protested.

'Perhaps,' Weston said. 'But he's not.'

'We should go,' Jimmy said.

'I'm in Room 132,' Weston said to someone on the other end of the phone. 'I need urgent assistance. There's a trespasser in the building.'

'Come on, Carrie,' Jimmy said. 'We have to leave.' He pulled at Carrie's arm and started to back out of the doorway, but she yanked her arm out of his grip, strode forward and grabbed the photo from the desk, making sure that she got right in the woman's face.

'OK,' Carrie said. 'You can call off your dogs. We're going. But don't think this is over.'

She slammed the door on her way back out. As they headed to the exit, Jimmy kept his eyes peeled for the security guard but saw no one. He wondered if Weston had been faking the call, just to get rid of them. He thought about the classic signs of lying he remembered from his training: the long pauses, the throat clearing, the face rubbing. She'd displayed them all.

'Did you believe her,' he said, 'that she's just a colleague?'

'Did I fuck,' Carrie said.

Some people didn't need the training.

Norma Weston left the building ten minutes after Jimmy and Carrie. They were watching the exit from a coffee shop across the road.

Carrie immediately got up and strode after her, Jimmy

reluctantly following behind. He'd tried to dissuade her from her plan to follow the woman, but she was adamant and there was no way he could let her go on her own – Mr Blond was still out there somewhere.

Weston's bright red hair made her an easy target, so they were able to maintain their distance while keeping her in sight. Just to be sure, they stayed on the opposite side of the road, avoiding her occasional glances behind. Wherever she was going she looked nervous. At the end of the road, she headed down a side street towards the Manors roundabout.

'If she takes the footbridge, we're screwed,' Jimmy said. The bridge led high over a wide dual carriageway that bypassed the city centre. Anyone walking on it was clearly visible; they'd never be able to follow her without being seen. Maybe that would be a good thing; give him time to think about what the hell he was doing.

Unfortunately, Weston turned away from the bridge's steps and headed towards a nearby car park, pulling some keys from her pocket. The lights on a blue Mini flickered on and off.

'She's got a car,' Jimmy said.

'So have we,' Carrie said, hailing an approaching taxi. Things were spiralling out of Jimmy's control, but Carrie clearly had the scent of blood in her nostrils. He almost wished he hadn't left Dog with Gadge; at least he'd have had an excuse to bail out now and let her get on with it.

Carrie clambered into the back of the cab, leaving the door open.

'Come on,' she shouted. Jimmy sighed and jumped in next to her. As he did, Weston pulled out of the car park.

'Where to?' the cab driver said.

'Follow that blue car,' Carrie said, pointing ahead.

The cab driver looked in his mirror and grinned, his gold tooth glinting in the reflected light.

'You serious?'

'As a heart attack,' she said.

'It's not one of them reality shows, is it? Have you got a hidden camera back there?'

'No! Now get going, will you.'

'Bloody marvellous,' the driver exclaimed. 'Waited years for this.'

As the Mini moved past them, he slipped into gear and slotted in behind it. When they stopped at a traffic light he glanced in the mirror again.

'You're not up to anything dodgy, mind? I mean you look alreet, pet, but . . .' His glance turned to Jimmy.

Carrie laughed. 'He's fine, a bit rough round the edges, right enough, but otherwise sound.'

'If you say so, pet,' the driver said, looking doubtful. The lights changed and he pulled off again, keeping close to the car in front.

'D'you really think she's got something to do with all this?' Jimmy said, keeping his voice low. The driver seemed like the nebby type. Carrie followed suit, taking the hint.

'Who knows?' she hissed. 'But like she said: she's a married woman. Maybe her husband's the jealous sort. I could imagine my dad keeping his head down if there was a mad husband running around out there.'

Jimmy frowned. She was still hoping for some kind of happy ending and he was pretty sure she wasn't going to get it.

Luckily it was rush hour and the roads were busy, so they were able to follow Weston's car through the outskirts of the city undetected until it turned into a small housing estate near the racecourse. A few yards in, she pulled onto a driveway. The taxi carried on past her house, stopping a few houses down.

'This do you?' the driver said.

'Perfect,' Carrie said.

Jimmy watched through the back window as Weston got out of her car and went into the semi-detached house. There was a small tricycle to the left of the front door.

'What now?' he said.

'Round Two.' Carrie was already getting out of the cab.

'D'you want me to wait?' the driver said. 'I don't mind, best thing that's happened to me all year.'

'No, you're alright,' Carrie said. 'What do I owe you?'

'Buggered if I knaa, pet. I was so excited I forgot to put the meter on. Just give us a couple of quid. Can't wait to get home and tell the wife.'

When Weston opened the door her face dropped and she tried to close it straight away, but Carrie already had her foot in the way.

'We're not going away, Mrs Weston. It's us or the police. Up to you.'

Weston opened the door again and stepped outside, pulling it half closed behind her.

'What do you want?' she said, keeping her voice low.

'The truth,' Carrie said. 'Not some utter bollocks like before.'

Weston frowned and moved closer, visibly upset now, almost whispering.

'Please leave me alone. I have a young child. My husband is in the kitchen feeding her.'

'Maybe we should ask *him* about my dad instead?' Carrie said.

'Don't you fucking dare.' Weston paused, lowered her voice. 'There's no need for that.'

'Spill then,' Carrie said.

Jimmy watched in admiration – the girl was relentless. He could see why the police were fed up with her. Weston glanced over her shoulder at the half-closed door.

'I don't know what's happened to your dad, I swear.'

'But you weren't just colleagues,' Carrie said.

Weston hesitated but Jimmy could tell she was going to answer. Carrie had her on the back foot now.

'A bit more than that. Friends.'

Carrie left space for Weston to continue. It was classic by-the-book stuff. She was a natural.

'We'd been, um, seeing each other. A drink after work, that sort of thing.'

They all knew what she meant by 'that sort of thing'.

'Does your husband know?' Jimmy asked.

'Of course not.'

'You sure?' he pressed.

'Positive.' She glanced behind again. 'And I'd like to keep it that way.'

'Anyone else know?' Carrie said.

'No. We were very discreet.'

'When's the last time you saw him?' Carrie said.

'At the demo. He said he was going for a drink and that he'd see me at work the next day. I haven't heard from him since.'

Going for a drink made sense. Jimmy remembered that Roger had seemed a bit unsteady on his feet.

'Everything alright, darling?' A man's voice came from inside the house.

Weston blanched.

'Fine, love,' she shouted.

The door opened. A dark-haired man stood there holding a young girl in his arms. He was short, about five four with a moustache and a neat goatee beard. Not the man Jimmy had seen on the Quayside. Nor the blond car driver.

'Oh, hello,' he said. The girl squirmed in his arms. She was wearing blue denim dungarees, which reminded Jimmy of Kate, who, until yesterday, was about the same age and dressed much the same the last time he'd seen her.

'They're collecting for charity, Martin,' Weston said, glancing at Jimmy, 'for Shelter.'

'Oh right,' the man said, 'don't be long though, love, dinner's nearly ready.'

He moved back inside. Jimmy touched Carrie on the shoulder and she turned around.

'We should get going.' He knew what a marriage break-up was like and he didn't want to be the cause of another one. Carrie was made of sterner stuff.

'Not yet.' She turned back to Weston. 'Some people think he's run away with a woman. Do you believe that?'

Weston hesitated. 'No,' she said. 'I don't.'

'Then what?' Carrie said. 'If you were *friends*, you must think something.'

Weston looked over her shoulder again then back at Carrie.

'Look, you didn't hear this from me, and if anyone asks, I'll deny it. I can't afford to lose my job. You understand?'

Carrie nodded.

'Talk to Andrew Lang, our boss. He's in some kind of trouble. It might be related.'

Weston turned to go back into the house.

'What kind of trouble?' Carrie pressed.

'I'm sorry, I can't say any more.'

And then she closed the door.

21

The Pit Stop, Newcastle, July 4, 2012

'You've been on the rob again, you thievin' little bastard!' Gadge yelled.

As Jimmy approached the Pit Stop, his mind was full of shite that he couldn't get rid of: murderous car drivers, dodgy coppers, broken families, absent fathers – he could feel a storm coming, but he didn't know which direction it was coming from or how to shelter from it. The last thing he needed was to find Gadge and Deano fighting outside, circling each other like mismatched sumo wrestlers, Dog running around them, barking like mad, thinking it was a game.

'I haven't done anything, man,' Deano yelled. 'Swear down.'

Behind them a couple of late-night shoppers crossed the street to avoid the fuss, heading for the car park near the Discovery Museum.

'Lyin' sod.' Gadge made a grab for Deano, but the kid was too quick. And Gadge was too pissed, his lame effort sending him spinning to the pavement, narrowly missing Dog who decided the game was over and moved well away, watching them cautiously.

'Li'l bastard,' Gadge shouted, rolling onto his back, trying to get back up, failing miserably. Deano could have given him a good kicking while he was down if he'd wanted, but was too busy laughing – a manic laugh; he was definitely on something.

'What's going on?' Jimmy said, grabbing Deano by his arm. The kid tried to focus on Jimmy's face but couldn't, his gaze shifting from one side to the other. It was a toss-up whether that was due to guilt or whatever shit he'd taken.

'Nothing,' Deano said.

'He's been on the rob, I tell ya,' Gadge yelled, trying to sit up again, but losing his balance and falling back down, screaming with frustration.

'Have you?' Jimmy asked Deano.

'No, man, I haven't.'

'Where d'you get that money then, eh?' Gadge yelled from the floor.

'I told ya.'

'It's a good one this, Jimmy. You'll love this. Go on, Deano, tell Jimmy what you telt me.'

'Well?' Jimmy said.

'You won't believe us, I knaa you won't. *He* didn't.' Deano pointed at a still-prone Gadge.

'Try me,' Jimmy said.

'I sold me begging sign,' Deano said. 'Swear doon, Jimmy, I'm not lying.'

'Who the hell would buy that?'

'I divvn't knaa, Jimmy man, he said he was an artist, wanted it for his what's-a-name . . . his instalment!'

'His installation, you pleb,' Gadge shouted, rolling onto his stomach and trying to push himself up with his arms. 'Can't even get your story right.'

'Gave me fifty quid for it,' Deano said.

'Bollocks,' Gadge said, as his arms collapsed, his face smacking into the pavement. Jimmy flinched, expecting another scream, but Gadge barely seemed to notice.

'He did, man,' Deano said, 'reckoned it was one of the best he'd seen.'

'What did it say?' Jimmy asked.

'*Will Dance For Money*,' Deano said. 'Spelled properly and everything, I think – I got a mate to write it. I'm not gonna lie, Jimmy man, I was surprised how much, like, but I'm not gonna ask questions, am I? Fifty squid is fifty squid. Didn't even have to dance for it.'

Jimmy half believed him. He'd heard rumours that Deano had done a lot of worse things for cash than dance; had tried hard not to imagine them.

Deano's eyes suddenly went blank.

'Deano?' Jimmy said.

The kid looked at him like he was surprised he was still there.

'Had something to tell you,' Deano said.

'What?'

'Can't remember.'

Behind them, Jimmy could hear Gadge still struggling to get to his feet.

'Wait there,' Jimmy said to Deano and walked over to Gadge, pulled him up by his arms and propped him up on his shoulder.

'Thanks, Jimbo,' Gadge said.

'What the hell have you been drinking?'

'Rough scrumpy,' Gadge laughed, 'gallons of it.' Jimmy sat Gadge down gently on the pavement, his back against a wall to keep him upright. Dog decided it was safe to join in again and came and sat beside him, licking Gadge's hand.

'Got it,' Deano suddenly cried. 'I remember what it was, Jimmy, I remember. There was someone round earlier, asking questions, looking for you.'

Jimmy knew exactly who that would be.

'Young, short, blond hair?' he said.

'No, man, it was the polis. Remember, Gadge? I told you, they wanted to knaa if I'd seen Jimmy, if I knew where he was.'

'Slow down,' Jimmy said. 'Who's they?'

'Not they, just one of them. A DC or something, asking for "Jimmy". Plain clothes. Big bastard. Like a brick shithouse, knaa what I mean.'

'Did you see his ID?' Maybe they were taking him seriously, Jimmy thought, wanting to follow up on his statement. Or they'd seen the paper and wanted to kick his arse for going public.

'No,' Deano said. 'Didn't think. Had to hide my stuff, he nearly saw me with it, that would've been—'

Deano stopped talking, realising that he'd said too much, slumped down against the wall next to Gadge, their stupid fight already forgotten.

'What are you on?' Jimmy said.

'Nothing,' Deano muttered.

'Don't lie to me, son,' Jimmy said, kneeling in front of him to get his attention.

'OK, Dad,' Deano said. Jimmy blinked. Hadn't been called that in a long time. Kate's smiling face flashed through his mind and he wished again that he'd said something to her. Deano's confession broke the spell.

'Had a little bit of spice, didn't I?'

'I thought you were trying to clean yourself up.'

Deano looked like he might cry. He tried to look away, but Jimmy wouldn't let him, putting his hand on the kid's chin and turning his head back towards him so he couldn't avoid looking at him.

'Gave it me for nowt, didn't he,' Deano said, sniffling.

'Who?' Jimmy said.

'Not saying.'

'Goldilocks,' Gadge muttered. 'Twat offered me some earlier; told him to stick it up his arse. Would have done it for him if I wasn't so pissed.'

Jimmy found Goldilocks at one of his regular spots, at the top of Dog Leap Stairs. He wasn't alone. He was sitting on a bench, deep in conversation with a fat, middle-aged man in a cheap, shiny suit. There were two possibilities: the guy in the suit was after either a fix or a fuck. As he had his hand on Goldilocks' knee, Jimmy was betting on the latter.

'If you're after a bit of rough, you're talking to the right man,' Jimmy said, startling the shit out of the fat man, who hadn't seen him coming. 'He's as rough as they get. As soon as you've handed over your cash, he'll beat the crap out of you.'

Goldilocks had made no secret of his gay-bashing sideline, bragging about it to all and sundry. Seemed to think it made him look hard.

'You can fuck off for a start,' Goldilocks said, without looking up.

The fat man moved along the bench, not wanting to get involved in whatever was kicking off. He looked nervously from Goldilocks to Jimmy and back again.

'You'd better run,' Jimmy said. 'Unless you fancy explaining to your missus how you got mugged in a well-known gay pick-up spot.'

'Ignore this twat, he's just—' Goldilocks was too late, the man had heard enough and was away on his toes.

'You prick,' he said. 'What did you do that for?'

'I want a word,' Jimmy said, closing the gap between them. Goldilocks tried to get up, but Jimmy pushed him back down on the bench.

'How about *wanker*?' Goldilocks said.

'Stop giving your crap to Deano,' Jimmy said.

'It's a free country,' Goldilocks said. It's not, Jimmy thought. Couldn't be arsed to argue though, not this time.

'He's just a kid. He's trying to get his shit together,' Jimmy said.

'Bollocks. He's a junkie pot-head. Anyway, it's mostly fucking oregano.'

'Don't give a shit what's in it, just pack it in.'

'Why should I?'

'Because I'm asking you nicely.'

'Ask me any way you want. Same answer.' Goldilocks reached into his pocket and took out a small tin of roll-ups. 'I didn't even charge the little twat. I'm like Oxfam for druggies, me.'

Jimmy didn't say anything, knew fine well that Goldilocks would just charge the kid more the next time and the time after that. Goldilocks looked back up at him.

'You still here?'

Jimmy thought about letting it go, *not his fight*. Sod that. He grabbed Goldilocks by his feet and wrenched him off the bench, slamming his arse onto the pavement.

'Jesus!' Goldilocks shouted, trying but failing to grab on to the bench. Jimmy dragged him through a small flower bed on his back, towards the steep stone steps that led down to the Quayside.

'For fuck's sake, let go,' Goldilocks shouted, twisting his body from left to right to try and disturb Jimmy's grip, leaving himself wide open to a firm kick in the bollocks which Jimmy happily gave him. As Goldilocks curled up into a ball Jimmy grabbed him by the seat of his pants and the scruff of his neck and dragged him towards the top step. He weighed next to nothing.

'What are you doing?' Goldilocks screamed.

A man with a camera around his neck started to climb the

steps until he saw what was happening at the top, thought better of it and disappeared around the corner.

Jimmy lifted Goldilocks off the ground, ready to heave him into the air and down the steps.

'Alright, you bastard, alright. I won't sell your bum-boy any more shit,' Goldilocks cried.

Jimmy swung him towards the drop but held on to him.

'On my mother's life,' Goldilocks shouted.

'Like you give a shit about your mother,' Jimmy muttered.

As Jimmy swung him back once more, ready to hurl him over the edge this time, a large plastic bag fell out of Goldilocks' coat. It was full of dozens of small packets: his supply.

Jimmy dropped Goldilocks face first on the concrete, probably breaking his nose. Then he picked up the large bag, gave him one last kick – just because – and started to walk down the steps, whistling as he went.

'That's mine,' Goldilocks shouted, his voice distorted by the hand he was no doubt holding to his damaged face. 'What are you doing with it?'

'Giving it a float test,' Jimmy yelled back, heading down towards the river.

'Bastard,' Goldilocks screamed. 'I'll kill you for this.'

Jimmy stopped, turned around. Goldilocks took his hand from his nose, which Jimmy *really* hoped was broken, and started scrabbling backwards on his hands and heels like a human crab.

Jimmy laughed and headed back down the steps. No need to rub it in, he'd made his point. As he reached the bottom he heard one last, much fainter 'Bastard.'

He turned and walked down past the taxi rank, crossed the road, went around the old fish-market building to the edge of the river and dumped the bag in, watching as it floated away downstream.

22

National Probation Service, Newcastle, July 5, 2012

Sandy pushed the newspaper across her desk.

'So this is what you meant by keeping your head down?' she said.

'No, I—'

'It was a rhetorical question, dipstick.'

Jimmy's last probation officer had been straight down the line, formal, like she had a stick up her arse. Sandy was different. Mad as a snake, but you could talk to her. If you dared.

She pointed at the story.

'Is all this accurate?'

He nodded.

'And you've given the police a statement?'

'Yes.'

She smiled.

'We'll make a proper citizen of you yet.'

Sandy reached down and patted Dog, who was asleep under her desk. Jimmy relaxed. It was going to be OK.

'Just one thing.'

Bollocks.

'Who gave you permission to sleep on the street?'

'I, um . . .'

She put a finger to her lips. 'Don't speak. The correct answer is *no one*. You have an approved address where you are required to sleep every night. Hastings Terrace – lodging with your old friend Gary. Nice man, proper job, upright, trustworthy, no previous offences.'

He nodded. Gary was divorced now; Liz long gone, the kids all grown up. Jimmy had persuaded him to help out while he settled back into the city. At least that was what he'd told Sandy. In reality it had been a one-night-only deal, when Sandy came for a home visit. And then he was off again.

'So why were you sleeping on the Quayside?'

'Gary and I had an, um, argument.'

She raised one eyebrow.

'Does this face look stupid to you? Don't answer that either. Do you think you're the first offender who's played the old fake-address trick on me?'

She had him bang to rights. No point arguing. Jimmy shook his head.

'D'you like football, Jimmy?'

'What?'

'Simple question: Do. You. Like. Football?'

'Not really.'

'In the wrong city then, aren't you? It's practically compulsory up here. Anyway, I'm sure you understand the basics: this is a red-card offence. Understand? I only gave you two instructions when you came to me, Jimmy, d'you remember what they were? You can speak now.'

'Don't lie to you.'

'And?'

'Don't be a twat.'

'Bingo. How's that working for you?'

She put a finger to her lips.

'You understand that if you breach the conditions of your licence, I can have you returned to prison, yes?'

He nodded. He was screwed.

'And that living at an approved address is one of those conditions?'

'Yes.'

'Then get a fucking grip. Sit-rep: I've got your balls in my hand and I can choose to stroke them or crush them. Or I can let them sit there to see what your next move is.' She sighed. 'Yellow card this time. One more chance. Understood?'

Jimmy breathed out. 'Thank you.'

'You did a good thing here,' Sandy said, indicating the newspaper. 'Don't go and spoil it. I'll see you in one week. If you haven't got a proper address for me by then, you can leave the dog with me because you won't be able to take him where you'll be going.'

23

The Free Trade, Newcastle, July 5, 2012

Knackered, Jimmy collapsed onto a bench in the beer garden of the Free Trade. Best views of the river in the city, they reckoned, especially at this time of night, but he was too tired to look.

After the meeting with Sandy, he'd spent the rest of the day keeping out of harm's way, constantly on the move, watching out for blond men, black cars and rogue policemen and trying to shake off the anger he felt that he had let himself get dragged into the middle of a shitstorm. Wasn't it the definition of madness to keep making the same mistake over and over again?

Eventually he'd reached the pub and Dog had sat on the pavement and refused to move, making it clear he wasn't going to be dragged around any longer. He couldn't even be arsed to bark at the large cat sitting on the pub's windowsill.

Like the garden, the pub was in darkness, well after closing time. He'd seen the last barman leave, locking the front door behind him, knew no one else was around. The garden was hidden behind a hedge, so he couldn't be seen from the road. No one would find him there. He could hear a man banging on a door and shouting in the nearby flats, trying to get someone to open up. Felt his eyes closing.

The school playground. The bell's ringing. Jimmy's dad slaps him around the head; yells something in his face, his mouth opening and closing, but no sound coming out. Slaps him again. The other kids are in a circle around them, laughing at him, pointing. He looks down. He's naked. Tries to cover up his dick, but his dad slaps him again and he has to raise his hands to defend himself. The laughter gets louder. He tries to run, but his feet are stuck. The circle of kids closes in on him, his dad gone now, leaving him alone, unprotected. The laughing gets louder and louder and louder. The kids are slapping him now, kicking him, pinching him; he's crying. The laughing is louder still, building to something – the sound of Hell. Suddenly the kids vanish, but he can still hear the laughter, still feel the punches and the kicks. He wants to hit back, but he can't – there's no one left to fight. So he stands there, frozen to the spot, taking the lumps, his hands over his ears, screaming for help. For his dad.

A searing pain woke Jimmy up, his left knee on fire. He screamed in agony. Someone was standing above him, a man, something in his hand glinting in the moonlight. A large kitchen knife. He could hear Dog growling, running around on the gravel, but couldn't see him. The man moved, kicking out at something. Dog yelped. Jimmy tried to sit up, but the pain was brutal. He reached down to his knee, could feel warm blood pouring out. Kept his hand pressed on it to stop the flow, but it seeped through his fingers. A clubbing blow to the head sent him reeling off the bench, his damaged knee smashing into the concrete floor as he fell. He screamed again. The attacker knelt on his back, put the knife to his throat.

'Don't fuckin' move.'

Goldilocks. The stink gave it away.

'My knee,' Jimmy said.

'You've got another one.'

Jimmy could feel the point of the knife jabbing into the side of his neck. He stayed as still as he could, trying not to think about the pain in his leg; about not being able to walk again.

'Think you're a big man, don't you?' Goldilocks hissed into his ear, his rank breath fouling the air. 'Think you're the king of the fuckin' castle.'

For a moment Jimmy felt the pressure of the knife ease, but it quickly returned, higher up, near his ear this time.

'Fancy going all Van Gogh, Jimmy?'

Jimmy had no idea what he was talking about.

'Please . . .' he said.

'Fuck please.'

Jimmy felt the knife slice through his ear, blood trickling onto his neck, the sharp pain momentarily overshadowing that from his knee.

Goldilocks stood up. 'Now who's gonna be the one crawling?' he said and stamped down on Jimmy's back, his kidney. Jimmy felt like he'd been turned inside out, like he would burst unless he threw up or shat himself.

'You'll piss blood for a fortnight,' Goldilocks said.

Somewhere close, Jimmy could hear Dog whimpering. He turned his head to look, but all he saw was a large boot coming towards his face.

Daylight. Jimmy woke up freezing, lying in a pool of his own blood, razor blades in his kidney. He tried to move, but the pain in his knee jagged through him, forcing him to stay still. He had been stripped down to a T-shirt, his Barbour jacket gone. He looked around. Rucksack gone too.

And Dog was nowhere to be seen. Had to find him. Jimmy grabbed hold of the bench seat and pulled himself up, ignoring the pain, clamping his teeth together, forcing himself to stand. His leg was a thick, clagged-up mess, but at least it had stopped bleeding. Holding himself up with one hand, he put the other to his ear, checking the damage. Didn't know what he was feeling; something still there, thank fuck, but torn, split, difficult to tell through more congealed blood.

Still no sign of Dog though. He whistled, then shouted, as near a shout as he could manage. 'Here, boy!'

Nothing. Then a bark. In the distance, but definitely a bark. Jimmy let go of the bench and tried to move towards the entrance of the beer garden, his head spinning from the blood loss so that he only managed two steps before his injured leg collapsed beneath him and he crashed to the ground.

'Help,' he croaked.

Nothing.

Using his arms, he pushed and pulled himself slowly along the ground and up a small set of steps to the road outside. He looked left and right. Nothing. He could feel himself starting to lose consciousness. He heard a car coming and forced himself to look up again, praying it wasn't the blond guy. It slowed down, the driver took one look at him and continued on his way.

Another bark. Suddenly, from around the corner, about twenty yards away, came a dog; a young boxer, too strong for the teenage girl desperately trying to keep a grip on its lead. Seeing Jimmy lying half on the path and half in the road, she stopped and let go of the dog, which raced towards him. Jimmy saw her pull out a phone and then everything went dark.

24

Visiting room, HMP Durham, 1992

Jimmy stares at the door in the corner, waiting for Bev to come through it. He's sitting on a chair in front of a small table, leaning forward, biting his nails. She's late.

Can't wait to see her. Been inside for sixteen months and it's only her third visit. He doesn't blame her, it's a long way to come and the public transport is shite. Hopes she brings Kate this time though; wants to see how much she's grown, how much she's changed.

There are about twenty other prisoners sitting at tables just like his, most of them already talking to their visitors, heads as close together as the watching screws will allow. The other exception is Wilkinson, a nasty jock psycho, short and constantly angry, the cause of more bother inside than the rest of them put together. He is also waiting on his own. Wilkinson sees Jimmy watching, sticks his tongue in his cheek and uses his hand to mime a blow job. Jimmy looks away; the twat doesn't need any encouragement.

'Keep your distance!' a screw shouts, clapping his hands loudly when an inmate right in front of Jimmy gets a little too close to his missus.

The outer door swings open and three more visitors are escorted in. And there she is. Bev, hair cropped short, elfin-style, and lighter than he's ever seen it before. She looks stunning. No Kate though. As she approaches the table, Jimmy stands up automatically, forgetting there are different rules here.

'Sit down,' one of the escorting screws shouts, 'or I'll walk her straight back out again.'

Jimmy does as he's told, holding his hand up in apology, doesn't want to mess things up again. She left early last time, upset that he lost his temper, that he kept swearing, just one of the many bad habits he's picked up inside.

Bev gets to the table and sits down on the chair on the opposite side, her handbag on her lap.

'Hi,' Jimmy says.

'You've lost weight,' she says.

'Prison food,' Jimmy says, 'not quite like home cooking.'

'How you doing?'

'Fine,' he says. 'Can't complain. You?'

'Fine.'

Silence. They're out of practice.

'How's Kate?'

Bev smiles for the first time.

'She's great. Loves school – never wants to come home, truth be told.'

Jimmy tries to hold it back, but he can't. It bursts out of him like he's got Tourette's.

'I was hoping she'd be here.'

'It's a school day, Jimmy, she's got school.'

'It's only a fucking primary school, Bév, not like she's got her fucking exams next week.'

'Jimmy . . . you promised.' He's blown it already. She looks like she's going to cry. She is crying. He reaches a hand across the desk.

'I'm sorry—'

'Keep your distance,' a screw yells, banging his baton on an empty desk for emphasis. Jimmy pulls his hand back.

Bev is staring down at her bag, tears streaming down her cheeks.

'I'm sorry, Bev,' he says. 'I just miss her, that's all.'

'You'll be out in a year,' she mumbles, still not looking at him.

Silence again. Doesn't know how to tell her. She feels his hesitation and looks up at him.

'Jimmy? What is it?'

He has no choice.

'There was a fight. In the dining hall.'

She's shaking her head.

'I didn't start it,' he says, knowing how pathetic that sounds, like something his dad would have belted him for. He glances across at Wilkinson, who, as usual, was to blame – he'd forced a server's hands into a saucepan of boiling hot soup for refusing him seconds. The psycho has visitors now: a downtrodden woman who is staring at the floor as

Wilkinson talks at her, his hands waving around wildly; and a young, fair-haired lad who looks terrified, like it's the last place in the world he wants to be. Poor little sod, Jimmy thinks, before Bev brings him back to his own problems.

'What are you saying?' she says. He hesitates, knowing she's not going to like this.

'I'll probably have to do the full sentence.'

'Five years!' she says.

He nods. 'But I've already done nearly two, what with the time in remand and that.'

She's looking at her bag again.

'Maybe you could bring her next time?'

Silence again. Unbearable fucking silence.

Eventually. 'Bev?' he says.

She looks up, looks at him properly for the first time.

'I've met someone else,' she says.

25

The Royal Victoria Infirmary, Newcastle, July 7, 2012

The beeping woke him up. Wires stuck to his chest. A tube in the back of his hand. He tried to look up, couldn't see out of one eye; a vicious, pounding headache made him wince and close the good eye. Slowly he opened it again and turned his head: a hospital bed, a small ward, like a cell. Two other patients maybe; the fourth bed looked empty. He closed his eye again, drifted off.

Woke again, someone leaning over him.

A searing pain . . . something glinting in the moonlight. A large kitchen knife.

He groaned, tried to push them away.

'Charming. You're awake then.' A female voice. A nurse. She moved back from the bed so he could see her properly, or as properly as it got through one eye. Older woman, lived-in face, smiling though.

'Just changing your drip. You lost a lot of blood.'

Jimmy looked around again. The same machine beeping,

the tube gone for the moment. Two other patients still, one asleep, the other reading a paper. Probably the same ones he saw the first time he looked – didn't think he'd been out for long this time.

'Where am I?' he croaked.

'The RVI.'

Then he remembered.

'Dog,' he said, trying to sit up.

'No dogs in here, bonny lad, the ward sister would have a blue fit.'

Jimmy started to cough, couldn't stop.

'D'you want a drink?' the nurse said.

Jimmy nodded. She picked up a cup, held it up to his lips as he edged up the bed – water, warm but welcome. He gulped it down.

'You got a dog at home then?' she asked.

At home? Too difficult to explain, so Jimmy just nodded.

'What's his name?'

'Dog,' he said, wondering what had happened to the poor creature, hoping he was safe.

The nurse looked at him as if he was taking the piss, eventually realising he wasn't.

'Well, it's original, I'll give you that,' she said.

'How long have I b—' He couldn't finish the question, started to cough again. She gave him some more water.

'They brought you in early yesterday morning, in a bad state you were. Doctor reckons you were lucky.'

He'd lost a whole day.

'Don't feel lucky.'

She smiled.

'Missed your femoral artery by about half an inch, apparently.'

Jimmy closed his eye again, weary beyond belief.

'Doctor will be around in about an hour,' she said. 'You've missed breakfast, but I could get you some toast if you're hungry?'

He shook his head.

'OK, but if you change your mind, there's a buzzer on there – the red button.'

He looked to the side. She was pointing to a device that looked like something you'd change the TV channel with.

'The police were in to talk to you yesterday, said they'd come back today.'

'The police?'

'They always get notified in stabbing cases.'

'I wasn't stabbed.'

The nurse stared at him, a glint of amusement around her eyes. 'Aye, right,' she said, 'fell on a knife, eh!'

He closed his eye again and when he opened it she was gone. Last thing he wanted was more police. He'd got away with his visit to the station, but the more contact he had with them, the greater the chance they would realise who he was – the police had long memories and he knew they'd never tire of paying him back for what he did to Kev. Anyway, he certainly didn't need their help on this, he could do payback as well and he intended to pay this one back himself, tenfold. He sat up a little and pulled the sheet down to look at his leg. There wasn't much to see; a large dressing covered his thigh from just above his knee.

'Noisy sod, you.'

Jimmy looked over to where the voice came from. An elderly man in the bed to his right – the newspaper reader – hairless except for a couple of tufts above both ears and a neat moustache. He was looking at Jimmy from above his paper, glasses perched high up on his nose.

'What?'

'Screaming and bawling half the night.'

Not the first time he'd heard that.

'Sorry.'

'Should think so. Need my beauty sleep, me; don't want to disappoint the lasses when I get out.' The man winked at him, he must have been well into his seventies, eighties even, gaunt and pale. Still had a twinkle though.

'Not got as many as you, mind, Bev, Kate . . . Carrie was it? Thought I was a ladies' man, but I'm not in your league.'

Jimmy wondered what else he'd said in his sleep, hoped it was nothing, hated someone knowing what he was thinking about; he tried to hide it from himself most of the time.

'Don't look so worried,' the man said, as if he could read his mind. 'You didn't say anything worth repeating, no national secrets or owt like that. I won't be going to the press just yet.'

Jimmy remembered the photo in the paper, wondered if the man had seen it, then realised it didn't matter, doubted he looked anything like that after the kicking he'd taken.

He tried to feel his face with his drip-free hand, grimaced at the pain as soon as he touched the right side. No wonder he couldn't see out of that eye, it felt huge.

'I've got a mirror if you want to see. Use it to trim my 'tache,' his room-mate said. 'It's not pretty, mind.'

Jimmy nodded his thanks and the man climbed out of bed, took a small hand mirror out of a drawer in his bedside cabinet and brought it over.

'You ready?' he asked.

Jimmy nodded again and the man held it up. He was right: it was a long way from pretty. Jimmy's right eye was swollen shut, he couldn't see the pupil at all. And that side of his face was dark, practically blue, and scratched to shit. The other side was almost untouched, which somehow made the whole thing look worse, like two different faces cut in half and joined together in the middle. He put his hand on the mirror and guided it around to the side; a series of black stitches ran up the middle of his ear from top to bottom. At least it was all still there.

'Hope you've got a good personality,' the man said and held out his hand. 'I'm Eric, by the way.'

'Jimmy,' he said, just about managing to shake the hand.

'Ex-military, eh?' Eric said.

'How d'you know that?' Jimmy said.

'Oh, you can always tell, just got to look at somebody and you know.'

He was definitely taking the piss, even without the bruises Jimmy looked nothing like a serviceman, not any more. The old man's face collapsed into laughter.

'Joking, man. Like I said, you were noisy last night. Navy was it? Falklands? Nasty business, eh?'

Jimmy nodded.

Eric tapped his chest.

'Royal Marines, me, 3 Commando, saw a bit of action in the Suez.' He snapped into a salute. 'Sergeant Eric Briggs reporting for duty, sir.'

'I was a Leading Regulator.'

'A Crusher, eh! Never got on much with them – bit too much of a mischief-maker back then, always in bother – but you seem alright.'

Jimmy wondered how far Eric would go to help out a fellow ex-serviceman, hoped the mischief-maker was still in there somewhere.

'Could you do me a favour, Eric?'

'Anything for a fellow comrade, young man. What do you need me to do?'

'Help me get out of here,' Jimmy said.

The old man was sceptical. Still had that military thing about following rules.

'Why d'you want to get out of here? Best place for you in your condition, surely?'

Jimmy looked around to make sure no one else was listening. The man in the other bed was still fast asleep. He beckoned Eric closer.

'Someone's after me.'

'Not being funny, old chap, but it looks like they found you.'

Too fucking sharp for his own good, this one.

'It's not the guy who did this I'm worried about.'

'Who is it then?' Eric asked.

Jimmy shook his head. 'Can't say.'

'Loose lips sink ships, eh?'

'Something like that.'

Jimmy could see the old man struggling with his conscience, but eventually he looked at Jimmy and smiled.

'What the hell! Let's do it.'

It wasn't easy. Taking the drip out was messy and Jimmy could barely put any weight on his leg when he got out of bed. If it hadn't been for Eric, he'd have fallen at the first hurdle.

'Long time since anybody needed my help,' Eric said, helping Jimmy stagger around the small ward until the feeling came back into his leg and he thought he could manage it on his own. He almost fell a couple of times but eventually he was shuffling around unaided. The biggest problem was his clothes. He didn't have any. There was a small locker by his bed but the only things in it were his boots.

'They probably had to cut you out of your trousers,' Eric said, indicating the size of his leg bandage.

I bet they burned everything else, Jimmy thought, remembering how he'd woken up with his coat gone. Goldilocks had probably had away with that, like everything else. Like Dog even.

'Try my stuff,' Eric said. 'I've lost a lot of weight recently, so it's all too big for me anyhow; probably fit you like a glove.'

He was right. With a lot of help Jimmy managed to squeeze into Eric's clothes – the regulation, ex-military civilian uniform combination of white shirt, grey trousers and a smart blue blazer. With a different face and some better shoes, he might have looked respectable.

He was ready to go.

'I owe you for this,' he said.

'Not at all,' Eric said. 'Makes a change to be useful to someone. I'll not be needing the clothes anyway; they'll be taking me out of here in a box.'

Jimmy didn't ask, figured that if Eric had wanted him to know what was wrong with him, he'd have let him know. Didn't need to ask anyway. Cancer had taken his dad, it wasn't hard to spot it.

'Get off with you, man. If the nurse comes back, I'll tell her you're in the loo, buy you a bit of time.'

Jimmy hobbled to the door. Taking it slowly. He looked out into the corridor. It was empty. About ten yards to his right he could see a lift. He moved gingerly towards it and hit the down button. A light came on. He heard a door opening. Somewhere around the corner someone started to whistle and there was a squeaking noise – the whistler was pushing a trolley, he guessed.

The lift pinged and the doors opened. The sole occupant was a doctor, white coat, clipboard in hand, the works. He looked up and Jimmy wondered if it was his doctor, the one who was supposed to be coming back to check on him. But he got lucky – the man showed no sign of recognising him.

'Morning,' Jimmy said and stepped inside, leaning against the wall for support.

'You alright?' the doctor said.

'Fighting fit,' Jimmy said.

As the lift descended, he remembered the last time he'd been in the RVI. When he'd come to take Kate home for the first time. When his biggest concern was making sure he didn't drop her. Another lifetime.

The lift reached the ground floor and Jimmy let the doctor leave first; didn't want him to see how much he was struggling. He kept his hand on the button to stop the doors from closing. Once the way was clear, he stepped out and headed towards the exit, keeping close to the wall in case he needed to rest. He was about thirty feet from freedom when things started to go wrong.

The glass doors at the entrance slid open and two uniformed policemen walked in. Not the usual suspects, Stevens and his mate, Duke, but probably just as lairy.

There were only two ways for them to go: straight on, where Jimmy stood, leaning against the wall, or down a corridor to their right. He willed whatever god might be looking out for him to send them down the corridor but, as always, his prayers went unanswered as they headed straight towards him. Fortunately, they were deep in conversation and hadn't yet seen him. There was a door on his left, about four feet in front of him, so he limped forward, opened it and stepped through. It was a small store cupboard, full of cleaning supplies, with barely enough room to stand. He closed the door and stood stock still, hoping that no one had seen him. He counted to a hundred before opening it again and walking back out. As he did, a woman trundled past pushing a tea trolley. For a moment, he thought she was going to say something, but he glowered at her and she thought better of it, which wasn't surprising given the state of his face.

There was no sign of the two policemen. Jimmy slowly made his way towards the entrance. It seemed to take hours, but there was a clock on the wall ahead of him, so he knew it wasn't as slow as it felt. Eventually he reached the doors, they parted automatically and he stepped outside. Two things on his mind: Dog and vengeance.

It was only about half a mile as the crow flies from the hospital to the Pit Stop, but Jimmy was far from flying. He had to sit down twice before he got out of Leazes Park and that was just across the road from the hospital. Luckily, a few trees had been damaged by the recent high winds and he managed to find a large branch to fashion into a makeshift crutch, which helped a lot. He slowly got used to the pain in his leg and the more he pushed on, the more it eased up. Still had a hell of a limp though and by the time he reached his destination he was completely shattered.

Not too shattered to notice the quiet though. Normally it was a human hive, the noise hitting you as soon as you got in the door: people preparing food, others arguing, someone weeping in the corner or screaming from withdrawal symptoms. But not this time.

As soon as he hobbled in, he knew there was something

off. A strange look from a young, bedraggled girl as she glanced up from her phone; a couple of others going quiet as he shuffled past them in the entrance hall. When he walked into the dining room everything went quieter still until someone in the queue dropped a tray on the floor and the loud clatter broke the silence.

Jimmy looked over and saw Gadge staring at him, seemingly oblivious to the food he had dropped over his feet and the floor.

'Fuck me,' Gadge said. 'You can't be here.'

'Why not?' Jimmy said.

'You're dead.'

26

The Pit Stop, Newcastle, July 7, 2012

Gadge and Jimmy sat huddled in the corner of the room, away from the others, who were all staring across, desperate to hear how a man had come back from the dead.

'Some poor sod got done in last night, doon under Byker Bridge,' Gadge said. 'Some bastard covered them in fucking petrol, burned them to a crisp. Deano wasn't far away, heard the sirens, said the smell was hideous.'

Jimmy closed his eyes. He knew that smell. For a second he was back on the ship, hiding under the ladder, could feel the smoke and heat, hear the screams.

'You OK, Jimmy?' Gadge said.

He looked up again, thought about it, nodded.

'Yeah . . . why did he think it was me?'

'He didn't, at first. The body was unrecognisable by the time people got there, could have been anybody. But then Deano saw the rucksack, near the body, thought it was yours. Then he saw—'

'Goldilocks.'

'What?' Gadge said.

'It must have been Goldilocks. It was him that did this.' Jimmy indicated his face, his leg. 'He nicked all my stuff as well.'

Gadge whistled.

'Shit. You reckon?'

'Aye, pretty sure. Who else could it be? Bastard cleaned me out.'

'Can't pretend I'm sorry, man was a shite-hawk. Not sure he deserved being barbecued though.'

'How's Deano?' Jimmy asked.

'He's in pieces, man, obviously. Fucking loves you, doesn't he.'

'I should go find him.'

'No bother, he's out in the yard, playing with Dog.'

'Dog's here?' Jimmy felt his eyes well up, suppressed it.

'Why aye, man, that's what I was trying to tell you. Deano thought he recognised the rucksack but then he heard Dog barking, saw him tied up to a fence across the road. That's what convinced him it was you smouldering away. Got Dog away from there before the police could pass him on to the dog catcher.'

When Jimmy walked out into the backyard Dog went mental, leaping up at him, yapping away, nearly knocking him off his makeshift crutch. Deano was almost as bad. At first, he'd turned pale, like he'd seen an actual ghost, but then he grinned, as if all his birthdays had come at once and wouldn't shut up. 'Thought you were brown bread! Where have you been? What happened to your leg, your face, your ear?'

Jimmy calmed them both down; Dog with a good scratch behind the ears, Deano with an elaborate handshake that they'd practised in the past to while away the long nights. Once they'd finished the handshake Deano prodded Jimmy's arm, as if making sure he was real.

'I don't understand, Jimmy. It was your stuff, and Dog was there. I was sure it was you.'

Jimmy explained about Goldilocks attacking him and taking his stuff, leaving out the reason why – didn't want the kid thinking it was all down to him.

'Poor bastard,' Deano said. 'I knaa he was a wanker, but he was still one of us. You should have smelled it, Jimmy. It was well rank.' Jimmy could see there were tear stains on Deano's face, tracking through the usual grime, couldn't help feeling moved. He sat down on a bench and Dog jumped up onto his lap, started licking his face. Jimmy turned his head slightly to keep him well away from the swelling.

Deano took a good look at him and grinned. 'Where d'you get those clothes from anyway? Your grandad?'

'Cheeky bastard,' Jimmy said, flicking out a hand to give him a clip around the ear, and then wincing with the pain of the sudden movement. He made a mental note to take things a bit more gently for a while. The kid was way too quick anyway, ducking underneath his arm, and darting out of reach straight into the arms of Gadge, who'd come out through the back door to join them.

'He giving you bother, Jimmy?' Gadge joked. 'D'you want me to sort him out?'

'Get off us, man,' Deano moaned, trying to wriggle free of Gadge, who was tickling him, driving him mad. Dog jumped off the bench and joined in the fun, leaping up at both of them, yapping away until the pair got tired of messing about and collapsed down onto the bench laughing.

Jimmy couldn't help thinking about Goldilocks' last few moments. Despite what the prick had done to him he hoped he hadn't known what was happening, that he'd been asleep or, even better, shit-faced, when it started. He'd heard stories of nutters roaming around, trying to set light to people sleeping rough, but had never thought it would happen in the Toon; most people around there were alright – sympathetic and that. He could see that Gadge was looking at him questioningly.

'Doesn't bear thinking about, does it?' Jimmy said. 'There but for the grace of God and that.'

'Not sure what God's got to do with it,' Gadge said.

'Why would someone want to toast Goldilocks though?' Deano said.

'It was probably nowt to do with him,' Jimmy said, 'just random, like. Could have been any of us.'

'D'you reckon?' Gadge said.

Jimmy could see Gadge's cogs turning, wondered if he was starting to think the same thoughts as he was; making the same crazy connections. Deano just looked puzzled.

'What d'you mean?' Deano said.

'Goldilocks nicked your stuff, right?' Gadge said.

Jimmy nodded. 'He took everything, my rucksack, my coat.'

'That canny new one?' Deano asked.

'Aye. Dog as well, of course,' Jimmy said, giving the still-excited animal another pat.

'That's what I'm on about,' Gadge said.

'I don't get it,' Deano said.

'They didn't mean to torch Goldilocks. They meant to torch Jimmy.'

Deano stared at Gadge in disbelief.

'Nah, man,' Deano said, 'that can't be right.'

'Can't it? He's got Jimmy's coat, he's got his rucksack, he's even got his dog.' Dog looked up at the mention of his name. 'Most people would think that was Jimmy.'

'And your hair's long like his was,' Deano added, quickly buying into Gadge's idea. 'Similar colour 'n' all.'

'I don't know,' Jimmy said.

'I do,' Gadge said, warming to his theme. 'It's something to do with what you saw on the Quayside. Think about it, man! One day there's some dodgy copper asking around after you, the next someone who looks like you – and has all your stuff – gets burned to death.'

'They *were* looking for you, Jimmy, remember, I told you that the other day,' Deano said excitedly. He never took much convincing.

'It's a state execution, man,' Gadge said. 'It's exactly like that scientist gadgee Kelly, ya knaa, the weapons inspector that MI5 killed cos he knew too much. Only this time they got the wrong man.'

Jimmy shook his head, not wanting to believe it, thinking about how much Gadge loved a conspiracy theory; then, thinking about policemen with long memories, about payback. He told them about the car attack. Deano just stared, his mouth wide open, but Gadge nodded knowingly.

'You need to get out of here, son,' he said, 'cos sooner or later they'll realise they made a mistake and they'll come back for you.'

Jimmy looked around his new hidey-hole. It was a huge, empty room, long neglected, with a high ceiling and animal droppings all over the place.

The sun was glinting off the small bits of glass that were left in the original windows, some of which were now completely boarded over. There was a long electrical cable hanging down from the ceiling; he imagined a grand chandelier must have hung from it at some point. At either end of the room were doors, the single one he had come through, which was hanging off one hinge, and a double set at the other end, which he'd already tested to make sure they still opened.

It used to be a banqueting hall. The place might have been a mess inside, but it was beautiful outside, smack bang in the middle of the Dene, which is maybe why people had stopped coming there – you'd have to drive and who wanted a banquet where they can't drink? It was big in the seventies, apparently, but drink-driving was a national pastime back then, his dad being one of its most enthusiastic players.

He'd seen the place when he'd come to meet Carrie by Pets Corner, made a mental note to check it out as a future sleep space. You never knew when you would need somewhere new to crash, so it always paid to stay on the lookout, to keep tabs on other places. He hadn't needed it at the time, but it was perfect for now, far away from his usual haunts, safe as.

He tried to inhale the lingering smells of the kind of meal he hadn't eaten in a long time, but there was nothing good to savour – just the stench of cat's piss and something worse . . . darker . . . long dead. Could have been the drains, but more likely there was something festering in the rafters or behind one of the walls. Dog was prowling around the edges of the room, sniffing in the corners, looking for where the smell was coming from, hoping to find some food or a place to crash out. Jimmy nodded to himself. It wasn't exactly comfortable, but it would do.

Even if they were wrong, and Goldilocks was just in the wrong place at the wrong time, it made sense to disappear for a bit. Nobody could try and run him over if he kept off the streets. He needed to rest, to get his energy back, give his leg time to heal a little. And this was as good a place as any. There was even a river right outside the gates, so he had a place to wash, both himself and his clothes. If it was winter, it might be different, the big windows doing nowt to keep the cold out, but it was July, so he'd live. Plenty of exits as well; that's why he'd tested the other doors – when Bev and he were looking for their first house they'd wanted a garden, a spare room for a nursery and a handy bus stop, but a quick getaway was his main requirement these days. It would be quiet at night too. Wouldn't help him sleep – nothing could do that – but he could hear if anything tried to get in. A predator, for instance.

That half-face painted on the wall though, that was definitely not OK. Fucking spooky. Clenched teeth, large and sharp, one eye staring at you wherever you were in the room; some sick mother had painted that. He was gonna have to cover it up somehow if he stayed.

He scratched his newly shaven head, which itched like a bastard. He probably shouldn't have let Gadge do it, but he needed to get away quickly, just in case whoever was looking for him – and he now had little doubt that someone was – came back again. And it didn't hurt to change his look; he'd stop shaving too, to see if he could grow a beard. As well as sorting his hair out he'd managed to clean himself up a bit – the bruises on his face were still pretty bad and his ear looked like something from a Frankenstein movie, but he couldn't do much about either of them. He'd also grabbed a newish sleeping bag, fresh toiletries and some more suitable clothes from the Pit Stop; Eric's gear had served its purpose – the trousers were still fine, but the blue blazer had made him stand out a bit too much on the streets. The black donkey jacket he'd got from the store wasn't in the best nick, but it would help him blend in with the crowd; everyone seemed to be wearing them.

Jimmy dropped his sleeping bag on the concrete floor, desperate to get some much-needed sleep. The floor was hard but not damp. He'd had worse. A lot worse.

He knew that once he'd rested it would be time to start kicking back; time to unearth the skills that had been drummed into him all those years ago. Someone had tried to kill him – twice now – so *not my fight* didn't work any more. He'd have to take on a new mantra, the watchwords of investigators all over the world – ABC: Accept nothing. Believe nothing. Challenge everything. There had been times, some quite recent, when he wouldn't have cared whether he lived or died, but he was way past that. He'd finally stuck his head above the parapet again and it hadn't been shot off; this time they'd missed. But they didn't know they'd missed. They thought he was dead. And the good thing about being dead was that nobody could see you coming.

27

The Ouseburn, Byker Bridge, July 9, 2012

The yellow and black police tape was still up, cordoning off the back half of the car park where Goldilocks' body had been found. Or what was left of it. Even from a hundred yards away Jimmy could see the black sooty deposit on the ground where the poor bastard had been cremated. Someone in a white protective suit was examining the area around the black stain, but he was the only one within the taped-off cordon. There was a uniformed policeman standing just outside it, no doubt there to discourage nosy sods like him. Jimmy wondered if there would be more going on if it wasn't a homeless guy who'd been the victim, if it had been someone 'normal'. Probably would, he reckoned.

A couple of days' rest had recharged the batteries, but he'd started to get restless; wanted to do something pro-active. He wasn't sure why he'd needed to see the place where he was supposed to have died, a bit morbid maybe, but sometimes you had to go with your gut. He'd half hoped they might have left his rucksack there, but there was no sign of it; he guessed that it counted as evidence of some sort. It wasn't like there had been anything of real value in it – his sleeping bag, some spare clothes, a wind-up radio, a pack of cards, his washbag and a water bowl for Dog were all that he could remember and he'd already replaced most of it; it was just that when you didn't have much in the way of possessions you got attached to what you did have.

He moved closer just to make sure the rucksack wasn't there somewhere, ignored by the police maybe, but then stopped. Shit. He recognised the copper standing guard, the big bastard who'd been patrolling with Stevens in the park, the one who'd lamped Deano. What had Stevens called him? Duke, was it? *Plain clothes. Big bastard. Like a brick shithouse.* Deano's description of the man who'd been looking for Jimmy the other day came back to him, along with a host of questions. Coincidence? Most policemen were big bastards – like the ones in the hospital. It went with the job. The kid would have recognised him, wouldn't he? Not if he was off his face. He'd said 'plain clothes' though; this guy's a uniform. But anybody can dress in plain clothes if they want. Jimmy tried to think clearly. Couldn't.

Remembered another big bastard. The one he'd seen on the Quayside arguing with Carrie's dad. But that was a different guy, wasn't it? As he watched, the scenes-of-crime guy walked over to the copper, taking off his hood to talk to him. The copper laughing at something he said.

Jimmy stepped back in shock. What the fuck?

Martin Weston. Norma Weston's husband was a

scenes-of-crime officer? Jimmy's head was spinning with the possibilities. He'd written the man off as a possible suspect, but now? It certainly wasn't Weston he saw attacking Carrie's dad – he was way too short – but that didn't mean he wasn't behind the attack. Jealousy could send you crazy, Jimmy knew that well enough. Weston was bound to know a few dodgy bastards who wouldn't mind doing him a favour – the cop standing next to him for starters. And who better to cover up a crime than a man who took all the evidence from the scene? Had Goldilocks been killed because Jimmy got too close, turning up at the man's house? Weston had looked so innocent, standing in the doorway, cradling his young daughter, but maybe, even then, he'd been calculating the risk of taking out a possible witness?

A shout.

'Can I help you, pal?'

Jimmy looked up, puzzled. He was much closer than he'd intended.

The SOCO had gone back to work – there was no way he would have recognised Jimmy with his newly shaven head anyway – but the copper was looking at him, quizzically, challenging him to come even closer, though he was now only twenty yards away.

'Um, no,' Jimmy said, turning away, walking as quickly as his gammy leg would allow. When he'd first woken up it had been stiff as hell, but he'd paced slowly around the banqueting hall, counting the steps both across and along, something he used to do in his cell to pass the time.

Jimmy looked back over his shoulder. The uniform was

still looking at him, but now he was doing something else – talking into his radio.

The library was a sight for sore eyes and a godsend for a sore leg. Jimmy had taken an age to get there, taking any turns available to him – left or right, small alleys, some of them blind, footpaths, cycle paths, whatever, keeping moving, changing direction, doubling back, going around in circles, resting when the leg got too sore – but eventually he'd reached the steps to the bridge which led over the main road and up to the library entrance. Refuge.

The new look seemed to be working. The nice librarian with the weird name hadn't noticed him as he'd come in. Maybe it helped that he'd left Dog with a *Big Issue* seller just down the street rather than tie him up outside. He didn't really know the lass, but he'd seen her in the Pit Stop a few times; she seemed a friendly sort, so he wasn't worried, just wanted to be extra careful in case anyone was watching the library for him. He may have changed his look, but Dog would be a dead giveaway.

He'd tried to remember what Gadge had taught him about using the computer and after a couple of false starts he'd managed to get it sorted. He'd hoped for some word from Carrie but there was nothing on his Facebook page, so he sent her a message instead, asking her to meet him. Carrie's page seemed different to Kate's; he could see a lot more stuff. He thought that was because they'd become 'Friends', wondered if they'd ever *actually* become friends. Doubtful, he reckoned. She had enough friends already by the look of it, lots of photos on her page, most of them in bars and clubs, always surrounded by lots of other girls. He wondered if she had a boyfriend, remembered the kid in the park who'd given them a lift to the police station. She'd said he was just a mate which was probably true; he was a bit of a wimp, whereas she had something about her. It felt like snooping, but he was fascinated, seeing how much of her life she was prepared to put out there while he spent most of his time hiding his.

There were other photos, cats and food mostly, but a couple with her dad, their arms around each other's shoulders, grinning at whoever was taking the photos, not a care in the world.

Kate on his knee. He's laughing, she's giggling, at him or at something on the TV. Someone singing in the background: 'Yoffy lifts a finger and a mouse is there.' Jimmy waggling his fingers in Kate's face, as if they're mice. Kate giggling, fit to burst.

'Are you OK?'

Jimmy opened his eyes, looked up, the nice librarian. He checked her name badge out. Aoife, that was it. Ee-fa.

'Oh, it's you,' she said. 'Didn't recognise you with that haircut.' He could see in her eyes that she'd registered the bruises but had chosen not to say anything. Even so, he was pissed off that she still recognised him. So much for lying low. He flicked the screen back to his own Facebook page, didn't want her to catch him snooping.

'You are OK, aren't you? See, you were humming a tune and laughing. Nothing wrong with that, it's just that it's a quiet zone, you know, shhhhhh!' she said, smiling and putting her finger to her lips.

Jimmy looked around. There were six other computers in that area for public use and the other five users were all looking at him, wondering what was going on. Nebby bastards.

'Oh, we can't have this,' Aoife said. Jimmy looked back at the screen, puzzled at what she might have seen.

'You've only got one friend – that's not right.'

She took the mouse from his hand and typed her own name in the search box. A list of identical names came up and Jimmy could see from the photo that she was the second one down. She clicked on 'Add Friend'.

'There you go. When I get home I'll have a think about whether I'll accept your request.' She patted him on the shoulder. 'Long as you behave yourself you should be alright.' To Jimmy's relief she went to move off, but then suddenly stopped, a look of horror on her face.

'Oh my God, what happened to your ear?'

'It's nothing,' Jimmy said. 'I'm sorry, I've got to go.' He quickly stood up, brushed past her and headed for the door, vowing not to go back, wishing he hadn't come, that he'd stayed dead.

'He's been no bother,' the *Big Issue* seller said when Jimmy went back for Dog.

'Never is,' Jimmy said. 'Thanks anyway though.' He grabbed Dog's lead and went to walk away, keen to leave the library behind him before word got out that he was very much alive.

'Any time, sweetheart, you know where to find me if you need anything. Maybe I should give you my business card?'

She winked at him when she said that. Or maybe he imagined it. Been a long time since anyone had flirted with him, wasn't sure he'd recognise it when they did. Or if he'd care. He knew it was crazy, but even after all this time he still couldn't imagine anyone taking Bev's place.

'Earth calling Jimmy,' she said.

She knew his name.

'I was joking ... about the card ... you know, I don't actually have one.'

'Right,' he said and walked off.

'Rude!' she said to his back, but when he glanced back she was laughing.

28

The library, HMP Durham, 1994

Jimmy sits at a desk in the deserted library staring at the sheet of paper in front of him. The words are unclear to him, even those he can see through his tear-blurred eyes: '... referring to the decree ... the marriage solemnised on ... be dissolved unless sufficient cause be shown ... made final and absolute ... said marriage was thereby dissolved.'

He knows that this means his marriage is over – that's the dissolved bit. On the grounds of his 'unreasonable behaviour'. The court had sent him a letter giving him six weeks to dispute that, but no matter how hard he'd thought about it, he couldn't find a way. His behaviour *had* been 'unreasonable' – worse than unreasonable. Whatever way you looked at it he was a worthless piece of shit. And now this. The first letter he's received since the last one from the court. Nothing from Bev, no letters, no new pictures of Kate – the last one he has, from months ago, is also on the desk in front of him. He picks it up and studies it, committing it to memory. Big blue eyes, brown hair, darker and curlier than it was, the little scar near her eye that he's tried to forget, that toothy smile that is never far from her face, *was* never far from her face. Maybe not any more. How would he know?

He looks around the room, grateful that it is his turn to tidy up at the end of the day; that he could be left alone to do this. He's been the assistant librarian for three months now – cost him a whole box of tabs to get the gig. Initially it was a good way to keep away from Wilkinson; he doubted the psycho had read a book since school, if he ever went to school. But that was then; now he knows it's the perfect place to escape from the black hole he's found himself in.

He checks the clock and puts the photo in his back pocket, leaving the sodden letter on the desk. The cleaner will be there in twenty minutes and he doesn't want him raising the alarm too soon. He walks to the back of the room and finds the steps, wheeling them over to the largest bookcase, positioning them perfectly for the task in hand.

He climbs to the top of the steps, reaches down to his sock and takes out the toothbrush he has spent the last six weeks sharpening on some ragged brickwork in his cell, turning it into a makeshift screwdriver. He stands tall and unscrews the metal grille of the ventilation panel in the ceiling, four long screws, one at a time, removing it completely. Then he takes it with him as he climbs back down.

At the bottom of the steps he removes his shirt. There is a seam that runs up the middle of its back which he has also been working on with the sharpened toothbrush, unpicking every third stitch to loosen it. Just enough to do the job but not so much that anyone would notice. He rips quickly through the other stitches then walks over to the small drinking fountain in the corner of the room and soaks the entire shirt, making sure that he drenches the sleeves and the two halves of the now-split back. He takes those halves and threads them through the grille of the ventilation panel, slipping them in and out before tying them on what will be the inside once he's put it back in place. He makes sure the knots are tight, the water making it difficult, if not impossible, for them to slip loose.

Jimmy climbs back up the steps and secures the grille back in place with the toothbrush, giving all four screws several extra turns to make sure they won't move. The arms of the shirt hang down from the grille, draped over his shoulders. He grabs them and pulls as hard as he can. The grille feels secure, so he takes the arms and ties them firmly around his neck. He leans forward to test the knot and it tightens even more. He reaches into his back pocket and takes out the photo of Kate, kisses her for the last time, then kicks the steps away.

29

The Old Banqueting Hall, Jesmond Dene, Newcastle,
July 9, 2012

The cat was almost entirely black but with a white streak on its belly that ran from its neck to where its balls used to be. It was dead. Jimmy was no vet, but he could tell as it was hanging by its neck from the long flex cable that dangled down from the ceiling. There were footprints in the dust beneath it, someone else's footprints, someone who had shoes that still had an actual grip on them, someone who had much bigger feet than him. Policemen had big feet. It was well known.

He touched the cat, just to be sure, and it moved, though not of its own volition; it just swung gently, to and fro, its shadow alerting Dog to its presence.

Dog yelped and tried to jump up to grab the cat, but it was way too high for him, so he sat below it and whined like a short kid at a piñata party.

Jimmy looked around. The painted face on the wall

appeared to be grinning at the bizarre spectacle. At least he didn't have to cover that up, no way was he staying there now. Dog tried to leap up at the cat again.

'Down, boy,' Jimmy said and, as usual, Dog obeyed.

His sleeping bag was still as he had left it. As was Dog's replacement bowl – a dish he'd nicked from the Pit Stop. Not kids then, they would have shat on the sleeping bag just because. A message then; someone had been watching him and they wanted to make sure he knew. At least he wasn't being paranoid.

Dog's whining was starting to get on his nerves. He patted him gently. 'Time to go.'

Jimmy had just started to roll up the sleeping bag when he heard the gate outside rattling. Dog growled.

'Shhh!' Jimmy said. He moved over to one of the boarded-up windows and looked through a small crack at the side. A young woman in a denim jacket and jeans was climbing over the gate. Carrie! Of course. He'd asked her to meet him there. A dead cat could play havoc with your memory.

Carrie jumped down into the courtyard, falling as she landed, scattering loose gravel all over the place. She scrambled back to her feet and looked around.

'Hello?' she shouted.

Jimmy waited, wondering if he should keep her from seeing the cat, but no, she was tougher than she looked. He'd seen what she did to Norma Weston.

'In here,' Jimmy shouted. He waited and watched as she crept towards the main door, nudged it open and peered around it.

'Oh,' she said, seeing him by the window as she came in. 'What happened to your face?'

'Long story,' he said.

Then the smell hit her. She grimaced and put her hand to her mouth. Jimmy remembered how bad it had seemed when he first got there. It was worse now, what with the cat and that.

'You get used to it,' he said.

She took her hand away and looked around.

'Home sweet ho-ly fuck.'

She'd seen the cat.

'Jesus Christ,' Carrie said, backing away towards the door. 'Who d-did that?'

'Not me,' Jimmy said.

She didn't look convinced. 'Who then?'

'Don't know. Think it's a warning. To stop talking to people.'

She glanced at the cat again then looked away, all the colour draining from her face.

'What are you going to do?' Carrie looked resigned to him quitting, disappearing on her.

'Cut the cat down,' Jimmy said.

Carrie smiled, but then her face changed. A grave look.

'Whoever did this might come back for you,' she said.

'Maybe.'

'But this is my problem, not yours,' she said.

'Not any more.'

She cocked her head slightly; he'd surprised her. Then she frowned again.

'Don't get mad at me.'

'Why would I do that?' Jimmy said.

'I've brought someone with me.'

'What?'

'He's waiting outside. I said I'd talk to you first.'

Jimmy moved back over to the window and glanced outside. Brian was hovering around by the gate in a sports jacket and chinos, like a boy dressing up as a man.

'He says he's got something else to show us.'

'About time.'

'He seems scared of you.'

'So he should be. Put my fucking picture in the paper.'

'He feels bad about that, Jimmy. I think he's trying to make up for it now.'

Too late for Goldilocks, Jimmy thought.

'Go get him,' Jimmy said, wondering if he was going soft in the head.

Carrie went back out. Jimmy watched as she called to Brian, saw him struggle to scale the gate, too many pies at his desk. Eventually he managed to swing himself over, landing in a heap on the inside. Carrie helped him up and brought him to the hall. As they pushed the door open a faint breeze got the cat swinging.

'Shitting hell,' Brian said, seeing it hanging. He backed away, looked like he might crap himself.

'Someone's trying to scare us off,' Carrie said.

'You think?' Brian said, pointing at the face painting on the wall.

'That was here before,' Jimmy said.

Brian saw the sleeping bag on the floor. 'You're sleeping here?'

'I was,' Jimmy said, as the cat's shadow swung across his face, Dog following its movement with his head. Jimmy crouched down and started to roll up the bag.

'Where are you going to go?' Carrie said.

'No idea. Somewhere.'

'You could stay at mine.'

Jimmy saw Brian give her a look as if to say, *Are you out of your mind?*

'What happened to your face?' Brian asked.

'I was attacked,' Jimmy said.

'By the blond guy?' Carrie asked.

'No.'

'Who then?'

'Doesn't matter, he's dead now.'

'Jesus, Jimmy!'

Carrie looked shocked and Jimmy realised how that had sounded. He couldn't blame her for thinking the worst. For a moment, when he'd first heard about Goldilocks, he'd wondered if he'd done it too, in some kind of murderous trance. Fortunately, he'd soon realised that he was unconscious in hospital at the time. A perfect alibi.

'It wasn't me. I didn't kill him.' Jimmy reluctantly gave them the short version, explained what had happened, told them about Goldilocks and Gadge's theory about mistaken identity. Brian looked like he wanted to throw up.

'It's all my fault for putting that picture in the paper,' Brian said.

'Hey, if it's anyone's fault, it's mine,' Carrie said. 'I'm the one who persuaded him to come forward.'

They both dropped their heads, too young to have to deal with this kind of crap.

'Look, if it makes you any happier, you're both to blame,' Jimmy said, 'but that ship has sailed now. Move on.'

'Have you told the police about any of this?' Brian said.

'No,' Jimmy said, a bit too quickly. He thought about telling them about Norma Weston's husband, but realised that throwing a police conspiracy into the mix would frighten them even more. He'd carry that one on his own shoulders for now. Keep things simple.

'No police.'

He turned to Brian. 'Carrie says you've got something to show us.'

'Yes, but not here,' Brian said, looking around as if someone was about to burst into the building. 'I need somewhere with Wi-Fi.'

'Why did you come here then?' Jimmy said.

'I was curious to see where you were living.'

'You know what curiosity did,' Jimmy said, glancing up at the cat.

The landlord at the Branstone pub didn't have his happy face on. He seemed to like Dog well enough, but he was keeping a wary eye on Jimmy, as if he'd steal the barstools given half a chance.

They'd settled down at a corner table, well away from the only other two people in the bar so they could speak without the locals listening in. Carrie and Brian were nursing bottles of lager, but Jimmy had asked for a glass of tap water – another thing that didn't exactly endear him to the landlord.

'It's not a dosshouse,' he'd muttered, only going to fetch the water when Carrie gave him a look that threatened imminent violence if he didn't. Just to wind him up Jimmy had then put Dog's new dish on the floor and poured half the water into it.

Brian took a small laptop out of his bag and placed it on the table.

'You know some of this already, but I'll go through everything and you can stop me if you get bored.' He looked across to Carrie.

'You told me your dad was a bit of a troublemaker, liked to get in people's faces, especially the local authorities,' he said. Carrie nodded. 'So I had a good look at some of the council agendas and minutes and stuff, to see if there was anything there, any meetings where he might have wanted to stick his oar in around the time he disappeared.'

'We get sent loads of papers but no one bothers with 'em any more,' he went on. 'We used to have an older guy who specialised in council stuff, but he got laid off – it's always the experienced ones they get rid of, saves more money . . .' He tailed off, seeming to realise that neither of them cared about the newspaper's internal problems.

'I did say to stop me if you got bored. I found a couple of things of interest. The afternoon your dad disappeared there was a meeting up in Morpeth – the county council were discussing an application from a fracking company to start some exploratory drilling up on the Northumberland coast. I reckoned your dad wouldn't be keen on that.'

'Obviously,' Carrie said, 'fracking's a complete catastro-fuck. Dad calls it chemical warfare.'

'Now,' Brian said, 'I don't know what happened up in Morpeth, we didn't cover it, nor did anyone else, but I've got some calls out, so hopefully I can find out if your dad was there. However, later that day there was a meeting at the City Council offices in Newcastle to discuss another planning application – a housing company wants to build a large new estate on some greenbelt land on the edge of the city. Big houses for the rich.'

'Was that what that demo was about? The photos you gave to Jimmy?'

Brian nodded.

'Yes, but they were only the hard copies, the ones they thought about using in the paper. I decided to do a bit more digging.'

'What does your boss say about all this?' Jimmy asked.

'He doesn't know I'm doing it. If I'd told him there might be a story, he'd probably give it to someone else, one of the staffers. He doesn't even know I'm here; thinks I'm on my lunch break.'

Jimmy closed his eyes. They needed an investigative journalist and they'd got the office boy.

'Anyway,' Brian went on, 'the point is I *did* find something else. I sweet-talked the photographer, mate of mine actually. I got him to upload everything he'd taken into our online library and look what I found.'

He clicked on something and turned the laptop around so they could see it properly. There were dozens of photos from the demonstration. He moved the cursor over them and clicked on one in particular, enlarging it so it filled the screen.

It was another photo of the protestors standing outside the council building waving placards, similar to the pictures Jimmy had pocketed, but taken from further away. Carrie's dad and Norma Weston were still front and centre, still looking like a couple to Jimmy. There was one banner that Jimmy hadn't noticed before proclaiming 'NO BUILDING ON THE GREENBELT', but that was it.

'We've seen these, Brian. I thought you had something new to show us,' Carrie said, clearly disappointed.

'This *is* new. I went through all of them, took me ages, but eventually I found something. At least I think it's something. This is why I picked this one,' he said, pointing to the left of the photo.

Standing at the back, a few yards apart from the group of protesters, lost slightly in the shadows of the building, was a large man, wearing a black jacket.

'The thing about house-builders,' Brian said, 'is that they know a lot of bricklayers.'

30

Grainger Towers, Fenham, Newcastle, July 9, 2012

The piss on the lift floor was still fresh enough to be steaming.

Dog tried to stick his nose in it, but Jimmy yanked him away and they headed for the stairs. Carrie's flat was on the sixth floor.

'Are you sure about this?' Jimmy said, as they climbed. 'There are plenty of other places I can go.'

'Don't be stupid,' Carrie said. 'It's safer here.'

He hoped so. Jimmy had resisted when she'd first suggested he crashed at hers, but she was adamant, claiming that she'd got him into this mess, that it was the least she could do.

They took a while to reach the top of the stairs – Jimmy's leg was still recovering from the stabbing – before heading through a heavily graffitied door into a dark corridor.

'Sorry,' she said, 'the lights are out at the moment, caretaker's a lazy twat.'

There were half a dozen doors on either side of the corridor, a couple of which had steel-barred gates bolted in front of them.

'It's like being back inside,' Jimmy said, immediately regretting it. Why couldn't he keep his big mouth shut?

Carrie gave him a look, slightly uncomfortable maybe, but didn't say anything. She stopped at the fourth door along on the left, turned a key in a strong-looking Chubb lock and then a second one higher up and showed him in.

The living room was surprisingly large and uncluttered apart from hundreds of books, standing in precarious piles along one wall. Aside from that there was only a desk with a computer on it, a TV on the wall, a chair and a large sofa. Dog immediately jumped on the sofa and settled down.

'Is that OK?' Jimmy said.

Carrie laughed. 'He's fine.'

'You a reader then?' Jimmy said, indicating the books.

'I am, but they're not mine, this is my friend's place.'

'Won't she mind?'

'No, course not. She's a student, gone home for the summer, won't be back for weeks.' She could see he wasn't convinced. 'It's fine, Jimmy, honestly.'

'Won't be a minute, make yourself at home.' Carrie went into another room, a bedroom, and closed the door behind her. Jimmy stood still for a moment, a bit out of practice; hadn't been in someone else's home for a long time. There were two other rooms – a kitchen and a small bathroom; only one bedroom.

There was no door to the kitchen, so he peeked in: all the

basics – a gas cooker, fridge and washing machine; a kettle and a microwave on the work surface which was otherwise as uncluttered as the other room.

It reminded him of the 'clear-desks routine' they had on board ship, where you had to make sure that everything was stowed away in cupboards, no stuff floating around, blocking up the pumps and that. Just in case there was a problem.

The impact of the first bomb hurls the stern up in the air. Jimmy shoots forward. He flings out his right arm to stop his head crashing into the underside of the ladder.

'Jimmy?'

He opened his eyes. Carrie was standing in the middle of the living room, staring at him. She'd changed into some kind of all-in-one jumpsuit.

'Nice place.'

'Not really, and it's only temporary, but it'll do for now,' she said. 'Had to get away from my mum for a bit. She was doing my head in, ranting about dad and his "slappers". Everything OK? You looked a bit out of it.'

'I'm fine.' She didn't need to know.

'The sofa's nice and comfy. I'm sure you'll sleep well.'

'It's not gonna cause you any bother, is it? Me being here.'

She looked puzzled.

'No. Why should it?'

'Just . . . you know, boyfriends and that. I don't want to get in the way.'

'You've no worries there,' she laughed. 'I don't do boy-friends. Not my scene.'

She moved past him into the kitchen, took a beer out of the fridge, opened it with her teeth. He was processing what she'd said, remembering the photos on her Facebook page, lots of girls, no boys.

'What do you think?' she said. 'About the man in the photo?' She'd already moved on.

'I don't know.' He wasn't pulling her chain, just genu-inely didn't have a clue. The image was too indistinct, his memory too unreliable. He could tell that Brian had been a little disappointed that he couldn't be sure. Carrie hadn't recognised him either though.

'Could have been him though, couldn't it? The man you saw arguing with Dad?'

She needed him to agree so he nodded. Carrie moved back into the room with her beer, sat next to Dog on the sofa. Jimmy took the computer chair.

'We need to talk to Andrew Lang, my dad's boss – that Weston woman said he might know something,' she said.

He wondered whether he liked that they were *we* now. Decided he did.

'I've got nothing else on tomorrow,' he said, making her laugh so loud that Dog looked like he might bolt.

'Did you want a drink?' Carrie said, once she'd stopped. 'I know you don't do beer but something else? A soft drink?'

'I'm fine.'

They sat in silence for a while, comfortable though, him

thinking about the man in the photo and whether now was the time to tell her about Martin Weston. She was playing with Dog, rubbing his ears. She seemed miles away, or so he thought.

'Why were you inside?' she said.

He knew as soon as it had slipped out in the corridor that she'd want to know.

'It's a long story.'

'I've got nothing else on tonight,' she said, smiling.

Jimmy lay on the sofa, wide awake, wondering if he should have kept his gob shut. He didn't like to talk about the fight, about the policeman bleeding on the road, any of that. He didn't want anyone to think he was looking for sympathy; he knew what happened wasn't down to bad luck, misfortune, whatever. Maybe he used to think like that, but not any more. It was all his own stupid fault. He'd never even mentioned it to Gadge, who was probably the nearest thing he had to a friend. So why Carrie? Was he using her as a dry run for Kate?

He thought she might throw him out once he'd told her, but she hadn't; she'd just found him a blanket and a pillow and gone to bed. He was pretty sure he'd heard a bolt slide closed just after she'd pulled the bedroom door shut, but you couldn't hold that against her.

Carrie's computer was making a little humming sound which he'd hoped would lull him to sleep, but was now irritating the piss out of him, so he got up to try to turn it off. As soon as he touched the mouse the screen sprang into life. She'd left it open on the *Chronicle*'s news page – Brian's story about Jimmy, his photo in the middle. He read it again, wondered if Bev had seen it, or Kate even, not that she would recognise him, though she might remember him as the man who caught her beret. He still wished he'd had the courage to say something to her. One day maybe, though not until all this was over.

Jimmy saw the Facebook symbol at the bottom of the screen, clicked on it and brought up Kate's page. She'd changed the picture at the top. In the new one she was on her own, on a beach – Tynemouth maybe – a big grin on her face. He wondered who had taken the photo. Bev? A boyfriend? Jimmy knew so little about her life. He noticed the 'Add Friend' button, remembered what Aoife had said in the library. He could do with more friends. If he couldn't risk seeing her in real life, maybe this was the next best thing. He moved the cursor over the button, paused for a moment, then clicked.

He woke with his head on the desk, a small pool of drool by his mouth. It was still dark, but that was probably because all the curtains were closed, the only light coming from the computer. Dog was growling.

Jimmy sat up. There was a noise at the door to the flat. Someone was trying the handle. Whoever had been watching him, following him, had finally caught him up. He should never have come to Carrie's flat, should never have put her in more danger. He looked quickly around, nowhere easy to hide – the bathroom was on the other side of the room and there was no door on the kitchen so that was out. He heard the lock click and ran to the door as it began to open, hiding behind it.

As the intruder came through the door Jimmy saw a flash of blond hair and pounced, grabbing them around the neck and pulling them backwards, inadvertently closing the door with his back at the same time.

A scream.

A *woman's* scream. He hadn't expected that. He tried to get a good look at her, but she screamed again and started to struggle fiercely, throwing her arms back and kicking at his shins with her heels. Dog had leapt off the sofa and was nipping at her ankles, yelping.

'Get off me, you prick,' the woman shrieked, catching Jimmy in the face with a flailing elbow, bang on the spot where Goldilocks' boot had connected just a few days before. He winced with pain. Dots of light flashed before his eyes. The blow loosened his grip and the woman wriggled free, turning to face him, fists clenched.

Behind her the bedroom door flew open and Carrie charged out, baseball bat in hand.

'D'you want some?' she screamed, lifting the bat before stopping in her tracks as the woman turned towards her, arms raised to protect herself from the swinging bat.

'Mum?' Carrie said, lowering her weapon.

'What are you doing?' her mum shouted. 'Hit the bastard, hit him.' She moved behind Carrie, putting herself out of Jimmy's reach. 'What you waiting for? Go on, fucking lamp him!'

Jimmy backed away towards the door, keeping his hands down, trying to look unthreatening. Dog was running around mindlessly, unsure who was friend and who was foe. Carrie turned to her mum.

'Mum, I—'

'Don't turn your back, you silly cow.' Carrie's mum grabbed the bat out of her hand and swung it hard towards Jimmy's head. He jerked his head back and felt the bat glance harmlessly off his shoulder.

'Get the fuck out of here,' she shouted.

'Mum!' Carrie shouted. 'Stop it, Mum, he's a friend, stop it.' She tried to grab the bat back, but her mum resisted.

'Friend? What sort of friend? He tried to bloody strangle me.'

She glared at Jimmy, daring him to contradict her.

'I'm sorry, I was asleep. I thought you were breaking in, I thought *you* were going to attack *me*,' he said.

She looked more closely at Jimmy, screwing up her face in obvious bewilderment, and turned back to Carrie.

'He's your friend? Him?'

'Yes,' Carrie said. 'I was trying to tell you.'

'I'm sorry, Carrie. I didn't know it was your mum,' Jimmy said.

'It's not her you should be apologising to, you prick, it's me. You nearly gave me a sodding heart attack.' Carrie's mum dropped the bat on the floor – the bang making Dog run under the desk – and flopped onto the sofa.

'Jesus Christ, my heart's going ten to the dozen.'

Carrie picked up the bat and tucked it away behind the sofa.

Her mum took a packet of cigarettes from her coat pocket,

took one out and put it in her mouth. Carrie snatched it away.

'Not here, Mum. No smoking, remember? Go outside if you're desperate.'

'Bloody hell, love, give me a break, it's six floors! And I just got attacked by a flipping . . .' She looked at Jimmy again. 'A flipping . . . ageing, skinhead tramp.'

Carrie laughed.

'Mum, this "ageing skinhead tramp" is Jimmy. Jimmy, this is Alice, my mum.'

Jimmy nodded. Pleased to meet you didn't seem appropriate after what had just happened.

'I'm sorry about . . . you know,' he said, waving towards the door.

'So you bloody should be,' Alice said. 'Don't expect to get mugged when you come to call on your daughter. I s'pose you're the one who dreamed he saw my ex-husband?'

It wasn't a dream, he wanted to say, but held his tongue. Wasn't the right time. Instead he just nodded and bent down to collect a trembling Dog from under the desk.

'What are you doing here anyway?' Carrie asked her mum, looking at her watch. 'It's eight o'clock in the morning. Bit early for a surprise visit.'

'Well, if a daughter won't return her mother's calls for three days and then switches her flipping phone off, what's she to do? My useless ex has done a runner' – she looked at Jimmy as if to say, *and not fallen in the bloody river like you say* – 'so the last thing I needed was you doing a disappearing act on me too. Thought I'd pop in on the way to work; it was the only time I knew you'd definitely be in, what with the hours you keep these days. Good job you gave me your spare key.'

'That was for emergencies, in case I lose mine; not so you can just wander in whenever you want.'

'Well, answer your phone next time!'

Carrie picked up her phone from the desk and checked it.

'Shit, I'm sorry, Mum. I turned it off last night, me and Jimmy were having a bit of a heart-to-heart.' She turned her phone back on and Jimmy heard it beep into life, several pings indicating a series of missed calls and messages coming in.

'Jesus wept, Mum, ten missed calls. That's a bit over the top, isn't it?'

'Wanted to say sorry, didn't I?' She looked over at Jimmy. 'I'm not normally that needy, we'd had a bit of a row about her feckless father. Anyway, I don't think it was ten.'

Carrie looked at her phone again, counting them, 'One, two, three, four, five . . . shit!'

'What is it?' Alice said.

Carrie hit a button on her phone and held it to her ear. She turned her back to them as if to help her concentrate on the call.

'Is DS Burns there?' she said. Jimmy remembered the name from their visit to the cop shop, the guy she'd asked for at the desk. The only one she said had actually listened to her when she'd tried to report her dad missing.

'D'you know when he'll be back?' she asked. There was a pause. Someone speaking on the other end.

'My name's Carrie Carpenter, he left a message asking

me to ring him . . . do you know what it's about?' Another longer pause. She'd turned back around to face them now and Jimmy could tell from her face that this was not good news.

'What is it, love?' Alice said. 'What's happened?'

'Shhhh!' Carrie said, turning her back to them again, putting her hand over her other ear to make sure she could hear whoever was on the other end of the phone without interference.

'I see . . . OK . . . yes please . . . yes, I will. Where is it?' She picked up a pen from the desk and scribbled something on a pad that was sat by the side of the computer.

'OK, I've got it. Thank you.' Carrie put the phone down on the desk but kept her back to them. Definitely bad news, Jimmy thought. Good news came quickly, there was always silence before bad news. The longer the silence, the worse the news.

Eventually Carrie turned around, her fists clenched to help keep her emotions in check. It wasn't really working. Her chin sank down to her chest and she moved her hand to her face as if she'd got a blinding headache. More silence. Very bad news, Jimmy thought. Her mum jumped up and grabbed her hands, pulling her close.

'What's wrong, love, what is it?' she said.

Carrie lifted her head up, her eyes filling with tears.

'They've found a body.'

31

Newcastle Mortuary, July 10, 2012

Jimmy rubbed the condensation from the inside of the taxi window. The rain was bouncing off the tarmac, ricocheting off the side of a bus shelter just outside the mortuary doors. A short, stocky man, like the human version of a bulldog, stood inside the shelter smoking a tab, staring through the spray at the cab.

'That's DS Burns,' Carrie said.

Jimmy didn't want to be there. He didn't want to see Burns and he definitely didn't want to see another dead body. Ever. But he couldn't let her do this on her own. Carrie's mum, Alice, should have been with her, not him, but she was a mess. The minute she'd heard that a body had been found she'd curled up into a ball and started whimpering, leaving Carrie to do the heavy lifting. In every relationship someone always had to do the hard yards. No wonder she was a tough kid. She would have to be even tougher now.

As soon as Burns saw them get out of the cab, he

dropped his cigarette on the ground and stubbed it out with his foot.

'Let's get out of this rain,' he shouted over the noise of the heavy drops clattering on the shelter's plastic roof, guiding them through the mortuary doors and into a large, deserted entrance hall.

'When can I see him?' Carrie said to Burns.

'It's not him,' Burns said.

Carrie stared at him as if he was speaking a foreign language, grabbing hold of Jimmy's sleeve for support. Eventually she found some words.

'What d'you mean?'

'The body – it's not your dad.'

'But the woman on the phone said—'

'She screwed up. I'm sorry, she shouldn't have said anything. She's just supposed to take messages.'

Jimmy could feel Carrie starting to tremble with relief. He didn't know what else to do, so he put his arm around her shoulders, held her tight.

'I don't understand,' she said.

'It's partly my fault,' Burns said. 'We found a body last night and the press had it, so I wanted to let you know what was happening, didn't want you to see it on the telly. At that stage we didn't know the man's identity, but of all the mispers, your dad—'

'The what?' she said.

'Sorry, jargon, mispers, missing persons – of all of them your dad was the best fit, right age, build, everything really. I didn't think it was him for various reasons, but I wanted to give you a heads-up, didn't want you to panic. Thought you'd call me back.'

'I didn't get your message till this morning. The woman on the phone just said you were at the mortuary, that you'd found a body . . . because you'd called me, I just assumed . . .' Despite Jimmy's arm around her, her shaking was getting worse.

'Can she sit down?' Jimmy said, worried that Carrie was going to collapse.

'Of course. And you are?' Burns said, looking at Jimmy curiously, waiting for a name. When he didn't get one he took his best shot. 'Jimmy?' he guessed, holding out his hand. 'I'm DS Burns.'

Jimmy wiped his rain-soaked hand on his trousers before accepting the handshake. He didn't trust the man, but Carrie had said he was OK so, for the moment, he'd go with her call.

They sat on a pair of sofas in the corner of the entrance hall, Jimmy and Carrie on one, Burns on the other, facing them.

'I'm sorry you were misled, Carrie,' Burns said. 'The woman you spoke to is new on the job, a civvy, cheaper than a uniform, but you get what you pay for. I've had smarter goldfish. She'll get her arse kicked, don't worry about that. At least, once she realised what she'd done, she rang me and fessed up. That's why I was waiting for you outside; I wanted to tell you as soon as I could. In person.'

'Are you sure it's not him?' she said quietly.

'Positive,' he said, nodding towards the corridor. 'Aside

from the bullet hole in his chest, the guy in there had form; his prints were on record.'

'Surely it wouldn't have taken long to find that out?'

'Not usually, no. Bit longer this time because someone had tried to burn his fingertips off.'

The hospital café was deserted. It could have been because the tea tasted like dog piss, but the rain was still pelting down outside, so it was a bit of a toss-up. Carrie had gone to the bathroom, leaving Jimmy to fend off DS Burns on his own. At least he hadn't had to pay for the tea.

Burns was looking him up and down, obviously not that impressed. Jimmy picked up a teaspoon and stirred his tea vigorously, hoping it would somehow improve the taste.

'Have we met before?' Burns said.

Had they? Was Burns one of the young coppers who'd kicked the shit out of him back in the station, all those years ago, when he'd been arrested for attacking one of their own? He was about the right age. Jimmy didn't have a clue, hadn't seen much of their faces, just the soles of their boots.

'I don't think so,' he said.

Burns didn't look convinced. 'What's your game?' he asked.

'What d'you mean? I don't have a game.'

'Young girl, pretty, vulnerable.' Burns ticked the three things off with his thumb and two fingers. 'Older man, grubby, looking for a roof over his head,' he repeated the counting-to-three thing with his other hand. 'Just doing the maths.'

'You should do them again then because you're getting the wrong answer,' Jimmy said, wondering if Burns' interest in Carrie was purely professional.

'That mouth of yours will get you in bother – from the look of your face it already has,' Burns said.

'Walked into a wall.'

'The drink'll do that.'

'I don't drink.'

'Aye, sure, and my dick's a kipper,' Burns said, putting his hand on Jimmy's to stop him stirring his tea. 'You're doing my head in with that, d'you mind?'

Jimmy pulled his hand away and Burns took the spoon out and put it in his pocket.

'Don't nick that,' Jimmy said, leaning towards Burns conspiratorially. 'There's a copper hanging around here somewhere.'

Burns smiled at that one. Maybe he had a sense of humour after all.

Jimmy could see Carrie making her way over to them. She looked calmer now.

'D'you want a cuppa?' Burns said.

'No thanks,' she said, sitting next to Jimmy.

Burns took a sip of his and pulled a face. 'Aye, you're probably wise.'

'I suppose this murder means you won't have any more time to look into my dad's disappearance? Not that you were anyway.'

Jimmy couldn't help admiring her powers of recovery. She was a machine.

'That's unfair, Carrie,' Burns said. 'I've done all I can, more than I ought if the truth be told.'

'He's still missing though, isn't he?'

'Well, that's a matter of opinion, love. Your mum and his boss both say he's gone off with some slapper and someone used his cashpoint card in Sheffield just last week.'

'Firstly, I'm not your *love*,' Carrie snapped.

That definitely pissed him off.

'Sorry, *darling*,' Burns said. 'I missed the political correctness seminar because I was busy that day – trying to catch murderers.'

'You'd think you'd be better at it then, wouldn't you?' she shot back. 'Secondly, anyone can have their cash card nicked. Don't they have cameras on cashpoints these days?'

'Yes, but—'

Burns couldn't get a word in. Jimmy almost felt sorry for him.

'You have been told what Jimmy saw?' Carrie added. 'You must have because you knew who he was.'

Burns looked a little embarrassed.

'Yes, of course, I read the note but—'

A loud buzzing noise erupted from Burns' jacket. He pulled out a pager with a flashing red light on it.

'That'll be the doc with the post-mortem results on Fingertips. I'm gonna have to go,' Burns said, getting up from his chair.

Carrie sighed. Jimmy could feel the energy draining away from her, but she gave it one last try.

'The man in there is dead, he's not going anywhere in a hurry; my dad might still be alive.'

Jimmy noticed the 'might'. He'd wondered how long it would take her to accept the possibility of doubt. Burns noticed it too and didn't walk off straight away; she'd got under his skin.

'He might,' he said softly. His buzzer went off again. 'Sorry, I really have to go.'

'We need to talk to you . . . properly. We've got new information,' she said. It was as near to begging as she was ever likely to get. 'We think my dad was seeing someone.'

Jimmy put his hand on Carrie's arm, stopping her in her tracks. He didn't want Burns to know about Norma Weston yet, didn't know how deeply her husband might be involved or whether he and Burns were mates. Could they trust him?

'What?' Carrie said, clearly irritated by his interruption.

Fortunately, Burns' buzzer went off for a third time.

'OK, we'll talk again, I promise,' Burns said. 'But I really do have to go now. I'll call you.'

He turned and hurried off, disappearing through a set of double doors which continued to swing to and fro after he'd gone.

Carrie shrugged Jimmy's hand off of her arm.

'You OK?' he asked.

'Not really,' she said. 'Why did you stop me telling him about Norma Weston?'

'Her husband's a SOCO – a scenes-of-crime officer. Burns might know him.'

'Shit,' she said. 'How do you know?'

'I went to see where Goldilocks was killed. He was there.'

'Why didn't you tell me before?'

'I didn't want to worry you, thought you had enough on your plate.'

'Don't fucking spare me, Jimmy, I'm not a fucking snow-flake.'

She took a breath, taking it all in.

'Jesus, d'you really think he's involved in my dad's dis-appearance?'

'I have no idea, but I don't think we should tell Burns yet. Not until we know for sure we can trust him. He and Weston could be best mates for all we know.'

She closed her eyes, as if seeking strength from some-where deep within.

'You OK?' he asked again. She opened her eyes. He hoped she'd found what she needed.

'Been better. I'd like to go home now. Need to tell Mum the good news.'

They picked Dog up on the way back. They'd left him, and her mum, with a nearby auntie – an animal lover who had cheerfully offered the opinion that she 'always knew Roger would come to a bad end'.

Carrie's mum took the good news in the same way she'd taken the bad, dramatically. She collapsed onto a sofa as if she'd had a fit of the vapours. Most of the people Jimmy knew living on the street were more balanced than Alice.

Carrie went to bed as soon as they got back to the flat, exhausted. Brian had e-mailed all the photos that his photographer friend had taken at the council meeting to Carrie so, while she slept, Jimmy spent most of the afternoon painstakingly going through each one. He worked out how to enlarge them, looking to see if there was a better image of the man Brian had flagged up to them in the pub, but it was useless; he was only in that one photo and so far back from the main shot that you couldn't make out his face at all.

There were also a couple of photos of the developer whose planning application had caused all the fuss, Ed Collins, but Jimmy had never seen him before in his life. He certainly wasn't the guy on the Quayside. Collins was big alright, but only because he was clearly the bloke who 'ate all the pies'. Nor was he the car driver; what hair he had left was greying, not blond. It seemed like a dead end. The only real progress Jimmy had made was on his computer skills.

After her afternoon kip, Carrie had got up and gone to work, leaving him on his own. Once she'd left he couldn't settle. One problem was the noise, or lack of it. He was used to the constant sounds of traffic or the police heli-copter that always seemed to be flying over his head. Even in the Pit Stop it was always loud – someone would be singing or praying or screaming. It was never this quiet. He thought about going down there, to see if Gadge or Deano was around, but he didn't know what or who was out there waiting for him. Maybe they thought he was dead, maybe not, but he wasn't going down the same way as Goldilocks. Best to keep away from his usual haunts for a while.

The second problem was the stars. He was used to having them there, maybe not always right above him – some kind of roof was useful in the North East – but somewhere in sight. He still couldn't really tell one from another, not like Gadge, but having them around was somehow comforting; gave him the illusion that there was a bigger and hopefully better world out there.

Jimmy tried to turn the TV on at one point, but couldn't work out how to do it. Then he attempted to cook some baked beans, but was defeated by Carrie's electric can opener, cutting his palm open on the jagged can lid and throwing the tin into the bin in frustration. Eventually he just sat there, on the sofa next to a sleeping Dog, staring at the walls, wondering what other people did to fill the time.

He would have probably stayed like that until Carrie got home, or until Dog needed a walk, if the phone hadn't rung. He let it ring, fearing it might be DS Burns keeping his promise, and not wanting to talk to him, not yet anyway. Then he thought it could be Carrie or even Brian ringing with new information, so after half a dozen rings he picked it up.

'Hello.'

'Oh, um, is Carrie there?' A woman's voice, local but posh.

'No. She's at work. Can I take a message?'

'I suppose, I just wanted to ask . . . look, um, who are you again?'

'I'm a friend, just staying with Carrie for a day or two.'

'Oh right, um, can you tell her that Wendy Lang rang, um, Andrew's wife . . . I just wanted to know if she'd heard anything? Only I saw the piece in the paper and then there was something on the TV about a body and I just . . . well, you know . . . I was worried.'

Andrew Lang. Roger's boss – and his occasional landlord from what Carrie had told Brian. Shit – they had planned to talk to him before it all kicked off with Carrie's mum and the mortuary. Norma Weston had suggested he might be in some kind of trouble.

'Hello?'

He was quiet for too long. Wasn't used to using the phone.

'It wasn't Roger,' he said.

'I'm sorry.'

'The body they found, it wasn't him.'

'Oh, right . . . I see, that's good.'

Something about her reaction seemed off. No joy, barely even relief.

'Can I come and talk to you?' Jimmy said. God knows where that came from. He hadn't thought it through, just needed to do something, get out of the flat, make something happen. Interviewing family and friends was supposed to be the first thing you did with a missing person. That's what he'd been taught – though they were called *deserters* in his old job. If anyone knew what Carrie's dad had been up to, surely it would be the people he lived with? And maybe he could find out exactly what kind of trouble Andrew Lang was in?

'Sorry, what? Talk to me about what? I just wanted to know if there had been any news about Roger. Who did you say you were again?'

'I'm Jimmy, I'm a friend of Carrie's, I'm trying to help

her to find her dad. It would be really useful to talk to you.'
Appeal to the woman's vanity. 'Be great to pick your brains,'
he added and then waited. And waited. He'd learned how
powerful silence could be. People often felt the need to fill
the space.

'You're the man from the paper . . . the homeless man?'
she said eventually.

'Yes,' Jimmy said. 'That's right.'

There was a longer silence. And then the line went dead.

32

The Langs' house, July 10, 2012

Jimmy was happier outdoors, at ease with the noise of the night: cars, sirens, bursts of music from people going in and out of pubs.

The rain had long since stopped so he and Dog had taken the leisurely route, skirting the edge of Exhibition Park, where he'd once got lost as a kid, his dad having fallen asleep in the sun after a couple of pints too many. Being out in the open also meant he was much harder to follow.

He found the house easily enough – the address was in a book by Carrie's phone; now it was written on the back of his hand. He hadn't seen a soul for five minutes; guessed that walking wasn't the local residents' preferred means of transport – nearly every house had at least two cars parked outside.

The Langs' house was in darkness – a lot bigger than he'd expected; semi-detached but with an attic conversion and a driveway that could seat a small tank. Lang's chosen tank was a Range Rover Evoque – Jimmy only knew that because it said so on the back. The whole place reeked of money; lecturing obviously paid more than he'd imagined.

As soon as he stepped onto the drive a light came on above the front door. No one came out or looked out of the window. A movement sensor, Jimmy guessed – people around here probably didn't encourage casual visitors either.

He knocked on the door and waited. No lights came on, no curtains twitched. And yet . . . it just didn't feel like an empty house. You got a sense for that living on the streets; it saved a lot of bother, kept you out of the odd turf war. He knocked again. Nothing. Or maybe a flicker of movement at the large bay window to the left of the door. Jimmy moved back a couple of yards to get a better view. As he did, the front door opened and a tall, balding man stepped out, the light glinting off his shiny head.

'You must be Jimmy,' he said. 'I'm Andrew Lang. Mind if we take a walk?' He didn't wait for an answer, didn't explain why he'd taken so long to answer the door, or why the house was in total darkness, just closed the door behind him and marched off down the drive.

Jimmy followed him down the quiet street, Dog in tow, still no one else in sight. When they turned the corner Lang stopped, leaned on the street sign and took out a tin of roll-ups from his coat pocket. Maybe he wasn't as loaded as he seemed?

'Don't tell Wendy. She thinks I've given up,' he said. 'Have to sneak them in when I can.'

He offered Jimmy one and looked surprised when he declined.

'Assumed you lot all smoked,' he said, pulling a box of matches out of his other pocket.

Jimmy must have frowned because Lang held his hand up in apology.

'Sorry. Call myself a professor – should know better than to generalise, shouldn't I?'

The man's hand trembled slightly as he tried to light up. He seemed nervous. Jimmy studied Lang closely, seeing if he could match him to the man on the Quayside. He was tall enough, but seemed too slim, his overcoat hanging off him. His face was sagging a little, like there was too much flesh for the bones to handle. Jimmy wondered if he was ill.

Lang finally managed to light his cigarette, taking a deep drag before blowing the smoke out.

'Bit pissed off with you, to be honest,' he said. 'You've upset the wife.'

'I'm sorry,' Jimmy said automatically. Didn't have a clue what he was supposed to have done.

'Her nerves are bad enough without you trying to get her involved in all this nonsense,' Lang said. 'She's taken to her bed again now.'

'I didn't mean any harm,' Jimmy said. 'She rang me . . . well, Carrie, I guess.'

'Yes, well, anyway, it's done now, I suppose. Just don't bother her again, there's a good chap. If you need anything, come straight to me.' Lang took a big drag from his cigarette and blew the smoke out just over Jimmy's right shoulder.

'How is Carrie anyway? This whole thing must be hard for her.'

'She's OK. She's a tough kid,' Jimmy said.

'Yes, sure, bit surprised she's making all this fuss though,' he said. 'I told her Roger'd gone off with some woman.'

'D'you know who she is?'

'Not a clue. He plays his cards close to his chest, old Rodge, doesn't want the likes of me sniffing around – not that I would, obviously.'

'Only Carrie heard he was seeing someone from work?'

Lang looked puzzled, alarmed even. 'Um, not to my knowledge. Does she have a name?'

Jimmy shook his head. He wasn't going to give up Norma Weston yet – and certainly not to this man.

'Look, I've known Roger since school, he's never changed.' Lang sighed, as if weary of telling the same story over and over again. 'He's a lovely man, do anything for anyone, but he's always had an eye for the ladies. Roger the Dodger we used to call him – constantly on the move, always thinking the grass is greener. He's off chasing skirt – I'd bet my life on it. Believe me; this is far from the first time he's buggered off with some woman he's just met.'

Jimmy nodded, as if an expert on all things Roger. 'Carrie's not convinced about the woman thing. She heard there might be trouble at work – in your department.'

'Who told her that?'

'I don't know.'

Lang took a deep drag from his roll-up and then released the smoke slowly. 'You seem to have a lot of anonymous sources. Carrie should know better than to listen to office tittle-tattle. Academia is riddled with gossips, malicious bastards most of them. Take it from the horse's mouth – there's no trouble, I would know.'

'What about his campaigning then? That must cause him a few problems.'

Lang laughed. 'Roger does tend to get up people's noses a bit, upsets the wrong ones sometimes probably.'

'What do you mean?' Jimmy said.

A car moved slowly past them, the driver glancing across, checking them out. Jimmy peered at him anxiously; he was getting worse than Dog where cars were concerned. Lang waited until it disappeared around the corner before turning back to Jimmy.

'Oh, you know, shouting the odds, getting in people's faces.'

'Like at that demonstration the other week?'

'Probably.'

'Were you there that night?'

'Me? Not likely. I like to support Roger's causes when I can but there are limits. Bit more to lose than him, eh?' He nodded at the houses behind him, not needing to spell out the obvious wealth you'd need to live there. 'And it would be a bit hypocritical; Ed Collins does a lot of work for the university.'

'That was the night he disappeared,' Jimmy said.

'Was it? I suppose you're right. Never put it together really.'

'Did the police not talk to you?'

'Not then. I've been away at a conference. Only got back a couple of days ago. First thing I knew about all this fuss was when the wife showed me the local rag with that story of yours in it. Obviously, I contacted them then. I'm not being funny, but I think you got it wrong. Maybe had a bit too much of the old Bucky wine that night, eh?'

Jimmy considered putting him right, couldn't be bothered, let him think what he wanted. Everyone living on the streets was a twenty-a-day, drug-addled pisshead, stands to reason.

'I know what I saw,' he said.

Lang clearly thought otherwise, shaking his head.

'Look, I tried to tell Carrie what he was up to, but I obviously should have spelled it out. It's like I told the police – he sent me a text, telling me he wasn't going to be around for a while.' Lang fumbled in his pocket. 'I might still have it, hold on.' He pulled out a phone and clicked a few buttons, scrolling through his messages. 'Yes, here you go.' He showed Jimmy the screen. 'I didn't show Carrie this; Wendy thought there was no need to upset her any more than necessary.'

Jimmy looked at the message on the screen.

'Going to disappear for a week or two. Thinking with my dick again! Cover for me?'

There was a yellow face at the end of the message which appeared to be winking.

As Jimmy headed back towards Carrie's flat, he tried to imagine what it was like to be Lang, successful, self-assured, confident of your place in the world, but it was too much of a stretch.

The man had been pretty clear – I'm right and you're wrong, don't care what you think you saw, this is what happened. Maybe the smug bastard was right? The text message seemed pretty straightforward – if it was Carrie's dad who sent it? Anyone could send a message from someone else's phone. He had a sudden image of the bricklayer picking up the bag from the ground and walking off.

He was still mulling that over as he turned the corner towards the tower block. Up ahead he could see flashing lights – a police car sat outside the building, a single uniformed officer standing by it. A group of young kids were milling around nearby, hoping to see something kick off. Jimmy's first instinct was to run. But what if something had happened to Carrie? He moved closer to the building, skirting around a manky patch of grass in front of the block, hoping to work his way behind the car. He got about halfway when the uniform saw him.

'Hey, you, where you going?'

Jimmy froze. The uniform started to move towards him but then stopped, glancing at the kids, not wanting to leave the car at their mercy. He had probably only been left there to stop it being vandalised.

'Come here,' the uniform said, beckoning Jimmy over.

Jimmy's second instinct was to run. He started to back away.

'Are you Jimmy?'

The kids were all staring at him now. The uniform held

his hands up to indicate he wasn't a danger. Aye, right, wasn't born yesterday. Jimmy stayed where he was but nodded. The uniform picked up his radio.

'2471 to Burns, come in, over.' The radio crackled into life.

'Burns.'

'He's here. He's safe.'

'Bring him up.'

The uniform looked back over to Jimmy.

'You'd better come with me.'

'What the actual fuck, Jimmy?'

Carrie was in his face as soon as he was escorted into the flat. He stopped abruptly in the doorway, the uniform bumping into his back. Dog carried on into the room and jumped onto his usual place on the sofa next to a pissed-off-looking DS Burns.

'I thought you'd been attacked again,' Carrie said.

Jimmy frowned. Why would she think that?

'Where have you been?' Burns said.

'Out.'

'There was blood in the kitchen,' Carrie said.

Jimmy held up his hand to show her the cut on his palm. He'd found some plasters in the bathroom earlier.

'It was just an accident. I'm fine.'

She looked like she wanted to punch him. He took a step back.

'I thought someone had got you,' she said, 'that they'd find you burned to a crisp like that other poor man or strung up like that bloody cat. I didn't know what to do, so

I called DS Burns, told him what's been going on – I'm sorry, I know you didn't want me to. You should have left a note.'

Jimmy nodded. She was right. He wasn't used to having someone care where he was.

'Let me have a look at that,' Carrie said, examining his hand. Up close he could see that her eyes were raw and there were splotches of mascara on her cheeks.

'It needs cleaning up.' She headed into the kitchen.

Burns shook his head wearily. 'You can go, Alex, thanks,' he said to the uniform, who left quietly, closing the door behind him.

Burns looked up at Jimmy.

'Sit down,' he said. 'We need to talk.'

Carrie and Jimmy sat on the sofa, while she cleaned his hand up. Burns had moved to the computer chair. Jimmy wondered if he thought it gave him a bit more authority sitting higher than them. Carrie had told Burns almost everything. About Goldilocks and the dead cat, about the blond guy, about it all happening after some rogue policeman came looking for him at the Pit Stop. She reckoned she'd had no choice, to make him take Jimmy's 'disappearance' seriously. Jimmy wasn't happy. Neither was Burns.

'I wish you'd told me all this earlier,' Burns said.

'You didn't give us the chance,' Jimmy said. 'You were too busy with your other dead body.'

'And what would you have done really?' Carrie added. 'Made another note!'

'You should have told me.'

Burns was probably right, Jimmy thought, but keeping things to himself was a hard habit to shake off. He winced as Carrie rubbed some antiseptic cream into the cut on his hand.

'Does it make a difference?' Carrie asked. 'To you looking for my dad, I mean.'

'Maybe,' Burns said. 'I'm not big on all this conspiracy stuff though.'

You should meet my friend, Jimmy thought, he'd soon put you right.

'For instance,' Burns continued, 'there was no rogue policeman looking for you at the Pit Stop.'

'You would say that,' Jimmy said.

'I would say that because it was me! I wanted to talk to you about your statement.'

Jimmy studied Burns. Built like a brick shithouse, Deano had said. Jimmy had imagined a tall guy, like the bricklayer, but Burns would fit the bill. He looked like a middleweight boxer, broad and muscular. Could have been him.

'Took you long enough,' Carrie said. 'That was almost a week after we came to the station.'

'You're right,' Burns admitted. 'But it's more cock-up than conspiracy. The PC – Barry Stevens – made a comprehensive note of Jimmy's story but it got left in the wrong place.'

Stevens. Jimmy snorted. Just a cock-up? Probably gave it to his mate Duke to file!

'I looked for you as soon as I read it, asked around all over, down under the bridges, the Pit Stop, places like that. Couldn't pin you down.'

Made sense, Jimmy thought. He'd been keeping out of the way, then he was in the hospital and after that hanging out in the old banqueting hall. Wouldn't have been easy to find him.

'The other stuff's not so easy to ignore though, is it?' Carrie said, pressing down a clean dressing on Jimmy's hand. 'It's pretty obvious someone's been after him – and me. How do you explain that?'

Burns nodded. 'I admit it's suspicious. And I don't know anything about the guy who got burned, not my case. I'll look into it. But there are a lot of nasty twats out there who think it's funny to attack the homeless.'

Some of them are policemen, Jimmy thought. He remembered Deano getting a kicking in the park from Duke – the same guy who'd been guarding the place where Goldilocks got done, laughing and joking with Norma Weston's husband.

'So you're putting that down to coincidence?' Carrie said. 'Convenient for you that!'

'Hold your horses, pet, I'm not putting it down to anything. I said I'll look into it. The cat's the same, kids messing about probably. There have been a few problems around there. Not that long ago someone broke into Pets Corner and attacked the goats, threw paint on them.'

'Didn't fucking hang them though, did they?' Jimmy said. He could see where this was going. Nowhere.

Burns glared at him. Carrie had finished bandaging Jimmy's hand and was now scratching at her arm; he could feel the heat coming from her, building up.

'This is bollocks,' she said. 'Jimmy talks to your people and suddenly all hell breaks loose. What about my dad? You going to put that down to kids? Was it a kid you saw arguing with him, Jimmy?'

Jimmy didn't see the need to answer. She'd made her point.

'That's the problem though, isn't it?' Burns said. 'Doesn't know what he saw really, does he?'

Burns was right about that. He was neither use nor ornament, as his dad used to say.

'So you're not going to do anything?' Carrie said.

'There's no case, Carrie. I can't do much until . . .' Burns stopped, embarrassed.

'Until what?' Carrie said. 'Until his body turns up? Is that what you were going to say?'

'I'm sorry but there's just no evidence to back up Jimmy's story. No one else saw anything.'

'What about CCTV?' Carrie said. 'There are cameras all over the place on the Quayside.

Burns didn't look optimistic. 'I'll try, but the chances are it's too late. The council's digital stuff will probably have been deleted and the private tapes will have been recorded over.' He looked pointedly at Jimmy. 'If the "incident" had been reported at the time, we might have had a chance of finding something, but now . . . well, we've lost over a month.'

As soon as Burns left, Jimmy told Carrie about his visit to the Langs – how Andrew Lang had dismissed the idea that

Roger had trouble at work as office tittle-tattle. It seemed a bit of a dead end. She barely seemed to hear him – there was a distance between them now and it felt like neither of them had the energy to talk about it. He was pissed off that she'd told Burns all about him – unfair, but there it was. And though she hadn't said anything, he knew that month gap was eating her up inside, could see it in the way she looked at him. Or didn't look at him. When she went to bed he heard her put the bolt across the door again. He lay down on the sofa on his side, Dog curled up behind his knees, and tried to sleep.

Smoke is pouring from under Carrie's door. Someone stumbles out of the bedroom. A man, his upper body wrapped in flames but still walking, like a zombie, coming straight for Jimmy. It's Goldilocks. A baseball bat appears in Jimmy's hand, he swings it at Goldilocks, shattering his jaw, but it doesn't stop him moving forward. Jimmy clubs Goldilocks again, there's blood everywhere, turning his arms scarlet. Goldilocks stumbles this time, the flames spreading to the sofa. Jimmy lifts the bat high and smashes it straight down on top of his head, driving him to his knees. More blood jets up through the air, splattering his face. He wipes it from his eyes and sees Goldilocks pushing himself back up on his knees, shuffling towards him, his entire body on fire now. Jimmy goes to swing the bat again, but it turns to ashes in his hand. He tries to run, but a hand grips his ankle. Goldilocks inches closer, his face gone, only a grinning skull left. Jimmy tries to kick out, but it's too late, his own legs are on fire. He can feel his skin melting. Goldilocks grabs him around the thighs and pulls him to the floor in a deathly hug, the flames engulfing them. The last thing Jimmy sees is Burns, standing in the bedroom doorway, laughing.

Jimmy woke up with a jolt, drenched in blood. He leapt off the sofa, pulling at his soaked shirt, desperately trying to peel it away from his skin. Slowly, he realised, not blood but sweat. His eyes flicked to the bedroom door. Closed. No fire. He jerked his head around the rest of the room. No fire, no one else there apart from Dog, cringing underneath the desk. He had to get out. It wasn't safe. Not for them and not for Carrie. Him being there put her in danger. Best to move on – they needed a bit of space to clear the air – and he wouldn't be able to sleep anyway. He had a quick shower, put a clean shirt on and left. This time he wrote her a note.

33

Premier allotments, Newcastle, July 11, 2012

'You're nicked, son!'

Jimmy leapt up, banging his head on a wheelbarrow that was hanging from the shed roof, knocking it off its hook, bringing the whole thing crashing down on top of him. He pushed it off, wriggled out from under it and kicked over a watering can as he did, the stagnant water soaking into his trousers.

A large, shadowy figure stood in the shed doorway, obscured by the blazing sun behind him. A flashback from his nightmare zoomed into his head then straight back out again. This was real.

Dog seemed strangely unfussed by both the noise and the intruder, jumping up at him gently, looking for attention more than anything else. The man laughed.

Gadge. The twat.

'Your face, man,' Gadge said. 'Funniest thing I've seen since wife number two fell off one of them plastic bananas at Gran Canaria. And that was fucking hilarious. She lost two of her teeth.'

Jimmy didn't see the funny side, too busy rubbing his head, could already feel a lump where he'd hit it, just to add to his recent war wounds.

'Thought I might find you here,' Gadge said. 'Creature of habit, our Jimmy, I said to Deano, a creature of habit.'

Gadge was right. They'd been here before, when Jimmy had been a novice at this, stumbling around trying shed-door handles, disturbing a three-quarters-cut Gadge who'd tried to take his head off with a garden hoe before falling into a marrow trench. The fact that Jimmy hadn't just left him there but dragged him back into the shed and put a blanket on him before finding a temporary home in another nearby shack had cemented their friendship, if that's what it was. He'd been coming back now and again ever since. There was always one shed that had been left unlocked and usually one or two tomatoes to scavenge if you were hungry.

'What do you want anyway?' Jimmy said, knowing that Gadge wasn't one for rose-tinted memories.

'That's nice. Come all this way for a chat and a cuppa and that's all I get?'

'There's no cuppa here, not after that stupid wake-up call. I'm soaked.'

'Good job I brought me own then, isn't it?' Gadge said, pulling a flask from his pocket. 'I hope you've got a cup.'

Jimmy found a spare mug on a bench and they sat on a couple of upturned pots outside the shed while they drank.

'We'll probably have to move doon here soon,' Gadge said.

'Why's that?'

'The Queen's coming, man. Diamond Jubilee tour, d'you not read the news? I applied to light one of them beacons. Didn't get picked, like, can't imagine why.'

'Maybe because you hate the royal family.'

'Aye, I knaa, I was gonna try and burn the council offices doon with the torch. Gan doon in history.' He laughed. 'Gadge Fawkes, what d'you reckon to that?'

'No bugger would pay a penny for you,' Jimmy said. 'What's all that gotta do with us anyway?' He took a sip of his lukewarm tea, pulled a face.

'They'll be clearing the streets when she comes, man, can't let Her Maj's royal eyes settle on the likes of us. Ya knaa they say she thinks everything smells of fresh paint; well, that's not all: she thinks all the roads are always empty and that everyone lives in a palace. She's proper delusional, like. It's the in-breeding.'

Jimmy started to laugh but still had tea in his gob and began to choke. Gadge jumped up and patted him on the back until he got his breath back.

'Good to see you're still in one piece anyway, bonny lad,' Gadge said. 'Me and the boy got a bit worried when we hadn't heard from you for a bit.' He started to grin. 'We weren't the only ones either.'

'What do you mean?' Jimmy had no idea who else would give a shit about him.

'Julie was asking after you. You kept that quiet. Have you been dipping your wick there, son?'

Jimmy was baffled.

'Who's Julie?'

'Howay, man, Julie, ya knaa, cute smile, cracking arse. Sells the *Big Issue* near the library.' The grin grew bigger. 'Look at you with a glint in your eye, you dirty bastard. Good kisser is she?'

'Better than you.'

'You reckon.' Gadge could move quickly when he wanted. Before Jimmy realised what was going down, Gadge had grabbed him by the collar and was trying to smack a lip-lock on him, his manky beard scouring Jimmy's chin.

'Get off, man,' Jimmy yelled, squirming out of his grip. Gadge sat back down, his chest heaving with a combination of laughter and the sudden exertion.

'You might have had a shave,' Jimmy said.

'At least I can grow a proper beard,' Gadge said, once he'd got his breath back.

Jimmy rubbed his chin; he hadn't shaved for about five days but there wasn't a lot to show for it.

'Bet you've missed all this banter,' Gadge said.

'You'd lose. Been happy keeping my head down.'

'And how's that working out for you?'

'Not great.' Jimmy brought Gadge up to speed on what Brian had discovered about Carrie's dad, the affair with the SOCO's wife and Roger's row with the developer.

'Sounds like a wrong 'un to me,' Gadge said.

'Who? Weston or this Collins guy, the developer?'

'Both of them. Roger 'n' all – he's no innocent.'

Jimmy wondered if there was anyone in the world, besides

him and Deano, that Gadge didn't think was a wrong 'un; decided there probably wasn't.

'To be honest, Gadge, I'm floundering here. I thought I'd be able to help Carrie but at the moment I don't know my arse from my elbow.'

'That's cos you're trying to do it all on your own, man. You're not utilising all your available resources.' Gadge tried a posh boss-man accent for the last bit but didn't really pull it off.

'What available resources? I haven't got any resources.'

Gadge was tapping his own chest, making it clear what he meant.

'Got heartburn, have you?' Jimmy said.

Gadge threw his tea dregs at him but Jimmy ducked out of the way.

'Can't believe you're using some cub reporter to do your digging around on the web when you've got an Internet expert at your disposal,' Gadge said.

'An Internet expert who doesn't have a computer and is banned from the library,' Jimmy said.

'There's more than one library, bonny lad. I'm not banned from all of them.'

Jimmy swallowed the thought that it was only because Gadge hadn't been into all of them.

'What are you still doing here then?' Jimmy said.

'Waiting for you to say please.'

It was a short walk from the allotment into Jesmond Dene where Jimmy had arranged to meet Carrie, provided she'd seen his note – on the same bench they'd met the first time, next to the goat pen at Pets Corner. As he wandered through the entrance, he could see her sitting there alone, reading a book. He knew she'd be a bit pissed off that he'd walked out but hoped the note had explained things. There was a stocky man in a fluorescent yellow jacket and a woollen hat behind the bench, trimming the bushes with a pair of shears and a young couple on a nearby bench sharing an ice cream. Aside from that the park was unusually empty.

Carrie didn't appear to see him coming until he was a few yards away. No wave. Not a good sign. No smile either.

'Can I sit down?' he said.

'Free country,' she said.

He sat on the end of the bench to give her some space.

'You're late,' she said.

'No watch,' he said and turned towards her; she was staring just over his shoulder, avoiding his eyes. She looked a little angry – no, more than that, there was disappointment in there too. And something else? Fear? No. Guilt? Maybe.

'What's wrong?' Jimmy said. She turned her head, her eyes blazing.

'Did you kill my dad?'

'What? No! Of course not. Why would you think—'

There was a noise behind him but before he could turn, he felt an arm tighten around his throat, putting him in a choke hold, lifting him up off the bench. The couple on the next bench jumped up and ran over towards him, the man taking something out of his pocket.

Jimmy turned his head slightly and caught a glimpse of the man holding him, the bush-trimmer in the yellow jacket. He was pulled over the back of the bench and onto the grass, surprised by the speed of the attack. He could hear Dog barking like mad, loud enough to send the goats scattering. Carrie didn't move or say anything. Jimmy tried to look up at his assailant, but before he could focus on the man's face he was flipped onto his stomach, a knee in his back pinning him to the floor. His arms were wrenched backwards and his wrists cuffed together.

'You're nicked,' said DS Burns.

34

Pilgrim Street Police Station, July 11, 2012

The camera didn't move. Jimmy had been staring at it since they'd left him there, but it just stared right back at him from its position in the top corner of the room, just above the door. Eventually he gave it the finger.

Suspicion of theft, Burns had said. Theft of what? Jimmy didn't have a clue. He'd been bundled into the back of a van by two other cops – the "couple" on the bench – and brought straight there, dumped in the chair.

Why had Carrie lured him into a trap? One day she's worried about him, the next she's serving him up on a plate. What happened in between? It couldn't just be because he left the flat without telling her; he'd explained why in his note. It made no sense.

He slammed his fist on the table in front of him, stood up and started to pace the room. Then the door opened.

'Sit down,' Burns said.

'I'd rather stand if it's alright with you,' Jimmy said.

'It's not.'

Jimmy thought about refusing but after a short show of resistance he shrugged and sat back down, keeping his powder dry for the battle to come. Burns sat opposite him, placing a box file on the table. He had another plain-clothes copper with him who was carrying a large bin bag. He wasn't introduced.

Burns unwrapped two tapes, placed them in the large recording device that sat on the end of the table and switched it on.

'It's 12.46. This interview is being tape recorded. This is an interview with . . .' He looked at Jimmy who wasn't giving him anything just yet.

'State your name, please.'

Jimmy said nothing.

'Look, Jimmy, or James Ian Mullen, if you prefer . . .'

Jimmy flinched. How did Burns know his full name? No one knew that, not Carrie, not Gadge, no one outside his immediate family . . . ex-family.

'That's right, I know who you are, so there's no point playing silly buggers.'

'How do you know my name?'

'I'm a detective.'

Burns pulled a plastic bag out of the box file and dropped it on the desk. The fucking teaspoon. Jimmy remembered Burns pocketing it in the café at the mortuary, pretending that he was annoyed by the noise. Bastard had got his fingerprints.

'Shall we start again?' Burns said.

Jimmy nodded. Burns went through an obviously pre-pre-pared speech, detailing those present – his silent partner was called Detective Constable Gibbs – the time, place, etc., etc. Jimmy zoned out for most of it, still pissed off that they knew his name. If they knew his name, they knew what he'd done. Maybe that was really why he was there? He started to pay attention again when Burns reminded him that he didn't need to say anything.

'... but it may harm your defence if you do not men-tion when questioned something which you later rely on in court. Anything you do say may be given in evidence. Do you understand?'

'No comment,' Jimmy said.

'Funny,' Burns said, though the look in his eyes said dif-ferent. Jimmy was suddenly glad the camera was there.

'You are entitled to free legal advice at any time,' Burns continued. 'And you may speak to a legal representative on the phone. Do you wish to do so?'

Fucking lawyers. Fat lot of good they'd ever done him. Plead this, plead that, throw yourself on the mercy of the court, talk to a shrink, the judge will look favourably on you, give you a lower sentence; bullshitters, every last one of them. Jimmy knew that he'd be drummed out of the ex-con fraternity for saying 'No', but he'd never really been a team player.

'No. I'm good, thanks.'

Burns got him to reconfirm explicitly that he didn't want a lawyer 'for the tape' and then settled back in his chair, clearly glad to have got the formalities over with. He took a piece of paper from the box file and skimmed through it. 'You reported seeing Roger Carpenter in a fight . . . is that right?'

'Yes.'

'And you thought that he was pushed or thrown into the River Tyne.'

'Yes.'

'But you didn't do anything to stop it?'

'No.'

'Why not?'

'I was scared.'

'Strong lad like you . . . ?'

Jimmy closed his eyes, ignored the bait, tried again to figure out why this was happening. Burns went again.

'You didn't report any of this for nearly a month?'

'Was that a question?'

'Why the delay?'

'I wasn't sure what I'd seen, but then I saw Carrie's appeal for witnesses in the paper.'

'Thought you'd do your civic duty, eh?'

'Something like that.'

'Took you long enough.'

Jimmy again refused to bite; just stared at his interrogator, waiting him out.

Burns cracked first. 'So you're telling me you didn't go anywhere near Mr Carpenter?'

'That's right.'

Burns delved into the bin bag and pulled out a larger clear plastic bag. He placed it on the table in front of Jimmy.

'D'you recognise this?'

Inside the plastic bag was a rucksack. Jimmy's rucksack. He could see the scratches on the side pocket where Dog had tried to take out his own biscuits. He nodded.

'For the tape, please.'

'Yes. It's my rucksack.'

Burns put the bag on the floor, reached into the box file and pulled out another plastic bag, smaller this time. Again, he placed it on the table.

'What about this?'

Jimmy looked closely. It was a cigarette lighter, a Zippo. Red used to have one with the ship's crest on. His was silver though, this one was gold. And instead of a crest it had a large 'D' inscribed on it. He'd never seen it before.

'Do you recognise it?' Burns said.

'It's a cigarette lighter – a Zippo.'

'Have you seen it before?'

'No.'

'You're sure?'

'Positive.'

'It was Roger Carpenter's lighter. His daughter has identified it. The D stands for Dodger – an old nickname of his, apparently.'

Jimmy remembered Andrew Lang saying something about that – Roger the Dodger.

'What's that got to do with me?' Jimmy said.

'We found it in your rucksack.'

'Fuck off,' Jimmy said, pushing his chair away from the table and starting to stand, pointing at Burns. Bastard was stitching him up. He'd expected some police payback but not this. 'I've never seen that before.'

'Sit down!' Burns shouted.

'Make me,' Jimmy said.

Gibbs started to get to his feet – he looked like he was going to enjoy putting Jimmy back on the chair.

'Sit down, Jimmy,' Burns said again, gentler this time.

Jimmy stayed half up. One name in his mind: Martin Weston, Norma's husband – he'd seen him working at the scene of Goldilocks' death. Who would have had a better opportunity to make sure that lighter got into Jimmy's rucksack?

He was well and truly screwed. Was that why Carrie had helped them? Because she thought he had her dad's lighter? Even though she knew about Martin Weston? It didn't seem enough. There was only one thing that was enough. He sat down again.

'Where did you get the lighter?' Burns asked.

'I didn't. I've never seen it before.'

'We found it in your rucksack.'

Jimmy almost started pointing fingers, but he didn't know who else was in on it. Duke? Almost certainly. Who else though? Gibbs maybe? He was silently glaring at Jimmy, still looking disappointed that he'd sat down of his own accord. Burns even? Probably all of them. The whole place could be rotten to the core.

'Someone else must have put it there – I bet you didn't find my fingerprints on it?'

For the first time Burns looked hesitant. 'Anyone can wipe prints off of something.'

'Anyone can plant something in a bag,' Jimmy fired back.

'You stole it when you attacked Roger Carpenter, didn't you?' Burns said.

'No.'

'And then, when you saw Carrie's appeal in the paper you thought there might be something in it for you, so you pretended you'd seen a fight, pretended to be her friend. Hoped for a reward.'

'No.'

'She trusted you, you know? Her dad's gone missing and she thought you were her friend. I bet you even got one of your dodgy mates to fake that attack on her in the hospital car park. To make her even more dependent on you.'

Jimmy just sat, shaking his head as Burns ploughed on.

'Look at the state of you, yet she put you up, gave you a bed when she thought you were in trouble. D'you think she'd have done that if she'd known you had her dad's lighter in your bag? That you were the one who attacked him?'

'I didn't attack him.'

'D'you think she'd have done all that if she'd known who you were?' D'you think she'd have let you anywhere near her, nice girl like that?'

Jimmy said nothing, looked down at the table. He could feel a trickle of cold sweat running down his back.

'D'you know how nice she is? She's even looking after your manky dog while you're in here. We were going to hand it over to the dog catcher, but she stopped us. After all you've done. After you've lied to her. After you've hidden things from her.'

'I haven't hidden things from her. I told her about my past.'

'Aye, some of it, she mentioned that. Bit economical with the truth though weren't you, *James*?'

Jimmy shook his head, didn't want to hear any more. Knew where this was going now. Understood why Carrie had done what she'd done.

'Told her about your time in the nick, did you?'

'Yes.'

'Told her how you got there, I'll bet. Easy to put your own spin on that one. Nice little sob story. Poor unlucky Jimmy, wrong time, wrong place, didn't mean to do it. Boo hoo hoo. Get the hankies out. Oh yes, I can see why you might have told her about that alright.'

Burns leaned forward, ready to play his ace.

'Didn't tell her why you stayed there so long though, did you?'

35

Healthcare Centre, HMP Durham, 1994

If Jimmy hears the male nurse tell the story to anybody else, he will probably kill him. He has been lying in this bed for three days now and heard the same thing a dozen times. It wasn't funny the first time and it's not funny now.

'And get this,' the nurse says. 'When he kicked over the steps, they made such a row that half the block went running into the library. When they got there, Jimmy here was lying on the floor holding his leg and screaming in agony. Only tried to hang himself with his prison-issue shirt, didn't he?' The nurse is creased up now, bending double with the strain of trying not to laugh. Jimmy wonders whether he can get to him before he looks up, wonders how many times he'd have to punch him to make him stop talking.

The nurse somehow manages to pull himself together for long enough to keep going: 'His made-in-Hong-Kong-for-about-50p-prison-issue shirt!' He's howling now, almost crying with laughter. 'Fell apart the minute he kicked the steps away, didn't it? He dropped like a stone, broke his ankle, his fibula and knackered his knee up something rotten.'

The other patient, a lifer – Jimmy doesn't know his name – isn't laughing. In fact, he's yawning. He only came in for an aspirin, probably wishes he hadn't now. Jimmy would bet that he's already heard the story; it will have been told a thousand times by now, passing from wing to wing like a massive game of Chinese whispers, getting more outlandish with every telling. At least the nurse's version is as near to the truth as makes no difference. Only thing that's wrong is that the shirt didn't split straight away, it took a few moments. A few moments where Jimmy hung there, thinking he'd got it right, thinking it was over.

'Not only that,' the nurse is saying, 'he tied the wrong knot, didn't he? Should have tied a slip knot, one that would tighten up with his weight; the doc reckons he'd more chance of breaking his neck when he fell than choking himself. Might have hung there for ages if the shirt wasn't shit and the noise of the steps falling hadn't brought the cavalry running.' The nurse finds the aspirin and dishes out two tablets to the lifer who quickly dry swallows them and leaves.

'You're welcome,' the nurse shouts after him. 'People, eh,' he says to Jimmy, as if he hasn't been the subject of his humiliating tale. When you're a total and utter fuck-up you lose the right to respect.

The itch under the plaster that's encasing Jimmy's leg, from just below his knee to the start of his toes, is driving him scatty but he can't reach it lying down, so he swings his legs off the bed and sits up, digging his fingers underneath the bottom edge to scratch away. As he's doing this, another prisoner comes in. This one's escorted by a screw. Jimmy grimaces. That's all he needs. He knows this one right enough: Wilkinson, the Jock psycho himself. Wilkinson sees him and winks, a wide grin appearing on his face that Jimmy would love to slap off. They've given him a pair of crutches and he considers using them to get away from the grief, but he's not long been back from a walkabout and the leg still aches a bit.

'Fancy seeing you here, son. What's wrong with you?' Wilkinson says, as if he doesn't already know. Everyone in the nick will know by now from the governor down to the woman who comes in once a week to teach drama. Nothing she can teach this week could be more dramatic than Jimmy's performance.

'I'm having my brain removed so I can put up with the levels of banter on the wing,' Jimmy says, not caring if he winds the twat up. Maybe suicide-by-provoking-psycho will work better than his other attempt.

Wilkinson stares at him, uncomprehendingly, until eventually the cogs click in and he gets it. 'Get to fuck, you wee prick,' he says, though he smiles when he says it, so that's another suicide bid down the Swanee.

'What can I do for you?' the nurse asks Wilkinson.

'He reckons he's having a migraine,' the screw says, his voice dripping with cynicism. Jimmy knows him too. Harris, a right hard bastard, hates everyone.

'Symptoms?' the nurse asks.

'I've been seeing spots and feeling a bit dizzy,' Wilkinson says.

'Probably from reading up migraine in the library,' Harris says without a smile.

'Fuck off,' Wilkinson says. 'I'm hurtin' here.'

Unseen by the nurse, but not by Jimmy, Harris jabs Wilkinson in the kidney – a short, sharp punch that brings him to his knees.

Wilkinson doesn't make a peep, wouldn't give Harris the satisfaction. The screw leans over, grabs his collar and pulls him up.

'You want to watch that mouth of yours, sonny, it might get you into trouble,' he says.

Without warning, Wilkinson smashes an elbow into Harris's nose, sending him flying backwards across the room, his head cracking against the door. As he falls forward, Wilkinson swings around and kicks him full in the face. Harris collapses on the floor and Wilkinson kicks him again. And again. And again.

The nurse doesn't move, his mouth gaping. There's a panic button on the wall but Wilkinson is between him and it, so there's no way he's going to get there. He glances at Jimmy who shakes his head: don't even think about it.

When Wilkinson's finished having his fun he turns around.

'Any other cunt got anything to say?'

No one has. The nurse looks away.

'Keys, now!' Wilkinson says, clicking his fingers and pointing at the nurse, who fumbles around in his pockets, inevitably finding them in the last one he tries. He hands them to Wilkinson who locks the door.

'Nobody move,' he says before turning the unconscious Harris over and pulling a pair of handcuffs from the man's back pocket. He puts one on Harris's wrist and snaps it into place. He drags him across the floor and snaps the other cuff to the radiator, leaving him slumped on the floor on his side.

'Right,' he says, 'that should do for now.' He looks up at the CCTV camera in the corner of the room. 'Shouldn't be long.'

Jimmy watches as Wilkinson starts to rummage through various drawers, pulling out several rolls of bandages and a pair of scissors. The nurse is trying to remain frozen in his chair, making damned sure he doesn't catch the man's eye, just in case, but he can't help himself. He's shaking like he's got hypothermia or something. Wilkinson grabs the nurse's face and turns it towards his.

'I said don't fuckin' move.' He pats the nurse down, taking his wallet, a pack of cigarettes and a disposable lighter from the man's pockets. Once he's satisfied there's no more treasure to be found he opens one of the bandage packs, ties one end to the back of the chair and starts winding it around the nurse's body and arms, making it impossible for him to move. He repeats the process until the man looks like an unfinished Egyptian mummy, white from his waist to his neck. Once Wilkinson's finished with his upper body, he does the same to the man's legs, securing them tightly to the chair legs before standing back to admire his efforts.

'Champion,' he says and turns his attention to Jimmy, who is still sitting on the edge of the bed. He has no plans to be a hero; without his crutches he'd be hard pressed to stand up anyway. Wilkinson laughs.

'You're good where you are. Play your cards right, son, I might let you hitch a ride – just for the entertainment value, you ken.' And then the phone rings.

Wilkinson lets it ring, five, six, seven times. Jimmy starts to get twitchy, the noise playing on his nerves, which are already pretty stretched. Suddenly Wilkinson grabs the receiver.

'Don't say a fuckin' word. You've got thirty minutes to get a helicopter on the roof or I kill the nurse. After that I get to work on Harris.' He slams the receiver down and grins at Jimmy.

'Fuckin' told them, eh? Last time they stop ma son visiting.' Wilkinson picks up the packet of fags he took from the nurse – whose face is now as white as his uniform – and offers one to Jimmy, who shakes his head.

'Looking after your health, are you?' he says, nodding at the cast on Jimmy's leg. Even Jimmy has to laugh. The man's a psycho, but at least he's got a sense of humour.

'They'll not let you get away,' Jimmy says.

'Maybe not, but you've got to try, eh?' Wilkinson lights a cigarette and blows the smoke into the nurse's face. 'Hope you're no' expendable, son.'

The nurse is now shaking so badly that Jimmy thinks his heart'll go before Wilkinson has the chance to do anything else to him. He might be an insensitive twat, but he doesn't deserve this. Jimmy tries to catch the man's eye, to reassure him in some way, but the nurse is keeping his head down, still making sure that he doesn't look at the psycho.

Time stands still like someone has hit the pause button. The only sound is Wilkinson playing with the lighter, clicking it on and off to test the flame, humming a tune that sounds an awful lot like Bruce Springsteen's 'I'm On Fire'. It's so quiet that when the phone rings again both Jimmy and the nurse jump; Wilkinson doesn't move. He's making a point: I'm in charge. Eventually, in his own time, he picks it up.

'Well?' There's a pause; this time he lets them speak. Jimmy can hear a tinny voice on the other end but can't make out any words.

'No fuckin' way,' Wilkinson says. 'No more time. The first one's on you, pal.' He slams the phone down and starts looking through the cupboards again, picking up and discarding several things: a pack of hypodermic needles, a blood-pressure test kit and all kinds of lotions and potions, all of which he tosses on to the floor. He finally finds something he likes: a large plastic bottle of antiseptic hand wash. He reads the writing on the back of it and smiles.

'Ninety per cent alcohol. That'll do nicely.' He takes the top off the bottle and for a moment Jimmy thinks he's going to drink it, but instead he starts to splash it all over the nurse, soaking the bandages. The nurse tries to back the chair away but he's right up against the wall so there's nowhere else to go. Wilkinson gives him a sharp slap.

'Stay still, you fucking arse bandit.'

The nurse is mewling like an animal in distress, the back of his chair banging rhythmically against the wall, and there's an acrid smell in the room. A pool of piss starts to gather under his chair. Once Wilkinson has emptied the bottle, he looks around the room again, seeing what he wants on the wall in the corner: a fire extinguisher. He pulls it out of its stand and hands it to Jimmy.

'If this gets out of hand, use this. I dinna want the whole room to catch on.'

The nurse is crying now, huge trails of snot hanging down from his nose. Jimmy thinks he's trying to say 'Please', but it's hard to make it out in between the sobs.

'Grow a pair, gaylord,' Wilkinson says, testing out the lighter again. 'Worse things happen at sea.'

Jimmy blinks and he's back on the ship. He can feel the heat, taste the smoke, smell the burning bodies at the other end of the passageway. He sees the firebomb hitting Red; his friend covered in flames, wheeling away and over the side of the ship.

He blinks again, lifts up the fire extinguisher and smashes it into the back of Wilkinson's head.

He closes his eyes, tries to make the sights and sounds go away, can hear the nurse howling, can feel something wet on his arms and face, can feel again the smoke and the heat, hear the nurse howling. He opens his eyes again. It's no dream; the nurse is howling for real. Jimmy's on his knees. His sleeves are soaking wet and stained dark. The fire extinguisher is still in his hands, the bottom of it covered in blood and little flakes of white bone and brain matter. Wilkinson is lying face down on the floor, the back of his head caved in, barely recognisable as a head at all. The nurse is leaning back in his chair, so his feet don't get covered by the growing pool of blood which is starting to mingle with his own piss. He's staring at Jimmy as if he's a demon.

'You wouldn't stop hitting him,' the nurse says, tears rolling down his face. 'I was shouting and screaming at you, but you just wouldn't stop.'

Jimmy drops the extinguisher and looks up at the camera in the corner, its winking red light telling him that someone is watching, was probably watching the whole time. He can hear footsteps and voices in the corridor, getting nearer.

'It's over,' he says, to whoever is watching.

36

Pilgrim Street Police Station, July 11, 2012

Jimmy opened his eyes. Burns and Gibbs sat opposite him waiting for an answer.

'No,' he said.

'No what?' Burns said. Gibbs still hadn't opened his mouth.

'I didn't tell her why I was inside for so long.'

'I'm not surprised. "I smashed a man's brains out" doesn't sound very nice, does it?'

'It wasn't like that.'

Burns sighed. 'Here's my problem, Jimmy. I've got a missing person. Last seen by you – a killer with a history of violence; a killer with the missing man's lighter in his rucksack.'

'I never touched him. And I've never seen that lighter before.'

'Tell that to the judge.'

Jimmy closed his eyes again. Him and judges didn't get

on. The tape from the sick bay CCTV had clinched it for the last one he'd stood in front of. Practically a textbook example of 'unreasonable force', the man had said. Jimmy couldn't watch it; didn't recognise the man on there, battering someone to death with a fire extinguisher. He opened his eyes again. Burns' gaze hadn't shifted. He'd probably watched the tape himself, knew what kind of man he was dealing with.

'What did you do to Carrie's dad, Jimmy?'

Jimmy hadn't said another word. They put him in a cell overnight. Trying to freak him out, remind him where he'd come from. Read him wrong though. He didn't mind. It was safe there. He'd done his usual pacing; it was small: five paces long and four wide. A wooden bench attached to the wall. That was it. It was only one night; he knew the law well enough – they couldn't hold him for any longer than twenty-four hours, not without something else to go on. They'd have one more crack at him, probably, and then he'd be kicked out. Though if Burns told his probation officer about any of this, he'd be back inside in days anyway.

Didn't know what the hell he was going to do if they did kick him out; was running out of safe spaces. He didn't sleep. It was too hot; but mostly he didn't dare – too much weird shit in his head that would leak out if he closed his eyes. Who had put that lighter in his rucksack? It couldn't have been Goldilocks. There was no shortage of contenders, but his money was still on Weston. He had both motive and opportunity. He decided to ask for a brief for the next session, even though he hadn't done anything. Had he? He pictured himself picking the lighter up, bringing the flame to life, watching it, mesmerised, before closing it again and dropping it in his bag. Shook his head. It never happened.

A uniform brought him breakfast in the morning. An egg sandwich and a milky cup of coffee. He'd bet someone had spat in both, so left well alone. Jimmy assumed they'd drag him back into the other room for another 'interview' but nothing else happened. Time ticked by. An hour or two later someone looked in on him through the hatch in the door, but they didn't speak, ignored his questions. He paced the room for a while, enjoying the mindless counting, until his leg got tired. He was beginning to think they'd somehow been given licence to hold him for longer when the door opened and a familiar face came in. A very pissed-off-looking familiar face.

'You're free to go,' Duke growled. At first Jimmy thought he'd imagined it.

'Sorry?'

'I said, you're free to go. I'll take you to the desk and they'll give you your stuff back – for what it's worth.'

'What's happened?'

'Mind your own fucking business.'

'Come on, Duke, I've a right to know.'

Duke stared at him, confusion writ large on his face. How did this scruffy prick know his name?

'It's PC Ellington to you, fuckface. And the only right you've got is to get your arse kicked if you get too fucking lippy.'

Best not to push it. He'd seen what the man was capable of, knew only too well what could happen on the inside of a police cell.

'Sorry, PC Ellington,' he said.

Jimmy followed Duke out of the cell and into an ante-room where a desk sergeant had a box containing Jimmy's meagre possessions. He signed for them and was then taken to a side door and shoved out.

'Don't get too comfortable on the outside, son,' Duke said. 'I'd bet good money you'll be back in here before too long. Your sort can't keep away. I'll be watching you.'

Jimmy ignored the taunt and walked around the side of the building, finding himself at the front of the station. Carrie was standing there waiting with Dog. One of them seemed pleased to see him. Dog pulled at the rope and she let go. He ran at Jimmy and jumped up into his arms, yapping away happily, trying to lick his face. Carrie started to leave.

'Carrie?' Jimmy said. She stopped but didn't turn around.

'What's going on?' he said. This time she turned, keeping her gaze away from his.

'Didn't they tell you?'

'No.'

'They've found some CCTV footage, from that night on the Quayside, a man walking away with what looks like dad's satchel over his shoulder. Don't know who it is, but it's not you.' Now she looked straight at him. 'Seems you weren't lying about *everything*.'

And then she turned again and walked away.

'I've never seen that lighter before,' he shouted. But it was too late. She was gone.

Jimmy sat in the corner of Rosie's Bar nursing a small glass of Coke and a bag of crisps. Dog was curled up under his chair. The place was quiet, the lunchtime drinkers having headed back to work. The sole barman had finished washing all the glasses and was now slowly cleaning the tables. Jimmy had been there for an hour. Spent half the time wondering who was on that CCTV footage, walking away with the satchel, the other half wondering how to get back in Carrie's good books; how he could prove that the lighter was planted.

He heard the door open and looked up. Gadge and Deano came in. Jimmy wondered if the barman might say something about the place going downhill – particularly as Deano had chosen to wear the outlandish gold jacket they'd found in the handouts the other day – but instead he waved at Gadge. Should have guessed they'd know him in here. The Pit Stop was just around the corner. Gadge was looking around constantly, over his shoulder, behind Deano, behaving oddly. Jimmy hoped he was sober. Eventually he came over and sat down, still looking around, casing the joint. Deano tagged along behind him, grinning.

'An old raincoat won't ever let you down,' Gadge said out of the corner of his mouth.

'What?' Jimmy said.

'An old raincoat won't ever let you down.'

'What are you on about?'

'You're supposed to say, "But you can't beat a really good umbrella."'

'What?'

'Come on, Jimmy, man, if we're going to play at spies we should do it properly.'

'Look, Gadge—'

'C'mon, Deano, we're obviously in the wrong place,' Gadge said. The pair of them got up to leave.

'For God's sake.' Jimmy sighed. 'But you can't beat an umbrella.'

'A *really good* umbrella,' Gadge corrected.

'A *really good* umbrella,' Jimmy said, wishing that he hadn't got one of the Pit Stop's regulars to pass on a note to Gadge saying, 'Meet me in Rosie's.' Should have known the twat would take that as licence to piss about.

'Right,' Gadge said. 'Thank God that's all ower and we can get doon to business. Where have you been, man? Me and the lad have been looking all ower the toon for you. That Julie's heartbroken. Typical, man, doing a bunk as soon as you've got your oats. I tried to tell her that there were better men than you available, but it was hopeless. She's smitten.'

Jimmy ignored the bait. The less encouragement you gave Gadge when he was in one of his moods the better.

'I've been helping the police with their enquiries,' he said. 'They seemed to think that I killed Carrie's dad. Kept me in overnight.'

He told him about the lighter.

'Should've seen that coming,' Gadge said. 'And they wonder why naebody ever reports anything. They don't want to get stitched up, that's why! I hope you kept your gob shut?'

'Course.'

'You still want to stick your nose in where it's not wanted?'

It was a fair question. Burns wanted to lock him up and Carrie didn't trust him. Couldn't blame her though. Hearing he'd got her dad's lighter would have been bad enough, but once Burns threw Wilkinson into the mix Jimmy's fate was sealed. He just hoped the bastard hadn't shown her the footage; no civilian should have to see that. He looked up, Gadge was still waiting, his head tilted to one side, curious.

'Got nothing better to do,' Jimmy said.

'I'm liking this new Jimmy more and more.' Gadge grinned and turned to Deano.

'Have you still got some of that dosh left from when you sold your sign?'

'Aye. A bit.'

'Well, get me a pint of foaming ale then, lad. Me and Jimmy have got business to attend to.'

While Deano trudged over to the bar, Gadge pulled out a few scraps of paper from his pockets, scraps that Jimmy suspected used to be pages in a library book.

'I need to find out more about this Martin Weston,' Jimmy said.

'Don't rush me, son. One thing at a time. Now where was it?' Gadge fumbled around with the scraps, reading and discarding two or three before he found the one he wanted.

'Right, here we go. Guess where Mr Collins has a builder's yard and offices?'

'No idea,' Jimmy said.

Gadge grinned like he'd just won a year's supply of free beer. He pushed a small, crumpled map over the table towards Jimmy.

'Only right here.' He jabbed his index finger down in the middle of the map. 'About two hundred yards from where our late friend Goldilocks – may he rest in hell – met his maker.'

Jimmy moved Gadge's finger and looked down. Gadge was right; Jimmy had walked right past the place when he'd gone down to look at the murder scene.

'Jesus.'

'I doubt that Jesus has anything to do with it. Small world, eh?'

'I should go down there. See what's what,' Jimmy said.

'Hold your horses, bonny lad. What have you got planned for this afternoon?'

'Same as I've got planned for every day. Nowt.'

'Grand,' Gadge said.

'Why?'

'Because Mr Collins, our favourite dodgy housing developer, is due to be making an on-site visit to his latest development, just ower Gosforth way.'

'How do you know that?'

Gadge tapped the side of his nose. 'That's for me to knaa,' he said, as Deano slapped a pint down on the table in front of him.

'He set up a fake e-mail account and pretended he was a journalist wanting to interview Collins for a feature on up-and-coming businessmen,' Deano said. 'The secretary sent him a screenshot of the man's diary.'

'Everyone's a media hoo-er these days,' Gadge explained, giving Deano a glare for giving away his trade secrets.

'He made me distract the librarian while he did it all. I had to pretend I couldn't speak English,' Deano said.

'Not much of a stretch,' Gadge said, grabbing Deano in a headlock and pinching his cheek.

'And who could resist this little face, eh? Even the stoniest-hearted librarian would drop everything to help this poor mite. Particularly when he's dressed up all smart, like. Am I right?'

'Get off, man,' Deano said, squirming out of his grip.

'So what's the plan?' Jimmy said.

'Like you said, we should head up there and see if we can have a cosy chat with Mr Collins,' Gadge said. 'Unless you've got a better idea, of course.'

'We?' Jimmy said.

'Why aye, man, the three musketeers here, all for one and all that shite. Did you think we'd leave you on your own? Well, you'd be wrong. And d'ya knaa why?'

'No, I don't, but I'm sure you're going to tell me.'

Gadge started a drum roll on the table but cut it short when beer started to spill from his pint.

'Because you'd balls it up, obviously,' he said.

37

The Grange, Gosforth, Newcastle, July 12, 2012

It was a small site. Half a dozen houses, all well on the way to being completed: roofs on but no windows or doors. There were a couple of huge rubbish skips, one of them full to the brim, set off to one side, and a stationary JCB idling by one of the houses. Builders wandered in and out of the empty doorways, some holding plans, some carrying buckets; *actual* bricklayers probably, but none of them familiar to Jimmy.

Jimmy and Gadge had parked themselves on a grass verge on the opposite side of the road to the site, right in front of a large, expensive-looking house, with manicured hedges. There was no car on the drive but, just in case, they'd sent Deano off on a recce to make sure it was empty. They didn't want a bolshie householder kicking off, causing a disturbance.

Gadge had bought a four-pack of lager from the offy on the way to use as camouflage – any excuse for another drink. He'd passed one to Deano when they got there, but made it clear he didn't expect him to open it – 'I'm not that fucking generous.'

Deano returned from his lookabout and reported the place was all clear.

'Canny house though, wouldn't mind having a neb around inside but they've got a right flash alarm system – probably one of them that goes straight through to the coppers.'

'It's not the alarm you'd need to worry about, man, it's that jacket – they could see you from outer space,' Gadge said. 'Thought you'd given up that robbing shite anyway.'

'I have, man, just saying, like.'

Neither of them really believed him.

The entrance to the site was open and there was a Portakabin just inside, but no one had gone in or come out of it since they'd got there.

Deano was getting agitated – the downside of him trying to clean himself up was that he never sat still. 'Aren't we gonna do something?' he said, kicking a loose stone onto the road in front of them.

'Like what?' Gadge said.

'I dunno. I could go and run around in there if you like, knock a few things over, shake things up, get them all radgee, see what happens?'

Jimmy shook his head. 'Just be patient. If Gadge is right, Collins should be turning up any minute.'

Ten minutes later and Deano was doing one, teasing Dog, tapping him on the tail and running around him in circles, getting him overexcited. A couple of the workmen had glanced their way, wondering what all the barking was about. Gadge was on to his third can and Jimmy was wondering why they'd bothered. Collins had obviously changed his plans.

Just as he was about to knock it on the head, a car turned into the street. Jimmy knew nothing about cars, but it looked like a decent one, black, shiny, well looked after, one of those personalised number plates giving the game away: BU17 DER.

The car turned into the site, looped around and pulled up outside the Portakabin, facing the entrance. The back doors opened on both sides and two men got out. The one on the side nearest to Jimmy was Collins; he recognised him from the photos that Brian had sent through – the giant belly was the clincher. The man liked to eat.

'That's our man,' he said. He was so intent on watching the developer that he didn't look at the other man who'd got out of the car until he was halfway to the Portakabin. It couldn't be? He looked again. There was no doubt. It was Andrew Lang, the secret smoker. What was he doing there?

Both men were greeted by a large, shaven-headed man at the door of the Portakabin – the site foreman, Jimmy guessed – and had gone inside, closing the door behind them. The car had driven off, suggesting they planned to be in there for some time. Jimmy brought Gadge up to speed, explaining who Lang was and his connection to Roger.

'Wheels within wheels,' Gadge said, nodding his head. 'Councillors, developers, academics – the ruling elite

– they'll all be mixed up in this, mark my words. Did I tell you that Collins is a Mason?'

'No, you didn't,' Jimmy said.

'Well, you can't remember everything, bonny lad, not when you drink as much as I do. It was on his list of engagements: dinner at the Masonic Lodge this evening – with most of Her Majesty's constabulary no doubt.'

'What do we do now?' Deano said.

'Fucked if I knaa,' Gadge said. 'I got us here. I've done my bit.'

'I wouldn't mind knowing what they're talking about,' Jimmy said.

'Well, gan and have a listen in, man,' Gadge said, taking another sip of lager.

'I can't just wander into the site; there are too many workmen about.'

'Bollocks, man. Most of them are inside, working and that, they'll not even notice. Especially if you've got a good reason to be there.'

'Like what?'

Gadge scratched his head like an actor who'd been told that was what someone thinking looked like. Jimmy almost laughed but somehow it seemed to work.

'Like trying to get your dog back,' Gadge said. He started fiddling around in his pockets, searching for something, eventually pulling out a Gregg's bag with half a steak bake left in it. Gadge always had a bit of scran on him somewhere. He pulled a bit off the edge of the pasty and fed it to Dog who swiftly devoured it. Gadge waved the rest of the pasty in front of the animal's face and then lobbed it through the open gate towards the Portakabin. Dog hared off in pursuit of the rest of his unexpected meal.

'Well, gan on then, man, what you waiting for?' Gadge said, pushing Jimmy in the back.

Jimmy got up, looked around to make sure no one was watching and moved towards the site. He stopped at the entrance and had another look. The JCB was now trundling along on the far side of the enclosure. It stopped and the driver got out and went into one of the half-built houses. Too far away to see what Jimmy was doing.

Dog had found the remains of the pasty a yard or two past the Portakabin and was sitting on the ground with it between his paws, happily wolfing it down. Jimmy crept inside the site and moved over to the side of the cabin nearest the fence. There was no way anyone on the site could see him there, but he couldn't see inside the Portakabin so that was no good. He edged around the front towards the one large window, took a deep breath and glanced in. Lang, Collins and the foreman were hunched over a table examining a small-scale model of the site, six perfectly formed mini-houses, all with beautifully manicured green plastic lawns – a replica of the kind of place Bev used to dream about living in.

Fortunately for Jimmy, the three men had their backs turned to him so he was safe for the moment. He moved closer, trying to hear what they were saying. It was no use. He could hear a faint mumble, as Collins pointed at one of the houses, explaining something to his visitor, but there was no chance of Jimmy hearing him.

'Oi! Who the fuck are you?'

Jimmy turned around. Two workmen, plasterers by the looks of them, were walking towards him: a fat guy with a bucket and a younger, shorter man, wearing a baseball cap and holding a large trowel. It was the fat guy who'd shouted, but the younger guy was staring at Jimmy like he'd seen a ghost.

'I, um, came in to get my dog back,' Jimmy said, pointing towards Dog, before suddenly realising that Dog was no longer there. He glanced out of the entrance and saw him, on the other side of the road, jumping up at Gadge, no doubt hoping for some more food.

'What dog?' the bucket man shouted, only yards away now. Jimmy started to indicate outside but was interrupted by the foreman, who had come out of the cabin to see what the fuss was about.

'What's going on?' he said.

'This bloke was snooping about, gaffer.'

The foreman turned to look at Jimmy.

'There's nothing to nick around here, son, so you may as well piss off before we set the dogs on you.'

Jimmy was pretty sure there weren't any dogs around, other than his – he'd have seen or heard them by now – but he was more than happy to go. He started to leave, but as the foreman moved forward to see him off the other two men came out of the cabin behind him.

'Problem?' Collins said.

'No, boss,' the foreman said. 'Just some hobo wandering in off the street. I've sent him packing.'

Jimmy was moving away as quickly as he could, trying to keep his face hidden, but he couldn't help glancing up and saw Lang staring at him.

'I know him,' Lang said.

'What?' Collins said.

'I know him . . . Jimmy something. He was hanging about outside my house the other day. He was trying to talk to my wife about Roger – you know, my, um, colleague.'

'Oh, I know Roger, alright,' Collins said.

'This is the man who told the police that Roger had been attacked – seems to think he's some sort of private detective,' Lang added.

Jimmy turned to run but the two workmen who'd first spotted him had moved around between him and the entrance to the site. There was no escape. He looked past them, but there was no sign of Gadge and Deano or even Dog. The miserable bastards had legged it.

'Does he now?' Collins said, laughing. 'Sherlock Homeless, eh? Well, he ain't gonna find anything here, is he? What you sneaking about for?' he said to Jimmy.

'I wasn't. I was looking for my dog.'

'Just happened to be passing, eh?'

'S'right.' That was such obvious bollocks that Jimmy could feel the atmosphere change. It was like the lull he'd always felt right before something kicked off in the prison dining hall. Collins came down the steps and walked towards him.

'Dangerous things, building sites. Kind of places where someone could have an unfortunate accident, if they just wandered in, like, if they didn't know what they were doing. Isn't that right, lads?'

The foreman and the other two men all laughed, but Lang was starting to look a bit uneasy. Jimmy glanced over his shoulder to see if the exit was still blocked; it was. Collins stopped a couple of yards away from him.

'I reckon half the houses around these parts have probably got a body buried underneath 'em. Built in the sixties, you see. The good old days – they knew how to deal with troublemakers then. Pity we've already laid all the foundations here, eh lads?'

Lang had come down the steps behind Collins. To his credit he tried to drag the conversation back to safer territory.

'Let's not get carried away. Maybe you should explain what you are really doing here?' Lang said.

In for a penny, Jimmy thought.

'I was going to ask you the same question.'

Collins laughed. 'Cheeky bastard, isn't he? Will you tell him or shall I?'

'Not that it's any of your business,' Lang said, 'but, as I think I told you before, Mr Collins gets quite a bit of work from the university. We like to use local companies when we can. In return he's offering to sponsor a PhD post in my department for someone to do some research into green housing. I was a bit dubious, for obvious reasons, given the recent greenbelt protests, so he invited me to come and look at what they were doing with this development.'

Jimmy couldn't think what to say. It sounded reasonable. Likely even.

'So that's what he's doing here,' Collins said. 'But I'm still at a bit of a loss as to what you're doing here.'

He wasn't the only one. Jimmy didn't really know what he'd expected to find. Started hoping that a hole would open up in the ground; was glad it didn't though – these bastards would probably try and bury him in it. He tried to buy some more time.

'I told you. I was looking for my dog. He ran in here.'

Collins shrugged. 'Ewan, why don't you, Taff and Jock take Jimmy here around the back and see if you can help him find his dog? Be careful, mind. Like I said, dangerous places, building sites.'

The foreman moved towards him, grinning. Jimmy stepped back, looking around for somewhere to run. Collins, Lang and the foreman were all in front of him, the other two men and the site fence behind him. He bent down and picked up a rock from the ground.

'That's close enough.'

The foreman paused, wary, his eyes on the rock. Behind him, Jimmy saw a flash of colour, somewhere near the back fence, moving quickly, someone running towards them. A gold jacket. Deano. The foreman edged closer, but Jimmy feinted as if to throw the rock at him and he backed away. Behind him, the two plasterers were holding their ground, waiting for a word from their boss. Deano had now reached the JCB which was still parked up outside one of the houses. Jimmy watched as the kid pulled the cab door open and climbed in. He heard the engine start.

'Put it down,' the foreman said. 'We don't want anyone to get hurt.'

'Back the fuck off and let me walk away then,' Jimmy said, still brandishing the rock. He looked behind him. The men on the gate had moved a couple of yards further in; they were closing in on him.

The JCB started to move, heading towards them, gathering speed. Nobody else had seen it yet, probably thought it was just one of the other workmen getting on with the job. It wouldn't be long before they noticed it though; Jimmy needed to distract them for a moment longer.

'The police are investigating Roger's disappearance now. They think it's suspicious,' he said.

'What?' Lang said.

'Is that right?' Collins asked Lang.

'First I've heard of it,' he said.

'Won't be the last though,' Jimmy said as the JCB came ever closer, the noise of the engine now loud enough to attract the attention of the foreman who looked behind him to see it heading towards them.

'What the hell?' he cried.

Collins and Lang turned to see the digger speeding towards them, only twenty yards away now; the bucket lowered to the front to cause maximum damage if it hit someone. They moved apart, trying to get out of its path and Jimmy saw his chance. He barged past the foreman, knocking him to the ground, and dashed in between Lang and Collins, sprinting to the JCB. Deano saw him coming and slowed slightly, starting to turn in the direction of the entrance.

As Jimmy drew alongside the cab, he saw Deano pointing and got the message. He grabbed hold of the side of the bucket and hauled himself up and in. Fortunately, there was a layer of claggy earth inside, so he had a soft, if filthy, landing. Jimmy pulled himself up and looked out of the bucket. The foreman was still lying on the ground where he'd fallen and neither Collins nor Lang had given chase, which left the two workmen guarding the entrance. He felt the JCB pick up speed and looked back, up into the cab. Deano was grinning madly, loving it. Jimmy turned back and held on tight as they careered over the rough ground, carving out a path towards the entrance, Jimmy at the front like the figurehead on a ship. The men stood their ground, trying to call Deano's bluff, until the digger got within ten feet or so, then they both hurled themselves to the side as Deano steered the JCB straight at them. As they scrambled away, the short one's cap fell off, revealing a shock of blond hair. Jimmy glanced back to try and see the guy's face, but his view was obscured by the cab. The JCB flew through the entrance and straight onto the road outside, clipping the edge of the site fence, with Deano yelling at the top of his voice, 'Yippee-ki-yay, motherfuckers.'

38

Swan House subway, Newcastle city centre, July 12, 2012

An elderly woman leant up on her elbows and spat into the face of the man leaning over her.

'I was just looking,' the man said, wiping the phlegm from his face as he backed away. 'Didn't mean nothing.'

It had been kicking off all night. Rumours of police clear-outs ahead of the Queen's visit were making the natives restless. Jimmy pulled his coat around him, turning his head away.

He normally avoided the subways at night. Too many others looking for a spot to rest, getting all territorial over a shitty bit of concrete. Jimmy preferred solitude. This night was different though. He was exhausted; he felt the need for safety in numbers – no one would try to set him alight in a crowded subway.

Swan House subway was the busiest as well; too central, no distance from the city centre where the begging was more fruitful. Every few feet another body lay in a sleeping bag or cardboard box, even the odd small tent, protecting their own bit of space, snarling at anyone coming within range. They'd mostly left him alone though, possibly because he was so filthy from his unscheduled JCB ride, but more likely that they were worried how Dog might react. Given that the mutt was exhausted from the walk and hadn't opened his eyes for several hours they didn't have much to fear there.

They'd left the JCB at the far end of the road, only a couple of hundred yards from the site, where Gadge had been waiting with Dog. Jimmy didn't think that Collins would bother reporting anything as long as he got it back, not with Andrew Lang having been there, a witness of some sort to the not-so-veiled threats that had been made. Unless Lang was more involved with the builder than he'd let on?

Gadge and Deano both had hostel beds to go to, so he'd headed alone to the subway, only stopping to grab a quick bite from the Pit Stop's mobile kitchen by the arches on Trafalgar Street. He needed somewhere to think without worrying about who was coming around the corner. Gadge had told him to make the most of it; reckoned the whole area would be cleaned out before Her Maj's visit, the authorities not wanting the underground wretchedness to leak out onto the busy streets above.

He shook his head; he'd been there for hours but was getting nowhere – all his ideas about what was going on were falling to pieces as soon he dreamed them up. The more he thought about it, the less he understood. Lang's reason for being at the building site seemed plausible enough but Jimmy didn't like coincidences. Which meant he really didn't like seeing a flash of blond hair when that plasterer's cap flew off. Was he the same guy who'd attacked Carrie and tried to run him down? If he was, then Collins must surely be behind it.

The one thing he thought he knew for certain was that neither Lang nor Collins was the man he'd seen arguing with Carrie's dad on the Quayside. The man the police had now seen on CCTV leaving the scene. Lang seemed too thin, Collins too short. He would love to see that tape; wondered if Burns would show it to him. He was the only eye witness after all.

A scuffle broke out opposite him. A drunk had tripped over the outstretched leg of a sleeping man. Once he'd staggered back up to his feet the drunk had lashed out at the sleeper, kicking him in the stomach. Others piled in, dragging the drunk off, sending him on his way with a few retaliatory kicks of their own. They might not like each other much but they hated outsiders even more.

Jimmy needed to see Carrie again. She was the only one he could talk to about her dad and his dealings with Collins and Andrew Lang, but he didn't know how to approach her, how to build a bridge of some sort. He'd tried to open up a little, giving her some pieces of the Jimmy jigsaw, thinking the whole screwed-up puzzle would be too much for her. And look how that turned out: SNAFU – Situation Normal All Fucked Up. He slapped both sides of his head with his fists, hoping that his dad's regular method of 'knocking some sense into him' could be self-inflicted.

He'd chosen a spot in the middle of the subway so he

could keep an eye on both ends and have enough time to do a runner if he saw something, or more importantly someone, he didn't like the look of. The problem with that was the overcrowding; for some reason, possibly the same as his, most of the rough sleepers liked to gather in the centre. Everyone was packed a little too close together. The man nearest to Jimmy was beginning to piss him off. He stank of something – knock-off whisky maybe – and when he'd first turned up, he'd tried to cadge a tab and didn't seem to believe that Jimmy didn't smoke. He'd then tried the same with everyone else within a ten-yard radius, getting angrier with each rejection. Now the stupid bastard seemed to be trying to build a fire.

Jimmy watched as he emptied his rucksack of old newspapers and started screwing the pages up into balls, piling them up in a small heap against the wall. He delved deeper into the bag and pulled out a handful of twigs and a tin of spaghetti hoops.

You've got to be joking, Jimmy thought.

'What you doing?' he asked.

'What does it fucking look like?' the man slurred. 'You got a light?'

Jimmy closed his eyes and started counting. Not this man's fault. He didn't know. How could he? He reached ten and opened his eyes again, calmer now. The man was staring at him, still waiting for an answer. He might be stupid, but he was certainly patient.

'I told you, I don't smoke,' Jimmy said.

'Don't mean you ain't gotta light.'

'Yes it does,' Jimmy said, turning away on his side.

He heard the man get up and ask the guy nearest him on the other side. No joy there either. Hopefully he'd give up.

A few moments later he heard him come back. Then rustling and the sound of metal on metal. A can opener. He turned over again. The man had moved the paper away from the wall and made a circular pile, putting the twigs on top; a foot away from Jimmy's nylon sleeping bag. He took a small disposable lighter from his pocket.

'Don't even think about it,' Jimmy said, pulling his sleeping bag away just in case.

'OK, I won't,' the man said and lit the paper.

Jimmy jumped up, stamped on the only piece that had caught light and kicked the shit out of what was left, sending balls of paper and twigs everywhere and knocking over the open can of spaghetti hoops which began to spill its bright orange contents on to the ground.

'You wanker,' the man said, trying to shovel the hoops back into the can with his hands. 'That's my dinner.'

Some of the other sleepers moved away, leaving them to it. Jimmy looked down at the man; half his teeth were missing and the lines on his face were so deep they could have been carved with a Stanley knife. He was much older than Jimmy had first thought, old enough to be his dad. Jimmy leaned forward to try and give him a hand but the man cringed, clearly expecting to get a slap to add to his troubles.

Instead, Jimmy reached into his own rucksack and dug around, pulling out a cheese sandwich he'd grabbed from the past-its-sell-by-date bin at the back of Greggs. It was only a day over, fine to eat. Better than nothing. He tried to hand it to the old man.

'Don't need charity,' the man said, waving it away.

'I'm not offering charity,' Jimmy said. 'Just paying what I owe you for ruining your dinner.'

The man looked at him, clearly wondering what the catch was.

'I'm not giving you a blow job,' he said.

Jimmy laughed. 'That's a relief,' he replied and put the sandwich on the floor next to the old man who looked at it for a moment then snaffled it up.

Behind the man Jimmy could see a commotion at the far end of the subway; whatever it was it caused a ripple effect, like a Mexican wave. People jumped up, either to see what was going on or to pack their stuff away. He saw a sleeping bag thrown through the air and then caught a glimpse of a big man moving through the subway; people scattering in front of him. As the man got closer, Jimmy could see it was the big cop from Leazes Park: Duke, the one who'd also threatened him in the cell, though this time he was in plain clothes. Bloody Collins must have reported him after all. He started to pack his stuff back into his rucksack. A shout echoed through the subway.

'Out of the way.'

He looked up. Duke had seen him and was pushing through the crowd, shoving people out of his path. Jimmy finished packing and went to grab Dog, but the stupid mutt had run towards the danger and was barking at the noise in front of him. He dashed over and picked Dog up just as

Duke broke through the crowd. The big cop lunged at him, grabbing a fistful of his sleeve, pulling Jimmy towards him.

'Gotcha,' Duke shouted, just as a shopping trolley smashed into his legs. He yelled with pain and crashed to the floor, his chin catching the edge of the trolley on the way down, blood spurting into the air. The toothless old man grinned at Jimmy.

'I divvn't like you much but I hate pigs even more,' he said. 'You'd better get on your toes, son.'

Jimmy quickly threw his rucksack over his shoulder and legged it out of the other end of the subway as fast as he could, still carrying Dog and heading to fuck-knows-where.

39

HMP Durham, 1995

The psychologist is reading through some notes as Jimmy is escorted into the office. He's younger than Jimmy expected, with neatly cropped hair and glasses like the ones John Lennon used to wear. He's wearing an open-necked shirt – no tie: his sign that he's not part of the system, Jimmy suspects. The screw sits Jimmy down and goes to stand at the back of the room.

'You can wait outside,' the psychologist says, putting the notes down.

'You sure?' the screw says.

'Yes, I'll be fine. We'll be fine, won't we, Jimmy?' he says, smiling.

Jimmy thinks about leaping over the desk and grabbing him around the throat but it's only a joke thought, he wouldn't do it really. Not today.

'Aye,' Jimmy says. 'We will.'

The screw seems a little unsure but then shrugs.

'On your own head,' he says. 'I'll be right outside, just in case.'

Once they're alone, the psychologist leans back in his chair and makes a little steeple with his hands, putting the tip of the spire against his lips.

'How are you feeling today, Jimmy?' he says, eventually, moving his hands back down and picking up his notes again, obscuring his face as he scans them.

'Top of the world,' Jimmy says.

The psychologist lowers his notes. 'Really?'

'No.'

'Why say it then?'

'Don't know. Just messin'.'

'Do you do that a lot?'

'What?'

'Act on instinct . . . say the first thing that comes into your head.'

'It wasn't the first thing, just the funniest.'

The steeple is back now. Jimmy wonders if they teach it at psychologist school, imagines him practising it in a mirror.

'And how are you feeling really?' the psychologist says eventually.

'Shitty.'

'Really?'

That's obviously his default question. Jimmy thinks about it for a moment.

'Yes, pretty much.'

'Why's that?'

'My wife has left me for another man. I haven't seen my

daughter in ages and can't imagine ever seeing her again. I've messed up everything I've ever tried to do. I couldn't even commit suicide properly.' Jimmy scratches his head. 'I'm sure there was something else . . . oh, yeah, I just murdered a man.'

'Murdered?'

'I smashed his brains out with a fire extinguisher. What would you call it?'

'I don't know. I'm a psychologist, not a lawyer. I'm just here to establish your state of mind. Your actual lawyer thinks it might help you.'

'I'm not mental.'

'That's not a term I like to use.'

Jimmy laughs.

'Sorry. I'm old school, Doctor, you know, nuthouses, loony bins and all that.'

The psychologist looks pleased for some reason. Given his age, Jimmy wonders if he's newly qualified, still getting a kick out of being called 'Doctor'.

'Tell me a bit about the attempted suicide.'

'It didn't work.'

'And are you glad about that?'

Is he? Jimmy's not sure. For the first time he doesn't have a glib answer. Maybe everything happens for a reason? If he hadn't completely screwed up killing himself, then it's highly likely the nurse and probably the screw would be dead now – maybe God had done some kind of weird, arse-about-face, two-for-one deal.

'I haven't decided yet,' he says.

'I see you were medically discharged from the Royal Navy?'

Jimmy's on the back foot now. Where's he going with this?

'Yes,' he says, hesitantly.

'After serving in the Falklands War.'

It's not a question, the man's reading through the notes, his face again hidden as he speaks, so Jimmy says nothing. He lowers the notes again.

'What happened out there?'

'What's that got to do with the price of fish?'

'I don't know yet. Maybe if you gave me some of the details.'

'Why? So you can get off on them?'

'Of course not. It would help me make an assessment though. And perhaps give you some kind of closure.'

'Which bit of "I'm not mental" didn't you get?' Jimmy doesn't know why he's happier being known as a killer than a crackpot; he just is.

The psychologist grimaces. 'Behaviour generally has causes; I'm just trying to establish what yours might be.'

'Have you ever been to war?'

'What?'

'Ever seen anyone blown up, shot . . . set on fire?'

'No.'

'Then what the fuck would you know about it?'

Jimmy stands behind a clear screen in the dock of the small courtroom. It's different to last time; then he was pleading not guilty, there was a jury watching his every move. This time there are far fewer eyes on him.

He wrote to Bev begging her not to come; she probably wouldn't have anyway, but he didn't want her here. There is only one person in the public gallery, a fresh-faced, fair-haired boy. Jimmy wonders if he's lied about his age because he asked his brief and you have to be eighteen to come on your own, over fourteen if you're with an adult. He'd been worried that Bev might bring Kate and was pleased to hear that she was way too young to be there; to hear and see what he'd done. Jimmy glances across at the boy. He is sitting right at the front of the gallery, leaning on a rail, staring directly at Jimmy, as he has been since he entered the courtroom.

The judge, who has been waiting for the rest of the court to settle down following the submissions from the prosecution and defence briefs, finally looks up.

'James Ian Mullen, the law requires me to impose a life sentence on you for the murder of Gregor Wilkinson. However, it is also my duty to recommend the minimum number of years you must serve before being considered for parole. I have heard the submissions from Mr Hearn, for the prosecution, who has emphasised the brutal nature of this murder and, having seen first-hand the CCTV evidence I can only concur with his argument that this was a particularly violent attack, clearly using unreasonable force. However, I have also read the statement from the witness to the attack, Mr Neil Hardy, who was in fear for his life until your intervention and the character reference from Mr Mark Harris, the prison officer. The defence counsel, Miss Monroe, has pointed to your guilty plea, and for that the court commends you, and she has also highlighted your service to your country, which I also commend. It is unfortunate, I believe, that you opted out of a proper psychiatric examination, as I can only think this would have been to your benefit. However, given the lack of medical support for Miss Monroe's supposition that you were mentally unhinged at the time of the attack, I cannot give any credence to this particular plea for mitigation. I therefore recommend that you serve a minimum of fifteen years.'

'Fifteen fucking years!'

Jimmy looks across to the public gallery where the shout came from. The boy is standing up, looking as if he might leap over the rail.

'That's no' right, he killed my dad,' the boy yells.

The judge is banging his gavel and shouting for order. The clerk of the court runs towards the public gallery and a policeman is heading the same way from the back of the room. The boy is pointing at Jimmy now.

'I'll be waiting for you,' the boy shouts as the policeman finally reaches him, pulling him out of the gallery and through the doors at the back.

'Get off me, you bastard,' is the last thing Jimmy hears as the doors shut behind them.

His brief looks over to him and nods. She'd pissed him off by sending him to the baby psychologist, trying to make out he was mad, but it could have been worse. He'd expected to get at least twenty years as a minimum. Jimmy revises the maths in his head. By the time he gets out Kate will be twenty-four. He wonders if he will see her before then. Probably not, he thinks, given that he writes to her every week and has never received a reply. He sits down and stares at his blurred reflection in the Perspex screen and for the first time realises that he's crying.

40

National Probation Service, Newcastle, July 13, 2012

Jimmy sat sweating in the reception area. Sandy was running late; probably organising an escort to take him to prison.

If Burns reported him, Sandy would have little choice but to recommend sending him back inside. He'd breached most of his licence conditions in the last few days. Arrested for theft. Suspected of murder. Not to mention taking a JCB without consent. She wouldn't need to give him a second yellow card, she could just go straight to red.

At least he'd managed to clean himself up in the washroom while he waited. The mud on his coat from the JCB's bucket had taken some shifting but he didn't want to give her any reason to question him any more than she usually did.

Sandy's door opened and she beckoned him in. He closed the door behind him. Dog headed straight under her desk where, as usual, she'd left a small pile of dog biscuits.

'Good boy,' she said, clearly not talking to Jimmy.

She lit a cigarette and sat on a chair next to an open window, so she could blow the smoke straight outside.

'It's demeaning having to do this, isn't it?' she said. 'Tried to explain that it was only me and some ex-cons who would get cancer, but they wouldn't listen.'

'Nobody ever does,' Jimmy said.

'Damned right. Apart from me, of course – what I'm here for. You keeping out of trouble?'

He nodded; waited for her to start talking about honesty again.

'They caught your guy yet?'

'No.'

'That's a shame. No one likes to see violent criminals roaming around on the street.'

He nodded but then wondered if she meant him. Somehow Sandy always managed to put him on the back foot.

'Any suspects?'

'One or two.' The police had one; he had two. Or maybe three if he counted Martin Weston.

'I hope they're looking after you. Their star witness.' She threw the cigarette out of the window, moved her chair opposite him and gave him her full attention. It was like being trapped in the beam of a prison-yard searchlight.

'Trouble is, Jimmy, I've been sent a note.'

'A note?'

'Says you're not a witness. Says you're a suspect.'

He held his breath and her gaze at the same time; tried desperately not to blink. Fucking Burns.

'You know what the problem with that is?' she said.

He did.

'The problem is it's anonymous . . .'

Not quite what he was thinking. Not Burns then. He would have made it official. Who else wanted him out of the way?

'. . . and I don't do anonymous. Could be anyone, couldn't it? Some gadgee you pushed in front of in the dinner queue. Some ex-con with a grudge. A rogue cop who remembers you from back in the day. Any number of possibilities. You're not shagging someone's missus, are you?'

'No.'

'Not that then . . . Any truth in it?'

Jimmy thought about lying, by omission at least. But he didn't. He told her almost everything – from nearly being run over to the dead cat, from Goldilocks to the planted lighter. Sandy didn't take her eyes off him for a moment; didn't react at all until he'd finished. Then she lit another cigarette, not even moving to the window this time.

'You have been busy,' she said. 'What happened to "Not my fight"?'

He'd been wondering about that himself.

She shook her head. 'I can't decide if you're stupid or just plain unlucky.'

She picked up a pen. A make-or-break moment. Jimmy held his breath.

'Just be careful. You got that address for me?'

He exhaled; told her he was staying with Carrie.

'Providing comfort to a pretty young woman? You sure that's wise?'

'It's not like that.'

Sandy looked him up and down.

'Now that I do believe. Even I wouldn't and it's been a while.'

She looked down at the address she'd scribbled on her pad.

'And she knows about this, does she, this Carrie?'

'Yes,' he lied.

Jimmy flinched at the explosion behind him. He turned to see a cloud of steam blowing out of the coffee machine as the lad behind the counter fiddled frantically with one of the switches. Eventually he found the right one and the loud hissing died down.

'Sorry about that,' the lad said. 'I'm new here.'

Jimmy picked up his glass of water and turned back to watch the early-morning shoppers passing by outside. Where was she?

Dog was sound asleep at his feet, oblivious to the noise around him. The poor creature wasn't getting any younger and they'd been walking around all night, after leaving the subway – Jimmy too restless to sleep, churning shit over in his mind, worrying about the meeting with Sandy.

After he'd left the Probation Office, he'd tried to find Carrie, wanting to make peace and ask her, no, beg her, to tell Sandy he was staying with her – even though he had no intention of actually doing that. He'd trekked to her flat, but she wasn't there. He'd try again later, but in the meantime, he needed to do something to get back into her good books.

Something that would help them discover what had really happened to her dad. He still wanted to find out more about Norma Weston's husband, Martin, but wasn't sure where to start. Ed Collins was different though; he knew exactly where to find him – him and his thuggish blond friend, perhaps.

The café door opened and a large policeman walked in. He flinched, thinking it was Duke, but then realised it was just another in a long line of well-built coppers. Even so, he turned his head away, just in case, pretended he was reading the paper. He stared at the headline 'City prepares for the Queen'. He glanced at the story below. The royal visit was just over a week away. Maybe that was it? Maybe Roger had discovered that Collins and Lang were planning an assassination attempt on the Queen and they'd killed him to keep him quiet. And now Jimmy was going to save the day, rescue Her Majesty from the treasonous plotters and get knighted for his services to the country. Arise, Sir Jimmy.

Get a fucking grip, he thought. You need some sleep.

'Hey!'

He looked up. The policeman was standing right in front of him. Jimmy started to reach for his rucksack, eyeing the door. Then he realised he was holding out a cup of coffee.

'Thought you might fancy a hot drink.'

Jimmy nodded.

'Thanks. That's good of you.'

'Least I can do,' the cop said. 'Look after yourself.'

Jimmy watched him carefully as he headed for the door, just in case it was a trick – so carefully that he almost missed the main event: Julie was outside, putting a pile of *Big Issue* magazines down on the pavement. He took a big glug of coffee, gave Dog a nudge with his foot and picked up a paper bag from the table in front of him.

The sun had shifted since he'd gone into the café and it was much warmer than an hour earlier. Julie's pitch was bathed in sunshine and she was wearing mirrored sunglasses, which was a shame, as he would have liked to have seen her eyes again. She was holding a pile of magazines in one hand, hopping around restlessly from foot to foot, buzzing with energy, a new dawn, a new day and all that. As soon as she saw him she smiled.

'Morning, handsome,' she said, eyeing the bag. 'That for me?'

Jimmy nodded.

'Hope it's gluten-free.'

'Oh,' he said. 'I didn't know ... I'll um, see if I can change—'

'Don't be daft, you divvy, I'm just winding you up. I'll eat owt, me.' She took the bag and looked inside. 'Yum, blueberry, my favourite.'

'I need a favour,' Jimmy said.

'And there was me thinking this was a love token.'

He could feel himself blushing. Tried to stop it, which just made it worse.

'Well? Out with it. You can't just stand there gawping, you'll frighten my customers away.'

'Would you look after Dog?'

'How long for?'

'Not sure. Couple of hours, maybe? Might be a bit longer.'

She took a bite of the muffin as she considered his request. He wouldn't have asked her, but Dog was knackered and he had places to go. Carrie had disappeared and Deano and Gadge wouldn't be up for hours.

'Why not?' she said eventually, ripping the remainder of the muffin in half and dropping it on the pavement where it was swallowed up by a grateful Dog.

'Thanks,' Jimmy said, turning to go. 'I owe you.'

'Yeah. Next time I want dinner,' she said.

Jimmy sat on a wall opposite the entrance to Collins' yard, partially hidden by the overhanging branches of the trees behind him. Above his head he could hear the traffic rumbling over Byker Bridge.

Surveillance was one of the few things he hadn't been trained in – there was nowhere to hide on one of Her Majesty's Ships – but he'd watched enough cop shows to know the basics. Familiarity with the neighbourhood? Check. A good vantage point? Check. A bottle to piss in? Nobody's perfect.

The yard gates were locked but the developer had offices in the building next to it, and that was open for business. Jimmy had been there for hours, seen several people come and go, recognised none of them. Collins wasn't the only occupant of the building. There were half a dozen other companies based there according to a sign outside. He'd wandered over to the door, but it was keypad controlled. And the woman at the small reception desk inside the foyer had waved him away when he'd knocked. He wished he'd brought some food, but more urgent than that the lack of a piss-bottle had come back to bite him; he badly needed a quick wazz.

He thought about sneaking into one of the nearby pubs but didn't want to take the risk of missing Collins, so instead lowered himself behind the wall among the trees. He found a handy spot, out of sight of the road and far enough away from the footpath on the other side of the trees, and unzipped, sighing with relief as he emptied his bursting bladder.

A branch snapped behind him.

Fuck, he thought, desperately trying to glance around and finish what he was doing at the same time, without pissing on his feet. He couldn't see anything, but the fear seemed to make him dry up anyway.

He tucked himself away and was doing his zip up when he felt something press up against the back of his neck. Something cold, hard and metallic. Something like a gun.

'Bang,' a voice whispered.

Jimmy froze.

'Just put your hands behind your head and turn around very slowly,' the voice said, recognisably male now, with a slight Scottish lilt. Jimmy did as he was told, sensing the gunman moving back at the same time, out of his reach.

Jimmy could feel his mouth drying up, his hands going cold, like his body was preparing to close down. It was the blond guy. He still had no idea who he was, though he'd definitely seen him before, firstly standing outside the Pit Stop and latterly at the building site – the builder with the baseball cap. He was pretty certain he was the car driver too. The spiky blond hair was a giveaway, though he had never been close enough before to register the thin scar that ran down the left side of the man's face from just below his eye to his chin, or the fading black eye – the latter Carrie's handiwork he guessed.

'There's no need for this,' Jimmy said. 'I just want to talk to Collins.'

'Collins can fuck off, you're mine. I've waited a long time for this,' the man said.

Jimmy looked at him blankly, needing more, hoping his ignorance might buy him some time. If he wasn't doing this for Collins, then who?

'You haven't a clue who I am, have you?' the man added, grinning. His teeth were as bad as the old man's from the subway, all of them stained, one or two missing.

The man's accent sounded familiar somehow. Jimmy looked closely at him again. Nothing at first; then a glimmer of an idea.

'Maybe I should beat you to death instead, see if that jogs your memory,' the man said and finally Jimmy knew.

'You're Wilkinson's kid,' he said, remembering the young boy from the public gallery all those years ago, recognising in him the same nervous, violent energy he'd seen in his father – like human nitroglycerin.

'And you're a murdering cunt,' Wilkinson said, suddenly smashing Jimmy in the side of the head with his gun.

Jimmy fell to his knees, holding his head, closing his eyes to stop the trees spinning around him.

'I told you I'd wait for you,' Wilkinson said.

Jimmy kept his head down, still trying to clear his vision.

'Been looking for you since you got out. Guessed you might head back to Newcastle eventually.'

Keep him talking, Jimmy thought. If he's anything like his dad, he'll like to talk, and when he's talking he won't shoot.

'Nice shiner you've got there.'

'Shut the fuck up.'

'Anyone I know give you that?'

Wilkinson kicked him in the stomach. Jimmy doubled over, could feel the coffee in his throat. He took a couple of deep breaths and pulled himself back up, needed to keep talking.

'I saw you outside the Pit Stop.'

'So fuckin' what?'

'How did you find me?' Jimmy said.

'Helps when you get your picture in the paper, ya fuckin' numpty.'

'Took you long enough to do anything about it.'

'Nine fuckin' lives, youse.'

'Like that poor cat.'

Wilkinson looked bemused.

'What fuckin' cat? I should've got you with the car. Did get you once. Turned out not to be you.'

'What?' Jimmy said, looking up, his turn to be confused.

'That's the burning question, eh?' Wilkinson said, his grin widening.

Goldilocks. It was Wilkinson. Not the bricklayer. Nothing

to do with Carrie's dad. Just the past coming back, like it always did. He should have guessed from the way the poor bastard died. Like father, like son where fire was concerned.

'You're a sick bastard,' Jimmy said.

'Takes one to know one,' Wilkinson said. 'Couldn't believe it when you turned up on the site, causing bother. I'd thought you were dead. Couldn't get you there though, too many witnesses. But I'm no' stupid, knew it wouldn't be long before you came sniffing around the boss's office next. Just had to be patient. Been waiting long enough for this, another day or two was no bother.'

Wilkinson stepped forward and pointed the gun right at the middle of Jimmy's face, just inches away from his nose.

'Pray for forgiveness, you filthy bastard.'

Jimmy closed his eyes and waited to die.

A dog barked close by. Jimmy pictured Dog pricking his ears up at the snap of a branch a mile away, sprinting off from Julie's pitch. Her shouting after him, wondering what was going on. Dog charging up the steps near the Blue Carpet, dashing over the flyover and back down again, really picking up speed. Barking loudly, dog-speak for 'Must save my master'. Flying along New Bridge Street, just like fucking Lassie, heading towards Byker Bridge, but veering off to the right at the last minute, down Stepney Bank, getting so close he could smell Jimmy's fear. Jumping over a stile, into the trees, seeing the man with the gun, leaping up, his teeth gripping the man's arm, ripping his jacket to shreds. The gun going flying . . .

Another bark. Jimmy opened his eyes. Not Dog. A small

Scottish terrier had appeared just behind Wilkinson. It stopped a yard or so away and crapped on the ground. Wilkinson glanced behind him, distracted. The terrier growled.

'Piss off,' Wilkinson said, trying to kick the dog but missing.

'Scotty,' a woman shouted. Not too far away. 'Scotty!'

The dog ignored her, and moved off to one side, giving Wilkinson a wide berth but staying in the trees, sniffing around for food.

'Come out, Scotty.' Her voice closer still.

Wilkinson put his gun down to his side and moved behind Jimmy.

'Stand up. Don't speak,' he said.

Jimmy did as he was told, grateful for the temporary reprieve. Wilkinson pushed the gun into his back, near the base of his spine.

'Make a move and I'll kill you and the woman.'

There was a rustling in the branches in front of them and an elderly woman appeared, late seventies, early eighties maybe. Despite the hot sun she had a striped woollen hat on and a big winter coat.

'There you are, you naughty boy,' she said. She picked the dog up, but as she did, she suddenly seemed to realise she wasn't alone and looked across to where the two men were standing, close together.

'Oh,' she said, her eyes flicking from Jimmy to Wilkinson and back again. She started to blush. 'I didn't mean . . . I'm sorry . . . come on, Scotty.'

She turned and headed back through the trees, towards the path, muttering to the dog as she went.

'She thought you were gay,' Jimmy said.

'Fuck right off,' Wilkinson said, jabbing the gun hard into his spine. Jimmy could tell he'd touched a nerve. He remembered the bastard's dad taunting that poor nurse, would bet that homophobia was another family trait.

'Just like your dad,' he added, seeing if he could press a few more of the kid's buttons, make him lose his focus completely.

Wilkinson shoved him to the ground.

'You're a fuckin' dead man,' he yelled, raising the gun.

'Too bad there's a witness now,' Jimmy said, keeping his eyes fixed on Wilkinson. 'She'll not forget you easily, that scar's a bit of a giveaway.'

Wilkinson glanced towards the path then shook his head.

'She'll no' remember me. She was fuckin' ancient; I doubt she knows her own name.'

'Hell of a chance to take,' Jimmy said.

Wilkinson looked back towards the path. Jimmy edged closer to him, shuffling on his back, getting ready to push him completely over the edge.

'*You'll* be in the paper this time. "Gay Lovers' Tragic Tiff." Your dad would be so proud.'

'Stop fuckin' talking about my da,' Wilkinson screamed, turning the gun back on Jimmy. One more nudge would do it.

'He was as bent as a nine-bob note, you know? Used to dish out blow jobs for chocolate,' Jimmy said.

Wilkinson was ranting incoherently now, his eyes popping with fury, spit flying all over the place. Eventually he found some words.

'You're f-fuckin' dead!' he yelled, leaning in close to Jimmy and pointing the gun in his face to make doubly sure he didn't miss.

Jimmy hurled a handful of dog shit into Wilkinson's eyes and, in the same movement, kicked his legs from under him. The gun flew out of his hand into the undergrowth.

'Bastard,' Wilkinson screamed, frantically wiping dog shit from his eyes.

Jimmy hurled himself at the blinded man and kneed him viciously in the balls, wiping more dog shit in his face as Wilkinson moved his hands down for protection. Then he climbed to his feet and kicked him once, twice, three times, Wilkinson curling up in a ball to protect himself. Jimmy looked around for the gun but couldn't see it anywhere. He gave him another firm kick in the stomach, turned and ran.

Jimmy exploded out of the trees and onto the path. He could see the old woman and her dog off to his left, heading back up towards Byker, so he turned and ran the other way, in the direction of the river, not wanting to drag her into trouble should Wilkinson try to follow him. As the path joined up with a small road, near a riding paddock, he glanced back. There was no sign of Wilkinson. He kept going, running along the road until it met a small towpath that ran behind some old industrial buildings alongside the Ouseburn River. Jimmy was starting to pant, unused to exercise; his injured leg was giving him some gyp – kicking lumps out of Wilkinson hadn't helped. He could see some children reading in a room at the back of one of the buildings. As he passed, one of them waved to him and he heard something ping off the railing beside him. Then he heard the gunshot. He glanced back. Wilkinson was standing on the small footbridge, fifty yards away, aiming the gun at him. Another bullet pinged off the railing. Jimmy turned and ran, doubling his efforts, heading around a bend and momentarily out of Wilkinson's sight. He dashed up some steps and across a road, narrowly missing a builder's van that swerved to avoid him, its horn blaring at him as he reached the other side. He glanced back again just as Wilkinson appeared on the lower path. Jimmy ducked and ran as the man fired off another shot, turning left down a smaller road. To his left he could see the river running down to the Tyne and in front of him the Toffee Factory, a brand-new building that he'd watched going up over the last few months. A sharp pain shot through his leg. Not a bullet though, no blood. A muscle tear. He slowed to a walk, couldn't run any further. To his right, a small group of people in hard hats were gathered in front of the entrance to the Victoria Tunnel. He'd forgotten it started there.

Gadge had dragged him to see it a couple of months back, banging on about how you had to know your history. The tunnel had originally been built to transport coal from the north of the city down to the river but had then lain dormant for years, until it was put to use as an air-raid shelter in World War II. Now it was a tourist attraction. And a hiding place where he could lie low until Wilkinson was long gone.

A guide was giving the group a briefing by a large information board.

'. . . the German planes used to pass over Newcastle on their way back across the North Sea to their airfields in occupied Denmark. Unfortunately, that meant that if they had any bombs left, they'd dump them on the poor Geordies doon below.'

Jimmy waited until the guide was distracted by a question, sneaked past the group and went into the unguarded entrance.

As he entered, he grabbed a large flashlight and a hard hat from a table on the left. He remembered that it was not only dark – the interior lighting not running all the way along – but also that the roof was very low in places. Jimmy was fastening his hard hat when he heard a shout from outside. The guide had turned to escort the group inside and seen him lingering by the table.

'Hey!' the guide shouted again.

Jimmy turned and headed into the tunnel proper, ignoring the pain in his leg and the shouts behind him. He couldn't ignore the gunshot though. Or the woman screaming. Wilkinson had caught up with him.

He splashed through some puddles, switching the flashlight on and moving as quickly as his leg allowed him. There was a small trail of lights on the floor, but he knew they didn't last long. Fuck, he thought. He'd made a trap for himself; one way in, one way out.

Then he remembered. Not one way out – two. At the end of the tunnel the tour guide had shown them one of the original entrances – now an escape hatch. He just had to make it there – half a mile maybe.

Behind him Jimmy could still hear faint screaming but nothing else. Maybe Wilkinson hadn't come into the tunnel? He wasn't going to stop to find out. The flashlight picked out one of the blast walls fifty yards in front of him. They'd put them up at regular intervals when they'd turned it into a shelter to try and contain bomb damage to small sections: two walls, one jutting out from the left-hand side for about two-thirds the width of the tunnel, then a second, a yard or so behind, jutting out from the right-hand wall to create a chicane effect.

Jimmy dodged through the first chicane and ploughed on, the flashlight taking over as the internal lights stopped. On one side of the tunnel were a series of small benches where people – including his grandparents – had sat during the air raids, probably even more frightened than he was now. He stopped for a moment, listening out for someone behind him. Nothing. He started to move off but then stopped again as he heard a noise. Footsteps, splashing quickly through the puddles behind him, but with the noise ricocheting in the narrow tunnel there was no telling how far away. Jimmy took off again, negotiating another blast wall chicane, his head clipping off the roof which had suddenly dropped several inches. Thank Christ he'd put the hard hat on. Hoped Wilkinson hadn't done the same. He crouched lower as he hobbled on as fast as his leg would carry him, passing a steel bucket – a toilet in the air-raid shelter days – which he pulled into the middle of the tunnel.

His flashlight picked out the next blast wall, about fifty yards ahead. A piece of the tunnel wall to his right flew into the air and he heard a gunshot. Shit. He tried to pick up speed but knew he was never going to get to the escape hatch before Wilkinson caught him. He slowed again, listening carefully. The footsteps were definitely louder. Then they stopped. Jimmy looked back down the tunnel. It was pitch black. He guessed that Wilkinson hadn't stopped to pick up a flashlight.

He heard a slight buzzing sound and then another gunshot as something tore through his upper arm. He'd been hit; no idea how badly, but it hurt like hell and he could feel blood leaking through the rip in his coat. He turned and limped towards the blast wall. From behind him came a clang of metal on brick and a yell of pain; the bucket had done its trick. It wouldn't kill Wilkinson, but it might slow him down.

Jimmy reached the chicane wall. He tried to shine the flashlight on his wounded arm but all he could see was blood; didn't have time to inspect the damage. He couldn't outrun Wilkinson; he was going to have to fight him. With one good arm and one good leg, the odds weren't great. He turned off the flashlight and placed it on the ground a couple of feet in front of the first blast wall, then hid himself out of sight behind the wall. He could now hear the footsteps getting nearer, splashing through the groundwater, getting louder. He waited, hoping the flashlight was bulky enough to do its work. If not, he was done.

There was a loud yell followed immediately by a huge

thud as Wilkinson crashed into the wall, so hard that Jimmy could feel the vibrations on the other side. He waited. Silence. Slowly he edged around it. There was a dark shape on the ground, a body, face down. Jimmy knelt down and turned it over. Wilkinson. He could feel his chest moving slightly; unconscious, not dead. He scrambled around and found the flashlight in the gutter on the right-hand side. He turned it on and shone the beam at Wilkinson, grateful that it was still working. Wilkinson's face was covered in blood. The flashlight had done its job, sending him flying head first into the wall as Jimmy had hoped.

The gun was lying on the floor a few feet away from the body. Jimmy put the flashlight down and picked the gun up, using his sleeve to avoid getting his fingerprints on it. He emptied out the remaining bullets, hurling them and the gun back into the pitch-black tunnel.

He picked up the flashlight, felt the heft of it, heavy enough to put the sick bastard out of his misery. Wilkinson wasn't going anywhere soon, but there was no point in taking any chances. Jimmy walked back towards the prone body and lifted up the flashlight.

You wouldn't stop hitting him . . . I was shouting and screaming at you, but you just wouldn't stop.

Jimmy blinked. He'd done enough damage for one lifetime. He lowered the flashlight and limped off, moving past the chicane and on towards the safety of the escape hatch.

41

Grainger Towers, Fenham, Newcastle, July 13, 2012

The lift was out of order. Jimmy limped up the stairs, leaving a trail of blood like the breadcrumbs in a fairy tale. If anyone else was looking for him, he wouldn't be hard to find. He'd already had a scare outside. As he approached the flats, he had seen a woman sitting in her car, right outside the entrance, staring at the doors. His first thought: plainclothes policewoman. But as he was thinking about what to do next, she had driven off.

By the time he reached the sixth floor he was exhausted and light-headed. He leaned against the banister for a few moments to try and regain some strength. Eventually he moved off again, along the corridor, to the flat. He tapped on the door, gently at first, but then, when no one answered, a little more urgently. He heard a sound from inside the flat, a door opening, then footsteps.

'Who is it?' Carrie said, from the other side of the door.

'It's me, Jimmy.'

'It's late.'

'I need your help,' he said. Silence.

'Please,' he said. Another noise. The chain going on, a key rattling in the lock.

Jimmy slumped against the wall on the other side of the corridor.

The door started to open and he caught a glimpse of Carrie standing there, baseball bat dangling down by her side.

'Burns told me to call him if you—' she stopped, suddenly aware that Jimmy was sitting on the floor, blood dripping from his arm.

'Jesus Christ. What happened?'

'I've been shot.'

She stared at him, open-mouthed, then shut the door. Jimmy waited. He heard the chain coming off and the door opened again, fully this time. Carrie came out and helped him up and into the flat.

'Jesus, Jimmy, you stink.' He'd tried to wipe the dog shit away on some grass, hadn't completely succeeded.

'We need to get you cleaned up,' she said. She led him over to the bathroom.

'Is this anything to do with Dad?' she said.

'No.'

'What then?'

'Someone from my past . . . it's a long story.'

'You can tell me once I've had a look at your arm. But first wash your hands.'

She disappeared into the kitchen. He could hear her opening drawers and cupboards.

Jimmy scrubbed his hands, practically taking the skin off. Once he'd finished, he had to clean the sink. Eventually Carrie emerged from the kitchen with an armful of dressings and a bowl of warm water. She helped him take his jacket off and then slowly removed his shirt, leaving the damaged arm till last, easing the ripped sleeve from the bleeding wound. Jimmy winced as she pulled the last piece of cloth – and a fair amount of skin – away.

Carrie gently wiped the blood with a damp cloth, examining the damage to his arm.

'You were lucky,' she said. 'It's just nicked your upper arm, a flesh wound, no permanent damage. Probably leave a nasty scar though.' She ripped open a clean dressing and placed it over the wound, pressing down firmly before taping it in place.

'You going to tell me what happened then?'

Jimmy hesitated, reluctant to drag her fully into his world.

'You don't want to know,' he said.

She sighed. 'I need you to be honest with me, Jimmy; if you'd been honest with me before, I might have been prepared for what Burns told me.'

'What did he tell you?'

'That you beat another prisoner to death with your bare hands.'

Not exactly, he thought. Jimmy closed his eyes, saw the extinguisher, covered in blood and bits of bone and hair. He opened them again, tried to keep her gaze, hoped that she could see him for what he really was.

'Wilkinson – the man I killed – he was a monster, Carrie.

He'd raped and strangled three women, he was going to set fire to the prison nurse.'

It was no excuse for what he'd done, how he'd done it. He knew that. The judge and Burns knew that. And now Carrie knew too.

'I know,' she said. 'I've been reading about it on the Internet. I should have given you a chance to explain before. I'm sorry. When Burns told me what you'd done, and about the lighter, I should have asked more questions. You deserved better.'

'I swear I'd never seen that lighter before,' he said. 'I have no idea how it got into my rucksack.'

She looked at him for a moment, hesitated, then nodded. 'I believe you.'

This wasn't going how Jimmy had expected it to; he'd been preparing his own apology for not being completely honest with her. If he deserved better, she deserved the truth this time.

'It was Wilkinson's son who shot me,' Jimmy said. 'He was the one who set Goldilocks on fire too. And it was him who tried to run me over.

Carrie gasped.

'The man who attacked me in the car park?' she asked, shaking now.

Jimmy nodded.

'You gave him a black eye.'

'Where is he now?' she said. He could see the real question in her eyes: *Did you kill him too?* She looked much younger than her twenty-two years; scared and vulnerable.

'He was chasing me and he hurt himself, ran into a wall, knocked himself out. He'll be fine. I'd imagine the police have got him now.'

He'd heard the sirens as he came out of the escape hatch, no doubt called by someone in the tour group after the shooting started. Even if Wilkinson had come to, he couldn't have got out the same way he had; ignoring the pain from his injured arm, Jimmy had managed to wheel a full, industrial-sized rubbish bin out of a nearby back alley and left it over the hatch. No way out.

A look of relief flashed across Carrie's face, but then her brow furrowed.

'What are you going to do now?' she said.

'What do you mean?'

'Well, you thought that people were after you because of what you'd seen with my dad, but that wasn't true, was it? It must have been Wilkinson's son. It was nothing to do with what you saw. My problems and your problems don't have anything to do with each other.'

In some ways she was right. Maybe he could just walk away. Leave it all behind; better for him, certainly. However, it wasn't Wilkinson who'd planted that lighter in his bag. Or killed that cat – the gobshite clearly hadn't known what he was talking about. Whichever way you looked at it there was still someone else out there who wanted to cause him harm.

And it was by no means one-way traffic.

'I brought Wilkinson to your door. He only tried to grab you to get to me. If anything, I owe you.'

'Burns thinks you're dangerous.'

'But what about you? What do you think?'

Carrie held his gaze while Jimmy held his breath.

'I don't believe you would hurt me.'

He exhaled, relief flooding through his veins.

'Thank you.' He stood up. 'And thanks for the treatment.'

She smiled. 'Any time you get shot again you know where I am.'

'I should get going,' he said, but suddenly felt dizzy, stumbled, started to fall. She caught him on his way down.

'When's the last time you slept?' she said.

He tried to work it out. Not the previous night. Once he'd left the subway, he'd walked the streets, trying to think stuff through. Not the night before either, in the cell.

'It's been a while.'

'You need to rest,' she said.

'I can't stay here again,' Jimmy said.

'Why not?'

'I have nightmares. It can get messy. It's better for me to sleep alone, away from other people. That way they don't hurt anybody but me. That's why I don't stay in hostels. I don't want to be confined, don't want anybody else getting caught up in my horrible fucking nightmares. I thought it might be different by now, but it isn't.'

'You had one the other day, didn't you? I heard you shouting in your sleep. Was that why you left in the middle of the night?'

'Yes, yes, I'm sorry, I didn't know you'd heard me. I didn't mean to scare you. But that's what I mean. I shouldn't have stayed here. I knew it was a mistake, I tried to say.'

Jimmy moved towards the door but stumbled again. Carrie held him up.

'You're not leaving now,' she said. 'If you try and leave, I'll call Burns. Tell him what's happened. He'll be here in a heartbeat and it'll take you ages to get down the stairs in your condition.'

Jimmy hesitated, his hand on the door handle. Carrie had that look on her face. He'd seen it a few times before – the one that told him she wasn't going to budge.

'OK,' Jimmy said. 'But I'm not staying for long. I'll rest for an hour. No more. Deal?'

She didn't look convinced, but eventually conceded defeat.

'Deal,' she said. 'I'll bet you haven't eaten anything either. I'll make you a sandwich.'

She led him to the sofa and sat him down gently before heading into the kitchen.

Jimmy leaned back, rested his head on a cushion and closed his eyes.

'Jimmy. Jimmy.'

He opened his eyes. Flinched. Someone was leaning over him. Carrie.

'Here, I made you a cuppa.'

He shuffled upright. 'What time is it?'

'Just before nine. You've been out for nearly twelve hours.'

He tried to move his arm. Sore, and a bit stiff, but not too bad; it wouldn't slow him down at least. He noticed a plate with a stale-looking sandwich sitting on the desk and smiled – he hadn't even stayed awake long enough to eat it. Carrie sat down next to him.

'Your probation officer rang,' she said.

Shit. He should have told her about that. Getting shot must have scrambled his brains.

'Don't look so worried,' she said. 'I confirmed you were staying here.'

'Thank you. I should have asked you first though.'

'No biggie. How you feeling?'

'Arm's a bit tender but apart from that . . . bit parched.'

She handed him the tea, waiting while he slurped it down. One of her feet was tapping gently on the floorboards and Jimmy could tell she wanted to say something else.

'What is it?'

'Who's Kate Mullen?' she said.

Jimmy could feel his heart racing. Why was Carrie asking about Kate? What had happened?

'She's my daughter.'

'Thought so.'

'Why are you asking me about her?'

'She accepted my friend request on Facebook.'

'Why would you send her a friend request?'

'I didn't. You did.'

Now he was completely lost.

'Did you use my computer when you were staying here?' Carrie asked.

'Yes, I couldn't sleep.'

'You didn't log me out. When you sent her a request you did it from my account. And she accepted. You might want to tell her off about that next time you see her; it's not clever to do that with strangers.'

Jimmy didn't really understand what Carrie was talking about and the possibility of him telling Kate off about anything was so remote that he couldn't begin to imagine what it would be like. He glanced across at the computer as if Kate herself was about to appear there. Somehow it felt like he was edging ever closer to her. A sudden pain from his arm dragged him back into the present.

'Right,' he said. He stood up, needing to stretch his legs, but immediately felt dizzy again.

'You'd better sit down, you look a bit pale,' Carrie said, steering him back down onto the sofa.

'You should eat something.'

Jimmy eyed the untouched sandwich.

'That'll be bone dry now,' she said. 'I'll get you some toast.'

'Could you put the TV on first?' he said. 'They might have something on the news about Wilkinson's kid.'

He sipped his tea as she reached for the remote. First drink he'd had since that nice copper had bought him a coffee the day before; it seemed like a lifetime ago. A newsreader appeared on the screen, a photo of the Queen behind him:

Thousands of people are gathering in Hereford and Worcester today hoping to catch a glimpse of Her Majesty, Queen Elizabeth II as she continues her tour of the UK to celebrate her Diamond Jubilee. She will be visiting the cathedrals in both cities and opening the new Hive library which has just been built on the banks of the River Severn. We'll go over now to Sarah Stone, who has been talking to some of the crowd, many of whom have been queuing overnight.

Carrie turned the volume down. 'The local news'll be up after this probably. I'll get that toast.'

Things were better between them, but it felt like an uneasy truce, every subject a potential minefield: Wilkinson, the lighter, Carrie's dad. He was drinking his tea slowly, mentally rehearsing each word before it left his lips. He sensed that she wanted to talk a bit more about Kate, but he wasn't ready for that. It should have been easier for him to talk about his daughter than for her to talk about her dad, yet she was stronger than him in so many ways.

'What's happening with the CCTV footage they found?' he asked when Carrie brought him the toast.

'I don't know. The man's face wasn't clear on it – the picture was pretty fuzzy, and he had some kind of scarf on which covered the bottom half of his face.'

Jimmy had no memory of a scarf.

'Burns said they were going to check more footage,' she added. 'To see if the man was picked up on any of the other cameras, but he didn't seem to hold out much hope. Too much time has passed.'

'How come they got anything at all?'

'They were lucky. It was a private company. They'd sent someone out to check around the Quayside, just on the off chance, and one of them still had some old tapes they hadn't recorded over.'

His fault. If he'd reported what he'd seen straight away, the footage would have been readily available – as Burns had pointed out.

'I'm sorry,' he said.

Carrie nodded; she obviously knew what he meant. She didn't need to say any more, but she did.

'The police probably wouldn't have done anything anyway,' she said. 'They didn't really believe you when you did go in. They only checked now because they thought it might prove you were involved.'

An olive branch. She was a good kid.

'What else have I missed?' he said.

'Brian rang me yesterday. He couldn't speak for long, said his editor has him on a very short leash. But he's done a bit more digging and reckons Dad was at that fracking meeting in Morpeth as well. He's not certain, but he spoke to someone, a councillor, who thought he remembered him. He's found something else too – guess who's a director of the company applying for the fracking licence?'

It didn't take Jimmy long to come up with a name, there was only one contender really.

'Collins.'

Carrie nodded.

It had to be. Put him right in the frame. Two projects and Carrie's dad was trying to stand in the way of both of them. Two reasons to get him moved out of the way. And like Brian said, the man was a builder; he knew plenty of bricklayers. And wasn't fussy about their criminal tendencies, if Wilkinson was anything to go by.

Jimmy told her what happened at the building site – just the broad brushstrokes: Lang showing up, Collins threatening him, Wilkinson's brief appearance.

'D'you really think that Collins and Lang have got something to do with my dad disappearing?'

'I don't know, maybe, maybe not. When I first saw Lang there I thought it was something, but the sponsorship thing ... it sounded genuine ... I believed him. And he tried to calm Collins down when he was threatening me.'

'Was he really going to have you beaten up?'

'He might have just been trying to scare me.'

'Because you'd been asking about my dad?'

'Hard to say. I was trespassing. Spying on them.'

'But now you know about the fracking thing as well? It makes more sense, doesn't it? That he'd try and scare you off, stop you digging any deeper.'

He could tell she was grasping for certainty, but he couldn't help her.

'I don't know. It could be something.'

'What do you think we should do?' she said.

He smiled. They were *we* again.

Behind Carrie he saw the images on the screen change. A different newsreader behind a desk, a woman this time. He picked up the remote and turned the volume back up.

A man is seriously ill in hospital following a shootout in the Victoria Tunnel in Newcastle yesterday. The man, believed to be a tour guide, was caught up in a gunfight outside the tunnel.

Not exactly a gunfight, Jimmy thought – there was only one gun.

Witnesses said that two men were seen running into the tunnel and further shots were heard. A man, who it is believed was found unconscious in the tunnel, is helping the police with their enquiries. Another man is believed to have fled the scene. Police are appealing for witnesses. If you were in the area or saw anything suspicious, please ring 0191 498 0999.

In other news, Newcastle is gearing up for the visit next week of Her Majesty, Queen Elizabeth II . . .

Jimmy turned the volume back down.

'It won't take them long to come looking for me, will it?' he said.

'How do you figure that out?'

'Well, as soon as they identify Wilkinson's kid, someone will put two and two together. Burns probably.'

'Did you know he'd shot someone else?'

'No. I heard gunshots and I heard a woman screaming, but I was inside the tunnel by then. I hoped he'd just been trying to scare them.'

'Maybe you should turn yourself in. You didn't do anything, did you?'

Jimmy shook his head. 'They could put me back inside, Carrie. It doesn't look like I've done anything, but they'll not want to take any chances. They'll find something that sounds like a probation violation – "consorting with a known gunman", something like that.'

'Burns isn't as bad as you think, you know.'

'Isn't he?' Jimmy remembered the interrogation, had no doubt the man wanted to fry him then. 'Someone planted that lighter in my rucksack.'

Carrie looked shocked. She obviously hadn't considered it might have been Burns. She shook her head.

'I don't believe he'd do that. He's the only one who seems to care about what happened to my dad. Isn't Norma Weston's husband the most likely candidate for that?'

Jimmy had stopped listening. Behind Carrie he could see a new image on the screen; a huge wooden structure on the edge of a river. He knew it well: Dunston Staiths, built in Victorian times, where the trains used to bring coal to be loaded onto boats and shipped all over the country. Jimmy lived near there as a kid.

But it wasn't the memories that had distracted him. It was something else. It was the boat on the river next to the Staiths and the diver in the water, holding his arm up, signalling to someone on the shoreline. The small crowd gathered on the banks of the Tyne. The police cars behind them, doors open. The white-suited SOCOs – Weston among them probably – searching the riverbank.

'I think we should try and talk to Burns again,' Carrie said. 'Tell him about Collins and—'

'Carrie,' he said. She stopped talking, puzzled.

'What?' she asked.

Jimmy nodded at the TV and turned the volume back up.

. . . It is believed the man's body was dislodged by a fisherman in the early hours of the morning. A police spokesman said that it looked like it had been trapped under the water, between two of the supporting pillars, for several weeks.

42

Newcastle Mortuary, July 14, 2012

Jimmy was used to having flashbacks but this was real.

It was pissing down and he was sitting with Carrie in the back seat of a taxi approaching the mortuary. It was a different taxi this time and there was no sign of Burns, but apart from that nothing had changed. For Carrie's sake, he hoped it would end the same.

They were met inside by a smartly dressed woman carrying a clipboard.

'Are you Carrie Carpenter?'

'Yes,' Carrie said.

'I'm DC Laura Moore, I'm a family liaison officer. Thank you for coming in so quickly.'

'I had to. I wanted to see him.'

Moore frowned and seemed to be about to say something, then hesitated and looked at Jimmy.

'And who's this?'

'A friend,' Carrie said. 'They said I could bring a friend.'

'Of course. That's fine,' Moore said, though her look suggested that she thought Carrie might have found someone a little more presentable. 'They did tell you that you don't have to do this, didn't they?' she asked. 'We're waiting on the dental records; that's all we really need.'

'I want to,' Carrie said. She hesitated. Jimmy had a pretty good idea what she wanted to ask. He was right.

'Do you really think it's my dad?'

'To be honest, pet, I don't know.'

Jimmy didn't think that Moore was going to add anything, but Carrie's face forced the issue; she so obviously needed more.

'Look, Carrie, I wish I could tell you for sure, one way or the other. It would save you from having to do this for a start. All I can tell you is that he's about the right age and height and the clothes, what's left of them, roughly match what we had on the misper report. Until we get the dental records, I can't say any more than that.'

'I'll know,' Carrie said.

Moore looked doubtful. 'I understand that the person who spoke to you on the phone filled you in on the circumstances?'

Carrie nodded. 'They said that the body was dislodged by a fisherman early this morning.'

'That's right. Look, there's no easy way of saying this – the body has been in the water for some time, it's really not a pretty sight.'

Jimmy had tried to persuade Carrie not to come. He had

known that if it was Carrie's dad, it would be a mess. Fish would eat anything.

'I can handle it,' Carrie said.

'Have you ever seen a dead body before?' Moore pressed.

Carrie shook her head; Jimmy wished he could do the same, images of a headless corpse caught in netting flickering behind his eyes. The first of too many.

'How about you?' Moore asked Jimmy.

He nodded. 'I fought in the Falklands War.'

Moore studied him again, like she was recalculating his worth, adding a touch more value.

'Look after her,' she said. 'Follow me.'

She led them through a pair of double doors and down a white-walled corridor to a small waiting room which had four chairs lined up along one of its walls. It smelled of disinfectant and something else . . . death, Jimmy thought. Carrie didn't seem to notice.

'You wait here,' Moore said, indicating the chairs. Carrie sat down, but Jimmy remained standing. Then, pointing to a door, she added, 'I'll go in there and make sure they're ready for you. The body will be on a trolley. It's not like on the telly. The face won't be covered, so you'll see it as soon as you go in. The rest of the body will be covered with a sheet and, if necessary, they can pull that down as well, though I wouldn't advise it. I won't be long.'

She went through the door, leaving them alone. Carrie stared ahead, picking at the skin around her thumbnail.

'You sure you want to do this?' Jimmy said.

'Positive,' she said. 'I need to know.'

'I'm not saying it's definitely him, right, but, if it is, then it's not the way you'll want to remember him,' Jimmy explained. Red's whirling body encased in orange flames spun past his eyes.

'It won't be,' she said.

Moore stuck her head around the door.

'They're ready for you.'

Carrie got up and headed for the door, pausing just as they went through to take hold of Jimmy's arm. Moore led them into the next room and placed them in front of a window. The room behind the window was in darkness, but almost immediately a fluorescent light was turned on and, as it flickered to life, Jimmy saw a trolley in front of the window and an attendant in a medical gown standing next to it. As Moore had explained, the body on the trolley was covered with a sheet up to its neck.

Carrie gasped and Jimmy felt her grip tighten on his arm. The dead man's head was hideously bloated and disfigured. The eyes were completely gone and the ear on the side nearest to them was reduced to a small bit of cartilage, hanging loosely from the side of the head. There was no flesh on the nose or chin and the only cheek they could see was a ragged mess. What skin there was left on the face had a darkish green tinge to it. Surprisingly, the man's hair still seemed relatively normal, long and brown, about shoulder length, a little matted. Jimmy looked automatically for a moustache but there were only gums and teeth where an upper lip should have been.

He felt Carrie's legs go and grabbed her arm to keep her

upright. He turned to look at her. Her eyes were closed, but tears were cascading down her cheeks and she was nodding.

'It's him,' she whispered. 'It's him.'

'How can you be sure?' Moore asked.

'I just know.'

'OK,' Moore said. It was pretty obvious she wasn't convinced, which was understandable – the corpse was barely recognisable as a human, let alone as Roger Carpenter.

'He has a birthmark,' Carrie said, suddenly.

'What?' Moore said. 'That wasn't mentioned on the misper report.'

'I didn't think . . . I mean, I thought he would just turn up, I wasn't thinking about him being . . . like this.'

'Where is it?'

'Under his hair, just behind his right ear. It's shaped a bit like a map of Australia.'

Moore nodded to the attendant who very carefully turned the body's head to one side, brushing back the hair as he did so. This time Carrie's legs went completely, and it was all Jimmy could do to stop her collapsing to the floor. Even Jimmy could see that there, just behind the remains of the ear, was the birthmark.

As he held her, he imagined Kate being put in the same position as Carrie, having to identify her dead father's body . . . *his* body. She wouldn't have had the faintest idea whether it was him or not, whatever state the body was in.

Carrie was sobbing heavily now.

'I was so sure it wasn't going to be him,' she cried. 'I

th-thought that if . . . something . . . had h-happened to him, I would feel it. And I didn't. I didn't feel anything. How is that possible?'

Jimmy pulled her into him, so that she could no longer see what was left of her dad. Moore nodded to him as if to say, 'Good job'. He watched as she went into the room behind the window and said something to the attendant who started to wheel the trolley out of the room. She paused a moment before coming back through the adjoining door to where they were standing.

'Let's go back into the waiting room,' she said.

Jimmy steered Carrie out, taking most of her weight on his arm, and sat her down on one of the chairs before sitting next to her so she could lean on him. She was still sobbing, but less forcefully now, and as he shifted his weight to support her, she took a deep breath, dug a tissue from her pocket and started to wipe the tears and snot from her face.

'Take your time, pet,' Moore said. 'There's no rush. I could rustle you up a cup of tea if you want?'

'No,' Carrie mumbled. 'I'm fine.' She pulled away from Jimmy slightly and brushed herself down a little before raising her head for the first time since seeing the birth-mark.

'Do you . . . do you know how he died yet?'

Moore hesitated, and Jimmy could see that she knew but didn't really want to say anything. Carrie seemed to sense this as well and pressed her.

'I need to know.'

'The doc thinks he drowned,' she said. 'He had taken a

blow to the head, but it doesn't look like that was enough to kill him. It's hard to know whether that was before he fell in the river though, he may have hit it when he fell in—'

'He didn't fall,' Carrie shot back. 'He was pushed.'

Moore held her hand up in apology. 'However, there was some water in his lungs which almost certainly means he was alive when he went in.'

It was Jimmy's turn to bow his head. He remembered the splash, remembered looking over the railing at the pitch-black water, wondered if there was anything he could have done. What if he'd jumped in? The poor bastard was still alive. He could have saved him. Chalk up another death, Jimmy. Well fucking done.

'It was dark,' he muttered to himself. 'I looked but I couldn't see anything. I—'

He felt a touch on his arm. 'It wasn't your fault,' Carrie said. 'No one thinks that.'

The door from the corridor flew open and DS Burns came dashing in.

'Sorry I'm late,' he began, but then saw Jimmy. 'What's he doing here?'

'He's the friend,' Moore said. 'He came with Carrie.'

'Are you insane?' he said. 'He can't be here, he's a suspect.'

'What?' Moore said. 'No one told me.' She was giving Jimmy daggers, but he gave them right back.

'Get outside,' Burns said to Jimmy, pointing with his thumb at the door he had just come through.

Jimmy went to stand up, but felt a tug on his sleeve.

'No,' Carrie said. 'I want him with me.'

Burns looked astonished.

'We spoke about this, Carrie. I told you who he was, what he's done.'

'I don't care,' she said, looking up at Burns. Her eyes were rimmed red, but still shone fiercely, pinning the DS in an angry spotlight. 'He didn't kill my dad and that's all that matters to me. The sooner you get that into your head, the quicker you might actually start looking for whoever did. Jimmy is a witness not a suspect – he's done way more to help me than you have so far.'

Moore was looking awkward now, half amused, half worried. But Carrie wasn't finished yet.

'Jimmy told you my dad had been pushed into the river weeks ago and you ignored him. You could have sent divers down and maybe he wouldn't look like that now.' She gestured at the door to the viewing room, a look of horror returning to her face.

'Haven't you got somewhere else to be?' Burns said to Moore, clearly embarrassed by Carrie's outburst.

'Yes, Sarge,' she said and headed out of the door in double-quick time.

Burns pulled up a chair in front of Carrie. He sat down, sighed and leaned towards her.

'How sure are you?' he said. 'About your identification, that is.'

'Very.'

'I'm sorry about your dad.' He waited a moment – trying hard to be 'appropriate' Jimmy thought. 'Assuming you're right, of course. I'll have to wait for verification from the dental records before we make it official. But if that confirms your identification, then we will be opening a murder investigation.'

'About time.'

'Look, Carrie, I'm sorry you feel that way, but I'm not sure what else I could have done. There's no way my boss would have approved divers on the say-so of a . . . vagrant. We just don't have the budget for it.'

'You think I give a shit about your budget?' Carrie snapped.

Burns held his hand up. 'No, no, obviously not, sorry. I'm not doing very well here. We will find out who did this, I promise you that.'

'I'll believe it when I see it,' she said, though Jimmy could tell from the way the tension was easing out of her body that she was feeling more appeased than she was letting on.

'You should talk to Ed Collins,' Jimmy said.

Burns glared at him, his discomfort at Jimmy's presence obvious. 'Who's Ed Collins?' Burns said eventually.

Jimmy and Carrie filled him in on what they knew about Collins' plans and how her dad had been instrumental in trying to stop them. He took out a pad and made a few notes, only pausing when Jimmy told him about what had happened at the building site, cutting out any mention of Wilkinson.

'Collins threatened to bury you in the foundations?'

'Sort of,' Jimmy said. 'You could ask Andrew Lang, he was there, maybe he'd confirm it?' Jimmy realised he'd been thinking about Lang, wasn't sure why though – something was niggling away in the back of his mind.

'I will, but in the meantime, I need to talk to you again about that night on the Quayside, see if you remember anything new that might help us.'

'No problem.'

'I'll get DC Moore to take you to the canteen, Carrie, while I talk to Jimmy here,' Burns said.

'No need,' she replied. 'I'm a big girl. And I need to clean myself up. Just point me towards a bathroom.' She turned to Jimmy. 'Will you be OK?' He nodded.

Once she had left, Jimmy turned back to face Burns, wondering if he was going to take a softer approach this time around.

'So, what do you think?' Burns asked.

Maybe he was. Maybe Carrie was right about him. Or maybe he was leading him gently into a trap.

'About what?' Jimmy said.

'Is it Roger Carpenter? The body.'

'I don't know,' Jimmy said. 'I never really met the man.'

'Put it another way: could it be the man you saw arguing on the Quayside?'

Jimmy thought a little longer about this one, trying yet again to conjure up an image of that night, the bricklayer and the social worker going head-to-head. He shook his head.

'I'm sorry, I just don't know.'

'Fair enough,' Burns said. 'The doc thinks the timeline is right though. It's only an estimate, obviously, but he thinks he's been in the water for around four to six weeks.'

And then Jimmy realised what it was about Andrew Lang that had been bugging him. The text.

'Did you know that Andrew Lang claimed to have got a text from Roger Carpenter on the night he disappeared?' he said.

Burns frowned. 'How did you know about that?'

'I went round to his house. He showed me.'

'Playing detective again? No more, OK?'

'But what about the text?'

'I'll be looking into it.'

'But—'

'I said I'll be looking into it. Obviously, it doesn't look like Roger Carpenter sent it.'

'So who did?' Jimmy said.

Burns sighed. 'Look, I know you and Carrie think we're a bunch of plodders, that we haven't done our job here – maybe you're right. But let's be clear: I'm the one asking the questions, not you. Understand?'

'But—'

Burns held his hand up. 'I said, *understand*?'

Jimmy nodded.

'Good. So how about you tell me what you were doing in the Victoria Tunnel yesterday?'

43

Newcastle Mortuary, July 14, 2012

The scream of an electric saw from a nearby room broke the silence. Jimmy tried hard not to imagine what it was being used for.

'Where's the Victoria Tunnel?' Jimmy said.

Burns just looked at him, a small grin playing on his lips.

'You gonna arrest me again?' Jimmy asked.

'Probably not.'

Jimmy couldn't get a read on Burns. The playful grin was now a full-on smile and it was bugging the shit out of him, almost as much as that saw – someone must have had a thick skull.

'Might give you a medal though,' Burns added.

Been there, done that, Jimmy thought. 'I don't need another medal, thanks.'

'You were there, then?' Burns asked. If anything, the smile got wider.

The screeching stopped. It felt like a sign. And anyway, Jimmy wanted to know what was going on.

'Aye. I was there.'

'Thought so. When I saw Wilkinson's name in the daily report, a little bulb lit up – I don't really do coincidence. Looks like you weren't being paranoid, after all; he's been in Newcastle for a couple of months at least. Chances are he was here looking for you all that time.'

'It was him who torched Goldilocks.'

'You're probably right. They found some paraffin in a lock-up he was renting. Might be hard to prove it though.'

'Bastard tried to shoot me.'

'Looks like he might have succeeded to me. I've seen how you're holding your arm. You should probably get it looked at.'

Jimmy didn't respond. Would it get Carrie into trouble if the police knew she'd treated a gunshot wound and hadn't said anything? Was there some kind of code nurses signed up to?

'Don't sweat it,' Burns said. 'Not important. I'll need you to come in later and make a statement though. You can go through your last one at the same time.'

'You're not going to charge me then?'

'What with? Being shot at? Can you imagine the paper-work?'

'He was working for Collins, you know – just temporarily, I think.'

'Really? Small world. I'll look into it.'

It seemed like Carrie was right about Burns after all. The man could have made life much more difficult for him if he'd wanted to. It didn't look like he'd said a word to Sandy for a start – about the arrest or Wilkinson.

'How is Wilkinson?' Jimmy said.

'I think the medical term is "completely fucked". Fractured skull; doesn't know what day it is, or what happened to him. At least we don't think he does; poor bastard can barely string two words together – though I'm not sure he ever could. It was a good job he had his driving licence in his pocket cos he couldn't even remember his name. Sadly, the docs don't think it's permanent.'

Jimmy had a vision of Wilkinson as a zombie, rising from his bed and coming back for him, never stopping until he managed to gain his revenge.

'Don't look so worried,' Burns said. 'He's not going anywhere – well, not anywhere he could get to you anyway. Putting aside his shooting of the tour guide – who's fine, thankfully – our Scottish colleagues have several outstanding arrest warrants for him: murder, torture, rape, you name it. He's going away for a long time. We owe you one.'

The sins of the father, Jimmy thought . . . it was hard to escape the shadow of a violent dad; he knew that and his had been nowhere near as bad as Wilkinson's. Carrie had been lucky to have a dad like Roger – he couldn't help but envy the close relationship they'd so obviously had.

The door opened and Carrie came back in. She'd cleaned herself up, but nothing could wash away the pain she was clearly feeling. Her entire body seemed folded in on itself, like she was trying to make herself as small a target as possible, just in case any more shit was about to rain down on her. He shouldn't have let her go on her own; it had given her too much time to think about what she'd lost and he knew fine well where that road normally led – straight off a cliff.

'You OK?' Jimmy said, more out of politeness than anything else. Of course she wasn't. A tiny nod was all she could manage.

'I need to go and see my mum,' she muttered.

Burns stood up.

'Come into the station tomorrow and we'll get those statements done,' he said to Jimmy. 'And no more vigilante shite, you understand? Both of you, that is. I'll check out Collins and talk to Andrew Lang as soon as I can and let you know what's going on.'

'You might want to look closer to home as well. Someone put that lighter in my bag,' Jimmy said.

A flash of anger crossed Burns's face.

'I don't—' He bit back whatever he was about to say and just nodded. 'I'll look into it.'

Jimmy could almost hear Gadge whispering in his ear: . . . *Wheels within wheels . . . Did I tell you that Collins is a Mason? . . . dinner this evening with most of Her Majesty's Constabulary . . .* Was Burns part of that shit?

Burns patted Carrie on the shoulder. 'Thanks for coming, love. It's been a big help. I know how hard it must have been.' And with that he turned and left.

Unusually Carrie didn't react to the 'love'; she seemed stuck, just staring into space.

'D'you want me to go with you?' Jimmy said. She looked at him blankly. 'To tell your mum,' he added.

'No,' she said, almost mustering a smile. 'No innocent bystanders should have to watch the fallout from that.'

Jimmy suddenly felt a little lost. They stood together quietly in the waiting room, neither seeming in a hurry to go anywhere, Carrie for obvious reasons, Jimmy because there was nowhere else to go. He tried to make a mental list, got as far as 'pick up Dog'.

'Are you going to do what Burns said?' Carrie asked.

'What do you mean?' Jimmy didn't think she'd been listening to the cop.

'Give up the *vigilante shite*?'

He smiled.

'Am I bollocks.'

He looked for Julie at her usual spot on Northumberland Street, anxious to see Dog again, but had no luck; it was possible the punters had been more generous than usual and bought her out, but it was getting late and more likely that she'd had enough and gone for some scran. He'd bet on the latter and, sure enough, there she was, out the back of the Pit Stop, throwing a ball to a still weary-looking Dog.

'That was a long "couple of hours",' she said, as Dog leapt up into Jimmy's arms.

'Sorry, about that,' he said, trying to keep Dog away from his still-sore wound. 'Has he been OK?'

'Oh, he's been grand,' Julie said. 'And you don't half shift a lot more magazines when you've got a dog. Everyone stops to give him a pat.'

Jimmy smiled as Dog licked his face, happy that he'd been spoiled in his absence.

'I've been fine too, seeing as you're asking,' she added. 'Better than your mate, anyway.'

'My mate?' Jimmy said, putting Dog down on the ground.

'The old guy with the beard . . . Gadge, is it? He's over on a bench, outside the Discovery Museum, drunk as a skunk. He was hurling dog's abuse – and empty beer cans – at a parking attendant last time I saw him.'

Jimmy instinctively turned to go, Dog following at his heel. Julie coughed theatrically.

'Ahem!'

He stopped. Turned back.

'I'm sorry.' He always seemed to be apologising to her. 'Thank you, you've been a lifesaver. I owe you one.'

'You owe me dinner.'

'Yes, right, dinner.' He was starting to get anxious. 'Look, um, do you mind if—'

'Get on with you,' she said. 'Sort your mate out. I'll find you when I'm hungry. I know where you live.'

'Thank you,' he said and legged it through the building and along the street, hoping the stupid bastard hadn't staggered off somewhere else or been arrested or worse. Dog chased after him, a fair way back. Jimmy ran through a gap in the hedge that led into the car park and there, sitting upright on the bench, fast asleep, was Gadge, more than a dozen empty cans scattered around his feet. Jimmy stopped in front of him and started to laugh. Some joker had put a cardboard sign on his lap. It had *Wake me up if you fancy a shag* scrawled on it in black felt-tip. It didn't look like there'd been any takers.

'Gadge,' Jimmy said, and then louder, 'GADGE.' Nothing. He shook his shoulder. 'Wake up, man.'

'Nnnnn,' Gadge grunted, slumping to one side, only the armrest stopping him from falling off the bench completely. Still he didn't wake. Jimmy glanced around. A couple of likely lads were watching on from the other side of the car park, pointing and laughing. He sighed and took off his coat, sat down next to Gadge and pulled the coat over both of them. It was going to be a long night.

44

Gosforth Park, July 15, 2012

The young girl in the blue denim dungarees stood three feet away from Jimmy, staring at Dog, who was lying at his feet.

'You can pat him if you want,' Jimmy said, 'he won't bite.'

She looked across to her dad who was sat on the next bench, smiling.

'Go ahead, Kelly,' he said. 'It's fine.'

The girl edged forward, knelt down next to Dog and stroked him behind his ears. Dog pushed his head towards her; she'd found his sweet spot.

'Nice dog,' the dad said.

'The best,' Jimmy said.

'Where did you get him? Is he a rescue dog?'

'I think it's the other way around,' Jimmy said. 'He rescued me.'

The man laughed. The girl ran over to her dad and whispered in his ear.

'You can ask him yourself, you know,' he said.

The girl thought about it then shook her head.

'Sometimes she takes "Don't talk to strangers" a little too far,' the dad said. 'She wants to know what your dog's called.'

'Dog,' Jimmy said. Seeing the girl's puzzled face, he reiterated: 'That's his name, his name is Dog.'

She stared at him for a moment longer and then a big grin appeared on her face and she ran back to Dog and continued to stroke him. After a couple of minutes the dad got up from the bench.

'C'mon then, Kelly, we need to get home and make your mum's dinner, see if she's feeling any better.'

The girl hesitated and Jimmy thought that she was going to protest, but in the end she gave Dog one last pat and stood up.

'Say thank you to the nice man for letting you play with his dog,' the dad said.

She looked at Jimmy, looked back at her dad, who nodded and then back to Jimmy again.

'Fank you,' she said, then turned and skipped away.

'Nice to meet you,' the dad said and hurried after her.

Jimmy watched them head towards the gates, pleased that he'd followed them to the park. It was clear in his mind: Martin Weston had no idea who Jimmy was. Whoever had put that lighter in his bag, whoever was coming after him, whoever had instigated the murder of Roger Carpenter, it wasn't Norma Weston's husband.

45

The Langs' house, July 16, 2012

The house looked bigger in daylight. Jimmy glanced at the clock on the dashboard: 7.30 a.m. There was no sign of life inside, but the flash Range Rover was still sitting in the driveway. Carrie yawned and glanced back at Dog who was asleep on the back seat, snoring quietly.

'Maybe we should come back later?' he said.

'I tried ringing them last night to arrange something but there was no answer,' she said. 'I thought I'd come here before my shift – catch them before they go to work.'

They'd come to get her dad's stuff. The police had taken most of it, but had left one or two personal possessions behind. Jimmy knew she'd need support so had volunteered to come along, though that wasn't his only motive – there was something off about Andrew Lang and he wanted a closer look. Not least because he was going to the police station straight afterwards to look at the CCTV images and, as far as he was concerned, Lang was still in the frame.

He realised Carrie had been staring at him, seemed concerned somehow.

'What is it?' he asked.

'You look terrible.'

'Not been sleeping great.'

'You were crying in your sleep the other night.'

He shrugged. At least he hadn't had another bloody nightmare.

'Wouldn't be the first time. I've learned to live with it.'

'You can get help, you know that, don't you?' she said.

'Tried it once, waste of time. The psychologist was like a war tourist, just wanted to hear the gory details. The only person who can help me is me and I've been doing the best I can.'

She shook her head. 'That's not true. There are others who could help you.'

'Like who?'

'Well, there's me for a start. Though I was really thinking about people with more qualifications.'

'We'll see,' he said, desperate to change the subject. 'Before we go in, tell me about them . . . the Langs.'

'How do you mean?' Carrie said.

'Not sure. Gut feeling. Can't really get a handle on them. What did your dad think of them?'

'Andrew was one of his best friends.' Jimmy noticed the past tense. People were surprisingly adaptable. 'They'd known each other since they were kids,' she continued. 'I don't know him that well, but he's always seemed really nice. I don't think he charged my dad much for staying in their attic room, for instance. And he was the one who got him the job, lecturing part-time.'

'He told the police your dad had sent him a text to say he was going off with a woman. He showed it to me.'

'First I've heard of it.'

'Yeah, sorry, I should have told you that as well, but Lang said he wanted to spare your feelings. To be fair, it was a bit crude.'

Carrie looked at him questioningly – his first truth test this time around.

'It said something about "thinking with his dick".'

She looked away, gazing out of the window. She already knew her dad wasn't perfect, it clearly wasn't news to her, but Jimmy knew that there was a breaking point when you stop forgiving your parents for stuff, when the balance sheet tips too far into debt. Maybe she'd just reached it? Jimmy had it with his dad when he was about twelve, one belt-thrashing too many. At least Kate hadn't had that problem; he was out of her life way before she would ever have had any expectations of him.

'I don't think your dad sent it though.'

Carrie looked across at him.

'You think it was whoever killed him?'

He nodded. 'Burns does too, I think. They were setting up a false trail.'

Carrie went quiet again and looked away. It was a lot to process.

But Jimmy hadn't finished.

'What about Lang's wife, um, Wendy is it?' he said.

Carrie turned back towards him. 'Yes, I think so. What about her?'

'What's she like?'

'Never met her. Dad seemed to like her.'

Jimmy hesitated. Sod it, she wanted him to be honest. 'A little too much maybe?'

'What do you mean?'

'I'm just wondering ... given your dad's reputation ... He was living in the same house as her – something might have happened between them?'

He expected her to protest but she didn't.

'It's possible,' she said sadly. 'I wouldn't have put it past him.'

'And if that was the case, I wonder how Andrew would have reacted? He seemed very twitchy when I spoke to him. Or even what *she* might have been prepared to do to keep their affair a secret? She has a lot to lose,' he added, nodding at the house.

'Where is this coming from, Jimmy?'

'When she rang the other day, after she'd seen the thing in the paper and heard that the police had found a body, she said she was worried.'

'And?' Carrie asked.

'Well, she'd seen the text your dad was supposed to have sent. Saying he'd gone off with a woman. So what did she have to worry about? I think she already knew it was bollocks.'

Finally, there was a sign of life inside the house, a light coming on downstairs. Five minutes later, they rang the bell. Then again. Another minute passed until they heard some keys jangling and the door finally opened. Andrew Lang stared out, bleary-eyed and unshaven, looking a lot worse than the last time Jimmy had seen him.

'Oh, it's you,' he said to Carrie, holding out his arms to embrace her. 'I'm so sorry about your dad.'

As they hugged, Jimmy studied the man's face; he really did look like shit, his face drawn and pale. He seemed to have lost weight since Jimmy first saw him. What was that – a week ago? He was pretty sure he could smell whisky on the man's breath as well; even Gadge might think it was a bit early for that.

'I can't believe he's gone,' Lang said as he released his grip on her. 'It's crazy. I can't get my head around it.' He seemed to notice Jimmy for the first time.

'Oh, hello.' He put his hand on Jimmy's shoulder. 'Look, I'm sorry about the other day. I should have listened to you. I was too quick to dismiss what you were saying.'

The apology seemed genuine. 'No problem,' Jimmy said. 'I didn't entirely believe it myself.'

'I was so sure that text was from Roger. It was exactly the kind of thing he'd do,' Lang said. 'I can't believe I was so naive. If I'd questioned it more, maybe things would have been different.'

'It's not your fault, Andrew,' Carrie said.

'I still feel responsible though . . . if there's anything I can do . . .'

'If it's OK, I'd like to get what's left of my dad's stuff,' Carrie said.

Jimmy could see tears welling up in her eyes. She was holding it together but only just. He put his hand on her arm to steady her.

'Of course, sorry, what am I thinking keeping you on the doorstep? Come in. I'll make some tea.' Lang stepped to one side and let them in, moving a set of golf clubs out of the way.

'I'm sorry it's so early,' Carrie said. 'I hope we haven't disturbed you and your wife.'

'Oh, don't worry,' Lang said. 'It's just me at the moment. Wendy's gone to stay with her brother in Elswick for a couple of days.'

The woman was never around. If he hadn't spoken to her on the phone, Jimmy might have started to wonder if she actually existed.

'D'you want to go straight up? It's the attic room at the top, just keep going up, second room on the left, you can't miss it. I'll get that tea sorted.'

Roger's room was more spartan than Jimmy had expected, not a massive upgrade on a cell. There was a small single bed, neatly made, a two-drawer bedside table with a lamp, a radio alarm clock, a framed photo and a small box of tissues on top of it. And a wardrobe. That was it; not exactly cosy.

Carrie sat down on the bed, absent-mindedly rubbing her hand over the bedspread. She looked lost.

'You stay there, pet,' Jimmy said. 'I'll sort this.' He picked up the photo – a younger version of Alice, holding a baby in her arms – and handed it to Carrie. She sighed and smiled at the same time.

Jimmy opened the wardrobe door. There were half a dozen shelves down the right-hand side, most of them empty. One had a couple of pairs of boxer shorts on it, another some socks. On the left-hand side there were just a few bare hangers. No wonder Lang thought Roger had gone away for a bit.

Carrie glanced over. 'Burns said they'd taken most of his things,' she said. 'Just in case there were any clues in the pockets, receipts and that. He travelled light anyway,' she added, 'and apart from his denim jackets he didn't care much about clothes.' A tear leaked out of the corner of her eye. Jimmy picked up the box of tissues and passed it over to her.

'Thanks.'

Jimmy took what little was left in the wardrobe and put it on the bed. The contents of the bedside table were equally sparse. The top drawer was empty except for a packet of condoms, which he discreetly tucked away before Carrie could see them – not that she was paying any attention. Maybe his theory about Roger and Wendy Lang was right? The bottom drawer had a pile of *National Geographic* magazines in it.

'D'you want to take these?' he said.

Carrie glanced over, smiled.

'He loved that magazine; used to read stuff out to me over breakfast when I was a kid. I always felt he was disappointed that I never shared his passion. I think he hoped I'd grow into it. Too late now.' She was going through the tissues rapidly.

'You should take them,' he said. 'Could do with something to put them in though.'

There was a dresser against the wall on the landing with a couple of drawers at the bottom, the kind of place you might stuff a few carrier bags. He rummaged through the top drawer, nothing useful at all. The bottom drawer was different.

Jimmy stared at the satchel. Roger's satchel. The one he'd been carrying when Jimmy saw him on the Quayside. The one the murderer had walked off with after throwing Roger in the River Tyne.

As he pulled it out of the drawer, he heard a noise to his right. Andrew Lang was walking up the stairs carrying two mugs of tea. Lang looked up, suddenly realising someone was standing at the top of the stairs. He eyed the satchel.

'What are you doing with that?' Lang asked.

'Where did you get this?' Jimmy said, holding the satchel in the air. He moved towards Lang who backed away, a glint of fear in his eyes. 'Was it you I saw that night?'

'What? No, no, I—'

'Throwing a man in the river . . . stealing his bag . . . this bag.'

As he moved backwards, Lang tripped on the bottom step, his back slamming against the wall. One of the mugs flew out of his hand, over the banister and down, eventually smashing on the stone tiles two floors below. The other fell to the carpet beside him, tea splashing everywhere.

Jimmy had followed Lang down and was almost on top of him now.

'You murdering bastard,' he yelled. Lang looked terrified.

'No . . . look . . . you've got it wrong . . .'

Jimmy moved a step closer. Lang put his hands over his head and sunk to his haunches, making himself as small as possible, talking quickly.

'Don't hit me . . . I didn't do anything. It's not . . .'

Jimmy reached down and grabbed the front of Lang's dressing gown, hauling him to his feet. Lang was trembling, little drops of sweat bursting out on his forehead. Jimmy pushed him back against the wall, about to unleash a punch.

'JIMMY, STOP!'

He held the punch back and glanced behind him. Carrie was standing at the top of the stairs.

'That's not Dad's,' she said.

'What?'

'Let him go. The satchel. It's not Dad's.'

Jimmy looked at the satchel and then back at Carrie.

'But—'

'His was newer than that, bigger too.'

'You sure?' Jimmy said.

'Positive,' Carrie said. 'I bought it for him, remember. It had his initials on it. That isn't it.'

Jimmy still had a tight grip on Lang's dressing gown. He let go and Lang slumped back against the wall, breathing heavily. Jimmy shut his eyes. It was either that or bang his own head against the wall. He was, without any shadow of doubt, the world's shittest detective, bar none. Sherlock Homeless? Sherlock fucking Clueless more like.

'It's mine,' Lang said, once he'd got his breath back. 'I was trying to tell you.'

Why wouldn't it be Lang's? It was in his dresser, in his house, after all. Jimmy opened his eyes again.

'I'm sorry,' Jimmy said. 'I didn't think. I just saw the satchel and thought . . . I should have given you a chance to explain.'

He sat down on the stairs facing Lang and put his head in his hands. He'd come so close to punching the poor man's lights out; so close to making a rapid trip back to a prison cell. That could still happen if Lang made a complaint. Carrie came down the steps and sat behind him, her hand on Jimmy's shoulder.

'You OK, Andrew?' she said.

Lang nodded slowly. 'A little shocked, but I'll live.'

Jimmy looked up again, Lang was still trembling. There was tea everywhere, on the walls, the banister and the carpet.

'Shit. What a mess. I'm so sorry,' Jimmy said again. 'I'll clean it all up.'

Lang shook his head. 'Don't worry. We're all a bit on edge after . . . what's happened. You weren't to know. The satchels were a bit of an in-joke, they made us use them at school. The head was ex-military, he liked neatness, order, you know, thought he was still in the army. Sad old sod even made us carry them on our right shoulders like rifles. Woe betide us if we put them on the wrong side – a week's detention on the spot.' He laughed at the memory.

'When we left, we carried on the tradition. Thought it made us characters.'

What it made you was twats, Jimmy thought, then mentally slapped himself. He should give the guy a break.

'I got bored of it after a while, aside from the occasional school reunion. But Roger never did.'

'Dad used his so much it got worn out,' Carrie said. 'That's why I bought him a new one.'

They sat in silence for a while as Jimmy felt the adrenalin drain out of him. Back to square one.

Lang was the first to speak.

'I should probably get ready for work,' he said.

'It helps to keep busy, doesn't it?' Carrie said. 'People think I'm mad still going in, but it takes my mind off what's happened.'

'I know what you mean,' Lang said. 'I feel awful but what else can you do? Wendy's taken it really badly and that's partly because she hasn't got a job to distract her. She reckoned she kept seeing things around the house that reminded her of Roger. That's why she's gone to her brother's for a bit.'

Taken it really badly? Jimmy wondered again about Wendy Lang's involvement in all this. Her involvement with Roger in particular. Could she be the key? This time he kept his thoughts to himself – he should probably give the Langs a wide berth for a while.

'We should get going,' Carrie said. 'Let you clean up the mess. Are you sure you don't want a hand?'

'Honestly, it's fine,' Lang said. 'Have you got everything?'

'Almost,' Carrie said. 'We still need a bag.'

Lang smiled. 'Maybe not the satchel, eh!' He disappeared downstairs and came back with a couple of carrier bags which they loaded up with Roger's meagre possessions.

'If I find anything else, I'll give you a call,' Lang said.

'Thank you,' she said. 'And sorry about the, um, misunderstanding.'

'Don't worry about it,' Lang said. 'It's already forgotten.'

As he showed them towards the door, Jimmy noticed a small collection of photos on the wall that he'd missed on the way in. One picture was of Andrew Lang – looking much bigger than he did now – and Roger Carpenter, taken just a couple of years earlier by the looks of it, probably at one of those school reunions Lang mentioned, both of them proudly carrying their old school satchels over their shoulders. But it was the one next to it that stopped him in his tracks. Two people – smiling faces, arms around each other's waists: one a tall, thin brunette, hair in a ponytail; the other a large, heavy-set man with short-cropped hair. They looked like the best of friends.

'Nice photo,' he said. Lang followed his gaze.

'Yes. Happier times.'

'That your wife?'

'Uh-huh.'

'She's pretty,' Jimmy said. She was also the woman he'd seen sitting in her car outside Carrie's flat the night he was shot.

'She is that,' Lang said.

'And the man?' Jimmy asked.

'That's her brother, David.'

Otherwise known to Jimmy as PC 'Duke' Ellington.

Jimmy waited until they were back in the car before he said anything. He felt like he had all of the pieces but was struggling to fit them together properly. Maybe Carrie could.

'Wendy Lang's brother is a copper.'

'Really?'

'Yes. Nasty bastard too. I've seen him around a lot lately.'

He told her about the attack on Deano in the park, the veiled threats in the police cell, the failed attempt to grab him in the subway.

'D'you think he's got something to do with all this?' she said.

'I think the whole bloody family have. She was the woman I saw hanging around outside your block the other night.'

'Wendy Lang? Why would she do that?'

'Fucked if I know. She was sitting in her car. Drove off as I came near.'

'That's weird.'

'It's not just that though. Andrew Lang looks like he's going to crumble at any minute.'

'You can hardly blame him for that. You nearly beat the crap out of him.'

That was true. He'd lost control for a moment. Had vowed never to let that happen again. He could feel his hands shaking a little, shoved them in his pockets so she wouldn't see.

'He was falling apart before that,' he said.

She didn't look convinced.

'When you get to the station you should tell Burns about all this.'

'Maybe,' he said.

'You still don't trust him, do you?'

'I don't trust anyone.' It was an automatic response.

'Nice.' She turned away from him and started the car up.

It had been true for so long; it shocked him to realise that it might not be true any more. 'I didn't mean . . . sorry,' he said. 'I trust you.'

'Then trust my judgement. Tell Burns – he's a good man and we're making him operate with one hand tied behind his back. I'll drop you at the police station.'

Jimmy took a deep breath and closed his eyes. Trust a cop? It was hard to change the habits of a lifetime. Well, most of a lifetime – he'd almost forgotten that he'd once wanted to be one. Would people have trusted him? He hoped so.

'Jimmy?' she said.

He let the breath go. 'OK,' he said.

46

Central Police Station, Newcastle, July 16, 2012

The killer strolled along the path as if he didn't have a care in the world, the satchel swinging over his left shoulder as he walked.

Burns stopped the tape.

'Anything?' he asked.

Jimmy wanted to say something positive, wanted to stand up and shout 'I know who that is', but he would have been lying. Carrie was right; the picture was fuzzy, as if it had been a foggy night, but apart from that they were pretty much the same images he'd pictured a hundred times behind his eyes, whenever he'd tried to remember what happened that night. The man never showed his face. He was big, dressed in black, with a scarf around his neck – a scarf, like Carrie had said, not a beard, as Jimmy had thought.

He closed his eyes, trying to think back, to find something lingering in his muddled brain, but all he got was a repeat of the brief snatches of the argument he'd overheard:

I saw you . . .

. . . fucking incensed . . .

. . . none of your business . . .

. . . your system . . . it's wrong.

He looked again at the image frozen on screen. The jacket was different from what he remembered.

'It's a padded jacket. I thought it was a donkey jacket. Gives him more bulk. Maybe he's not as big as I thought. It could even be Andrew Lang – he's lost some weight now, but he was bigger, and he's certainly tall enough. Does he ever turn around?'

'No,' Burns said. 'You'd almost think he knows where the camera is.'

Like a policeman, Jimmy thought, immediately thinking of Duke Ellington. He looked at the screen again. Could it be him? A gun for hire for Andrew Lang or Ed Collins?

'We'll release the footage on TV to see if it sparks anything, but I'm not holding my breath,' Burns added. He reached into his desk and pulled a folder out onto the desk. 'I want you to look at some photos.' He took out a dozen pictures – mug-shots, Jimmy supposed – and spread them on the desk facing Jimmy. 'Take a good look, see if you recognise any of them.'

Jimmy scanned the photos. Got nothing on the first pass. Half the men seemed way too old and most of the others too young. 'I don't know,' he said. 'Can't be sure.'

Burns tutted, clearly frustrated. 'Have another look,' he said. As he did, Jimmy sensed him nodding slightly towards the photo nearest to him in the centre of the bottom row. A rugged-looking guy with a shaven head. It could have been unconscious, but Jimmy was beginning to think that Burns never did anything by accident. He stared hard at the photo.

'There is something familiar about this one,' Jimmy said, picking up the photo for a closer look. It wasn't just Burns's prompting; he'd seen the guy somewhere, fairly recently, he was sure of that.

'So it could be him?' Burns was leaning forward, practically drooling.

'I guess . . . it *could* be.'

'Great,' Burns said, putting the other photos back in the folder.

'Who is it?'

'His name's Ewan Milburn. He works in the building industry, not a bricklayer but a bit of a jack-of-all-trades. Current employer – a certain Mr Ed Collins. After you told me that Wilkinson had been working for Collins, I thought I'd check out what other deviants he employed. I think it's fair to say his recruitment procedures aren't exactly exemplary.'

Jimmy had a lightbulb moment. He took the photo back and had another look. 'That's where I've seen him, on Collins' building site. He's the foreman.'

'You were lucky,' Burns said. 'Milburn has a string of convictions for violence.'

You could easily say that about me, Jimmy thought. 'What are you going to do now?' he said.

'Bring him in for questioning. Depending on what he's got to say, I might set up an ID parade, so don't disappear on me.'

Jimmy nodded.

'And I need to have a long conversation with Mr Collins himself. With this ID and what you've told me about the threats he made against you I might even be able to get a search warrant.'

Jimmy wasn't entirely convinced. And he had to tell Burns about Ellington, not least because he'd promised Carrie he would.

'You're still looking at other people though, aren't you?'

'Never say never, but one thing at a time,' Burns said. 'If there's one thing I've learned in this game, it's to follow the money. Collins has a lot invested in that development; he would have lost out big time if anything stopped it. He's top of my list – unless there's something else you haven't told me?'

It was now or never.

'You should check out Wendy Lang as well,' Jimmy said. 'There's something going on with her.' He filled Burns in on her odd behaviour outside Carrie's flat and how she seemed to have gone into hiding at her brother's house.

Then he dropped the bomb.

'Her brother is a cop at this station. Duke Ellington.'

Burns sighed. 'What are you saying?'

'I don't know. You should check him out, that's all. It's a bit of a coincidence, isn't it?'

'Is it? Do you know how small this city is? There's no six degrees of separation here. It's not London – it's more like a village. If every time there was a crime I pulled in everyone with some connection to the victim, no matter how tenuous, they'd have to shut the city down.'

'I just thought—'

'What *did* you think exactly? Another bent cop?'

'He threatened me when I was in the station the other day and tried to grab me in a subway the other night.'

'I threatened you when you were in the station! And they're trying to clear the streets for the Queen's visit – you know that.'

'He didn't try and grab anyone else.'

Burns sighed and pointed at the screen.

'D'you think that's Ellington?'

'Could be.'

'Jesus wept, Jimmy, it could be anyone. Look at it – it's like someone smeared Vaseline all over the lens and filmed it underwater. I was only really showing you in the hope it might spark off some other memory of that night.' He looked closer at the screen. 'It could be me, for fuck's sake!'

Jimmy said nothing.

'Christ, you actually think it could be, don't you?'

Jimmy shrugged. Burns shook his head, his face the perfect mixture of despair and disbelief.

'Can I go now?' Jimmy said. He knew he was being childish, but he'd told Carrie it would be a waste of time bringing Ellington's name into things and he wished he'd stuck to his guns. He'd played his cards now and had nothing left up his sleeve.

'No you can't. While we're on the subject of my colleagues – leave the Westons alone.'

Fuck. Where did that come from?

'I don't know what you mean.'

'Yes, you do. I wasn't going to talk to you about this – mainly because it's none of your bloody business – but given that you seem to suspect everyone involved in investigating this case I'll spell it out for you. Martin Weston came to see me this morning. He's recused himself from the Carpenter case and handed all his work on it over to one of his colleagues.'

'I don't understand.'

'Don't piss me about, Jimmy. As you well know, his wife was having an affair with Roger Carpenter. When she heard that we'd found his body she went to pieces. Confessed everything. She told him that you and Carrie had been sniffing around. Martin is taking compassionate leave and they're going to go for counselling – see if they can save their marriage.'

He pointed at Jimmy.

'The last thing they need is some amateur sleuth bumbling about, giving them a hard time. Understand? Take it from me, Martin is in pieces,' Burns continued. 'He knew nothing about his wife's affair until last night. He is not a suspect. OK?'

Jimmy thought about explaining that he'd already come to the same conclusion but realised that would be like throwing oil on a raging bonfire, so he kept the details of his park exploits to himself and just nodded.

'I know what you think, Jimmy, but I'm not stuck on a single track here. I'm interviewing Norma Weston later today – just in case she can tell me what Roger Carpenter was up to – apparently, she blames herself for his death and I'm interested to know why. I'm open to any new lines of enquiry.'

As long as those lines didn't include fellow policemen, Jimmy thought.

47

Byker Library, July 16, 2012

'You owe me for this,' Gadge said, as Jimmy steered him towards the library doors.

'I looked after you all night, the other night, you ungrateful bastard,' Jimmy said.

'I never asked you to. I could have looked after meself.'

'Aye, right, those kids could have cut your dick off and stuffed it in your ear and the first you'd have known about it would have been when you woke up and couldn't hear the dawn chorus.'

'Hadaway and shite, man.'

Jimmy tied Dog up outside. Still grumbling, Gadge stumbled into the library and headed towards the unguarded computers.

'It'll cost you this time, bonny lad. A pint a minute.'

'I think you had enough the other day to last you a lifetime,' Jimmy said. 'You could still get half-cut on your breath alone.'

Gadge stopped and folded his arms against his chest. 'Those are me terms. Take it or leave it.'

Jimmy sighed and nodded. 'Fine. Just get me that address.'

'It's not gonna be easy. Can't just look on the electoral roll like the old days – most people opt out now. D'you want an estimate before I start? Be at least ten pints, I reckon. Gonna have to call in a few favours, like.'

'Just crack on, man. I'll make sure the librarian's occupied.'

Jimmy could see a grey-haired woman on the far side of the room pinning something to the noticeboard. He wandered over towards her, racking his brains to think of an author he could ask about. Nothing came. He was just going to have to busk it.

As he got near, she turned. It was Aoife.

'What are you doing here?' he said.

'I was just about to ask you the same thing. It's not your usual patch.'

Jimmy waited, knowing that she'd fold first. She was too nice not to.

'I'm filling in for holiday gaps. Here all week.'

Over her shoulder, Jimmy could see what she'd been pinning on the board: a flyer advertising a veterans' therapy group. She noticed him staring at it.

'Are you interested?' she asked.

'Why would I be?' he said.

She looked at him curiously, like she was wondering whether or not to say something.

'My grandson goes. He finds it . . . helpful.'

'Good for him.' Jimmy thought that would close the conversation down, but it didn't.

'He was in Afghanistan . . . he was . . .' She paused, clearly disturbed by whatever memory she had dredged up. 'Doesn't matter. You have the same look as him sometimes, that's all,' she said. 'What do they call it? A thousand-yard stare, is it?'

'I don't know,' he said, though he did.

'You are ex-forces though?' she said.

A month ago, he'd have probably told her to mind her own business, but things had changed.

'Long time ago.'

'Doesn't matter to them. You should try it. There's no doctors; just a group of ex-servicemen talking to each other, sharing stories. Like I said, Mark finds it helpful.'

'Maybe I will,' Jimmy said, eventually. She was the kind of woman you wanted to please.

Aoife smiled but the smile turned quickly to a frown.

'What's wrong?' Jimmy said.

'Is that your friend over there?' she said.

Shit, Jimmy thought. Basic error. He'd forgotten his mission – hadn't bought Gadge much time to get his act together.

'Um, where?'

'On the computer,' she said, moving past him. He almost grabbed her arm to stop her but as he turned, he understood why she was moving so fast and looked so concerned. Gadge was slumped face down on the keyboard, his arms hanging down by his side, a pencil rolling across the floor.

Aoife got there first.

'Are you alright?' she said, leaning over to try and look in Gadge's face. As she did, his wheeled chair spun around and he fell off it, onto the floor, on his back. His eyes fluttered for a moment, but then he lapsed back into unconsciousness.

Jimmy knelt down by his side. 'Gadge,' he shouted, shaking his friend by the shoulders. Nothing. He leaned in close, placing his cheek over Gadge's mouth. Nothing. Shit, shit, shit, shit, shit.

'He's not breathing,' he shouted. 'Call an ambulance.'

Aoife was already on it, phone in hand, pecking away at the keypad. Jimmy closed his eyes, searching for a memory of his first-aid training all those years ago, practising on 'Freda' – a dummy that used to be 'Fred' until some joker had drawn tits on it . . . something . . . anything. And there it was. Thank God the chaplain did the training – *Psalms* 30:2: *Lord, my God, I called to you for help and you healed me.*

He made sure that Gadge was lying flat on his back, knelt over him and placed both hands on his chest, just below his breastbone. Thirty compressions, two every second. One, two, three . . .

Behind him he could hear Aoife giving the operator the address of the library.

Ten, eleven, twelve . . .

'Hurry, please, he's not breathing,' Aoife said.

Eighteen, nineteen, twenty . . .

Gadge was motionless, his face showing nothing.

Twenty-eight, twenty-nine, thirty. Still nothing.

Psalms 30:2. Thirty compressions: two rescue breaths.

Jimmy moved to one side, tilted Gadge's head back, cov-ered the man's mouth with his own and blew firmly into his mouth, watching his friend's chest rise as he did. Then he did it all again. Gadge remained lifeless.

Another thirty. Another two breaths. Nothing. Maybe he'd got it wrong, maybe it was the wrong way around. Useless twat. One more try.

One, two, three, four, five, six ... He'd reached twenty when he heard a door fly open behind him somewhere, and then at twenty-five he felt a hand on his shoulder. He looked up. A paramedic, thank Christ for that.

'I couldn't remember how ...' Jimmy mumbled. 'I don't know if I've done it right.'

The newcomer eased him out of the way.

'I've got it, sir,' she said.

Jimmy rolled away. The paramedic leaned over Gadge, checked his pulse, placing her cheek against Gadge's mouth at the same time. She looked over at Jimmy and nodded.

'He's breathing. You did good.'

48

Central station, Newcastle, January 10, 2012

Jimmy steps down from the train. The old home town looks the same, he thinks, smiling at his own joke – his mum would have laughed at that one. She had loved Tom Jones.

A new year, a fresh start. It feels good to be back. It's been six months since he got out of prison; half a year of slumming around in Glasgow, trying to get his shit together before heading home. Dossing down wherever he could, finding his feet, keeping out of trouble; pretending he was living at his aunt's to keep his probation officer happy. All that time Newcastle calling to him with its siren song. He just hopes he can avoid the rocks.

He heads straight for the Pit Stop, been told it's a safe place to start. No beds, but showers, hot food and shelter; people to talk to, if that's what you want. He doesn't. Just wants to settle back down slowly, then maybe try and catch up with Kate when he's ready; when she's ready. Bev is a lost cause, he knows that. She made it very clear in the last letter he got, after he'd written to tell her he was finally being released.

Jimmy takes his time. He's got plenty, no forthcoming engagements. Strolls up Pink Lane, past the old town wall and Chinatown, which is bigger than he remembers, crossing St James Boulevard which he doesn't remember at all – must have been built while he was . . . away. In the distance he can see the building where he did his interview for the police. It's been a long time.

The Pit Stop is bigger than he expected, but apart from that it's just the job, warm and welcoming. As soon as he's through the door a woman approaches him, smiling.

'New here?' she asks.

Jimmy nods.

'Thought so,' she says. 'I know most of our friends. I'm Maggie. Don't worry, we don't bite.'

Aye, but what if *I* do? Jimmy does his best to hide the thought. His nose twitches as he catches a whiff of something cooking. He can hear a clatter of plates from somewhere close.

'You hungry?' she says.

He nods again.

'We've just started serving. Go through the doors on the left, grab some food and find yourself a seat. If you need anything, come and find me or one of the other volunteers. OK?'

He nods again.

'Mr Chatty, eh!' she laughs and heads off.

Jimmy pushes through the doors. It's a large, bog-standard

room, trestle tables laid out in three rows, thirty or so people already eating, another handful waiting to get their food. They're all men except one, a short-haired woman wearing mirrored sunglasses who smiles at him as he walks in. He nods in return, feeling his way, keeping his own counsel for now.

He takes a tray and stands in line, grabbing a plate of shepherd's pie and some rice pudding before heading for one of the tables, making sure not to invade anybody's space.

A few feet down, on the opposite side of the table, a young, too-skinny kid wearing a weird Cossack-style hat is playing with his food without actually eating anything. An older man, stocky with a big grey beard, who is a shoo-in for a few weeks playing Santa in Fenwick at Christmas, nudges the kid.

'You need to eat, bonny lad,' the older man says.

'Not hungry.'

If they didn't look so different, Jimmy would think they were father and son. He watches as the older man picks up a spoon and scoops up some rice pudding.

'Open up,' the man says, shoving the spoon towards the kid's mouth.

The kid laughs. 'Piss off, I'm not twelve.'

He actually could be, Jimmy thinks.

The kid keeps his mouth shut, so the older man starts moving the spoon around and making aeroplane noises.

'Nyoooooooooooooooooooom!' He does loop-the-loops with the spoon, somehow keeping the rice on it. The kid is laughing harder now, fit to burst.

'Here comes the aeroplane, coming into land,' the older man says. 'Open up, now. Nyoooooooooooooooooooom!' He moves the spoon towards the kid's mouth again and this time he does as he's told, opening wide and accepting the food.

'That's better,' the older man says, handing the spoon over. 'Now eat the rest properly or I'll lamp ya.'

Jimmy laughs. Can't help himself. The two of them look over at him.

'Think it's funny, do you?' the older man says.

Jimmy tries to stop laughing but he can't. He's never been threatened by Santa before. No Christmas presents for Jimmy this year. Eventually the older man smiles and joins in.

'Aye, fair play to you,' he says. 'It must have looked pretty stupid.' He shuffles along the bench so that he's in front of Jimmy. 'New boy, eh?'

Jimmy nods.

The older man points his thumb towards the kid. 'The Twat in the Hat calls himself Deano.' He sticks his hand across the table, waiting for a shake. 'I'm Gadge.'

49

Freeman Hospital, July 17, 2012

Jimmy had been sitting there for hours. Nobody seemed to know anything about Gadge; either that or they didn't want to tell. The paramedic reckoned it was a heart attack. She nearly wouldn't let him in the ambulance; he'd had to pretend Gadge was his brother. Aoife had given him a look, but she hadn't said anything. She'd even agreed to take care of Dog; she'd probably do a better job than he had lately.

At the hospital, his story had fallen apart the minute they'd quizzed him for details; he had no idea what Gadge's last name was – didn't even know his proper Christian name. Gadge had been rushed through the double doors on a trolley and Jimmy had been sitting there in the waiting room ever since, ignored by everyone, fretting that he'd been the cause of it somehow – putting the poor bastard under too much pressure or something? Waste of time as well; didn't even get the address he'd wanted. He'd used a payphone to leave a message at the Pit Stop for Deano, but didn't know if he'd got it.

He noticed a few new faces appearing behind the desk; reckoned it was probably a shift change. He'd try asking again once they'd settled down; maybe the new lot would be less guarded. Then the door opened and Carrie walked in, in uniform. She saw him immediately. It was a toss-up which one of them was more surprised. He'd forgotten this was where she was doing her training. She had dark bags under her eyes and looked shattered.

'You shouldn't be working,' he said.

'Don't you start. It's bad enough having Mum banging on at me,' Carrie said. 'I couldn't sit around at her place doing nothing; it was driving me mad – she was driving me mad. And I didn't want to sit in an empty flat climbing the walls. Thought I'd be better off here. But what are you doing here? Are you OK? Is it your arm?'

'No, I'm fine. Gadge is here somewhere. I think he's had a heart attack,' he said. 'No one will tell me anything.'

'What time was he brought in?' she said.

'About 4 p.m.'

'Leave it with me.'

Carrie went over to the desk and spoke to the duty sister. She turned around a couple of times and pointed to Jimmy. The sister picked up the phone, spoke briefly to someone, and then to Carrie. Eventually she came back over.

'He's out of surgery but still hasn't regained consciousness.'

'Can I see him?' Jimmy said.

Carrie looked doubtful. 'I'll see what I can do,' she said, walking away.

Ten minutes later, she was back.

'You've got five minutes. Follow me.'

They took a lift up to the third floor.

'Thanks for this,' he said.

'Least I could do. Luckily, I know one of the nurses on the ward.'

'D'you know how he is?' Jimmy asked.

'They say he's stable,' Carrie said.

'Was it a heart attack?'

'Arrhythmia, they think.' She could obviously tell that meant nothing to Jimmy. 'It's an irregular heartbeat, probably brought on by excessive alcohol use from what you've told me about him.'

Relief washed over him. Not his fault at least. Maybe he could have tried to stem Gadge's drinking, but it would take a brave man to get between Gadge and his beer.

At the third floor Carrie guided him to Ward 21 and handed him over to another nurse.

'This is Jimmy, the man I was telling you about; your patient is his best friend.'

Jimmy wondered if that was true, decided it was. It worked the other way around too, he thought. It wasn't the biggest field in the world these days.

'This is Helen, she'll look after you,' Carrie said. 'I've got to get to work. I'll try and catch up with you later.'

'I'm not going anywhere,' Jimmy said. 'Not until I know what's going on with Gadge.'

'I know,' she said and left.

'Follow me,' Helen said. 'We need to be quick; the ward sister's on a break and if she finds you here, she'll have my head on a stick.'

Helen took him into a four-bed room. Three of the beds had sleeping patients in them; the fourth was curtained off. She pulled the curtain aside to let Jimmy in. Gadge was lying there, almost unrecognisable due to the large plastic mask clamped over his mouth and nose where his beard used to be – he was completely clean shaven now. A thick blue hose snaked out of the mask to one of several machines that surrounded him. He looked like an alien from an old *Doctor Who* episode.

'Jesus,' Jimmy whispered.

'It's not as bad as it looks,' the nurse said. 'It's just helping regulate his breathing post-op.'

One of the other machines was emitting an occasional beep. A heart monitor, Jimmy guessed, relieved that the sound seemed to occur at regular intervals – not that he knew a thing about it.

'Is he going to be OK?' he said.

'It's a bit early to tell. But we're hopeful. Most patients with arrhythmia make a full recovery.'

'How long will he be unconscious?'

'It varies,' said Helen. 'Could be an hour, could be a day, could be two days. No two patients are the same. The surgery took several hours, so it's unlikely to be any time soon.'

'What about ...' – he paused, trying to choose better words, couldn't find any – '... brain damage?' he said. 'He stopped breathing for a while.'

'I'm sorry,' she said. 'We won't know what effect it's had until he comes round, and even then it'll be some time before we know for sure.'

Jimmy could feel himself welling up. He took Gadge's lifeless hand in his.

'Can I wait here?' he said.

'No, I'm sorry, that's not possible. You can wait in the reception downstairs though, and if anything happens, I'll get someone to let you know.'

'Thanks,' he said.

'You'd better get off now, before the Wicked Witch comes back,' she smiled.

'OK.' Jimmy patted Gadge's hand. 'See you soon, mate,' he said, turning to leave.

'Oh, just a second,' Helen said, opening a drawer by the side of the bed.

'Maybe you could keep this safe for him? The doctor found it clenched in his fist when he examined him earlier – had to prise it out of his hand before they operated.'

She handed him a small piece of paper with an address in Elswick scrawled on it. Gadge had come through.

The corridor is full of trolleys. And all the trolleys have people on them. At least, Jimmy thinks they're people; they're all covered with sheets. He walks slowly along the line, in among the dead men, pulling back each sheet in turn. On the first trolley is a headless body – all that's missing is the netting. Next up is Red, his skin melted by flames, unblinking eyes staring straight into Jimmy's. Then it's Wilkinson – the head is an unrecognisable mess, but the prison uniform gives the game away. Goldilocks is similar to Red, apart from the smoke still drifting from his blackened corpse. Last but one is easy: Roger, the catch of the day only a few days ago, his remaining skin still tinged seaweed green. Jimmy looks back down the line; how many of them would be alive if he'd done things differently? There's only one trolley left. Who's next? Not Gadge, he mutters under his breath, not Gadge, please. He pulls back the sheet. His prayers are answered; his own face stares back at him.

Loud banging woke Jimmy up. He looked around, blinking at the bright fluorescent lights. The waiting room was almost empty. So were the corridors, thankfully. The almost bit was Deano, who was slapping the shit out of a vending machine.

'Thievin' metal-bastard-box,' Deano yelled.

'Oi!' the nurse behind the desk said. 'Stop that or I'll call security. And keep the noise down.'

'What for?' Deano shouted. 'It's the middle of the night – there's no bastard here. This thing's ripped me off a quid. I only wanted a Snickers.' He gave it another slap.

Jimmy yawned. He'd decided to stay in the waiting room overnight. Had to ask Aoife if she could keep hold of Dog for a while; he could sneak him into most places, but the hospital was a definite no-no. Hadn't thought he would sleep at all. Had just sat staring into space, running the CCTV images through his head over and over again, sure there was something he was missing, only vaguely aware of the procession of drunks stumbling in and out of the place. Exhaustion must have finally kicked in.

He stretched his arms out, his back stiff as hell.

Deano was now administering a good kicking to the coin slot.

'Oi,' Jimmy shouted. 'You heard the nurse, keep the noise down.'

'You can piss off as—' Deano yelled, cutting his cursing off when he realised who was shouting at him this time. 'Shagging hell, it's Sleeping Beauty, back from the grave,' he said. 'You took your time; I've been sat here all night playing wi' meself.'

Jimmy knew that wasn't true. It had been pretty late when he'd eventually conked out and there'd been no sign of the kid, but he let the lie pass. He was just glad he'd come at all. Deano came and sat down next to him.

'I was worried about you,' Jimmy said. 'Where you been?'

The kid looked sheepish, guilty even.

'Ya knaa, round and about and that.'

He was back on something, just coming down by the look of it. MDMA maybe – the chocolate craving was a dead giveaway. Still, he was there and that was all that mattered for now.

'You OK?' Jimmy said.

'Aye, I s'pose. Worried about the Gadge-meister, like.'

'Me too, son, me too.' He sat back, closed his eyes and started running the CCTV images through his head again and again.

Jimmy felt someone tapping him on the arm. He opened his eyes and knew immediately what had been bothering him about those images: the devil in the detail.

'Thought you might need this.' Carrie was sitting next to him holding out a paper cup – strong coffee by the smell of it. He sat up and took it from her. Deano was fast asleep, lying across three or four chairs, his head on Jimmy's lap.

'No news on Gadge, I'm afraid,' she added. 'He still hasn't recovered consciousness.'

Jimmy was beginning to fear the worst. He knew there was nothing he could do about Gadge. He'd even considered praying but knew the man would have punched him for even thinking about it. He needed to do something though; something to stop him thinking about his friend. And he now knew what that was.

'It's not Andrew Lang,' Jimmy said.

'What isn't?' Carrie said, puzzled by the sudden leap.

'The killer. The man on the Quayside. He picks up your dad's satchel and puts it on his left shoulder.'

'And?'

'Your dad and Lang were trained to carry the satchels on their right shoulders – remember what Lang said: instant detention on the spot if you got it wrong. The head was ex-military – he'd drilled it into them. It's like rifle drill in the services. It's ingrained. You would never put your rifle on your left shoulder, you just wouldn't. It's second nature.'

He could see Carrie trying to work it through, to picture her dad walking along, carrying his bag.

'I don't know, it's hard to remember. It seems a bit tenuous.'

'What about that photo on Lang's wall? Remember that? Even then, years later, they had the satchels on their right shoulders. Second nature. I'm telling you – Andrew Lang isn't the killer.'

'Maybe,' she said. 'It certainly fits in with the other news I had for you.'

'What's that?'

'Burns has been in touch . . . they've arrested Ed Collins.'

50

Elswick, Newcastle, July 18, 2012

Jimmy had never broken into a house before but there was a first time for everything. He just wished the first time could have been someone else's house. Policemen were touchy about being robbed.

He knew that he was taking a massive risk, but he was sure that Burns was on the wrong track. He could believe that Collins was involved in something dodgy, maybe Lang too; no bother at all believing that, in fact. But he didn't believe that either man was the killer.

Trouble was, he didn't have any evidence – and without it Burns wouldn't shift. The satchel was the key. Ever since he'd made the mistake in Andrew Lang's house it had been bugging him. That was probably why he'd stumbled upon the shoulder thing; he'd thought of little else since. The killer walked off with it – but what if he'd kept it? Didn't they often keep souvenirs? Someone had kept Roger's lighter, so maybe they'd kept the satchel too. And if Martin

Weston was no longer a suspect, – and, for once, Jimmy was in agreement with Burns that he wasn't – then the increasingly dodgy-looking Duke Ellington was right in the frame.

Wendy Lang's odd behaviour had also continued to nag away at him. Having a nose around the house the two of them were now staying in was the obvious option – two birds, one stone; ideally a big bastard thrown through the window so he could get in. He knew it was a long shot, but it felt like the only shot he had left.

The house seemed empty. He knew that Ellington was on duty – the Queen was visiting the city later that day and every low-level grunt would be on crowd control – but didn't know where Wendy Lang was. The Volkswagen Beetle he'd seen her sitting in outside Carrie's flat – one of the few cars he could actually recognise – was nowhere to be seen.

He'd rung the doorbell twice. Either she was ignoring it or she couldn't get to the door. Then he'd heard the phone ringing inside. He'd rung the bell again, just in case anyone was watching. Inside, the phone continued to ring. No one answered. Eventually it stopped. In for a penny. There was a gate at the side of the house; he opened it and crept through to the fenced-in back garden. A conservatory had been added to the back of the house, so he could see inside; no sign of life. He tried the door, but it was locked.

He contemplated smashing one of the windows to get in – that had been the plan as he made his way to the house – but Jimmy now realised he didn't want Ellington to know anyone had been there. He stepped out into the middle of the neatly mown lawn and looked up at the rest of the house. There was a window open on the first floor – a bathroom probably – but it was too high and too small for Jimmy to get through. He needed someone smaller.

Deano looked up at the open window.

'You might've mentioned the alarm,' he said, pointing to a box with a small flashing light attached to the back wall.

'Shit,' Jimmy said. 'I didn't even see it.'

'Divvn't worry, man, it's a fake box. You can tell by the crappy LED light.'

'You reckon you can get in then?'

'No bother,' Deano said.

It had taken Jimmy ages to find a phone box to ring the hospital. Deano had moaned a bit about trekking out this far but it wasn't like he had anything else to do – Gadge was still out for the count. Even so, he'd demanded a slap-up at Maccy Ds in exchange for his services. The kid had already checked the outside doors, but the back door was dead-bolted vertically and the front had a very solid-looking mortice lock on it. Ellington might have saved money on his alarm system but he hadn't skimped on the locks. Maybe he did have something to hide?

Deano hoisted himself up onto the conservatory roof, sat on the edge, his feet dangling down, and smiled at Jimmy.

'Piece of piss, eh?' He stood up and walked around the edge of the roof, where it was sturdier, and grabbed hold of the drainpipe that ran up the wall towards the open window. He yanked it a couple of times to test it, but it held firm. He glanced back down at Jimmy.

'You'd better go round the front, keep an eye out just in case. I'll flick the curtains once I'm in, then you can come back round and I'll let you in.'

'Shouldn't I wait here, just in case you fall or something?' Jimmy said.

'You gonna catch us, like?' Deano laughed. 'No danger, man, I could do this in me sleep.' He started to climb.

'Remember to keep your eyes peeled for the bag,' Jimmy shouted. He waited a moment, just to make sure Deano wasn't waffling about his climbing skills, and then went back to the front of the house. There was still no one around – it was like a ghost town that morning. He reckoned everyone must have gone to see the Queen drive through town – hoped that included Wendy Lang. Still, couldn't be too careful, so he stayed tucked out of the way, behind a hedge at the front, just in case the neighbours were a bit nebby, while keeping one eye on the curtains for Deano's sign.

Several minutes passed. Jimmy was starting to get worried; he felt guilty enough that he hadn't told Deano it was a policeman's house – didn't want the kid to brick it – but would feel a lot worse if anything went wrong. He hadn't heard any screams or the smashing of glass as a body fell through the conservatory roof though, so worst-case scenario was probably that Deano had got stuck trying to get through the window or maybe that the room it led to was also locked? If the external doors were anything to go by, Ellington seemed very keen on security.

He was just about to head back around the house to check

when he heard a car coming down the road. He waited for it to pass, but then heard it slowing down as it got near the house, so he legged it quickly down to the side gate, out of sight of the driveway, only just making it around the corner before a car pulled into the entrance and parked in front of the house. The Volkswagen Beetle he'd seen outside Carrie's flat. A woman got out. Wendy Lang. She'd changed her hairstyle from the photo he'd seen – it was swept over one side of her face now – but it was definitely her.

He watched as she opened the boot, keeping himself hidden around the side of the house. What should he do? He edged back, out of her line of sight. He thought about running around to the back of the house to shout a warning to Deano, but she'd almost certainly hear him. She opened the front door. Surely Deano would have heard the car pull up?

Jimmy looked back around the corner. She had gone into the house but had left the boot open, so chances were, she'd be straight back out. That made his mind up for him. He sprinted out, past the car and onto the pavement outside, standing there as if looking for something. A few moments later she came back out and saw him immediately.

'Oh,' she said. 'Can I help you?' She sounded like the woman he'd spoken to on the phone, local but posh.

'Are you Wendy Lang?' he said, far louder than he needed to, hoping Deano would hear him.

'Um, yes.' She looked over her shoulder, whether for help or for an escape route from the mad, shouty man he wasn't sure.

'I'm Jimmy. We spoke the other day.'

She stared at him, a slight glimmer of distaste around her lips which she was trying hard to hide. He was used to that.

'I don't think so,' she said.

'On the phone,' he said.

'I don't remember.' She took two bags of shopping out of the boot and closed it behind her, clearly intending that to be the end of the conversation.

'I'm a friend of Carrie's. Your husband can vouch for me. You could check with him if you like. He's the one who told me where to find you.' He hoped she wouldn't call his bluff; after his mistake over the satchel, Andrew Lang would almost certainly call the police and scream about harassment.

She didn't respond, heading towards the open door with her shopping.

'I was wondering if I could have a quick word? About you and Roger Carpenter.'

That got her attention. She stopped, her back to him, shoulders stiff. Slowly, she turned back to face him.

'Me and Roger?'

'Carrie said the two of you were close.'

'I wouldn't say *close*.'

'Oh, I'm sorry, maybe I got the wrong idea. She's just trying to find out a bit more about his last few days. She needs, um . . .' – he racked his brains for the wank-speak word that therapist had used all those years ago – 'closure.'

Wendy Lang looked behind her again and for a moment Jimmy wondered if she'd heard a noise in the house, like

Deano had knocked a vase over or something. More likely she was wondering whether she could make it inside and slam the door before Jimmy could get to her. She turned back to face him.

'You'd better come in,' she said.

Jimmy was crapping himself. Where the hell was Deano?

Wendy Lang had sat him down on a stool in the kitchen and then excused herself for a moment, conspicuously taking her handbag with her and glancing around to make sure there was nothing else he could steal before she left. He thought she'd gone upstairs. Either that or she was ringing her husband to check on his story. Neither was good. He heard someone moving around above his head. Upstairs it was. Unless that was Deano?

The kitchen opened out into the conservatory, where there was a dining table and chairs, meaning Jimmy could see straight out into the back garden. It was mostly neat and tidy, all gleaming surfaces, everything tucked away in cupboards apart from a kettle and a knife block, both of which sat on an otherwise bare island in the middle of the room. He suspected she had tidied the place up a bit, couldn't imagine Ellington keeping it that clean.

There was another noise upstairs. He wondered about going after her, shouting up the stairs, pretending that he cared whether she was OK. Then the door opened and she came back in – without her bag, he noticed.

'Sorry about that,' she said. 'Thought I smelled gas.'

'No problem,' Jimmy said, relieved. She was probably

telling the truth, though the smell was more likely Deano; he wasn't the most hygienic kid around, a typical teenager.

She started to fill the kettle.

'Can I get you a cup of tea?' she said.

Jimmy didn't want one, but he nodded anyway. It would keep her occupied and, if he was still there, give Deano more time to escape – maybe even a chance to sniff around for the satchel.

'Aye, thank you,' he said. 'Two sugars.'

'I don't think there is any sugar,' she said.

Even though she'd just been shopping. He wasn't surprised. There wasn't a spare ounce of fat on her. Unlike her brother.

'No problem, wet and warm is fine,' Jimmy said.

She took some milk out of the fridge, sniffed it, doing everything she could to avoid his gaze.

'Are you staying here for long?' he said.

She looked concerned, like he knew too much about her.

'Um, I'm not sure, at least a couple more days.'

'Did you hear that the police have arrested someone?'

That got her attention. She turned around rapidly, spilling a small drop of milk as she did.

'In connection with Roger?'

'I think so.'

'Who?'

'Ed Collins.'

She seemed relieved. She turned away again, picked up a cloth and wiped the milk away.

'Andrew's friend?' she said.

Friend? That was an interesting choice of words. Were they friends? How close?

'I believe so.'

'Who told you that?' she asked.

'You wouldn't believe what I hear on the grapevine. Who did what to whom. Who's sleeping with who.'

She flicked a glance at him then turned back to the cups, clearly wondering if he was playing with her. Which he was.

'What was it you wanted to know about Roger?' she said, still keeping her back to him as she got two mugs out of a cupboard, wiping the already spotless surface with a cloth before putting them down.

'Did he have a girlfriend?'

'Not to my knowledge.' She didn't turn around. Jimmy wanted to see her face when she answered his questions, so he got up and started to pace a bit.

'Mind if I stretch my legs?' he said. 'My back's not what it was, can't sit still for too long.'

She didn't say anything, just carried on making the tea, putting the bags in a pot, the milk in a jug, then back in the fridge – all the while keeping her back to him.

'Your husband showed me a text a while back; it said Roger had gone off with some woman. Did you ever believe that?'

She seemed fascinated by the inside of the fridge. 'Why shouldn't I have?'

'It's just that you said you were worried about him.'

'Did I?'

'Yes. On the phone.'

The kettle boiled and she finally closed the fridge and poured the water into the teapot, still not looking at him, playing for time.

'I was . . . concerned. Roger was like a brother . . .' She hesitated, distracted by something, before continuing. 'He was my friend. I don't think it's odd to worry about a friend.'

'Suppose not,' Jimmy said. He walked around the island, milking the idea that he was stretching his legs, until he was on the other side, facing her, which also gave him a good view into the garden. Jimmy was getting a bit pissed off with her avoiding things. He remembered how Carrie had got Norma Weston flustered, what seemed an age ago.

'Were you sleeping with him?'

She jerked her head up and glared at him.

'With Roger? No! What on earth gave you that idea?'

Over her shoulder he saw a flash of movement in the upper corner of the window. Something fell to the ground outside. It must have landed on the lawn as there was no sound. Deano was on the move. He needed to keep her looking at him.

'Oh, I don't know. Good-looking housewife, well-known womaniser, workaholic husband, just putting two and two together . . .'

He let her do the maths. Through the window he could now clearly see a foot, a black-and-white-trainer-clad foot: Deano's. Then another one. The kid was perched on the edge of the conservatory roof, waiting for the chance to jump down unobserved.

'There was nothing remotely like that,' she said, clearly

angry. 'Roger was a chancer where women were concerned, everyone knew that, but he, um, knew better than to try anything like that with me.'

'Don't shit on your own doorstep,' Jimmy said.

'What?'

'It's something they used to say when I was in the Navy; the married lads used to play away, but never where they lived.'

A look flickered across Wendy Lang's face that Jimmy couldn't quite pin down – regret maybe? Then she blinked and was back in the present.

'You were in the Navy?' she said, clearly surprised, as if he'd suddenly whipped off a mask to reveal a whole new Jimmy. She passed him the tea.

Jimmy took the cup and immediately dropped it onto the stone floor where it smashed to pieces, hot tea flying everywhere. Wendy Lang jumped as if a bomb had gone off. He remembered Andrew Lang saying something about her nerves – he wasn't wrong.

'Shit, sorry,' Jimmy said. As he'd hoped, she immediately grabbed a cloth, fell to her knees and started wiping up tea. There was no way she could see the window from there. Outside, Deano, took his sound cue, lowering himself from the roof and dropping the last few feet to the ground. As soon as he landed, he glanced through the window, winked at Jimmy, picked something up from the ground and ran off, disappearing from sight around the side of the house. Jimmy exhaled. Job done.

He knelt down next to Wendy Lang and started to pick

up bits of broken china. She was still wiping furiously at the spilled liquid as if it was blood. She looked up at him properly for the second time.

'What do you really want?' she said.

She pushed her hair behind her ears. That's when he saw the remnants of a black eye; she'd tried to cover it with both her hair and make-up, but there were still tell-tale traces of purple bruising on her pale skin. He couldn't help remembering Ellington's brutal attack on Deano in the park – the man was handy with his fists.

'Did someone hit you?' he asked.

'No,' she said. A little too quickly. He could see her hands trembling. He held her gaze, leaving the question out there; using the silence again to see if she'd give him something else. The move paid a surprising dividend.

'Look, it's nothing, a spur of the moment thing, that's all. Andrew's been under a lot of stress, barely eating or sleeping. Especially since Roger's body was found.'

At first Jimmy thought he'd misheard her. She didn't seem the kind of woman who let things slip. Admitting that Andrew had hit her was one thing, but was she deliberately putting her husband in the frame for murder?

'What are you saying?'

'Nothing. Ignore me, I talk too much when I'm nervous. We'll be fine. He just needed a bit of space for a few days, that's all.'

She glanced at her watch like she was waiting for something to happen. Jimmy wondered if she *had* called someone when she'd gone upstairs.

'Maybe I should go,' he said.

She grabbed hold of his arm.

'No, don't. I'll make you another cup. Then we can talk a bit more about Roger. Properly talk. Just let me clean this up first.'

Jimmy could feel desperation coming off her; he'd seen that a lot inside, knew what it looked like. And suddenly the realisation hit him – he thought he'd been the one playing for time, giving Deano a chance to get away. But in reality, she'd been slowing things down, keeping him there; casually dropping in the bombshell about Andrew to give the cavalry time to arrive, whoever that was.

'No, you're alright, I'll get myself off,' he said. 'Sorry to have bothered you.'

She kept a firm grip on his sleeve, leaned in closer. For one bizarre moment he thought she was going to kiss him.

'It's no bother. It's good to have someone to talk to for a change. I could make you a sandwich.' She tried to smile but it didn't reach her eyes.

'It's OK, I'm not hungry. I've got to go,' Jimmy said.

He shrugged her hand off and headed out of the kitchen to the front door. It was locked. He turned around. She had followed him into the hallway.

'It's locked,' he said.

'Is it? Sorry about that. Force of habit. Always lock it behind me when I'm on my own.'

He knew she was lying. When you've spent years having doors locked to keep you inside it was the kind of thing you noticed. She hadn't done it when they came into the house;

it must have been when she went out of the kitchen. To make sure he couldn't leave.

'Can you open it, please?'

'Sure. I'll just have to find my bag.'

She went back into the kitchen. More playing for time. He knew she hadn't brought her bag back in with her earlier. She'd left it upstairs. He was suddenly very afraid. He thought about running up the stairs and getting out the same way Deano had, but there was no way he'd get through the small window.

He looked around the hallway, hoping that there was a place for spare keys somewhere, a small hook or a dish or something – Bev had always liked to keep a spare handy just in case. Nothing. But there was a coat rack in the corner. He tried the pockets on a couple of coats, a red fleece and a blue denim jacket but no joy. Pulling them aside, he saw another coat – a large black jacket. He stared at it, running the CCTV image through his head again. He wasn't going to make the satchel mistake again. It wasn't the same jacket. This one had a white stripe running down the sleeve. He tried the pockets. Bingo. A small key ring. He grabbed it and ran to the door, fumbling the keys as he tried to find the right one. The third one he tried worked. He was out.

Deano was sitting on a small wall at the far end of the street, wired, his heels tap-tap-tapping on the bricks.

'Shit, man, that was a blast.'

'Don't get a taste for it,' Jimmy said.

'You should try it. The rush is nearly as good as poppers.'

'I'll take your word for it. What happened in there?'

'Oh man, you did great. I was halfway doon the stairs when I heard you shouting out the front. Double-backed and hid on the landing, didn't I? Thought I'd wait until things settled doon before sneaking out the front door. But then I heard her coming up, so I nipped back upstairs, into one of the bedrooms.'

'What did she do?'

'Only followed me up there, didn't she? Had to dive under a bed, hold me breath and hope for the best.'

'And?'

'Not sure, couldn't see much. I heard her moving on the landing. Walking and talking. On the phone. Then she put something in one of the cupboards. Didn't knaa what at the time.'

Jimmy again wondered who she'd called.

'Did you hear what she was saying?'

'Not really, too far away.'

'Then what?' Jimmy asked.

'Got out of there, didn't I? Heard her go back doon, didn't want to risk getting caught on the stairs again, so I nipped back out the bathroom window. Had to wait on the roof of the conservatory till the coast was clear – great cup smash, by the way.'

'Thanks. Sorry it went a bit pear-shaped. I shouldn't have got you involved. Gadge'll have my balls on a plate when he hears about it.'

'Divvn't be daft, man, I won't tell him it was your idea. Haven't had so much fun for yonks.'

'Waste of time though, wasn't it?'

'I wouldn't say that,' Deano said, grinning.

'Why not?'

'Well, I said she put something in one of the cupboards, didn't I? So I had a little sniff around before I left. Found this, didn't I?' He reached behind the wall and pulled something up from behind it. Jimmy saw the strap first and felt his heart start to race.

'Da-daaa,' Deano said, revealing the bag in full.

Jimmy's heart sank again. It was Wendy Lang's bag. Not the satchel. He tried but failed to keep the disappointment from his face.

'You divvn't look ower-pleased, like,' Deano said, his grin slowly disappearing. 'Isn't it what you were looking for?'

'No, sorry, it's great,' Jimmy said. 'We might find something useful in there.' The kid had done his best.

'Already looked. Her phone's in the inside pocket,' Deano said enthusiastically. 'She'll have a password on it or something, but I bet Gadge'll be able to get into it. He can get into anything.'

Maybe they would get lucky. Find some incriminating texts or something. As if cued by the conversation, Deano took his own phone out of his pocket and glanced at it.

'Carrie's left a message,' he said, tapping the screen and putting the phone to his ear.

'Gadge is awake,' he said, grinning. 'I knew the old bastard wouldn't go quietly.'

As they stood up to head for the hospital, Jimmy heard a

screech of tyres and looked up. A police car had pulled up outside the house.

They watched as a uniform got out and ran towards the house. Not just any uniform. It was Duke. Now he knew for sure who she'd been calling, who she'd been trying to keep him in the house for. What he didn't know was why?

Before he'd had a chance to get his head around that he heard a shout and looked up. Duke was standing on the pavement outside the house looking directly at them.

'Shit the bed,' Deano said and started to run.

51

Freeman Hospital, July 18, 2012

The flag wavers were everywhere, hundreds of them lining the streets, hours ahead of the Queen's visit, flapping their Union Jacks around their heads, as if tormented by flying insects. Jimmy hadn't seen anything like it since his return from the Falklands, when he'd sailed into Southampton on the *QE2* with the other ship-less casualties, a tearful Bev waiting on the quayside, her own small flag in hand. A lifetime ago.

They'd managed to get away from Ellington, diving down an alley, through an allotment and out the other side before he could get anywhere near them. It still took them ages to get back to the hospital, what with the royalists and the roadblocks; police everywhere. Eventually they cut their losses and jumped the Metro to South Gosforth. From there they took the back roads, sneaking through the edge of Paddy Freeman's Park, all the time listening out for sirens. The nearer they got, the more they heard, Deano jumping at every one, even though he must have known they were mostly ambulances.

All that time Jimmy had been trying to piece it all together: the Langs, Collins and Ellington – all four of them involved in one way or another, he was certain of that now. What the hell was Wendy Lang up to? Trying to keep him locked in until Duke got there, for sure. But why? To have him arrested? Or something much worse? Was it Duke who Jimmy had seen on the Quayside? He was big enough, no doubt about that, and it would explain how the lighter ended up in his rucksack. Jimmy had tried to rerun the CCTV camera images through his head once again but it was no good; it really could have been anybody – especially with that padded coat beefing them up, making them look way bigger than they probably were. And how did Collins' foreman fit into it all?

As they approached the hospital, he saw two familiar faces sitting on the smokers' bench outside: Carrie and Brian. He packed Deano off to see Gadge and sat on the bench next to them.

'Doing a bit of ambulance chasing, are you?' he said to Brian.

'No!' the reporter said. 'Came to see Carrie, actually. I've got some news.'

'About time,' Jimmy said. 'Thought you must have been on holiday. What's the news, Scoop?'

'Bin the sarcasm, Jimmy,' Carrie said. 'Give him a break – he got into trouble digging around for us. Nearly lost his job.'

He was being harsh on the lad, he knew that, the disappointment over not finding the satchel still bugging him.

'Sorry,' he said. 'Just being a twat for a change.'

'Apology accepted,' Brian said graciously. 'Listen up, and don't pass this on, it's confidential.' He pulled them in closer, looking around to make sure no one was was snooping around. The lad loved his job; there was no doubt about that.

'I was talking to our education specialist and he's got a bit of an exclusive up his sleeve. He can't publish it yet because it's part of an ongoing fraud investigation involving the university. Apparently, Ed Collins the builder is part of it. He's been submitting inflated invoices for work he's done there. He's trousered thousands of pounds. There's a warrant out for his arrest.'

'He's already been arrested,' Carrie said. 'DS Burns told me that this morning.'

Brian looked a little deflated. 'Oh, right, didn't know that. However, that's not the best bit. It takes two to tango – someone on the inside had to sign off the dodgy invoices.'

He paused for dramatic effect, nodding as he saw they had both quickly worked it out for themselves.

'Andrew Lang. They think he's been pocketing half of the money. They've still got to dot the i's and cross the t's but the word on the street is that he'll be arrested this afternoon. We're waiting on confirmation so we can publish the story.'

'Jesus,' Carrie said. 'No wonder he seemed stressed.'

'Apparently, the university were trying to deal with it

internally, but there's a whistle-blower on the staff, one of the registrars.'

'Norma Weston!' Carrie exclaimed. Jimmy nodded – Burns had said he was going to interview her, it sounded like she'd given him something solid.

'Thing is,' Brian said, 'that might not be the end of it.'

'How do you mean?' Carrie asked.

Jimmy knew exactly what he meant. Could see it coming a mile off. Maybe Wendy Lang had been steering him in the right direction after all?

'They think your dad found out about it,' Brian said. 'Tried to get Lang to come clean and Collins had him killed to shut him up. Some ex-jailbird who works for Collins is in the frame.'

Jimmy took the lift up to Gadge's floor, dying to see his ugly face again. He was wondering if Brian was right – that the foreman, Ewan Milburn, had murdered Roger Carpenter. He certainly seemed to have all the right qualifications.

. . . your system, it's wrong.

Roger's anguished shout on the Quayside came back to him. That seemed to fit as well. Something to do with finances maybe? Burns had said they should follow the money. He'd also said something about Norma Weston blaming herself for Roger's death – if she'd told Carrie's dad what was going on, he might have tried to do something about it. And got himself killed in the process.

He was still thinking about this when he was stopped at the reception desk by the young nurse he'd met the last time he'd been on the ward.

'Here to see your friend?'

'That's right,' Jimmy said.

'You're cutting it fine, visiting ends in ten minutes.'

'I know, I won't be long,' he said, heading towards the room.

'Just a minute,' the nurse said. She looked over her shoulder as if to check that the coast was clear. He hoped she didn't have more bad news.

'Look, I probably shouldn't tell you this, but did you know he was admitted last year?'

'No,' Jimmy said.

'He'd had heart palpitations. The doctor who saw him told him he had to stop drinking immediately or he probably wouldn't see the year out. Said he had to choose between alcohol and life.'

Jimmy tried to imagine Gadge without a drink in his hand, but the image wouldn't come.

'He should get help,' she said. 'It's such a waste.'

Jimmy avoided her gaze, knowing that the same thing applied to him, half wondering if she'd been coached by Carrie.

'I'll, um, have a word,' he mumbled, knowing he would probably do no such thing. The man had made his choice.

His friend was sitting up in bed, as pale as the bedsheets, and with tubes coming out of everywhere, but he was alive and that was all that Jimmy cared about for now.

'Divvn't start blurting like this one,' Gadge said, pointing to Deano, his voice even more gravelly than usual. 'Or you'll get me going again.'

Deano was sat on the far edge of the bed, his hand on Gadge's arm, his tear-stained face breaking into a cheesy grin as he held up a packet of Maltesers.

'I bought him some chocolates,' he said, throwing one up and catching it in his mouth. 'What did you get?'

'It better be grapes,' Gadge croaked. 'And by that I mean wine, obviously.'

Jimmy thought he should at least make the effort. 'Strictly teetotal from now on, the nurse says.'

'Teetotal, my arse,' Gadge said and that was the end of that. 'You can get off me now, son,' he said to Deano. 'Give a man a little bit of breathing space.'

Deano moved his arm away and slipped off the bed.

'And since when did you start carrying a man bag?' Gadge said, pointing at the handbag hanging off Deano's shoulder. 'I leave you alone for five minutes and you gan all metro-sexual on me!'

'It's not mine,' Deano protested, looking at Jimmy for help. 'Jimmy can explain.'

'It's Wendy Lang's. We "borrowed" it from Ellington's house,' Jimmy said.

'You got the address then.'

Jimmy nodded. 'Aye, thanks for that.'

Gadge grinned. 'I'll send you my bill.'

'Waste of time really,' Jimmy said. 'We thought Wendy Lang's phone might have a story to tell but that's been overtaken by events now.' He explained what Brian had told them about Collins and Andrew Lang.

'It's always about money in the end,' Gadge said.

'That's what Burns said. Looks like he was right.'

'Greedy bastards,' Gadge said.

Jimmy and Deano nodded.

'I could still look at the phone if you want,' Gadge added. 'It'll cost you extra, mind.'

Jimmy laughed. The man was incorrigible.

'Nowt to lose, I suppose.' He nodded to Deano who took the phone out of Wendy Lang's bag and handed it over. Gadge began to examine it.

'Password protected,' he said. 'Might be tricky.'

Jimmy shrugged. It didn't matter anyway. Carrie had got a resolution of some sort, but he was screwed either way. Ellington was bound to report the theft of the bag and once Sandy found out she'd have no choice but to return him into custody. No one else to blame – he knew the risks. He suddenly felt very tired.

'Bingo,' Gadge said. 'What do you want me to look for?'

Jimmy looked up.

'What?'

'1-2-3-4,' he said, 'most common PIN number in the world. People are inherently lazy-slash-stupid – take your pick.'

Gadge clicked through various screens.

'Nothing much here,' he said. 'All the baskets are pretty empty, she must delete her texts regularly. I'll try her photos. Most people don't realise they have to delete them twice. The first time they just go into another folder.' Jimmy watched as Gadge tapped the screen several times before pausing, swiping through something, his eyes widening, his hand moving over his heart.

'Heavens-to-fucking-Betsy,' Gadge said. 'This is not the kind of thing a man with a dodgy ticker should be looking at. You need to see this.'

Jimmy took the phone. The screen was a blur of fleshy pink and swollen red. It took him a moment or two to register what he was looking at – an extreme close-up of a couple fucking. So close that you could see where their pubic hair entwined. He flicked through several photos, the first ones more of the same from slightly different angles, each more graphic than the last. Then a shot of the woman's small breasts and then one of her face. It was Wendy Lang.

'Christ,' he said.

The last photo was the same as the first, but it had an arrow on the middle of the screen.

'What's this?' he said, holding the phone out to Gadge.

'A video. Press the arrow.'

The video followed the same pattern, gradually moving up from their genitals, over Wendy Lang's body to her face, her eyes closed, mouth slightly open, shoulders shaking. The shot was held there for a few moments, then went fuzzy as the camera was turned around, taking in a quick shot of a wardrobe. Eventually it settled down again. Staring out at Jimmy from the small screen was the grinning face of David 'Duke' Ellington, his uniform jacket still buttoned up. Wendy Lang was fucking her brother.

Jimmy and Carrie sat in the canteen staring at the phone, which was lying on the table in front of them, face down, neither of them wanting to see the images ever again. Deano was at the counter trying to persuade the server to give him more chips.

The ward sister had cleared them out of Gadge's room, having walked in as Jimmy was watching the video. He was thankful that there was no sound.

'I feel sick,' Carrie said. 'It's incest – you can't *do it* with your sister.'

Jimmy sat up.

'Say that again.'

'I said, "I feel sick."'

'No, not that, the other bit.'

'It's incest, you can't do it with your sister.'

And just like that he knew. What happened that night on the Quayside suddenly crystal clear: *I saw you . . . fucking incest . . . your sister.*

'Carrie . . .'

'What?'

'I think . . . I think it was Ellington.'

'What was Ellington?'

'He's the one who killed your dad.'

'What are you talking about? I thought it was this guy who worked for Collins.'

He talked her through it, reminding her what he'd heard that night, Carrie nodding as each piece of the jigsaw came together, tears forming in her eyes. She took a breath or two, clearly fighting to hold back much stronger emotions.

'We have to tell Burns,' she said. She reached for Wendy Lang's phone, but then pulled back, reluctant even to touch it. Instead she pulled her own phone out.

'We're not supposed to carry these on duty,' she said. 'Been keeping it in my bra today, so I could contact you about Gadge.'

She tried to call Burns, but Jimmy could hear the phone ringing and ringing at the other end. No answer. That seemed strange – surely policemen always answered their phones, just in case? He knew that wouldn't be the end of it for Carrie though. She was dogged, like he guessed her dad must have been. He suddenly wished he'd met him . . . before.

'That's odd,' she said. 'I'll try his office number.'

Someone answered this time; a tinny voice on the other end.

'DS Burns, please,' Carrie said. She frowned. 'Where is he?' Another frown. 'No, I don't want to leave a message. I need to speak to him urgently and he's not answering his phone.' A small blue vein started to pulse on the side of her head. He could see her hand beginning to tremble.

'I don't give a rat's arse about procedure,' she said. 'You just pulled my dead father out of the river and I think I know who put him there. I'm pretty sure that DS Burns will want to know that too. And if you're the person who stops him from knowing it, he'll probably ram a truncheon up your arse.'

Jimmy put his hand on her arm to try and calm her down.

She glanced at him, saw his concern, put her hand over the phone.

'It's that civvy again, the one that Burns was telling us about. She's the only one in the office, pretty much everyone else is out on the street for the Queen's visit. She's gone to try and find someone.'

'Hello,' Carrie said eventually.

The tinny voice came out of the phone again. The explanation took some time.

'Can't you tell me a little more than that? Right. Thanks for nothing.' She switched the phone off and turned to Jimmy.

'They won't tell me exactly where he's gone – just that he's gone to execute an arrest warrant.' She smiled. 'But we know where that is, don't we?'

'Andrew Lang's house,' Jimmy said, offering up a silent thank you to Brian for his inside information. The lad had done good in the end. 'I could go there. See if I can catch him. Let him know he's got the wrong man. Show him this,' he added, picking up Wendy Lang's phone.

'There's no need for that,' Carrie began, but then stopped, as it started to ring. Jimmy almost dropped it, but recovered from his initial shock and looked at the screen.

'It's Ellington.'

'Answer it,' Carrie said. 'See what the sick bastard has to say.' She leaned in close to Jimmy and pressed to accept the call, switching it to speakerphone.

'Hello,' a man's voice said.

Neither of them said anything, letting him make the first move.

'Listen, you fucking lowlife, I know it's you. I want that phone back. If you don't get it back to me within the hour, I'll hunt you down like the vermin you are. I know where to find you. There's a tracker on the phone, you fucking moron.'

Before Jimmy could react, Carrie grabbed the phone.

'I know what you did, you murdering twat. You're the vermin. You killed my dad.'

There was a long pause. They could hear Ellington breathing on the other end.

'I don't know who you are or what you're talking about,' he said eventually, worried about being recorded Jimmy guessed.

'Fuck you,' Carrie said. 'We've seen the photos.'

'What photos?'

'Don't even . . .' she stopped, almost hyperventilating.

Jimmy put his hand on her shoulder as she took several breaths. He couldn't believe that she'd got this far without falling to pieces. She was like the Terminator. You could knock her down, but she just bounced back up and kept on coming at you. Once she'd calmed down, she went again.

'Listen, you piece of shit. I am going to send those photos to DS Burns. Then with one fucking touch of a button I'm going to send them to every single person on your perverted sister's contact list. Then I'm going to send them to every local and national paper I can find. Then we'll see who's going to be hunted down. How do you like them apples?'

There was a long silence. Then the call was cut off. Jimmy stared at Carrie in admiration.

'Well, that told him,' he said.

She closed her eyes and let out a long breath before

putting the phone back on the table. 'What do you think he'll do?' she asked. 'He might come after us.'

Jimmy shook his head.

'He'll run,' Jimmy said. 'Him and Wendy Lang. What choice do they have? I'm sure he killed your dad, but finding real proof won't be easy, even if Burns can be persuaded to look for it. But incest's still a crime. Ellington could go to prison and no cop wants that. And even if that doesn't happen, those photos will end his career and humiliate both of them. They couldn't live with people around them knowing about this. Trust me, they'll run.'

Carrie picked up Wendy Lang's phone again.

'Do you even know how to do that?' Jimmy asked. 'Send them out to everyone at the touch of a button.'

'Not a clue,' she said. 'I could do it one at a time, but it would take forever.'

'Gadge'll know, but visiting hours are over.'

'Not for nurses,' she said.

52

Gosforth, Newcastle, July 18, 2012

The empty police car felt like an omen.

It was parked up a couple of streets away from the Langs' house but there was no sign of its occupants; there was never a copper in sight when you needed one. Jimmy looked around for a moment or two then moved on. No time to waste. He'd already lost too much working his way around the roadblocks.

After Carrie went to seek out Gadge he'd sat in the canteen for some time thinking that it was almost over. But then he started fretting that Ellington and Wendy Lang were going to escape justice. Jimmy was sure they'd already be on the road, but felt he had to try and stop them before they were out of the country. The only way he could think of doing that was to find Burns – he knew from his time chasing down deserters that you needed someone in authority to set things in motion, alert the airports and that. He just hoped he wasn't too late.

As he neared the Langs' house he could hear doors being slammed, and when he turned into the driveway, he saw Andrew Lang throwing something into the boot of his own car. There was no sign of DS Burns. And there was a suitcase on the ground next to the car. Was Lang doing a runner as well?

'Going somewhere nice?' Jimmy said.

Lang jumped, catching the back of his head on the lid of the open boot.

'Fuck!' he shouted, rubbing his head. 'You again? What do you want this time?'

'I'm looking for DS Burns,' Jimmy said.

Lang looked even worse than he had the last time, still unshaven, sweating heavily, shirt unironed, a button hanging off his jacket. His eyes flicked towards the house, then back to Jimmy.

'Never heard of him.'

Lang reached back into the boot again. Jimmy knew he was lying, just wasn't sure why. He moved closer to the car.

'He's the man investigating Roger Carpenter's murder.'

Lang reappeared from under the boot, a golf club in his hand.

'Keep away from me,' he said.

Jimmy backed off a fraction, holding his hands up to try and calm the man. 'There's no need for that,' he said.

Lang blinked, his eyes flicking towards the house again. 'Isn't there? You've been harassing me for weeks, turning up at the house uninvited, attacking me in my own home. Threatening behaviour, the police call it.'

'I'm not the one with a golf club in my hand,' Jimmy said, edging closer, so close that he could now see there was blood on the head of the club and a dark stain on the sleeve of Lang's jacket.

'Not sure that's how the law will see it,' Lang said. 'A respected academic attacked on his own property by a vagrant, trying to steal his car. I'd bet you've got a criminal record to boot. If I was you, I'd walk away while you still can.'

Jimmy shook his head. He was way past that. It was obvious Lang was bluffing. He was doing a runner. From the fraud investigation or something worse – Jimmy wasn't sure. What he did know was that he wasn't going to let him go.

'Respected academic?' Jimmy said. 'Not what I've been hearing. I hear Burns has a warrant out for your arrest.'

Lang took a pace towards Jimmy.

'Roger's death was nothing to do with me.'

'No, that was your brother-in-law's responsibility.'

That stopped him. Lang looked bemused.

'What are you talking about? Who told you that?'

'I know about your wife and her brother – I think Roger did too.'

Lang's arms started to shake; he looked like he was going to explode.

'Everyone knows about those perverts now.'

'Have you seen the photos?' Jimmy asked.

'I fucking have now . . . the bitch sent them to me her-self . . . just to rub my nose in it. I can't even begin to . . . it's obscene – *they're* obscene.'

Carrie had obviously managed to get Gadge to work his magic. He could have corrected Lang's assumption as to who had sent them but it was working to his benefit. Lang seemed lost in his own angry world. Jimmy took a step closer.

'Back off,' Lang screamed, raising the club. 'Are you saying that you think David killed Roger? Because he knew about them?'

'I know he did. I think Roger saw them together and threatened to tell everyone if they didn't stop what they were doing.'

Lang's expression softened and he lowered the club slightly. 'Roger always thought he could fix things. He would have known this would destroy me . . . Christ, I miss him.' He paused for a moment, clearly trying to digest the implications of what he'd just learned.

'Didn't you know about them?' Jimmy said.

'No, of course not. I'd guessed she was having an affair, but I never dreamed it was with her brother. We had a fight. I thought that was why she'd moved out – to give us time to think; not so she could fuck him whenever she liked.'

Jimmy remembered her black eye. He almost admired the way Wendy Lang had turned that into something else, implying that Andrew was cracking up over Roger's death.

'D'you think Wendy knew what he'd done?' Lang asked. He was starting to fall apart in front of Jimmy's eyes – the depth of his wife's betrayal sinking into his bone marrow.

It was a good question. Maybe not from the start, Jimmy thought, though she'd clearly considered it: the phone call, hovering around Carrie's apartment – all those things pointed to her fearing the worst, looking for confirmation, one way or the other. But she knew now, he was certain of that. And she was still with Ellington.

Jimmy nodded. 'Probably.'

Lang seemed to shrivel up in front of him.

'And she still wanted him more than me? Her own fucking brother. Sold my fucking soul for her – I'm up to my ears in debt – and that's how she pays me back? Sleeps with her brother and helps kill my best fucking friend.'

'If she's an accessory to murder, she'll get what's coming to her,' Jimmy said.

'You can take that to the bank,' Lang said, his brow furrowing, a look of pain on his face. 'She was sterilised, you know. Before we even met. Said she'd always known she didn't want kids. Now I know the real reason.' He shook his head vigorously, as if trying to eject the image of his wife and her brother together, and refocused on Jimmy.

'D'you have kids?'

Jimmy nodded, distracted by something over Lang's shoulder.

'I would have liked to,' Lang said, wistfully.

Jimmy could see a hazy light flickering behind the closed front door of the house. Couldn't quite make it out. But then he smelled it. The smell that haunted his nightmares. Fire. The fucking house was on fire.

'What the hell?' Jimmy started to move towards the house. Out of the corner of his eye he saw Lang take a pace forward, the club swinging at his head. He swayed back, out of the way, his old boxing instincts kicking in, as the club passed inches in front of his face. To his attacker's obvious surprise, Jimmy stepped in closer, restricting the space, making Lang readjust, forcing him to step backwards himself.

Jimmy could see large patches of sweat forming under the man's armpits, could smell the booze seeping out of him. He guessed his hands were equally sweaty, his grip on the club slipping.

'You should go now,' Lang said. 'I'll not miss again. This isn't your problem.'

It was true, but Jimmy had come a long way from *not my fight*.

'Looks like you've already hit someone,' he said, nodding at the blood on the end of the club. Lang followed his gaze and Jimmy pounced, stepping even closer. Lang tried to swing for his head again, but he was too late. Jimmy threw his left arm up to block the swing, sending the club flying out of Lang's hands. At the same time he threw the perfect uppercut with his right, hitting his attacker smack on the point of his chin. Lang's knees buckled and he fell backwards, cracking his head on the side of the car.

A memory of Kev's head bouncing off the pavement tried to force its way into Jimmy's mind, but this time he closed it down before it kicked in fully. There wasn't time.

Jimmy kicked the club further away, towards the house, but there was no need – Lang was spark out. Jimmy pulled him up, bundled him into the boot, ripped out the escape handle and slammed the lid down, only then noticing the pain in his own left arm – something broken, he reckoned.

Doing his best to ignore it, Jimmy ran over to the house, certain that there was someone in there – that was the only explanation for Lang's behaviour. The smell of burning was much stronger now, more light flickering through the frosted-glass door. He tried the handle, but the door was locked. He picked up the golf club and swung it at the glass. A few cracks appeared. Another swing. More cracks. The third swing did the trick, the top pane shattering completely. Smoke poured out of the hole. Through the smoke he could see someone lying in the hallway. It was DS Burns – his head nearest to Jimmy, feet pointing towards the kitchen. Jimmy leaned through the door frame and flicked open the lock from the inside, yanking the door open.

Burns was unconscious, blood seeping slowly from the back of his head. Jimmy reached down to grab him under his arms, but the pain in his own arm was unbearable; definitely something broken. Instead he grabbed Burns by the collar with his good arm and heaved him along the floor, over the broken glass and out into the fresh air, pulling him onto the lawn in front of the house.

He knelt over him. Still breathing. Checked the head wound; nasty, but it didn't look life threatening. He pulled off Burns's jacket and lifted his head up, placing the bulk of the jacket underneath it and tying the arms around it as best he could to try and put pressure on the wound. Makeshift, but hopefully effective. Why the hell had Lang attacked Burns? It seemed too extreme – a fraud charge was bad, but it didn't seem enough to warrant attacking a cop and leaving him lying in a burning building.

Jimmy looked up and saw the answer right in front of him. He should have noticed it sooner. Parked on the other side of the road was Wendy Lang's car, the Volkswagen Beetle. He'd thought that she and Ellington would have been long gone by now. He remembered Lang's boast when Jimmy had said she would get what was coming. *You can take that to the bank.*

He ran to her car and opened the boot, fearing there would be a body in it. No body, but a suitcase and one other bag. Why had she come back to the house and not gone straight to the airport? To get the rest of her stuff maybe?

Jimmy looked back at the house. Was she in there as well? The smoke was getting worse, pouring out of the shattered front door now but he didn't know where the fire was; hadn't had time to look around before dragging Burns out. If it was at the back of the house, he might have time to check. If he wanted to. Like Lang said, it wasn't his problem. He could just sit there and let the cards fall where they may.

He shook his head. That was the old Jimmy. He ran back to the front of the house, but froze as a flame shot into the hallway from under the kitchen door.

A fireball hits Red square in the chest, shooting him backwards through the air like a blazing rag doll, crashing into the guard rail. For a moment he hangs there, a vaguely human shape in a haze of flame, a pair of orange and black arm-like shadows windmilling for balance. And then he's gone.

Fuck it. He ran back in. The kitchen door was just about holding up, but smoke was now pouring underneath it and the occasional flame licking out around its sides – he'd bet that was the source of the fire. He ran towards it, but felt the heat building up behind it, the fire searching for new oxygen to feed on. No way he was opening that door; the whole place would go up in moments. It was solid though and should hold back the fire long enough that he could search elsewhere. He looked in the small front room. Sofa. TV. Nothing else. Nowhere to hide a body. Back in the hallway, an under-stairs cupboard, again nothing. He glanced at the stairs. No time to waste. Up he went. Small bedroom to the left. Neat and tidy but empty. Big bedroom to the right. Wardrobe doors flung open, all empty. Another suitcase on the bed, packed with women's clothes. He'd guessed right – she'd come back for the rest of her stuff.

There was an open door in the corner of the bedroom, the frame around the lock splintered; an en-suite bathroom. He glanced in, again nobody there, but full of lotions and potions, several bottles scattered on the floor and the shower curtain hanging off its rail. A fight of some kind? Out of the rear window he could see flames shooting out of the conservatory; hoped someone had called the fire brigade.

Back out into the hallway, the smoke much heavier now. He dashed back into the bedroom, ripped off a pillowcase, soaked it in the sink and held it over his mouth. One more floor to go. Not much time. He heard something collapsing downstairs, hesitated, maybe he should get out? But then another noise; not the fire this time, something human. A groan maybe? He sprinted up to the top floor and there she was, Wendy Lang, lying on the landing, face down, a scarf tied tightly around her neck. He turned her over, loosened the scarf, her eyes flickered open but then closed again, a small sound slipping from her lips. Her nose was crusted in blood, bent to one side, broken by the look of it. He tried to lift her, but an agonising pain shot through his damaged arm again. Somehow, he managed to pull her upright with his good arm and propped her against the wall. Then he leaned into her stomach, so she flopped over his right shoulder and pushed up with his legs, gripping her skirt with his good hand to hold her steady. He headed down the first flight of stairs, his left hand only good for keeping the wet pillowcase over his mouth. On the first floor he could see that the fire had taken hold downstairs now; flames climbing the stairs from below, the paint on the banister starting to blister. He took a deep breath and scrambled down to the halfway point. The bottom half of the stairway was ablaze, the flames the only things visible through the thick black smoke. No time to think about it. Ten steps to freedom. He headed down. Nine. Eight. The heat was intense now. He could smell singed hair and realised it was probably his own. Seven. Six. The fifth step collapsed under his feet and he plummeted to the floor. As he landed, he felt his ankle crack and Wendy Lang was catapulted forward into the open front doorway. Jimmy tried to stand but his ankle was knacked. He clawed his way towards her, pushing off the floor with his good arm, fortunate that the air was clearer at that level, the smoke rising to the ceiling. As he reached her, the burning banister crashed to the floor behind him, flames licking at his legs. She coughed a little, seemingly kick-started by the fall. He grabbed hold of her by the waist and dragged her forward, feeling the broken glass beneath him ripping through his shirt. On he crawled, pulling her with him until they hit clean air, but still he didn't stop. Over the gravel path and onto the lawn, where Burns lay, still unconscious. Then he heard the siren.

They sat on a wall on the opposite side of the road watching the firemen at work. The upper storeys of the Langs' house were now completely ablaze, the men's hoses focused on the ground floor. They'd been lucky: Jimmy's arm and ankle would probably require surgery, but most of their cuts and bruises were superficial. The paramedics had given them a quick once-over and handed Wendy Lang a bottle of water, carrying Jimmy over to the wall, before concentrating on the more immediate problem of Burns, who was alive but still unconscious. Jimmy hadn't even told them about Andrew Lang. The police were on their way, held up by all the road closures apparently. Hopefully, by the time they arrived, Burns would have come round and be able to clear everything up. Until then, Lang could stay in the boot.

'You saved my life,' Wendy Lang said – the first words she'd uttered since he pulled her out of the house. Even when the paramedics had checked her out she'd remained silent, seemingly in shock at her entire world going up in smoke. The words didn't come easy, her voice a strangled rasp, and he saw her reach to her throat where a thick red weal from the scarf was plainly visible.

He said nothing.

'Why?' she croaked.

He shrugged, glanced at the house, the fire still raging. 'No one deserves to die like that.'

'Where's Andrew?' she said.

'You don't need to worry about Andrew,' Jimmy said, glancing across at the car.

Jimmy could feel her staring at him, knew she would be testing him out, trying to work out how much he knew.

'I didn't know at first. Honestly, not for sure,' she said quietly. 'I didn't believe Roger had gone off with a woman, but I never thought that he had been ...'

'... murdered,' Jimmy added. 'Just so we're clear.'

'He said it was an accident,' she croaked, taking a big glug of water to ease the pain.

'I was there,' Jimmy said. 'It was no accident.' If he closed his eyes, he could still hear Roger's body being dragged towards the edge. 'Roger was knocked out and thrown in the river.'

She was crying silently, nodding her head, an occasional tear falling to the pavement.

'I knew something was wrong, though, before he finally confessed,' she continued. 'It changed him.'

Jimmy nodded, he could relate to that. The dead stayed with you, sitting on your shoulders, mocking you, weighing you down.

'He had stopped eating, he couldn't sleep, he was drinking – and he was never a drinker. He lost so much weight. It was like he was ... haunted.'

'Wait a minute – you're saying *Andrew* killed Roger?' he said, failing to hide his astonishment at her nerve.

She nodded, wiping away the tears with the back of her hand. He shook his head. She was keeping everything as close to the truth as she could, except the identity of the killer. It was one hell of a performance under the circumstances.

'Carrie deserves to know the truth, Wendy. She needs to know what happened to her dad.'

'I'm telling you the truth,' she said, glaring at him, willing him to accept her nonsense.

'I was leaving him, that's why he tried to kill me.'

Jimmy remembered the suitcase on the bed. She was good, weaving the truth and the lies together expertly.

'I came here to get the rest of my stuff. David was supposed to pick me up. We were going to go away for a few days, get away from all this mess. I didn't think Andrew would be home so early, didn't know he'd been suspended. He came up the stairs, saw the suitcase and started shouting at me. I locked myself in the bathroom, thought I was safe. But he smashed the door down, punched me in the face, pulled me out by my hair. Accused me of all kinds of things, having an affair, telling the police about his financial problems. I don't remember much else, think I blanked out.'

She put her hands to her face, openly sobbing.

Across the road Jimmy could see Burns sitting up now, the paramedics giving him some space. He could hear more sirens on the way. He had one last chance to get to some semblance of the truth before the police got hold of her and she hid behind the lawyers.

'I've seen the photos, Wendy, and the video. Andrew has

seen them. *Everyone* has seen them. I know what happened that night.'

She didn't look at him. Didn't say anything; just stared at the ground, slowly shaking her head.

'You were fucking your brother. That's what this was all about. Roger saw you together – in the house, I'm guessing – and threatened to tell everyone unless you stopped. Everything else you've said is probably true. I can believe you didn't know, at first, maybe even believed that Roger had done a runner. But one thing you and I both know for sure is that it wasn't Andrew who killed him. It was Duke.'

She almost laughed, a dark, bitter noise escaping her lips.

'I hate that nickname. His name is David.' She glared at Jimmy. 'Anyway, you don't *know* anything. You certainly can't prove anything.'

'You're probably right,' Jimmy said. 'But once the police have seen the photos . . .'

Wendy Lang looked over at Burns who was still talking to the paramedics.

'How much do you want?' she said.

'For what?' he said. 'The photos are out there, everyone has seen them. You can't buy them back.'

'Not for the photos. To say it was Andrew, to say that you saw *him* kill Roger, not David.'

Jimmy stared at her. She was a piece of work. Even though she knew what Ellington had done, she still wanted to save him. And crucify her husband into the bargain.

'I'll pay you whatever you want. Just give me a number.'

Jimmy shook his head. It was always about fucking money with these people.

'You couldn't afford me,' he said.

There was a sudden flurry of activity outside the house. Burns was on his feet now, looking across at them. The fire seemed to be under control, the flames dying down, but there was a lot of discussion going on. Jimmy watched as a fireman went back into the house, a paramedic close behind.

'You can't help who you fall in love with,' Wendy Lang said.

Was that true? Before Jimmy could say anything more he saw Burns heading across the road, walking slowly, his head bandaged.

He nodded at Jimmy. 'I owe you one apparently.'

'No bother,' Jimmy said. 'You'd have done the same for me.'

'Where's Andrew Lang?' Burns asked.

'He's in the boot of that car,' he added, pointing back across the road.

Burns laughed but Wendy Lang barely glanced up; she didn't seem to care one way or the other.

There was more activity across the road; the paramedic came out of the house, shaking his head.

'What's going on over there?' Jimmy said.

'That's why I asked about Lang,' Burns said. 'They've found a body in the kitchen, burned to a crisp.'

Now Wendy looked up, her eyes moving from Burns to the house and back again.

A fireman came out of the driveway and walked towards them. 'Did you have someone with you?' he asked Burns.

'No, course not,' Burns said. 'I'd have told you if I had. Why?'

'The body in the kitchen – looks like it's a cop.'

Right on cue two police cars sped into view, pulling up in front of the house, sirens wailing. Even that wasn't enough to drown out Wendy Lang's screams.

53

MEA House, Newcastle, August 4, 2012

'He was my best mate. And I saw him die. I think that should stay with you, it's only right. What kind of person would forget something like that? It would be disloyal, wouldn't it? I was depressed for a long time. Still am, I s'pose, sad at least. But that's natural, I reckon.'

He took a deep breath, looked around at the six other men in the room, all of them bar one looking at the floor, concentrating though, not ignoring him.

'I've done some stupid things, some really stupid things; things I regret deeply, and if there's a God of any kind, I've no doubt that I'll pay a heavy price. But at the end of the day I'm still here, still battling away. What else can I do? I owe it to my friend. He died that day, but I didn't. I've just got to keep going. It's my duty. Thanks for listening.'

Jimmy watched as the young kid got off the speaking chair and rejoined the others. He wondered if it was Aoife's grandson; would probably never know. Not that he was complaining. He liked the anonymity of the group – it felt safer.

No one else wanted to speak. It was Jimmy's third session and he hadn't spoken yet. Wasn't ready. Small steps, Carrie reckoned. Just keep going. Like the kid just said. Like she was doing, despite everything that had happened.

There was always tea afterwards. Someone got Jimmy a cup, taking pity on him because his arm was in a splint – cracked ulna the doc had said. He'd been luckier with the ankle, a small break – he had to wear a special boot for a few weeks and use a cane. He told anyone who asked that he'd been mugged.

When the tea came out it was like a switch had been thrown. Any talk of the horrors they'd all been through was off the agenda. Football was normally the safer ground. But not today.

'D'you read about the Homeless Hero?' one of the older guys asked.

'The guy who dragged that wifey and a cop out of a house fire?' another said.

'Yeah. D'you reckon he was ex-forces?'

'Deffo. No civvy would be mad enough to run into a burning house without all the proper gear on.'

Jimmy had given an exclusive to Brian. The lad deserved a leg-up after he had tried to help them. Some of the more salacious details were still under wraps – at least until the trials were under way; if they ever got under way – but it was still a great story. And this time the paper stuck by its no-names, no-photos promise. Burns had sung his praises in the piece; he was the one who'd coined the Homeless Hero name.

Jimmy and Burns had met up for a cup of coffee a couple of days earlier; Carrie too. It was awkward at first, each of them embarrassed by their own shortcomings. Burns because he'd been wrong about Ellington and then let Lang get the jump on him, having to be saved by Jimmy; Carrie because she'd sent the photos to Andrew Lang, which had inadvertently prompted his attack on Burns; and Jimmy because he hadn't identified Roger's attacker until it was almost too late.

'Don't beat yourself up, Jimmy. You wouldn't believe how unreliable eyewitness testimony is,' Burns said graciously. 'Don't tell the juries, mind, we like to keep that one secret. And you shouldn't be so hard on yourself either,' he said to Carrie. 'If you hadn't sent the photos out, Wendy Lang and Ellington would probably be sunning themselves on a Caribbean beach somewhere. We found false passports for both of them in Ellington's car.

'It looks like he was going to pick his sister up once she'd got all her stuff and head straight to the airport. Unfortunately for him, by the time he got to the house Andrew Lang had seen the photos. Ellington interrupted Lang's attack on his wife and got stabbed in the back with a kitchen knife for his troubles. Lang's admitted all of that.'

Burns put his hand to the small scar on his forehead, the only real sign of the injury he'd sustained that day.

'It's no wonder he battered me with that golf club the minute I walked through the door, he already had a dead cop lying in his kitchen, one more wasn't going to make any difference. I'm the real fuck-up here,' he added. 'If I'd listened more to you two, some of this might have been averted. I didn't know your dad, Carrie, but I do know that he'd be proud of you for how you've fought to get to the truth.'

A small smile crept onto Carrie's lips. Jimmy even thought he saw signs of a blush. He'd never seen her look so uncomfortable.

'What's happening with the Langs?' he asked, changing the subject to give her a break.

'What a pair,' Burns said. 'Wendy Lang will barely say a word and Andrew Lang won't shut up. He'll go down for the murder of Ellington and the assaults on his wife and yours truly, but he doesn't care – he's looking forward to his day in court. He seems to think of it as some kind of honour killing, for having his name tainted by incest. He can't wait to wash his wife's filthy laundry in public.

'We probably had enough to convict him anyway. Lang had Ellington's blood all over his sleeve and we found his fingerprints in the man's car – he'd moved it to try and confuse the issue.'

Jimmy remembered standing by the empty police car on his way to the Langs' house. He'd been waiting for a dead man.

'He'd probably have got away as well if it hadn't been for you,' Burns added.

'I was lucky,' Jimmy said.

Burns laughed. 'You don't look lucky. You look like you've

been hit by a bus. Anyway, Lang got the better of two trained cops, but you stopped him. That's not luck.'

It was Jimmy's turn to feel embarrassed. This time Carrie came to his rescue.

'What about Ellington?' Carrie said. 'Will there ever be a trial?'

Burns shook his head.

'No chance. There was plenty of evidence: you were right about the satchel, Jimmy, we found it in his attic; and we found the anonymous note he sent to your probation officer on his computer. But the CPS won't touch it when the suspect's dead. Way too difficult for them.

'Wendy Lang might be charged with assisting an offender, but I reckon the pen-pushers will even find it hard to make that stick. I'm afraid she'll probably walk ultimately. I'm sorry, Carrie. I know how pissed off you must be that no one will be brought to justice for your dad's murder.'

Carrie's response was typically robust.

'Actually, I don't give a stuff,' she said. 'The truth is out there. Ellington is dead and Wendy Lang will forever be known as the brother-fucker. I know that because even if she tries to move on, I'll be following her around the country painting it on her front door.'

Burns started to laugh.

'I'm not joking,' she said.

The cop looked unsure how to react. Jimmy thought he'd break it to him another day: she definitely wasn't joking. Carrie was a loyal friend, but he really wouldn't want her for an enemy.

Burns shook his head and got up to leave.

'I'd like to say I'm going to miss you two, but I'd be lying. It's hard to decide which one of you is the biggest pain in the arse. I won't be at all surprised if our paths cross again though.' He grinned at Jimmy. 'You know that if you save someone's life, you're responsible for them forever?'

'Sod that for a game of soldiers,' Jimmy said. 'I'm not good at responsibility. And you can look after yourself. What is that anyway? Buddhism or something?'

'No. *Star Wars*,' Burns laughed.

'You OK?' asked the kid who'd been the last to talk.

'What?' Jimmy said, and then realised he'd laughed out loud. He could see all the other lads in the group looking across at him, wondering what was going on. 'Sorry, yeah, fine. Just remembering something.'

'Care to share it?'

Jimmy knew what he was really asking. 'Maybe next time,' he said.

When he came outside the gang were there to greet him. He knew they were checking up on him really, making sure he was going to the therapy group. But what the hell, at least they cared. Dog was with Julie, sitting patiently, waiting to be told it was OK to move. Julie had been trying to teach him some obedience stuff, mainly because he kept jumping up on Jimmy's knackered arm. Maybe you could teach an old dog new tricks. He hoped so. Deano was behind them, pushing Gadge around in his new wheelchair, throwing in the occasional wheelie, just because he could; Carrie off to one side, talking to a friend, their backs to him. All in all, they looked like the perfect poster children for a dysfunctional-family ad campaign.

It had been a couple of weeks since Roger's funeral, a packed crem saying their goodbyes. Carrie had asked him to go with her, knowing that her mum would be useless and she'd need all the help she could get. He'd held her hand as several speakers said how much her dad had helped them, or their causes. Hearing how much he'd been appreciated had lifted her spirits. Jimmy noticed that most of them were women, but he didn't say anything.

As Jimmy hobbled towards them Carrie turned around and caught sight of him. 'Here comes Robocop,' she said, laughing with her friend.

Jimmy stopped hobbling, halted by the friend's smile. He knew that smile.

'Hello, Dad,' Kate said.

ACKNOWLEDGEMENTS

I first thought I'd like to write a book when I was fourteen. I blame Agatha Christie. A week trapped on a barge on the Norfolk Broads led to me reading a large chunk of her back catalogue and thinking 'Could I do that?'. It's a question that's taken a long time to answer. In the interim I've been a supermarket shelf-stacker, a sailor, a journalist, a spin-doctor and a playwright.

I'm sure that the fourteen-year-old me had an image of a writer bashing out his novel on an old typewriter in an attic room, isolated from the world, but the truth is no one can do this alone. To get here I had to first go back to Norfolk and the essential Base Camp of my assault on Mount First Novel, the UEA MA in Creative Writing – Crime Fiction. Anyone who wants to attempt the same climb should sign up immediately; the teaching, support and encouragement of the staff there, Henry Sutton, Tom Benn and, in particular, Laura Joyce were without parallel. As the first Crime Fiction course the 2015 cohort were very much guinea pigs but to a man and woman they were pedigree guinea pigs: Harriet

Tyce, Kate Simants, Caroline Jennett, Merle Nygate, Suzanne Mustacich, Marie Ogee, Geoff Smith, Jenny Stone, Shane Horsell and Steven Collier were the finest and most enthusiastic classmates I could have hoped for and were unstinting in their efforts to help me make this the best book possible. Many of them are now published authors; others are well on the way; they all richly deserve everything they achieve.

This novel was a product of that course and enabled me to secure the next foothold on my climb, my fabulous agent Oli Munson, who read the book almost overnight and offered to represent me the next day. His support, advice and knowledge are valued beyond measure. He is my Sherpa Tenzing and he led me to my legendary editor Jane Wood and the wonderful Quercus team who took me to the summit.

Jane has been a joy to work with, her wealth of experience guiding me through the publication process with relative ease. From our first telephone conversation to the present day she has had my back. I can't thank her enough. The same goes for the rest of the team, in particular Therese Keating, Ella Patel and Sushmi Shyam. Thanks are also due to Anne Newman, my copyeditor, and to cover designer Joe Mills at Blacksheep.

There are many others who have helped. My Newcastle-based writing group, who meet up regularly to offer considered, constructive criticism on our latest offerings have kept me going when the Muse has deserted me. Many thanks to Simon Van der Velde, John Hickman, Karon Alderman and Ben Appleby-Dean. A big shout-out to Victoria Watson too. The driving force behind the Newcastle version of Noir at the Bar, Vic has been a constant supporter and provided me with the opportunity to road test my work in front of a discerning audience. Find your nearest NATB and give it a go, it really will help improve your writing.

I also must thank my theatrical partner Ed Waugh for getting me started on this creative writing lark. Together we wrote umpteen plays, many of which are still touring. It was an absolute blast. Without his belief, determination and constant cajoling I would still be sitting in an office wondering where it all went wrong.

There are also the many experts who have contributed sage advice and real-world knowledge to this book. From New-castle City Council to the Port of Tyne Authority, everyone I've sought for help has responded immediately no matter how weird the question, such as: where would a body end up if it went into the Tyne by the Millennium Bridge? There are too many to name but I should give specific thanks to my good friend, former Detective Superintendent Tony Hutchinson, for his advice on all police matters. Any mis-takes are mine, any deviations from the norm in service of the story and none of the policemen in this novel bear any resemblance to my advisor. He would probably have sorted all this out in an afternoon, even with a tab break.

For those interested in finding out more about PTSD, I would strongly recommend *The Veterans Survival Guide* by Jimmy Johnson, a raw, honest and disturbing examination of a disorder which affects so many ex-servicemen.

I would also like to mention the inspiration for the fictional Pit Stop. The People's Kitchen in Newcastle is a fantastic organisation which provides essential comfort to the homeless and disadvantaged. Entirely funded by donations, its unpaid staff provide food, clothes and support to hundreds of people every week. I am honoured to volunteer there for an afternoon a week. If you have the means to help them, whether financially or with your time, please try to. For more information see www.peopleskitchen.co.uk

Finally, last but most definitely first in every sense, my wife Pam and daughter Becca, without whom none of this would matter a jot. Pam's absolute support throughout this journey has been remarkable, never a moment's doubt or hesitation, and her belief and constant support has made it all possible. Becca has been an equally staunch supporter, attending every public reading and critically devouring every draft with a copyeditor's eye – she is available at very reasonable rates, I believe. I genuinely couldn't have done it without them.